IN
SHEEP'S
CLOTHING

IN SHEEP'S CLOTHING

L.D. BEYER

OLD STONE MILL
Publishing

This is a work of fiction. The events that unfold within these pages as
well as the characters depicted are products of the author's imagination.
Any connection to specific people, living or dead, is purely coincidental.

Cover and interior design by Lindsey Andrews

ISBN: 978-0-9963857-0-1

Old Stone Mill Publishing
Battle Creek, MI
http://www.ldbeyer.com

For Mona, who patiently supported my follies from the very beginning

NEARLY ALL MEN CAN STAND ADVERSITY,
BUT IF YOU WANT TO TEST A MAN'S CHARACTER,
GIVE HIM POWER.

—*Abraham Lincoln*

PROLOGUE

September

As the clay disk sailed out of the trap house, the president swung his gun, tracking the target. A gentle squeeze of the trigger and the target exploded, nothing left but dust in the air.

One for one.

The Secret Service agent standing ten feet behind him nodded. President Thomas Walters was a life-long member of the NRA and former winner of the Marines' Expert Marksmanship Badge. The man was lethal with a gun.

It was a typical fall day for northern Maine. The morning sun had just cleared the tree line but wasn't yet strong enough to burn away the fog seeping out of the woods. Although the air was chilly, the president and his entourage of agents didn't seem to mind. Trap shooting was something that the many demands of his office prevented the president from enjoying as often as he would have liked. The way he looked at it, he could escape for a few moments while his Secret Service detail enjoyed a change of scenery. Besides, today it seemed the foliage was at its peak.

The red, orange, and yellow leaves, together with the scent of autumn, reminded him of hunting trips with his father long ago.

The clay bird shot off to the president's left, but he swiftly adjusted his aim and fired.

Two for two.

His father was the one who had taught him how to shoot, the one who had told him again and again that ammunition was expensive—a precious commodity not to be wasted by a bad shot. His skill had come from necessity.

The president changed his angle as another target sailed past the shooting line.

Three for three.

One of his father's friends, a buddy from his old platoon, owned a cabin on a lake up in Michigan. Every year in November, his father had gone hunting while the future president had stayed home with his mother and sister. Tom Walters was thirteen when his dad had first asked him to come along. He remembered how excited he'd been on the ride up to the cabin; how happy he'd been that his dad thought that he was old enough, man enough, to go. Almost instantly, the happy memory vanished as he recalled how humiliated he'd felt on the way home.

Another clay bird exploded over the field.

Four for four.

On the second day of the trip, he had missed a buck that was grazing fifty yards away. He had hesitated, waiting for the animal to turn for a better shot, a perfect shot. That one second had cost him, as the deer, sensing danger, bolted. He had squeezed off a wild shot, knowing as he did so that it was hopeless. God, how he had wished he could relive those few seconds. He had wanted so much to hear his father tell him how proud he was. The rest of the week was horrible as he dreaded the long ride home....

"What the hell's the matter with you, boy? There's no reason you shoulda missed that shot. Hell, I'll bet your sister coulda hit that buck. Maybe I'll bring her next year and leave you home!"

It was four more years before his father asked him to go again.

Five for five.

His father was the one who had pressured him to enlist, told him that the Corps would make a man out of him. The president felt a twinge of guilt wondering what his dad would think now when the story broke. Jesus! The press would be all over him like vultures on an animal carcass and all for something that happened almost forty years ago.

Six for six.

At one point, back when his career was beginning, he dreaded that his past "indiscretions" would suddenly surface and his budding political career would wither and die. But, as time passed and his career progressed, the fears had faded.

The target shot out in front of the president. He swung the gun, but not with the same fluid motion. The clay bird broke into several large pieces.

Seven for seven.

As the president reloaded his shotgun, he could almost hear his father:

"Concentrate now, boy! You almost missed that time! People will think I'm raisin' a sissy!"

He had just been discharged from the service and entered college on the GI bill. Like many young men away from home for the first time, away from authority, he lived the life of a rebellious freshman, going to beer parties, skipping classes, trying to get every girl he met in the sack. In a few short months, the disciplined life he had led while in the Corps seemed a vague memory. At the end of his first semester, after final exams, he celebrated with his roommate and some coed friends by drinking shots of tequila and playing strip poker. The poker game soon gave way to sex, and after they each had made love to both women, Walters and his roommate watched as the two women made love to each other. He must have had a lot of tequila—before he realized what he was doing, he was having sex with his roommate.

What might have been excused as a drunken college stunt or youthful experimentation probably would have been except for two things. First, over the next several years, he and his roommate had continued to fool around. Second, one of the women managed to capture a few intimate moments of the future president and his roommate on her camera.

He had thought the whole incident long forgotten until two months ago. Tyler Rumson, an aggressive, two-term Republican Senator from New Jersey, showed him the pictures and suggested that he reconsider running for reelection. When he refused, Rumson had threatened to leak the pictures to the press. He had increased the pressure over the last several weeks, and the president had finally realized that even if he agreed to drop out of the race, Rumson would give the pictures to the press anyway. It was odd, Walters thought, that the possibility of losing the presidency, of losing his wife, and possibly being cast aside as a social pariah didn't bother him nearly as much as the prospect of facing his father. He was a sixty-six-year-old man, he was the President of the United States, and he was still afraid of his father.

The president called for the next target. As the clay bird flew out of the trap house, he turned the gun, stuck the barrel in his mouth, and pulled the trigger.

CHAPTER ONE

November

President David Kendall swore under his breath. He had been hurrying to finish his speech before the technical staff invaded and converted the Oval Office into a TV studio with lighting, teleprompters, cameras, boom microphones, and wires snaking all over the floor. After his speech writer left to make the final changes and to load the speech onto the teleprompter, he found his Chief of Staff, Charles Howell, waiting, with news that the Secretary of State was resigning.

"What reason did he give?" the president asked.

Howell frowned. "He believes that he no longer has the support he needs to be effective."

The president cursed again. Bill Duggan had been instrumental in representing U.S. interests around the globe, especially in Asia, where China's growing influence on world affairs was a concern. The president both liked and trusted the man. But now, for some reason, Secretary of State Duggan had just submitted his resignation. The president shook his head, frustrated both at the timing and at the impact Duggan's loss would likely have.

He sighed. It had been eight weeks since President Walters' tragic death, and the nation was struggling to move on. The fact that Walters' death was due to his own bullet and not an assassin's made it that much more difficult to comprehend. David Kendall had chosen that evening to address the nation—again. He needed to reassure the country that the initiatives President Walters had started, the promises he had made during his campaign, the reason so many voters had selected him as their president, had not been forgotten. This would be the fourth time Kendall would address the nation as president, but this time he needed to bring a different message to the American people: one of moving forward, not looking back. He had to restore the nation's confidence in their government and in themselves.

President Kendall glanced at his watch. Although the speech was not until eight o'clock, still several hours away, he had two more meetings and then dinner with his family. The latter was something he had promised his daughters he wouldn't miss.

"I have Felicia next?" he asked, referring to Commerce Secretary Felicia Jackson.

Howell nodded. "Yes, sir."

"Postpone her. I need to speak to Bill."

———

Thirty minutes later, the president hung up the phone and cursed again. Bill Duggan had been adamant. Despite Kendall's reassurances, Duggan insisted that foreign policy decisions were being made by others without the State Department's involvement and that he no longer felt he had the president's confidence and support. When pressed for details, Duggan provided little. The president sat back and sighed. Although Duggan had agreed to meet the following day, he made it clear that it was only to submit a formal letter of resignation. Kendall had been surprised by the frustration, the anger and hurt in the voice of someone he had respected and supported for the last two years. *What the hell happened?* He wondered.

He stood, stepped to the windows behind his desk, and stared out over the South Lawn. His frustration clouded the picture-perfect fall day. People needed stability, and they needed to have faith in their government, especially so soon after President Walters' death. And a change within the administration right now—his administration—wouldn't help.

He sighed again. When he had taken the oath of office almost two years ago—then as vice president—he never expected to be standing here, inside the Oval Office. At the time, he was familiar with the line of succession and the role the vice president played in ensuring continuity of government. And if he hadn't been, the briefings by the White House Chief Usher, the legal scholars, and the Secret Service would have corrected that. The meetings had been sobering, and he had dutifully listened and asked questions and prepared himself for the day that he thought would never come.

But then it did.

———

He had been in Paris meeting with the United States' major economic allies on the recent rise of the U.S. dollar. President Walters had thought it important for the U.S. to demonstrate its commitment to other G-7 nations and had insisted that Vice President Kendall attend the meetings along with the Chairman of the Federal Reserve and the Secretary of the Treasury.

The U.S. delegation had just arrived at a reception at the German Embassy when, without warning, his Secret Service detail grabbed him and forced him back into the limousine. Kendall remembered the surreal feeling as his bodyguards barked orders into the microphones hidden in their sleeves while the limo raced away. It had seemed an eternity before one of them told him that the president was dead. At the airport, he was hustled onto the plane and, minutes later, they were airborne.

The Chief Justice of the Supreme Court had been waiting at Andrews Air Force Base when Kendall landed, and he had taken the oath of office on the plane. Then, under heavy guard, he was rushed to Marine One for the quick flight to the White House. The rest of the night was a blur as he met with congressional leaders, legal scholars, and constitutional experts to discuss succession, chain of command, and transition. At some point during the long night, he had been given the nuclear launch codes and instructed on the hows, whens, and whys of sending the world into oblivion. Then, at sunrise, he was escorted up to the second floor, where he met with President Walters' family.

Hours later, he was in the Oval Office, reviewing drafts of a speech—his first as Commander-in-Chief—trying to figure out what he was going to say that could bring some sense of comfort to a shocked nation.

———

Now, tonight, he would speak to the nation again and, this time, he hoped to bring a sense of closure to a tragic chapter in America's history. As much as he had admired and respected Thomas Walters, the man was gone. The baton had been passed to him, and it was time to move forward.

Since he'd assumed office, he hadn't traveled out of the country. For that matter, he hadn't spent much time away from Washington. His initial focus had been on succession and transition. The meetings with foreign leaders, the state visits and summits that had been on President Walters' schedule had all been postponed, and thankfully there hadn't been a major foreign crisis. The handful of issues that had arisen so far had been deftly handled by Bill Duggan and the State Department through diplomatic channels. And Kendall had spoken personally to counterparts throughout the world, reassuring them of America's stance and offering promises to meet soon. It was only four weeks ago that he traveled for the first time: to the University of Chicago where he spoke to a summit of educators. Nonetheless, there were many pressing matters outside of Washington, both at home and abroad, that were demanding his attention.

He turned from the window, his face grim. Now, it seemed, there was another crisis that had to be managed before he could give his full attention to doing the job he had been elected to do—if not directly, then as a stand-in for the man who'd been.

———

At six-thirty the following morning, the president sat down, as he did most days, with Charles Howell. It was a chance to review the schedule over a cup of coffee and, with the perspective that comes only after a night's sleep, to discuss the events and issues of the prior day.

His address to the nation had been well received, and more than one advisor told him that the tone and message were exactly what the nation needed. They must have been right, because the political commentary that followed had been overwhelmingly positive, and his approval rating had surged overnight. The discussion soon turned to the Secretary of State.

"I can't figure out what happened," the president said, frowning. He picked up his cup of coffee then hesitated. "Who's he close to?"

Howell was silent a moment. "Amalu, in Homeland Security," he finally said.

"Okay. Speak to Henry. See what you can find out."

Howell nodded and scribbled a note. "We need to think about a replacement."

"I know." The president sighed. "We also need to think about what we're going to say."

Howell nodded again. "I already spoke to the Communications Office. They're drafting something."

The president took a sip of coffee. "Okay. Let's set some time up with Linda Huff," he said, referring to the White House

Counsel. "We need to start developing a list of potential candidates."

"She's already on it," Howell responded.

The president smiled weakly. Howell, as usual, was a step ahead of him. As he took another sip of coffee, he wondered again what was troubling Duggan. There had been no misunderstandings, no disagreements, no warning signs as far as he could tell.

Just three weeks ago he had invited his Cabinet and the White House staff to Camp David for the weekend. Although he had worked with most of them for almost two years, the dynamics in the White House had changed when he assumed the presidency and, he reminded himself, when the new vice president had joined the team. The two days were a chance to get away from the hyper-charged environment in Washington, to focus on the future and on the team that would be responsible for helping guide the nation forward. By the end of the weekend, he sensed optimism again.

But after they returned to Washington, he could feel an undercurrent—a tension—that he attributed to President Walters' death. This was, after all, an environment that allowed little time to grieve.

———

Vice President Tyler Rumson seemed to agree. They were sitting in the private dining room next to the Oval Office, something they did once a week. It was a practice that President Walters had instituted when Kendall was vice president. The lunches provided a private forum for the president to share his views on the issues, events, and decisions that concerned him with the man who, in a heartbeat—or more aptly, Kendall thought, the lack of one—would take over. As he knew all too well, the next man in line had to be prepared.

Kendall looked forward to these meetings. Like his early morning coffee with Charles Howell, it was an opportunity to put things in perspective, to focus on the big picture and to prioritize.

The salads had just been served. President Kendall waited until the Navy Steward retreated before he shared his concerns with Rumson. He had met with Bill Duggan earlier in the day, but Duggan hadn't changed his position.

"Have you noticed anything?" the president asked.

"With Duggan specifically?" Rumson responded. "No. But people are under stress. Walters' death was a shock and, all of a sudden," he smiled and nodded in Kendall's direction, "there's a new boss. Change is difficult, especially sudden change. And with the pace everyone works around here, it's not surprising."

The president nodded. There was a heightened sense of urgency in the White House and, by extension, in the agencies and departments that were part of the Executive Branch. The pace was frantic and people tended to work brutal hours, very often through the weekend and, many times, through the night.

"Do you think we need to get away again?" he asked. "Maybe do something different this time?"

Rumson shook his head. "If it were me, I would give people some time, some space."

The president frowned. Time and space were luxuries those in the White House could not afford.

"Washington's not for the weak-hearted," Rumson continued after a moment, seemingly changing the subject. "You need to have tough skin to survive here."

The president scowled as he studied Rumson. "Meaning what?" he asked.

"Duggan probably made a few enemies over the years. From what I understand, he's territorial and insists that foreign policy concerns trump everything else. It wouldn't surprise me if someone was out to get him."

"So someone planted the idea that I wanted him to resign?" the president asked. "A game of political one-upmanship?"

Rumson shrugged. "Hey, this is Washington."

Kendall sat back, wondering. He had seen his share of political battles over the years. He had seen firsthand how Washington and the White House could bring out the best in people. He had also seen how they could bring out the worst. It wasn't surprising. It was a politically charged environment, where knowledge and proximity to the Oval Office conveyed power. People guarded what they knew and with whom they shared it. Invisible walls seemed to rise on their own. And the majority of the people in Washington were Type A personalities, most plagued with an exaggerated sense of self-importance. He had been in Washington long enough to know that battling egos thought nothing of stepping on each other's toes—or worse, throwing potential adversaries under the bus.

As the discussion continued, he realized that Rumson was

probably right; Duggan had likely made an enemy or two along the way. But he didn't agree that he should sit back and do nothing, not when the people who worked for him—the people in charge of the government—were worried and tense. That was a recipe for disaster.

He and Tyler Rumson had different styles. Kendall believed in creating a vision and setting the agenda and then getting out of his team's way so they could do their jobs. Rumson had a take-charge approach. But, like Charles Howell, Rumson's focus on execution—on pushing the agenda forward and getting things done—was a good compliment to his own focus on steering the country in the right direction.

Strange bedfellows, his wife had said when he told her he had chosen Tyler Rumson as his vice president. He didn't see it that way, at least not anymore; though he understood her initial reluctance.

Mere hours after he had assumed the presidency, in the chaos that had followed President Walters' death, Phil Perry, the Chairman of the Republican National Committee, had called to ask who he intended to choose as vice president. Kendall had been stunned by the question. Perry told him that, under the Constitution, he had to appoint someone to fill the office he had so recently vacated and that, in order to preserve the line of succession, he had to do so soon. He hadn't considered this; not at the time anyway. There were more pressing issues to contend with.

Yet, Perry had been persistent, insisting that Kendall choose Tyler Rumson, claiming the New Jersey Senator was the only man for the job. Kendall had worked with Perry during the last campaign and, although he had found him abrasive, the man had been effective in organizing the Republican machine behind the Walters-Kendall ticket.

Kendall hadn't acquiesced to Perry's demands. At least not right away. He had taken a week to review other candidates and solicit the opinions of key advisors and party elders. The line on Rumson was that he often resorted to strong-arm tactics to get his way. A bull in a china shop was how one person described him. But he had a good record in the Senate, got things done, and was able to raise considerable donations, which would be critical for an eventual reelection campaign.

President Kendall had taken four more days to meet with six final candidates. He had to admit that the meeting with Rumson had gone far better than he had expected. Rumson had been professional, respectful—deferential even—and had an air of statesmanship that was impressive. They discussed policy and, although they hadn't agreed on several points, Rumson seemed to understand the issues at a detailed level and was able to take an informed position.

It had been clear that the Republican Party supported Rumson. And after the expedited background check found nothing negative, Kendall had made his decision. He needed as much backing as he could get within both houses of Congress, and Rumson seemed to have a well-established network.

The confirmation hearings had been quick, and Tyler Rumson had become Vice President of the United States.

CHAPTER TWO

Humpty Dumpty sat on a wall.

Something was wrong, Matthew Richter thought. He watched as the smile on Humpty's face began to fade. Humpty looked sad, which puzzled Richter because he had never seen Humpty like this before.

Humpty Dumpty had a great fall.

Richter tried to move, he knew he had to move, but his body refused to respond. God! He felt like his limbs were stuck in cement. He reached for Humpty, trying to grab onto something, anything.

He watched in horror as Humpty tumbled past.

All the King's horses and all the King's men,
Couldn't put Humpty together again.

It was almost comical, to see everyone running around, no one sure what to do, panic in their eyes. It might have been funny, except that Humpty was bleeding. No matter what Richter did, he couldn't stop the bleeding.

The blood began to drip from the ceiling onto his bed. He

struggled to wipe the blood from his face, and when his eyes cleared he was staring at Humpty's head. The head turned and, suddenly, a lopsided, perverted grin began to form on what was left of Humpty's face.

I didn't fall. I jumped!

———

Richter awoke with a start. It took him a moment to realize where he was. He sat up, shivering. The sheets were on the floor, and he was covered in a cold sweat. He jumped out of bed and hurried from his room to escape the grisly scene in his head. In the kitchen, he busied himself brewing a pot of coffee. He was no psychiatrist, but it was obvious what the dream meant. He didn't need some pompous, high-priced shrink to explain it.

He couldn't shake the feeling that he should have done something to prevent what had happened on that chilly fall day two months before. He had replayed the scene over and over in his mind to see if there was anything, any hint to what President Walters had been thinking, but he found nothing.

After an internal investigation, the Secret Service had ruled there was nothing the agents on the scene could have done to prevent the president from committing suicide. Maybe one day Richter would be able to accept that, but that day seemed a long way off. The investigation had turned up nothing concrete. There was no suicide note. The president's health was excellent. There had been no prior signs of depression or mental illness. His approval rating was the envy of his predecessors. His family and his closest advisors were at a complete loss. The question of blackmail had come up, but no one was aware of any skeletons in the president's closet.

As an agent assigned to the president's security detail, Richter had to ignore politics and the constant stream of negative comments by the pundits, the columnists, and the president's opponents. His job was to protect the office of the presidency regardless of his personal feelings for the man occupying it at the time. Nonetheless, there had been very few negative articles about the president throughout his campaign or during the short time he had held office. While there had been one allegation of illegal campaign contributions and another of an illegitimate child, those had turned out to be false. As it was, there was very little in the president's past for the press and his opponents to sink their teeth into. The blackmail theory didn't make sense to Richter, but what else could it be?

The director had told him that if he requested a transfer, the Service would accommodate him. None of the other agents on duty that day had taken the director up on his offer. But, lately, Richter was thinking that working in the field again, maybe on the West Coast this time, would be a relief. Maybe then his nightly torture would cease.

Matthew Richter was thirty years old and single. He was a good-looking man who never seemed to be at a loss for female companionship, if he wanted it. The trouble was he had never met a woman who was willing to take a backseat to his job. That seemed to be the case with his current girlfriend, and he was beginning to wonder how much longer it would last.

In high school, he had watched a clip of the attempted assassination of President Ronald Reagan. The images were powerful. After the first shot rang out, the agents instantly formed a human shield around the president, forced him into his limo, and sped away. Their quick reactions had saved his life. Ever since that moment, Richter had known what he wanted to be when he grew up.

His high school guidance counselor had told him to aim higher. But after Richter had insisted that this was what he was meant to do, they discussed how he might better prepare himself. The counselor had told him that military service would improve his chances of landing his dream job. He had also suggested that Richter consider studying business and computer science in college. Besides guarding the president, he had explained, the Secret Service also investigated increasingly sophisticated crimes like counterfeiting and software piracy. Finally, with a twinkle in his eye, he had recommended that Richter take up karate. Although he knew the counselor had only been humoring him, he had taken the suggestions to heart. After sixteen years, he still went to the dojo three times a week.

Right after high school, Richter had joined the Army, and after basic training, had been selected for the Army Ranger program. Ranger school was brutal, but he had excelled. He spent two years in the Army and four more in college before he joined the Secret Service. He had been assigned to the White Plains, New York, field office where he learned the basics of investigative police work. After five years there, with several high-profile arrests under his belt, he had requested a transfer to the presidential detail. The Service ordinarily preferred that its agents spend more time in the field, honing their craft, before taking on one of the most stressful jobs in law enforcement. But the Special Agent in Charge of the White Plains office was so impressed with Richter's performance and potential that he continued to push the idea with headquarters. One year ago, the promotion had been approved and Richter had packed up his meager possessions, bid goodbye to White Plains, and set out for Washington.

He sighed. It was sad. This was the only job he'd ever wanted, and now he was considering giving it up.

CHAPTER THREE

The president shook his head, frustrated. In the two weeks since Duggan had resigned, they had narrowed the list of potential replacements down to two people. He and Charles Howell were in favor of Carol Hettinger, a career diplomat and current ambassador to the United Nations. Rumson favored Lyle Burdick, the former ambassador to Mexico. The vice president believed that Hettinger would not be able to survive the confirmation hearings, pointing to a left-wing organization, United For Change, which she had supposedly belonged to in college.

"She's already explained that," the president pointed out. "She attended one meeting—just one—out of curiosity. She never joined."

"It doesn't matter," Rumson responded. "The only thing that people will remember is that six, seven years later, two officials from UFC were charged with voter fraud and that Hettinger was somehow connected to the group." He paused. "That's what the press and the Democratic spin machine will say."

"So we'll fight it," the president said immediately. "We'll set the record straight." He paused, eyes steady on Rumson. "You know she had nothing to do with that scandal."

Rumson shook his head. "That's irrelevant. All of the negative press is going to be a bone of contention with the Senate. They're not going to want to touch it." He shook his head again. "Dave, you're better off avoiding the fight."

"Look," the president said. "Carol is a seasoned diplomat. She's been posted to half a dozen countries, including China, and has earned the respect of the folks over at State."

Rumson frowned. "I'm not debating her record. Frankly, I agree with you on that point. My concern is about her ability to survive the confirmation hearings and our ability to sell her to Congress."

They had debated for several more minutes when Rumson finally held up his hands in defense.

"Look, if Carol's your choice, I'll support you. But I think it's a mistake."

The president frowned. He leaned forward, his gaze steady on Rumson. "Tyler, I need you fully on board."

Rumson held his hands up again. "Dave, I'm behind you. But I think part of my job is to tell you what I think. And I think you and I might burn up a lot of political capital and, at the end of the day, still lose the fight."

Rumson was probably right about one thing, Kendall concluded. The press, the democratic minority in the senate, and even some in his own party might try to make a big deal of Hettinger's college activities. But it was a non-issue, the president knew, and one that was likely to die just as quickly as it surfaced.

And, he believed, on the heels of Walters' death, he had unprecedented support within Congress and with the American public. If he was going to push a controversial nomination—not that he believed this one would be—now was the time.

He studied Rumson for a moment before speaking. "I want Carol, Tyler. She's the best person for the job." His eyes narrowed. "Are you with me on this one?" It was more of a demand than a question.

Rumson was silent for a moment before he nodded. "Okay. Okay. I'm with you, Dave. I'll do whatever I can to support her."

The president nodded. Although relieved to have Rumson on his side, he was still frustrated, sensing there was something else driving the vice president's reluctance. While his argument, at first blush made sense, it was weak. Trying to connect Hettinger to UFC was a stretch. Even UFC, he remembered, had publically stated that Hettinger had never been a member. Besides, Hettinger was the best person for the job. Why didn't Rumson see that?

———

He sighed. Life was easier before he entered politics.

Six years ago, he had been the president and chief executive officer of Montclair Capital, a large portfolio management firm based in Colorado Springs. It was difficult to believe, but now here he was, sitting in the Oval Office.

He had built the firm single-handedly, from one small mutual fund to a publicly held company managing eighteen funds with a combined market value in excess of fifty-two billion dollars. Along the way, David Kendall had made a name for himself on both Wall Street and on Main Street. After his wife's battle with breast cancer, he had decided that twenty-eight years was enough and it was time to move on. He sold his stake in the company to a large German investment bank.

Several months later, he was invited onto a news talk show and asked for his opinion on some of the issues facing the country. The looming collapse of the Social Security System was the current hot topic and, without any preparation, Kendall had provided some specific recommendations on what needed to be done immediately and in the longer term. Much of his proposal was a combination of the better components of various ideas being tossed about, along with a few tweaks of his own. He soon found himself a regular guest on a handful of shows.

It didn't take long before an editorial in the Denver Times suggested that if he really wanted to fix the problem, he would have a much better chance working inside the system, as a member of Congress. He had resisted the idea of running, then his wife's doctors had given them the news they had been praying for—Maria's cancer was in remission. With Maria as his strongest supporter, eighteen months later, David Kendall became one of several dozen freshman senators taking the oath of office. His knowledge of Social Security and his experience as a money manager landed him on a newly formed committee to study the problem. They spent three years drafting a bill that ultimately resembled Kendall's initial plan. Being a freshman, he hadn't been designated as the committee's chairman, the position that typically received all the media attention. Nonetheless, the resulting legislation became known as "The Kendall Act."

Although it was too soon to tell whether the new law would fix the Social Security problem over the long term, his ability to get things done, and his obvious appeal to voters, didn't go unnoticed. The presidential primary race was heating up, and the man who would eventually win the Republican nomination, Governor Thomas Walters of Florida, began courting him. Three weeks before the convention, he had invited Kendall to dinner and wasted no time in making his intentions clear.

"I want to show the American voter that the Walters Administration will be a 'can do' administration," he had stated. "The public is sick and tired of the gridlock in Washington. Nothing ever seems to get done, and when we actually do something, it's half-assed at best. That's why I like your Social Security plan. You fix the problem once, and you fix it for good." Walters had paused, stared him in the eye. "I want you to be my vice president, Dave. I think the American people want you too."

Governor Walters had been persuasive. Although Kendall was getting used to living under a microscope, with the press analyzing his every move, he wondered how his family would handle the intrusion. Surprising him, they had brushed off his concerns.

After Walters won the nomination, the polls showed overwhelming support for the Walters-Kendall ticket and they had maintained that lead all the way up to the election.

———

There were times when he wondered whether he had made the right decision when he'd said yes to Tom Walters two-and-a-half years ago. Despite his family's support, their lives had changed forever. The constant presence of the media was stressful—as president, it was far more intrusive than it had been for the behind-the-scenes number-two man—but it was something his family had, somewhat reluctantly, come to accept. And then there were the daily reminders that the world was a dangerous place, especially for the man living in the White House. His interactions with the public were carefully orchestrated and limited. There were times when he found himself staring out the windows of the second floor residence at the tourists and the occasional protestors in the distance on the other side of the fence. The times he had ventured out beyond the gates had been behind the bulletproof glass of an armored limousine, with scores of Secret Service agents intent on keeping the public at a distance. And each time, they had urged, if not insisted, that he wear a bulletproof vest. He liked the agents assigned to him, and he knew they meant well. Still, it was odd, he thought. Never had he felt so exposed, where his every move was watched. And yet, never had he felt so isolated.

CHAPTER FOUR

The Secret Service Command Center was located on the ground floor of the West Wing, directly below the Oval Office and the Cabinet Room. Matthew Richter had just signed out at the end of his shift and was anxious to leave. As he stepped into the hall, he heard a voice behind him and tensed. *Oh, shit*, he thought. *Not again.* He turned to the hostile face of Agent Cal Mosby. What the hell did he want now?

"Did you put in for the transfer yet?" There was no disguising the threat in Mosby's tone.

"Back off, Mosby," Richter hissed then turned to walk away.

"Face it, Richter. You fucked up. You're not cut out for this."

Anger flaring, Richter spun back around. Before he could respond, Keith O'Rourke stepped into the hallway.

"Mosby! Get your ass in here, now!"

Mosby glared at Richter then backed away, leaving him cursing under his breath.

Mosby was an old-timer in the White House. Currently assigned to the vice president's protective detail, he had guarded presidents and various First Family members over the years. Richter had heard that Mosby had worked for the New Jersey State Police at one time, then the FBI, before he joined the Service. When Richter joined the White House team, Mosby had been cold and distant, having no time for rookies. From his time in the military and in a field office, Richter was used to hazing. He had to prove himself first, before the old guard would admit him to their circle. He had put up with the practical jokes and the teasing, stoically accepting that it came with the territory. It hadn't taken long before the older agents welcomed him as part of the elite guard. All except for Mosby; he had never acknowledged that Richter had earned his spot on the president's detail. After President Walters' death, other agents had been sympathetic, assuring Richter that there was nothing he could have done. Not Mosby.

To make matters worse, shortly after Walters' death, Mosby had been transferred to Vice President Rumson's detail. If anyone should have been transferred, Mosby had told him angrily, it should have been Richter. After all, Richter had been the closest agent to President Walters, the only one who might have had a chance to prevent his suicide. No one else saw it that way, but Mosby's words kept coming back to him.

"You froze. And now the man's dead."

Although he tried to ignore it, the confrontation and Mosby's stinging words followed him home.

—

Richter woke the next morning to noises coming from the kitchen. Feeling disoriented, he sat on the edge of the bed, rubbing his face while he waited for the feeling to pass. The sheets and quilt, as usual, were on the floor. He shuffled to the bathroom, catching a glimpse of himself in the mirror, not liking what he saw. The bloodshot eyes and sunken cheeks made him look hungover although he hadn't had anything to drink.

He made his way to the kitchen and found Karen, dressed and sitting at the counter.

She handed him a cup of coffee. "You look awful."

Richter grunted as he sat. Her bag, he noticed, was sitting by the door. A pillow and blanket lay on the couch. They sat quietly for several minutes.

"Matthew, you're making this too hard."

He sighed and put his cup down. "What do you want from me?"

"You know what I want." She paused. "I want you to quit."

He had met Karen Boyle seven months before at a SCUBA certification course. She was a flight attendant, twenty-nine years old, and gorgeous. They had been dating ever since.

"You're not going to say anything?"

He shook his head. "I can't quit. You know that."

He put his head in his hands, massaging his temples with his thumbs. He heard the scrape of her stool and the jingle of keys.

"Call me when you figure yourself out."

The door shut—not quite a slam, but hard enough to let him know she was pissed. He frowned. The trouble was they had fun together, or at least they used to.

When they first met, they were excited to discover that they were both active and adventurous. Their first date had been a hike along a section of the Appalachian Trail. This was followed by horseback riding, hang gliding, and mountain biking. Despite their conflicting schedules, they usually found time for each other once a week. They had planned on playing racquet ball this morning before Karen's flight, Richter remembered with a sigh.

For the last few months, he had been preoccupied and tense, and their times together had been strained. He knew that it was his fault, but now, when he needed her support and understanding, it had become clear that it was more than she was willing to give.

———

The rest of the day, Matthew Richter felt like he was in a fog. Exhausted, he checked in at the command center at the start of his shift and was just leaving when Keith O'Rourke motioned him over.

"Hey, do you have a minute?"

He followed O'Rourke to his office.

"You don't look good," O'Rourke said. "Everything okay?"

Richter hesitated a moment. O'Rourke was in charge of the command center. Although he wasn't technically the boss, he was a senior agent and was well respected within the Service. Richter enjoyed working with O'Rourke and, over the past year and a half, had come to value his guidance.

"I'm fine." Richter covered a yawn. "Sorry. I didn't sleep too well last night."

O'Rourke studied him for a moment. "Walters still weighing on you?"

Richter hesitated. "Yeah. I guess."

"You were cleared by the review board. There was nothing you could have done. I don't care what Mosby says."

Richter shook his head. "I know. I know."

O'Rourke sat forward. "Listen, Matthew. Go see the doctor. The Service is paying for it, and it's confidential, so you have no reason not to go. You've got to work this out. If you're not one hundred percent on top of your game, you become a liability."

Richter's stomach felt hollow.

"Why not take some time off? You know, go somewhere. Decompress."

Richter nodded again as he stood. "I'd better get upstairs."

CHAPTER FIVE

December

Pat Monahan, Deputy Director of the FBI, frowned at the traffic, looked at his watch, and swore. Being late for a meeting with the president would not be wise. Unfortunately, thirty minutes ago he hadn't known that he would be going to the White House today. He had been on his way to CIA headquarters for the weekly meeting of the Project Boston Task Force when FBI Director Emil Broder had called.

"The president wants an update on Project Boston."

"When?" Monahan had asked.

"At nine," Broder had barked then hung up before Monahan could protest.

What a way to start a week! Monahan had told his driver to turn around. His position as deputy director came with a driver, who also acted as his bodyguard. There was nothing he could do about the traffic, so he decided to let the young agent worry about it while he focused on Project Boston.

The goal of the task force was to put so much pressure

on the Mexican drug cartels that they would re-evaluate their desire to distribute narcotics in the U.S. Daunting, to say the least. But for the first time, they weren't bound by the rules that had hampered previous efforts. The Boston team employed guerrilla warfare tactics: cutting communication, jamming cell phone transmissions, kidnapping high-ranking cartel members, fire-bombing cartel processing and storage sites, confiscating cartel assets, freezing bank accounts—in effect, just about everything short of assassination. Their goal was to so decimate the cartel, effectively strangling it, which led one task force member to suggest the code name. The team was named after the Boston Strangler.

While it might appear odd, corrupt even, that the FBI would participate in what appeared to be illegal activities, Monahan's very presence on the task force was to ensure that they operated within the boundaries of the presidential directive. The plan was unusual in that it had the explicit agreement and participation of the Mexican government. All operations were carried out jointly between teams from both countries, including U.S. Navy Seals and CIA Field Operatives, as well as Mexican Special Forces.

Monahan had been summoned to explain to President Kendall exactly what Project Boston was. He glanced out the window as they pulled up to the gate. After showing their IDs, they waited as Uniformed Secret Service officers checked the trunk of the car and looked underneath with large rolling mirrors.

"Thank you, Mr. Monahan. Mr. Broder is waiting for you inside."

As Monahan jumped out, he glanced at his watch again.

Damn! He was cutting it close.

———

"We have a problem, sir." Howell began with a frown.

The Chief of Staff was one of the few people who were permitted to interrupt what was normally a quiet time in the late afternoon that the president reserved for reading or making phone calls.

"I had a conversation with Melinda Lentz. I don't know if you remember her, but she was an intern in your office five years ago."

The president shook his head. The name didn't ring a bell.

"Anyway, she's now an aide in Senator Miller's office," Howell continued.

"Arnie Miller? From Georgia?"

"Yes, sir. We've kept in touch over the years." Howell paused a moment. "She told me that Miller isn't going to support Hettinger's nomination."

The president flinched. "They haven't even had the hearings yet!"

"What's more concerning," Howell continued, "is that she overheard part of a phone conversation between Senator Miller and the vice president. Before the Senator closed the door, she heard him say…" he glanced down at his notes, "…'don't worry. I have no intention of voting for her.'"

The president took a deep breath. "How does she know it was Rumson?"

"She answered the phone, sir. She transferred the call in."

"God damn it!" the president swore softly.

Howell shook his head. "That's not all, sir. I also spoke to someone in Senator Broussard's office," he said. "Apparently he's already made up his mind too."

"Shit! I thought we were aligned on this!" The president sat back and stared at the ceiling for a moment. "He's trying to sabotage my nomination?"

Howell's face was grim. "It would appear so."

———

It was cold and dark as Monahan left his office and climbed into the back of the Suburban. Not a fan of winter, he was looking forward to the glass of wine he would have when he got home. That would warm him up, he thought. As the driver pulled out into traffic, he reflected on the day. It hadn't been too bad. The meeting with the president had gone well, even though he hadn't been given any opportunity to prepare. At least that was his impression. Unfortunately, the occasional pat on the back wasn't Director Broder's style. He shook his head as he recalled Broder's pep talk, a harsh whisper right before they entered the Oval Office.

"Don't fuck this up, Monahan!"

Motivation through fear—and public humiliation when you slipped up—wasn't the style leadership consultants were recommending these days. Still, Broder had let him meet with the president, which was something he had never expected. It must have been at the president's request, Monahan figured. Oh well, he sighed. Everyone has a cross to bear. He just needed to hang on a few more years before he could retire.

His cell phone rang, interrupting his thoughts.

"This is the White House Operator. Please hold for the president."

Monahan sat upright; seconds later the president came on the line.

"Pat. It's Dave Kendall. How are you?"

"Good, Mr. President. Is there something I can do for you, sir?"

"I wanted to thank you for the update today. Your summary was concise and to the point."

Monahan smiled.

"I know I said it earlier, Pat, but your role on this team is crucial. While I agree with the intent of President Walters' directive, we need to make sure that the team does not cross the line. Okay?"

"Absolutely, sir. You have my word." In the rearview mirror, Monahan noticed the young driver was smiling too.

After he hung up, Monahan sat back and sighed contentedly. No, today wasn't too bad after all.

———

In the Oval Office, President Kendall hung up the phone. He picked up the file on Carol Hettinger. He stared at it for a second before dropping it back on the desk with a sigh. Despite his conversation with Pat Monahan—the only bright spot in the last fifteen hours—his day had not gone well at all.

CHAPTER SIX

It was almost 9:00 p.m. when President Kendall left the Oval Office. Agents Brad Lansing and Stephanie Sartori snapped to attention and began to scan the quiet hallways for any signs of danger. Lansing brought his hand up to his mouth and, using Kendall's Secret Service code name, spoke into the microphone on his wrist.

"Falcon's moving."

Richter, standing watch at the foot of a stairway to the second floor residence, heard the call in his earpiece and scanned the hallway. A moment later he saw the president round the corner, Agents Lansing and Sartori trailing behind.

"Hey, Matthew!" Unlike some of his predecessors, President Kendall treated the Secret Service agents who protected him with both fondness and a deep respect for their mission.

"Good evening, sir."

"Did you catch the Flyers game last night?"

"Just the last few minutes of the third period, sir."

The president patted Richter on the shoulder. "That's about

all I caught too. See you tomorrow."

Richter remained at his post while the president climbed the stairs. Lansing and Sartori followed.

Although the president could have taken the elevator, Richter noted, he always chose the stairs. And unlike many before him, President Kendall was enjoyable to work for. This was the biggest factor that kept Richter from leaving.

———

On the landing just below the second floor, Lansing radioed the Secret Service Command Center and all other agents on duty that night.

"Falcon's in the nest."

In the command center, another agent updated the Location Board, noting that "POTUS," the Secret Service acronym for President of the United States, was now in the residence section of the White House. It was a low-tech way of making sure every agent on the protective detail knew exactly where the President was at all times.

If they didn't know, they couldn't protect him.

———

Stephanie Sartori walked back to her post. She had been on presidential detail for two years. Thirty-two years old and divorced, the prospect of another marriage, let alone any halfway serious relationship, was dim, given her job. In fact, her commitment to being an investigative agent and her desire to further her career were the primary reasons her marriage had failed three years before. Shocked when her husband had demanded a divorce, she soon began to look on it as a blessing. Without the distraction, she devoted herself to her job, distinguishing herself on numerous occasions, eventually earning the coveted promotion to presidential bodyguard.

Relationships were tough for those in the Service, she knew, especially for those on presidential detail. Many agents burnt out and, after paying their dues, were eventually reassigned to a field office. Hopefully their families were still with them, but not always.

To make matters worse, many agents were still haunted by President Walters' death. Although she hadn't been on duty when he took his life, she still experienced the feelings of failure. After all, the Secret Service was a team job, and the only way to win was to never lose. Unfortunately, the team had lost big time last year when Walters had pulled the trigger.

———

With his wife and daughters in bed, the residence section of the White House was quiet as President Kendall stepped into the Treaty Room. Located down the center hall from his bedroom, he had been using the room as his private study. Filled with antique furniture dating back to the eighteen hundreds, including the table that had been used in 1898 to sign the peace treaty ending the Spanish-American War, the sense of history was powerful. As he sat, he glanced at the oil painting depicting the event over the fireplace; then his eyes swept over the paintings of Lincoln and Grant and over the various treaties and historical documents displayed around the room. More of a place to think and reflect than to plow through paperwork, he had found himself drawn to the room in the evening.

He left the lights dim, reminiscent of the gas lighting that had been used in Lincoln's time, and sat quietly in the armchair behind the Treaty Table. As he rubbed his hand across the polished surface, he reflected on the day.

He had to make a decision on Project Boston. He had cautiously supported the program when it had been proposed three months earlier but had counseled his predecessor to be careful with how much leeway he granted to the Drug Enforcement Administration and to the CIA. Now that he had inherited the program, he had to be certain that they were still able to achieve their objectives while operating within the law. He had insisted that someone from the FBI, not a Justice Department lawyer, be involved. He didn't want to deal with shades of gray and had reasoned that a by-the-book agent would be better suited for the role. After speaking to Pat Monahan, he knew he had made the right decision.

Unfortunately, the rest of the day had not gone as well, starting with the news that his vice president might be trying to undermine him.

"Absolutely not, Dave," Rumson had said defensively when Kendall confronted him. "I've spoken to a few people and explained how important the Hettinger nomination is to this administration and that I personally believe she's the right person to head up State. Never once," he said, his voice firm, "did I give anyone the impression that I wasn't one hundred percent behind Carol."

The president noted the anger in Rumson's eyes. It was clear that he felt his integrity was being called into question.

Rumson demanded to know who was spreading false rumors about him.

The president considered the source. He had known Charles Howell for over ten years, having met him when he was a money manager and Howell was the President of Cornell University. Then, when he had been elected to the Senate, he had convinced Howell to join his staff. Of all of his advisors, he spent the most time with Howell. From their morning coffees to countless impromptu meetings throughout the day, Howell was always there offering his opinion, his advice. He trusted the man and never had reason to doubt him.

"Tyler, I have it from a source I trust."

"For God's sake, Dave!" Rumson threw his hands up in frustration. "This is the same thing that happened to Duggan! Someone over in the Senate is out to get me!"

He sat back in the darkened room and sighed. It was a long time before he finally stood and made his way down the hall.

CHAPTER SEVEN

Richter grabbed a bottle of water and began pacing back and forth to cool down after his ten-mile run. He glanced up at the clock on the kitchen wall. It was just after seven in the morning and his shift, the last before vacation, didn't start until four. Picking up his cell phone, he walked to the window and stared out at the overcast sky.

Last night had been rough. After waking in a cold sweat, he'd tossed and turned for two hours. He couldn't shake the feeling that his life was crashing down around him. He had finally given up trying to fall back to sleep and gone for a run.

He knew his job was at risk. Although his shift supervisor, Brad Lansing, hadn't said anything to him yet, it was only a matter of time. Keith O'Rourke, nonetheless, had pulled him aside again. The conversation had stung.

"You're putting POTUS at risk. I don't want to do it, but unless you get some help, I'll have to speak to Lansing and Kroger."

Richter had cringed at that. Secret Service Director Gerry Kroger had no tolerance for anything less than perfection.

"Listen, I'm going to do you a favor. I'm adjusting the schedule. You've got two weeks coming to you. Take them now. Go see your family. Enjoy the holidays." O'Rourke had paused. "But I want you to make an appointment with the shrink before you head out of town."

Richter stared at his phone for several seconds before pressing the buttons.

"Good morning. Doctor Hastings' office."

———

The snow began to fall as Richter walked down the steps to the metro platform. Washington traffic was challenge enough on a clear day. With six inches of snow forecasted, he decided to leave his car at home.

He had been somewhat disconcerted by his conversation with Dr. Hastings. After they had discussed his dream, she had surprised him when she asked what he wanted in life. A family? A wife? Kids? What did he do for fun? What made him laugh? What made him happy? What was his passion? What made Matthew Richter tick? If he could live his life again, would he do anything differently?

Richter had struggled with most of the questions.

"Are you telling me I should quit?" he had asked.

"Not at all," she had responded. "I can't make that decision for you. And I don't think you're ready to make it either. Not yet. Not until you know more about who you are and not until you know more about what you want."

It was odd, he thought as he waited for the train. He had

never considered that there might come a day when he wasn't with the Service.

They had talked for over two hours, and he had surprised himself by agreeing to meet again.

———

Later that day, as Richter took up his post outside the Oval Office, inside, President Kendall glanced at the calendar then looked up at Charles Howell.

"What's this meeting with Phil Perry?" he asked.

Howell shook his head. "Rumson set it up directly with Arlene, last night."

Arlene Reardon was the president's secretary. Howell explained that although she had informed him, he assumed that the president had requested it.

"Rumson set it up?" The president frowned. "Charles, I review everything with you. If I wanted to discuss the election, I would have told you."

Howell apologized for not verifying it with him, and the president knew it was unlikely to happen again. Howell was a trusted aide and skilled Chief of Staff, effectively coordinating the work of the Executive Branch while deftly balancing the president's time with a keen sense of what was urgent and critical and what could be handled without his involvement. It was Howell's job to control the schedule. From the Presidential Daily Briefs and national security updates in the mornings to the meet-and-greets with visiting groups and dignitaries in the afternoon, and then the Cabinet meetings and countless policy discussions in between,

Howell was responsible for controlling access to the Oval Office. The president's only free time was the few hours in the late afternoon that he reserved for reading briefing documents or making phone calls. The president frowned. It appeared that Rumson had done an end run around his Chief of Staff.

He knew he would have to make a decision soon. In the remaining time he had left in office—only two years—he wouldn't be able to accomplish all of the things he had resolved to do. Washington didn't move that fast. But running for reelection wasn't something he could decide on his own. He had to speak to his family first.

"Should I cancel it, sir?"

The president hesitated, then shook his head. "No. Let me see what he has to say."

———

Phil Perry leaned forward. "Sir, I've been thinking about the election."

Kendall nodded. He glanced at Rumson, who was sitting quietly, watching.

"As you know," Perry continued, "it's only twenty-four months away. I'm not sure how much thought you've given to this yet, but there are a few things you should be doing at this stage."

Kendall nodded.

"You need to start thinking about strategy. You need to start thinking about fundraising. And you need to start putting a campaign team together. That's the most critical component right now," Perry said as he slid a document across the table. "I've put together a recommendation for you."

Kendall nodded again but left the report unopened on the table. The fact that Perry had already been thinking about the upcoming election was expected. But why had he gone to Rumson first? Rumson, he noticed, was still silent.

"Give me the summary, Phil."

"As I said, at this stage, the organization is the priority. Once you select a campaign manager, a lot of the other pieces will fall into place."

Kendall sat silently, waiting for him to continue.

Perry leaned forward. "You need a top-notch manager running your campaign, sir." He paused. "And Tad Davinsky is the best there is."

Davinsky? It took him a moment to remember where he'd heard the name before. Wasn't Davinsky the one who had worked on Arnie Miller's senatorial campaign? The one that had been noteworthy for being negative? That was it, he remembered. One after another, Miller's opponents had fallen to scandal. As it later turned out, he remembered, many of the allegations had proven to be false, part of a carefully orchestrated smear campaign. And Davinsky had been in the middle of it.

He shook his head. "I haven't even announced yet if I'm running. So any talk about a campaign manager is premature." The president glanced at Rumson, then back at Perry. "Is that what you wanted to discuss today?"

"Well, sir, the clock's ticking, and the earlier you start making some key decisions…."

The president held his hand up. "Phil, I'm not ready to make any decisions yet."

"Sir…" Perry persisted.

The president held his hand up again. "I appreciate your position, but I'm not ready to discuss this."

He stood, signaling the meeting was over.

———

President Kendall turned from the window and sighed.

"I know I have to make a decision soon. Perry's right about that. But I'm troubled by why he went to Rumson to set up the meeting and not to you. And why recommend Davinsky?"

Charles Howell frowned. "I need to check, but I'm pretty sure Davinsky was also involved in Rumson's senatorial campaigns."

"Really?" The president's face was grim. If true, that meant that Rumson hadn't merely set up the meeting, he had been working side by side with Perry and, likely, had played a larger role in Perry's plan than he had let on.

"So Rumson has his own agenda," he concluded.

"That's hardly surprising," Howell said, leaning forward. "He clearly has his own aspirations."

The president nodded slowly as Howell continued.

"If I had to guess, he wants to run on his own in six years. If you lose in two years, that would likely hurt his chances and delay his plans."

So the vice president wanted his job. No, that wasn't surprising, he thought. Still, instead of speaking to him first, Rumson had gone directly to Perry to lay out a strategy. That troubled him. Usually a good judge of character, he began to wonder if he had misread Tyler Rumson.

CHAPTER EIGHT

His eyes dark, Rumson hissed at the waiter. "I asked for my steak rare!"

There was a momentary lull in conversations, a few puzzled looks from nearby tables. They were quickly replaced by smiles as people returned Rumson's friendly nods and waves. George's was a favorite of the Washington elite, a place to see and be seen. Getting in was difficult, unless you met the criteria. On any given day, congressmen, White House staffers, lobbyists, foreign diplomats, occasional members of the press—the movers and shakers in Washington—could be seen dining there.

The red-faced waiter retreated, dish in hand, while the vice president's protective detail, sitting two tables away, exchanged glances.

As conversations at nearby tables resumed, Phil Perry shot Rumson a look. He leaned forward, his voice low. "There's a room full of people," he stated, the implication obvious.

Rumson scowled at him for a moment then shrugged and smirked.

Perry sat back and, as he took a sip of wine, studied Rumson over the top of his glass. As if following Perry's lead, Rumson reached for his own glass and sat back.

"Don't give me that look, Phil." Rumson smirked again then took a sip. "I'm no worse than that prick Johnson was."

Frowning, Perry nodded. "Lyndon Johnson was a prick and, as time passes, that's all history seems to remember."

Rumson eyes narrowed. "Spare me the lecture, will you, Phil?"

Perry sat back again and took another sip, a moment to ease the tension. He was one of the few people who could speak bluntly with Rumson, but he had to be careful to not push too hard. The man was amazing, he thought. Despite the occasional short fuse, Rumson had tremendous potential. He was able to raise money, and he seemed to have a way of bending even his most ardent and vocal enemies to his will. He seemed to know where all the skeletons were buried, and he used that knowledge to eliminate opposition to his pet programs, to get legislation passed, and to gain financial backing. This man was going places, Perry thought, and if he played his own cards right, well, then the future would be bright.

Rumson swirled the wine in his glass then leaned forward.

"We may have a problem," he said quietly.

Perry nodded but remained silent as the waiter approached with a new dish.

"I hope this is prepared more to your liking, sir."

Rumson gently grabbed the man's elbow. "Sorry about that before. Just a tough day. I shouldn't have taken it out on you."

The waiter smiled. After he left, Perry caught Rumson's eye, smiling himself.

Rumson waved his hand dismissively. "Forget that. Listen, I'm not going to sit back and watch him fuck up this campaign. This is the big leagues, and he's got to realize that."

"Come on, Tyler." Perry shook his head. "You don't think he knows that? He knows how the game is played. And if he decides on someone other than Davinsky, I don't think it's going to hurt us. Besides, don't you think his record in the Senate, the Social Security reform, indicate that he can build the necessary alliances and cut the deals needed to get what he wants?"

"Oh, for God's sake, Phil! The country was hungry for a solution. He brought one. It didn't take much to rally people behind it. Okay, he's smart. I'll give him that. But he doesn't have a lot of experience in this game. This isn't like running some small-town bank in Colorado."

Perry shook his head. "Tyler, his mutual fund company managed over fifty billion dollars. It wasn't some small-town bank. He's not a rookie."

Rumson stared at him, and Perry caught the look in his eyes and realized he had missed something earlier.

"You're thinking of challenging him, aren't you?"

Rumson glared. "If he's going to be a lame duck, I'm not going to crash and burn with him."

Perry frowned. A sitting VP challenging a sitting president for the party's nomination? That could tear the party apart. The best way to play this was to help Kendall win the reelection, and then, in the next, run on his coattails. Rumson knew that, didn't he? He studied Rumson again, noting the look in his eyes: an almost single-minded focus on getting what he wanted.

He shook his head, his voice dropping to a whisper. "That's a dangerous move, Tyler."

———

If it weren't for the decorations, it would have been hard to tell that Christmas was three days away. Congress had broken for recess and the lawyers, the lobbyists, and the diplomats had already fled town. But in the West Wing it looked like any other day and would continue to until the president left for the holidays. Kendall was planning a few days off with Maria and the girls but, until then, there was work to be done.

He was seated in front of the fireplace in the Oval Office.

"I figured you'd be on your way home by now, Pete."

"I'm heading out this afternoon, sir." Pete Ortega, a Democrat from the State of Washington, was the chairman of the House Ways and Means Committee. It was one of the most influential and powerful committees on the Hill. Despite their party affiliations, he and Kendall had developed a mutual respect for each other. While Kendall was in the Senate, promoting his vision for Social Security reform, Ortega had worked on the House version of the bill that had ultimately been approved.

They spent some time discussing the upcoming holidays and their respective travel plans.

Then the president sat back and crossed his legs. "So, what can I do for you?"

"I've been hearing a lot of rumblings on the Global Free

Trade Alliance. Listen, I support what you're trying to do. But I wanted to let you know that there are some folks in your administration who are stirring the pot."

The president frowned. "How so?"

"Raising questions mostly. Will U.S. workers be left holding the short end of the stick if this agreement comes to fruition? Will this result in a sudden shift of jobs out of the U.S.? Nothing overtly negative. More like policy debate."

Kendall cursed silently. He knew that, while debate was essential to ensure that the ultimate agreement was well thought out and considered all of the implications, those debates were best left to the lawmaking bodies, the House and the Senate. It was good that the White House and key Cabinet members argued over the provisions of the agreement, but it was crucial that, publicly, the administration speak with one voice. Nothing would derail a proposal faster than mixed signals from the White House.

"Who specifically?" Kendall asked.

"I don't know for certain, but rumor has it that it's coming from Rumson's camp."

CHAPTER NINE

January

On the second day of the new year, his first day back on duty, Richter had just stepped out of the command center when he saw Stephanie Sartori walking up the hall. He smiled. A first-rate agent, she was also a very attractive woman.

Sartori smiled back. "Hi! How was your holiday?"

"Good. But after two weeks visiting family, I was anxious to get back to work."

She laughed. "I know what you mean."

They chatted for a moment before she turned serious.

"Hey, do you remember that guy you busted a few years ago in New York? The cannibal?"

Richter grimaced. Reginald Tempest was a self-confessed cannibal suspected in the murders of eight people. His fetish for dismembering and eating the organs of his victims came to light after his initial arrest. If not for a threatening letter to the president, he likely would have gone on to kill again. In the neat, hand-written note, Tempest promised not only to kill the president, but also to eat his heart and post the video online.

Richter had driven up to Dutchess County to interview him and assess whether he was a practical joker, some guy blowing off steam or a real threat. He remembered being surprised when a seemingly easygoing sixty-one-year-old man answered the door. With gray hair and a pleasant smile, he looked more like a grandfather than a violent criminal. Tempest had invited Richter in and they'd sat at the kitchen table. He told Richter that he was a widower and had been living on his own for some time. Richter studied the man before him, gently probing into his background. Then he asked Tempest his opinion of the president. Tempest readily admitted to sending the letter. Richter asked if he really intended to eat the president's organs. As if surprised by the question, Tempest said that he always ate his victims. Then he opened his freezer, and, as if he were sharing a stamp collection, proudly pointed to some two dozen packages, each labeled with a victim's name.

The ensuing investigation discovered eight shallow graves on Tempest's thirty-four-acre wooded property. Forensic tests had confirmed that the remains and the frozen organs belonged to eight missing men and women, including Tempest's wife, who hadn't been seen for fifteen years.

From what Richter remembered, Tempest was now in a state-run psychiatric hospital, committed until that time when doctors decided he was stable enough to re-enter society. For men like Tempest, that day rarely came.

Sartori frowned. "He sent another letter."

The White House received mail every month from would be

assassins, lunatics, and others who, for one reason or another, had a gripe with the current occupant of 1600 Pennsylvania Avenue. The Secret Service investigated them all, dispatching teams of agents from its field offices as the first line of defense.

"Listen, Matthew. This time, he's also threatened you."

Richter felt a chill. "He's still in the hospital, isn't he?"

Sartori nodded. "I don't think you have anything to worry about, but I wanted you to know." She squeezed his arm. "Just be careful. Okay?"

———

With a cup of coffee in hand, the president sat down across from his Chief of Staff. The five days out of the office—time he had spent reconnecting with his family—had helped him put things in perspective. By the time he had returned to the White House, he had made up his mind.

"I've made two decisions," he began. "First, I am going to run for reelection."

Howell nodded, apparently not surprised.

"But," he continued, "Rumson is not going to be on the ticket."

It was clear that Howell had been expecting this too.

"I'm not sure I can trust him anymore." The president shook his head. "I realize now that I made a mistake."

"I agree with your decision, sir. But, I'm concerned about how he's going to react when he finds out."

"I am too. I'm not sure how to manage that yet. But, for now, I want you and Linda Huff to start developing a list of potential running mates."

The two men spent several minutes discussing criteria.

Howell closed his notebook and stood to leave, but President Kendall caught his arm.

"This cannot go any further than you and Linda."

———

The large screen showed a Mexican hacienda, with over a dozen buildings, all surrounded by a fifteen-foot stone wall topped with an electric fence. The main house was four separate buildings arranged in a square around a large stone courtyard shaded by citrus trees. In the middle was a pool, the morning sun shimmering on its surface.

A trellised and vine-covered walkway connected the main house to a covered parking area, the front ends of several Mercedes and Porsches visible in the shade. Behind this were some outbuildings and another parking area—this one uncovered—with a dozen or more cars and trucks. These appeared to belong to the guards and workers.

Half a dozen guards were patrolling the perimeter, while others clustered together, talking and smoking, their automatic weapons casually slung over their shoulders. A few men were sitting in the shade of a jacaranda tree, possibly taking a siesta. In the courtyard, gardeners were trimming bushes and trees, while two men cleaned the pool. To the side, below a pergola, four men sat at a table. A second screen showed three armed men in the shade of the guard booth at the end of the driveway, three hundred yards from the hacienda.

Pat Monahan was amazed at the detail and the clarity of the

video feed. A colonel from the National Reconnaissance Office told him that the video was courtesy of one of the NRO's Lacrosse satellites. According to the colonel, the satellite was capable of capturing high-resolution images of objects the size of a football, all the while orbiting four hundred miles above the earth. The satellite employed highly sophisticated radar-imaging technology and was able to "see" through clouds, through all kinds of weather, and at night. The only drawback was that the satellite flew a geosynchronous orbit and passed over the target area just twice a day. They had been fortunate that the timing of the mission coincided with the satellite pass. Although, that probably wasn't a coincidence, Monahan realized.

The CIA analyst pointed to the men at the table.

"This is Pedro Aguilar, 'El Jefe.' The men with him are his key lieutenants: his brother Jayme Aguilar, his cousin Manuel Hernandez, and Roberto Calzada. Calzada is the enforcer."

"Do we know who's inside the buildings?" Monahan was nervous.

The analyst pointed to the largest house on the courtyard. "We believe El Jefe's wife and two daughters are inside this house. His brother's and his cousin's families live in the houses on either side. His mother and an aunt and uncle live in this one, across the courtyard. There will also be maids and domestic servants inside each building." The analyst pointed to two other buildings. "The chauffeurs and mechanics live in this one here, by the covered parking area. And the one in the back is for the security force. We expect there to be at least a dozen armed men in that building as well."

"Can you assure me that the family will not be harmed in the process? That none of the servants will be hurt?" Monahan was paid to worry.

"Mr. Monahan," a new voice boomed, "we will do everything in our power to prevent them from being harmed."

The speaker was Rear Admiral Walt Magers, from the Joint Chiefs of Staff. Magers was responsible for the Sea, Air and Land Team—more commonly known as the Navy SEALS—tasked with this mission.

"We are employing non-lethal technology," the Admiral continued. "We hope to neutralize any resistance, at least from the group out in the open. However, make no mistake, this is a combat operation, and we are going up against a heavily armed enemy who has demonstrated a willingness to use extreme violence. Rules of engagement are that no lethal force may be used unless we are fired upon first." The admiral explained that the guards would be immobilized using a sophisticated military adaptation of stun-gun technology initiated from a remote location. When pressed, he declined to provide details, citing need-to-know protocol. Although Monahan had a top-secret security clearance, he decided, for the moment, not to press the point.

Monahan knew that the SEALS were leading the planned strike in conjunction with Mexican Special Forces. Similar to their U.S. Navy SEAL counterparts, the Fuerzas Especiales, or FES, specialized in unconventional warfare, assault, counter-terrorism, and special reconnaissance operations. Compared to conventional forces, both were highly trained and disciplined and had a far greater chance of executing a mission like this without spilling innocent blood.

Rear Admiral Magers looked at the clock. "The strike should commence any moment now."

It looked like a normal, peaceful morning at the hacienda when, suddenly, as if on cue, everyone in view fell to the ground. Three men at the breakfast table slumped forward, their faces landing in their plates, scattering glasses and dishes in the process. El Jefe fell off his chair and landed like a rag doll on the stone patio. One of the pool cleaners fell onto the tile apron. The other wasn't so lucky and fell into the pool.

Monahan jumped up. "Admiral, we can't leave that man there! He'll drown!"

The admiral waved him back down. "The assault team is inbound now."

The screens went bright for a fraction of a second then returned to normal.

"Electromagnetic pulse," the admiral explained. "We just knocked out all communications in the hacienda and disabled every piece of electronic equipment within a one-mile radius. Cars, ATVs, computers, microwave ovens, refrigerators—everything's dead."

Seconds later, half a dozen guards rushed out from the main house and the security building, their weapons drawn. Seconds later, they began shooting into the sky, only to be met with a devastating hail of bullets from above. A helicopter entered the scene, the thirty-caliber mini-gun in its door still smoking. It hovered, and the assault team began to rappel down. Three more helicopters quickly followed; additional troops could be seen entering the compound from all sides.

The admiral turned to Monahan. "There are medical corpsmen on the ground now."

The assault was precisely orchestrated as the SEALS and FES broke into individual teams, each tasked with a specific objective. Individual teams assaulted each building, first tossing stun grenades. In the courtyard, the hands and feet of the still unconscious prisoners were bound, while two medical corpsmen pulled the body from the pool. They began to perform CPR. Another medical team rushed to El Jefe and his henchman. After ensuring that their injuries were not life-threatening, the corpsmen carried them off screen to waiting helicopters.

A number of well-dressed women and children, their faces filled with terror, were led out of the main house. Most were crying. They too were escorted off screen.

There was an audible click from the speakers in the room. "Tango Alpha is secure. Package in possession. Zero casualties."

The admiral smiled. "That, ladies and gentlemen, means that the head of the Zacatecas Cartel and his key lieutenants are now in our custody."

"Admiral," the colonel from the NRO interrupted, "we will be losing satellite coverage in thirty seconds."

"Thank you, Colonel."

The assault teams began to search the buildings for criminal evidence and to seize guns, weapons, computers, and anything else tied to cartel activities.

The screens went blank.

Monahan was surprised when the task force members—military and civilian alike—began to clap. A few congratulated each other on the successful mission. Monahan, though, was troubled. Although the team had stayed within the parameters of the presidential directive and there had been no fatalities, there was no hiding the fact that the game had just changed. The U.S. had drawn first blood and he wondered what the repercussions would be.

———

"How was your vacation?" Dr. Hastings asked.

Richter smiled. "Good, Doctor. It felt good to go back to work."

The doctor smiled back. "You look more relaxed. That's a good sign." She waited a second or two. "Have you given more thought to some of the questions we discussed last time?"

"You mean, like what I want out of life?"

The doctor nodded.

"I have, although I don't think I have all the answers yet. What I do know is that I want to make this work. For practical reasons, I can't leave the protective detail yet. If I want any other job in law enforcement, I need to demonstrate that I succeeded here. If I leave now, it will look like I failed."

"Okay. I can see that. How much time are you thinking?"

"I don't know. Two, maybe three years."

She was silent for a moment. "We discussed your dream last time. Can you tell me what happened that day in Maine? I know what the press is saying, but I'd like your perspective."

Richter shifted in his seat, an uncomfortable silence before he spoke.

"I was standing behind him," he began in a monotone. "He had shot six, maybe seven birds and hit them all. It was impressive; the man could shoot." He smiled weakly. "I really don't know what happened. He spun the gun so fast. The next thing I knew, he crumpled to the ground." Richter shuddered as he took a deep breath. "I didn't even think that was possible with a shotgun. He was tall, and I think the investigators even measured his arms and...well..." His voice trailed off as he shuddered again.

"Where were you exactly?"

"I was directly behind him, about ten feet away. There were agents on each side, maybe fifteen feet from me, and another six agents behind us. I was the closest." He sighed. "Right before he did it, I saw his arms move, and something didn't feel right. I took two steps forward, thinking he was ill or something. Suddenly, I was splattered with blood and he was falling."

They sat silently.

"I read the review board's report." Hastings said after a moment. "Director Kroger shared it with me. I obviously can't give you names, but several other agents are patients of mine as well."

Richter nodded.

"After talking to witnesses and reviewing the security camera footage, the investigators determined that there was nothing any of you could have done. Not even you, Matthew."

Maybe so, Richter frowned. But why, then, didn't he believe it?

CHAPTER TEN

"Are you too busy to say hi?"

David Kendall looked up. Maria was standing at the door to the Oval Office. He grinned and came around his desk.

"Never too busy for you." He gave his wife a kiss. "So, to what do I owe this pleasure?"

"My, aren't you formal?" Her smile was mischievous. "I stopped by to invite you to an early dinner." Before the president could respond, she added, "I already checked with Arlene, and she says you're free."

The president grinned. "Well if Arlene says so, I guess I am. So what's the occasion?"

"Oh, I don't know. How about the girls miss you and would like to have dinner with you tonight. They tell me you haven't been home before nine o'clock for the last week. Of course I told them you were busy doing......what is it you do again? Oh, yeah, running the country or saving the free world or herding cats. Something silly like that. Right?"

He smiled and saluted his wife. "Message received loud and

clear, boss. What time?"

"How does 5:30 sound?"

"I'll definitely be there."

"Well, just in case, the girls will be here at 5:30 on the dot to escort you upstairs."

"So you're resorting to strong-arm tactics, huh?"

"You bet I am." She dismissed him with a flip of her hand. "Now go back to that cat thing."

The president smiled as his wife left. He stood for a moment, thinking how lucky he was to have Maria and the girls. They were his anchor to reality. He had a tendency to become engrossed in his work. But his family always helped him regain his balance when they saw him leaning too much in one direction.

This was, by far, the most challenging job he'd ever had. Building a mutual fund powerhouse had been tough, but Kendall found that the federal government was in a league all its own. There seemed to be a very strong momentum that continued, administration after administration, Congress after Congress. It was a wonder that anything was ever accomplished. Special interest groups, weak campaign finance laws, and the outright support and acceptance of pork-stuffed bills had corrupted the legislative process. The executive branch was just as bad. It was a large, dysfunctional family, a bizarre combination of short-term political appointees and a much larger permanent staff. The former craved power and looked for every opportunity to flex their muscles, while the latter resisted any attempts to upset the status quo.

The team he had inherited from President Walters, with one or two exceptions, was good. They were making progress on some key initiatives, like the Global Free Trade Alliance, education reform, and the drug problem. But the rate of progress was agonizingly slow. President Walters had told him that some days it felt like he was trying to herd cats. After almost two years as vice president and several months in this office, he understood what Walters had meant.

He looked at his watch—three more hours herding cats, and then a quiet evening with the family.

He felt reenergized as he walked back to his desk.

———

Rumson's office was located in the West Wing of the White House, next to the Chief of Staff's, around the corner from the Oval Office. Historically, the vice president's office had been located in the Eisenhower Office Building, formerly known as the Old Executive Office Building, next to the White House. That had changed when Dick Cheney became vice president. During the transition, Cheney had his office moved to the West Wing. He then proceeded to dramatically expand the power and control wielded by the office of the vice president, often making policy decisions on his own. After Cheney left office, many complained that the vice president's role and influence had expanded too far. Now that he sat in the chair, Rumson thought that Cheney hadn't gone far enough.

The intercom buzzed, interrupting his thoughts and, moments later, a troubled Phil Perry sat on the couch.

"I just learned," Perry said softly, despite the closed door, "that the White House Counsel's office is compiling a list of A players in the Republican Party."

"Really?" Rumson asked as he joined Perry. "Any idea why?

"No. But I have my suspicions. What I do know is that the Counsel's office has called the committee staff several times over the last three days asking for specific data on certain people. Based on the names, it looks like they're preparing a profile of the party up-and-comers. Oh," Perry added, "here's the other thing. Linda Huff is the one asking. Linda herself, not one of her staff."

"Shit." Rumson sat forward. Linda Huff was the White House Counsel, and her responsibilities included vetting presidential appointments.

"What key positions are open?" Rumson rubbed his chin, thinking through the possibilities. "It's not a Cabinet seat. Was the request specifically for lawyers or judges?"

Perry shook his head. "I thought of that. It's not the Supreme Court or a federal judge, because the list includes non-lawyers. And you're right. The Cabinet's full." Perry sat back, thinking, "Do you think anyone is planning on resigning?"

"I haven't heard anything, and I'm pretty plugged into what's going on. What about an ambassadorship?"

"My gut tells me no. That's a good place to stick your enemies, as far away from Washington as possible. Not a party leader or a rising star."

"You think he's starting to fight back?

Perry let out a breath. "That's my fear. I think we may have pushed him too far."

Rumson was silent for a moment before he exploded.

"That son of a bitch!"

Richter smiled as the president walked by with his daughters: sixteen-year-old Angela on one arm and fourteen-year-old Michelle on the other. As they disappeared up the stairs, Stephanie Sartori joined him.

"Agent Sartori. Wipe that smile off your face. You're a disgrace to the Secret Service."

She swatted him in the arm. "Oh, stop. I saw you smiling too."

"Yeah." Richter laughed. "It is kind of cute. They're a nice family. I hope this place doesn't change that."

"Why, Agent Richter. You're turning red." She could see that if he wasn't before, he was now. She decided to let him off the hook. "Anyway, I know what you mean. This is the first family that I've worked with that seems to enjoy being together."

"The first family? Or the first 'First Family'?"

She swatted him playfully again. "Very funny. If you ever lose this job, you could do stand up."

As she walked back to her station, Sartori once again felt like she was in the wrong place at the wrong time. Over the last two months, she had found that her attraction to Matthew, which she had resisted at first, was growing. A romance between them would never work, not while both were assigned to the presidential detail. Not only could they both lose their jobs, but it could compromise the president's security if both of them weren't one hundred percent focused on their task.

Her ex-husband had never understood. Oh, there were some

things she could never discuss, but even when she did share what she could, he had no way of comprehending what she did. Her day could vary from absolute boredom as she stood guard for hours at a time to an intense adrenaline rush as she responded to potential risks. She could be in four different cities in the course of one day. She could also, as part of a small team, manage the dynamics of a large, excited, and often volatile crowd. And there were an almost infinite number of scenarios, related dangers, and emotions in between. She had the highest level of security clearance and was routinely exposed to classified information. She had witnessed all sorts of personal failures by the politicians she had been charged to protect over the years. Unethical behavior like infidelity, lying, stealing, drug addiction, and obsession with pornography—it seemed to come with the territory. It seemed the higher some people climbed up the ladder of success, the less they believed that society's rules applied to them. Unlike her former husband, Matthew did comprehend all of that. He lived it every day.

It was clear that Matthew was still fighting his demons from President Walters' suicide. But she knew in her heart that she would feel the same way had she been on duty that day. She had wanted to say something to him, to let him know that she understood, but she couldn't figure out how to say it without exposing how she felt about him.

And over the past two weeks, she had begun to suspect that Matthew might feel the same way about her. Which only made it worse.

CHAPTER ELEVEN

It was eleven o'clock at night when they left the fundraiser for Louisiana Senator Ray Broussard. Broussard was facing a very tough reelection campaign and had been surprised when Phil Perry had called and told him that the vice president was a supporter. The vice president, Perry had said, would be happy to lend his assistance. The Senator had quickly accepted. Over the last few months, his approval rating had begun to plummet. His democratic opponent was hammering him in TV ads, and Broussard didn't have the resources to fight back, at least not on the scale required. His opponent was distorting his record, finding ways to make him look bad with innuendos and allegations that were not truthful. Well, not completely anyway.

He was amazed. He had been struggling to raise money when Perry and the State's Republican organization had, without much effort, organized a dinner for the movers and shakers in the Louisiana political and business communities, not to mention the old-money families that had grown cotton and sugar on plantations for generations. The night had been a tremendous success, and they had raised over three hundred thousand dollars. Vice President Rumson's endorsement had been huge, and they were able to charge two thousand dollars a plate for the pleasure of listening to the vice president speak. And, this being New Orleans, the food had been superb.

"Mr. Vice President. I can't thank you enough for this. The evening was amazing. I think you helped reenergize my campaign."

"Oh, I'm sure you'll get a chance to return the favor someday."

Broussard laughed as they said goodnight. As he walked to his hotel room, he pondered the vice president's parting comment. Actually, it wasn't the comment that was troubling but the look and tone that had accompanied it.

Phil Perry sat down on the couch in the vice president's room. "Well, what do you think?"

"What? About Broussard? He's an asshole! He would be dead in the water right now if we hadn't helped him out!" Rumson sighed. "What an evening! All those inbred, Cajun dipshits with their prim and proper southern manners….." He waved his hand in dismissal. "Anyway, I'm sure he'll be useful to us at some point. It's like putting money in the bank, Phil."

Perry suppressed a smile. He had heard this lecture many times before. *I can go back at any time and make a withdrawal. When I ask for something, these fuckers will jump all over each other trying to help me.*

"Any thoughts on the reelection?"

"Yeah. There's only one option as far as I'm concerned."

After a moment, Perry asked, "And what's that?"

"It's pretty obvious." Rumson growled.

Perry waited; it wasn't so obvious to him. He didn't have to wait long.

"He's got to go!" Rumson slammed his fist on the table.

The flower vase fell and shattered on the tile floor.

———

One week later, Rumson looked up from his newspaper as Agent C.J. Timmons, the head of his Secret Service detail, stepped into his study.

"Your niece is here."

Rumson folded the newspaper and stood as the woman strode into the room.

"Hello, Uncle Tyler." She gave him a hug and a kiss on the cheek, then stepped back and took in the room. "I like your house." Her eyes sparkled. "But how come it's taken you so long to invite me?"

Rumson smiled. "I've been somewhat busy. But you know you're always welcome."

Rumson's house was located on the grounds of the United States Naval Observatory in Washington, DC. Originally built for the observatory's superintendent in 1893, it was taken over by the Chief of Naval Operations in 1923, when, after a visit, he decided the Queen Anne style house was more befitting a man of his stature than a mere superintendent. The Navy continued to use the mansion to house its Chief until 1974, when Congress, in an ironic turn of events, kicked the CNO out and the building was converted to the official residence of the vice president.

As Julie sat, Rumson offered refreshments. He wasn't surprised when she asked for water. He had never known her to drink. He added a twist of lemon to her glass and prepared himself a scotch.

They sipped their drinks and made small talk. Although his wife wasn't home, he expected her shortly. After twenty-nine years of marriage, she had learned never to disturb him when he was in his office. This, and the fact that Julie wasn't really his niece, would likely lead to speculation by the household staff and the Secret Service that Julie was a dalliance for a man whose marriage, while cordial, was devoid of emotion. While that couldn't be further from the truth, it suited Rumson for now.

He had met Julie's father when she was fourteen. Her father had been a New Jersey State Trooper who had landed in trouble when it was alleged that he had "mishandled evidence," a polite way of saying that some items he had been charged with protecting until they were needed for trial went missing. The fact that all of the items in question during Trooper Stapleton's short tenure as head of the State Police evidence locker were deemed high value didn't help. Nor did it help when several pieces of jewelry confiscated during the arrest of a suspected mobster were later discovered in a series of pawnshops owned by Trooper Stapleton's neighbor. Rumson had intervened with the state attorney general, the charges were quietly dropped, and Trooper Stapleton was reassigned back to patrol duty.

Stapleton had been killed less than a month later, when he

was shot twice in the face during a routine traffic stop on the Garden State Parkway. The crime had never been solved, but Rumson had seen to it that the trooper's family was taken care of financially, including sending the trooper's only child, Jane, to college. It wasn't until she applied that Rumson learned her name was Julie, not Jane as he still called her. Jane was a nickname that had stuck when Julie, as a four-year-old on the first day of preschool, had combined her first initial with her misspelled middle name, Ann.

Julie's mother had died seven years later of lung cancer, but not before seeing her daughter graduate from college. After graduation, Julie, like her father, had enlisted in the Army. All the while, she continued to hold a grudge against the New Jersey State Police and, as her Army record indicated, authority in general. Despite her occasional insubordination, she was honorably discharged three years later. She then joined a private security firm, again with the help of her uncle's connections.

After almost twenty years, Julie still referred to Rumson as her uncle, as she had since her father's death. Rumson considered Julie the daughter he never had.

He studied her for a few moments. As if she could read his mind, the sparkle was gone.

"Jane, I need your help."

CHAPTER TWELVE

President Kendall glanced at his watch. In ten minutes, he was scheduled to meet with Rumson. Their weekly lunch had been cancelled for the last three weeks due to both his and the vice president's travel schedules. Outside of a few short meetings about the budget and one on his State of the Union address, this was their first private meeting in several weeks.

He stepped to the windows overlooking the South Lawn. There was no mistaking that it was winter in Washington. There were several inches of snow on the ground and the overcast skies seemed to hint that more was on the way. He noticed the wind blowing through the bushes, the snow piling up. And he noted once again that it was difficult to tell that he wasn't looking through glass but through a very heavy, glass-clad polycarbonate that was designed to withstand the force of a high-caliber bullet. The Secret Service had assured him that he was safe in the Oval Office. He shivered. Despite the glass, he suddenly felt uneasy.

———

"Hey, Dave." Rumson said. "Before we begin, I wanted to apologize for the meeting several weeks ago. The meeting with Phil Perry?"

Despite Rumson's apparent sincerity, the president was wary. Nonetheless, he smiled back. "The election meeting?"

Rumson nodded.

"I remember," the president said evenly.

Rumson sighed. "Listen, Phil and I only wanted to make sure that the team we put together and the plan we developed were the best. We thought with everything you had going on that we were being helpful. But," he held his hands up in a conciliatory fashion, "we didn't consult you first or ask for your input. I'm sorry for that."

The president smiled again. "Thank you, Tyler."

"The reelection team, the strategy, the plan….well, it's your call." Rumson paused. "Look, things have been a little tense lately, and I want to apologize for that too. I know you don't think I'm behind you on Hettinger's nomination, but I wanted to let you know that I've spoken to a number of people over the last few days." He paused and smiled. "I think we have the votes we need."

"Really?" The president feigned. Although the vote wasn't scheduled for another week, Charles Howell had told him the good news that morning.

Smiling, Rumson nodded.

"That's great news! Thanks, Tyler. I appreciate your support on this one."

———

Thirty minutes later, when their meeting ended, Kendall walked back to the window behind his desk. The meeting had been cordial, and he and Rumson had discussed a number of issues, including the economy and the Global Free Trade Agreement. He had subtly asked questions, trying to determine Rumson's position.

"I'm behind it, Dave." Rumson had smiled. "You know, I wasn't a supporter of NAFTA when it was first announced. I was certain that we would lose jobs to Mexico. But I was wrong. NAFTA has been good for the country, and I think the GFTA will be as well."

Kendall had smiled back. "I'll need all the support you can help me drum up on this one. It's going to be a challenge in Congress. Too many lobbyists have already lined up against it."

"I can definitely help you there," Rumson had said confidently.

Yes, he had seemed sincere, the president thought as he stared out the window. But he couldn't shake the feeling that Rumson was playing chess. The problem was, he wasn't sure what move Rumson had just made.

———

Vice President Rumson walked out of the Oval Office and, with a brief nod at Charles Howell, turned towards his office. He ignored the Secret Service agents standing in the corridor. Matthew Richter couldn't help but notice the smug smile as Rumson passed by. He watched as Rumson, spotting the Deputy National Security Advisor, barked an order. The young woman's face fell. Richter knew that the junior staff, the assistants, aides, and interns were afraid of Rumson. He treated them like servants or like they didn't even exist. Most of the agents assigned to protect him complained. Rumson stopped and said something to Cal Mosby. Mosby nodded and, for a brief second, the hint of a smile flashed across his face then was gone.

How fitting, Richter thought as Rumson continued down the hall with Mosby trailing close behind. He glanced over at Sartori and rolled his eyes. She hid her smile. God, he hoped he was never assigned to Rumson's detail. If anyone ever had to take a bullet for that asshole, he hoped it was Mosby and not him.

———

Kendall waved Charles Howell into the room. When they were seated, he described his meeting with Rumson.

"You know," Howell said, "the younger aides around here talk a lot." He offered a thin smile. "Makes them look important, I suppose. Anyway, there's speculation that he's making a power play. That he may try to steal the nomination from you and run on his own."

The president frowned as he thought about the chessboard again. If that was Rumson's move, what was his?

CHAPTER THIRTEEN

February

As he was leaving the coffee shop, Lieutenant Francis McKay held the door for the woman behind him.

"Thanks, Frank." She had a warm smile.

McKay paused. He usually had no problem remembering names, especially those of young, attractive women.

"I'm sorry, have we met before?"

She laughed. "My name is Jane."

McKay sized her up. She had a pretty face; her eyes sparkled. There was something sexy about her, he thought, something about her smile, her eyes, and the way she stood. He noticed that despite the heavy coat, she was slim, athletic. Still a young man in his late twenties, he started to contemplate the possibilities.

"Do you mind if I join you?" She flashed her smile again as she pointed down the sidewalk. He smiled back and they began to walk. To any casual observer, they appeared to be two friends out for a stroll.

"So, Lieutenant Francis McKay."

He was surprised by the sudden change in her voice. "Do I know you....Jane?"

"No. But I know you." She turned and the sparkle was gone. Her dark eyes bore into him. "All about you."

———

Later that night, after his mother had gone to bed, McKay sat in her living room and wondered what he was going to do. For the last ten years, things had been going well. He had built a nice life for himself. He enjoyed what he did and had plans for the future. But now, it appeared that some of the things he had done when he was younger were coming back to haunt him. Now, not only could he lose his job, this could destroy his life.

The woman, Jane, or whatever her real name was, told him that she knew he had been caught cheating on an exam when he was a cadet at the Academy. She also told him she knew that some powerful forces had intervened at the time and persuaded the commandant to find a way to grant an exception to the Air Force's zero-tolerance rule.

Although he had worked hard over the years, without the help of powerful benefactors his life would be different. He wouldn't be where he was today, part of an elite team tasked with providing safe transportation to the most powerful man on earth. He would still be here in Newark, New Jersey, working in some dead end job. Still getting into fights, probably going to the strip clubs and bars every weekend; still flirting with the law. Like many of his former friends, he was also likely to be married to a woman he could no longer stand, with a couple of kids to support.

He had grown up poor in Newark and, like many boys in his neighborhood, had gone through the rites of passage of fighting to defend himself and to establish his place in the social pecking order, both on the streets and in school. As he grew older, his anti-social expressions expanded to petty theft and vandalism. The paradox, however, was that he maintained a B+ average in school. Sure, at times cheating helped, but the fact was, he never had to try very hard. The many aptitude tests he took during his school years confirmed his above average intelligence.

One day, after he broke the nose of a kid simply because the boy had made the mistake of sitting in McKay's seat, he was sent to the principal's office. Again.

"You, young man, are headed for trouble," the principal had said. "I've seen many punks like you come through this school. Some of them are able to rise up and break free of the streets. But the majority of punks like you go nowhere. Some end up in prison. And some." He paused. "End up dead." The principal sat back and stared at the ceiling for a moment, then shot forward. "You know that you have potential, son. You have good grades. You can make something of your life." He paused again. "You have a choice to make."

McKay was curious. This wasn't the principal's typical lecture.

"Do you remember Senator Rumson?" The principal asked.

McKay nodded, remembering the senator who had come to speak at their school several months earlier.

"He grew up on these same streets. He went to this same school."

McKay remembered the senator's speech. It had struck a chord as the senator described a childhood similar to his own.

"He would like to meet you."

"Why?" McKay spoke for the first time.

"Because you have potential."

They met after school one day and the Senator had offered McKay a path out. Rumson had told him that he could arrange for McKay to be accepted into a top college, but that McKay had to meet him halfway. He had to stop fighting, had to stop breaking the law and, further, had to apply himself in school and demonstrate to his teachers that he did indeed have the capacity to rise above the streets of Newark.

McKay had accepted the challenge and Senator Rumson, Vice President Rumson now, had been true to his word. He had written the congressional recommendation required for McKay's application to the Air Force Academy. Later, the senator had intervened in his life again when he had been caught cheating. And now, even though Jane had never mentioned the connection, it was clear the Senator was demanding payback.

His normal reaction to threats or manipulation was violence, the coping mechanism he had learned early in life. But over the last dozen years, he had worked hard to temper that reaction. While physical domination might work for a teenager on the streets, he had enough sense to know that it wouldn't work for him now.

When he had asked Jane what she wanted, she had flashed her sexy smile and told him that she wanted to meet with him again tomorrow, before he headed back to Washington.

———

The next morning, they met again at the coffee shop and, with cups in hand, began to walk. It was clear from the bags below his eyes that McKay hadn't slept much the night before.

"You have a choice to make, Frank." The sexy woman was nowhere to be found this morning. "Your life is over. At least the life you know." Jane was silent for a moment, letting this sink in. "You will lose your job. There's no doubt about that." She stopped and turned; her eyes bore into him. "How you lose your job and what you do next is up to you."

She started walking again. McKay hurried to catch up.

"Wait! What the fuck do you want from me?"

She walked on, letting him hang in the silence. It was an agonizing fifteen seconds.

"We want you to do us a favor."

They entered a small park overlooking the Passaic River. She steered him to a bench where they sat and watched as an older couple walked by. Jane waited until the couple crossed the street before she told him exactly what she wanted.

McKay jumped off the bench. "You're out of your fucking mind!"

Jane grabbed him and pulled him back down. She was surprisingly strong.

"Sit down and shut up," she commanded. "Earlier, I told you that you had a choice." She looked as menacing as some of the gang members he had run into in his youth. "Well you don't. You don't have a choice, Frank."

"For God's sake, why?" He was both confused and scared.

"That's not your concern."

"Fuck you!"

He began to stand up again when she squeezed his arm, finding the pressure point in his elbow. He winced in pain, broke her hold, and jumped up, ready to fight. She stood and stepped toward him, their faces mere inches apart. When she spoke, every word was measured.

"Do not ever try something like that again. I promise you, if you do, you will experience pain like you never have before."

———

His mind was reeling as he drove back to Washington later that day. Jane had told him that they would meet again in one week. He considered speaking to his commander, but she had been very clear that if she found out he had discussed this with anyone, anyone at all except her, his life, as well as the lives of anyone he spoke to, would be in danger. Although he had spent just one hour in total with the woman, his intuition told him that she meant what she said.

"We'll be watching you," she had told him as they parted.

McKay didn't notice the police car behind him until he saw the flashing lights. He swore and slammed his hand on the wheel. As he pulled over onto the shoulder, he was surprised to realize that he was on Route 295 just south of Baltimore. He must have been driving on autopilot; he didn't remember leaving New Jersey.

He handed his license and registration to the State Trooper

along with his military identification.

The Trooper studied the cards for a moment. "You're going a little fast, Lieutenant. Don't you think?"

"I'm sorry, Officer. I just got called back to base." The lie came without even thinking. He struggled to appear calm. He could see the doubt in the officer's eyes and worried that the policeman would check to see if he was sober or, worse, if he was hiding something. Not that the policeman would find anything, but still. He didn't need the added stress.

"Are you okay, Lieutenant?"

"Look, Officer. I spent two sleepless nights in New Jersey with my mother. She's been very sick. Then this afternoon, I got called back to base. CO said it was urgent."

The trooper studied him for a moment before a smile crept across his face.

"We're watching you, Lieutenant."

The trooper stared at him for another moment, then handed McKay's cards back and left him shaking on the side of the road.

———

The days that followed were agonizing. He spent the first few days working out in the gym in the mornings and then going on long runs in the afternoon. He avoided his friends and fellow officers, saying that he had put on a few pounds and had to get his ass back in shape. He didn't want anything negative in his Officer Evaluation Report. His friends shook their heads, but left him alone. It seemed that all McKay talked about was his next promotion.

What sealed his fate was a message he received on Wednesday afternoon. He had just returned from a six-mile run and decided to check his email. He felt a sense of doom as he read the message.

I saw your mother today. Such a sweet lady. You need to be a good son and take care of her. She's all you have.

When he scrolled down, there was a picture of his seventy-two-year-old mother, looking old and frail, as she stepped out of her apartment building. *Oh shit! They're watching her!* He realized then that they were going to do whatever they needed to do, including hurting his mother, to force his cooperation. *Oh God*, he thought, as his face went pale; he didn't have a choice.

CHAPTER FOURTEEN

Richter moved along the rope line, all the while looking for the face that didn't belong. It might be someone sweating profusely on a cold, winter day like today. Or a face in the middle of a sea of smiles; a pair of eyes that returned his own piercing stare. Such was the life of an agent on protective detail, where a stony mask was often a more effective weapon than the gun he carried.

Wearing a pair of Ray-Bans, Richter scanned the crowd. Although many misunderstood the Secret Service's fondness for shades, they allowed an agent to appear as if he was looking directly at several people at the same time.

Like most agents, Richter believed the mere presence of the president's security detail, with their cold, hard stares and the subtle display of weaponry, probably scared off many a would-be assassin. Of course, the large number of uniformed cops who lent assistance to the Service and the sheer size of the motorcade created the image of an impenetrable fortress. And that was just the way the Service wanted it.

The Service spent a considerable sum of money determining

the psychological profiles of would-be assassins. Most attempts on the president's life were the work of lone gunmen, deviants with one or two screws loose who, after a lifetime of being ignored by society, were looking to secure their fame in one brilliant moment. Or the David Berkowitz types, so out of touch with reality that a neighbor's dog became their connection to the world. John Hinkley, Squeaky Fromme, they each fit the profile.

After watching the Zapruder film, the uncut version that the public never saw, Richter concluded, like most agents, that even Lee Harvey Oswald was another lone psycho seeking to right what was wrong in his own little world. And that was the threat that worried him the most.

President Kendall stepped off the stage to the cheers of the crowd. With the Lincoln Memorial behind him and the Washington Monument in the distance, his address had been a fitting tribute to two great men on Presidents' Day. Like his predecessors, Kendall always took the opportunity to "press the flesh," but nothing made the agents protecting him more nervous than when POTUS wandered amongst the crowd.

Richter was a step behind the president, Brad Lansing a step ahead, Agent Sartori right behind. She carried the Fast Action Gun Bag, which agents referred to, in a rare breach of political correctness, as the Fag Bag. The Fag Bag appeared to be an ordinary laptop computer case, but inside was an Israeli-manufactured Uzi submachine gun. As the name implied, the agent was able to deploy the weapon with incredible speed.

Like many professional athletes, Richter found that when he was "working the man," escorting the president through the crowd, he was in "the zone." His eyes shifted from face to hand, always on the alert for the hand that darted out, always expecting to hear his earpiece scream, "Gun left!" or "Gun right!" He usually was able to tune out the distractions, the background noise, the day-to-day problems that weighed on him. Usually.

Richter watched as the president exchanged a few words with an excited group of school children and their teachers. Suddenly there was a flash and a loud pop. Richter lunged forward, grabbing Kendall's arm.

"Gun!" He yelled into his sleeve.

The crowd flinched, stepping back, confusion and fear in their eyes. President Kendall, confused himself, began to turn.

With one arm circling the president's waist, Richter pushed Kendall's head forward, bending him over, making him a smaller target and hiding him in the crowd. Pushing an aide out of the way, Richter began moving Kendall away as the protective detail converged on them.

After several seconds, with agents shouting and nervously scanning the crowd, Richter realized his mistake. Unfortunately, it was all captured on national television.

———

"A little exciting out there today, wouldn't you say, Mr. Richter?"

Sitting in the back of the limo for the short ride back to the White House, Matthew Richter glanced over at the president.

"I'm sorry, sir." Richter felt his face flush. Again.

The president reached over and patted his shoulder.

"Don't worry about it. Just a false alarm. I'm alive, right?"

Richter sighed. At least the president was forgiving, but Richter knew that for the next few weeks, he would have to endure the jokes from the other agents. All because he jumped at the sound of a truck backfiring. The camera flash didn't help. In hindsight, Richter realized that he remained on edge, still plagued by feelings of failure and the images that came to him at night. Lately, though, the dreams hadn't been as bad—his sessions with Dr. Hastings, as painful as they sometimes were, had made a difference. However, despite the doctor, and despite his evening regimen of brutally exhausting workouts, he still woke frequently, anxious and nervous. The lack of sleep was taking its toll.

His last vacation was…what? Richter wondered. Seven weeks ago, he remembered. Jesus, he felt like he needed another one already.

As if reading his mind, the president reached over and squeezed his shoulder again.

———

After filing an Incident Report and being debriefed by Keith O'Rourke, Richter finished his day in relative peace, standing watch outside the Cabinet Room and then the Oval Office. He knew he would have to meet with the review board, but O'Rourke told him that it could wait a day or two. Brad Lansing had been supportive as well.

"Hey, listen. Although the president's handlers are pissed, I'd much rather have you err on the side of caution then not react at all. Our job is to keep the man alive and you showed that we take that charge seriously." Lansing had smiled. "And frankly, the Big Man likes you, so don't lose too much sleep over it."

At the end of his shift, Richter clocked out in the command center then walked through the lobby, passing through the doors into the foyer. He waved to the uniformed agents manning the metal detector and stepped out into the frigid air. He took two steps when there was a loud pop behind him. He spun, reaching for his gun, only to find Cal Mosby, laughing, the remains of a burst balloon in his hand.

———

It took a therapy session and several difficult nights before Richter began to put the incident behind him. Late one evening, after his shift, he stepped onto the metro platform. The First Family had dined out at a small restaurant in Georgetown and it was ten o'clock at night when he left the White House. His eyes scanned the station, noting each person. Without thinking about it, he subconsciously assessed the risk, in this case not to his principal, but to himself. He had never had any trouble in the Metro, DC's subway system. His bearing, his situational awareness, and his physical presence were usually more than enough to convince any would-be assailant to bypass him for an easier mark. But there were times, like now, when he just wanted to turn it off.

He walked to the end of the platform and stood by the pillar, waiting for the next train. He let his mind wander, trying to decompress after the long day. As he contemplated the upcoming weekend, his first off in a month, he heard a shout on the other end of the platform. He stepped from behind the pillar and saw a young woman, her back to him, fending off two men. Alarm bells ringing in his head, Richter started running, unbuttoning his coat along the way. Suddenly, one of the men pulled a knife and lunged at the woman. Richter drew his gun and shouted. The woman sidestepped the man's thrust and grabbed his arm, twisting it to an unnatural angle until he dropped the knife and fell to his knee. She struck him once in the face and he went down. The second man hesitated, saw Richter charging, then turned and bounded up the steps. Richter got there just as the second assailant disappeared up the stairs. He pointed his gun at the man on the ground.

"Police! Put your hands behind your head! Now!" The assailant, writhing in pain, rolled on his belly and put his uninjured arm behind his head. Richter turned to the woman. "Ma'am, are you all right?" He did a double take when she smiled. "Stephanie?"

"Agent Richter. Thank you for coming to my rescue. I don't know what I would have done without you." Before he could answer, the sound of rapid footsteps came from the stairwell. Sartori pulled out her Secret Service credentials. Two uniformed Metro cops ran into the station, their guns drawn.

"Federal agents!" Richter yelled, his weapon still pointed at the assailant on the ground. The cops slowed, their eyes darting from one agent to the other. One cop stopped twenty feet away, while the second moved around to the side. Their guns were angled down, but they were clearly tense.

"What's going on?"

"Attempted assault." Richter, maintaining eye contact, spoke slowly and clearly. "I'm going to holster my weapon and cuff him. I need you guys to cover."

Three minutes later, the young thug was being led up the stairs by a second pair of uniformed officers.

"You both need to come down to the station and make a statement."

Richter sighed. *There go my plans for a workout.*

They were interviewed separately and both positively identified the second assailant, who had been arrested several blocks from the station. An hour and a half later, they were told that they were no longer needed. Richter called the incident into the Secret Service Command Center at the White House while Sartori asked the sergeant to forward a copy of the report.

As they left the police station, Sartori sighed. "I'm sorry."

"What do you mean?"

"I ruined all of your fun. Big federal agent tries to break up a purse snatching only to find that the assailant has already been subdued by the intended victim." She patted his arm and smiled. "I am so sorry."

"I was going to say the same to you. I'm sure you wanted to beat the crap out of those two. You probably would have if I hadn't shown up."

"Well then, you can make it up to me and buy me dinner." She made a show of checking her watch. "My date probably gave up on me by now."

Richter laughed. "Oh, I'm sure. But what the heck. I'll buy."

By the time he got back to his apartment, it was after two in the morning and, although they had only eaten burgers at a nearby bar, he realized that he had enjoyed the time with Stephanie.

CHAPTER FIFTEEN

Once McKay made his decision, he surprised himself by how quickly he shifted to the logistics of what he had to do. He was, after all, a survivor. He would find a way to do what Jane wanted and, somehow, still come out on top. He needed to focus on it, to think it through. There was always a solution if he took the time to look for it. If he could get his hands on the right supplies, it was possible. The big issue was what he did after. Well, he thought, he had two more days to come up with a plan before he would see Jane again.

———

They met in a large park and walked in silence to the middle of a soccer field. Despite the cold morning, a group of kids was playing flag football two fields away. Other than that, they were alone.

"You were very well behaved this week." Jane gave him a playful smile as she put her hands on his chest and feigned surprise.

"Have you been working out?" She let her hands play over his chest for a second, then the smile vanished.

"What I want to know, Frank, is…" she paused, "…are you on board or not?"

It was scary how she could turn it on and off. The woman was either mentally unbalanced, he realized, or very good at what she did. She had the resources and means to watch him, and probably a lot more. But she also needed him. *Two can play this game*, he thought. He let his anger show.

"Why don't you drop the psycho shit? Okay, Jane? Or whatever the hell your name is."

Her smile returned. "Okay. Whatever you say."

She was very, very good. But he was prepared.

"There are some conditions that we need to discuss first."

"My, my, my, Frank. Did you get your balls back?"

McKay ignored the jab.

"What do you want?"

He pulled a piece of paper from his pocket and handed it to her. Jane studied the list. It was cryptic but she had no problem translating.

"So, you want a safe place to hide for a while, stocked with food and supplies. You want a new identity. And a way out of the country." She looked up.

"Those are the big items. I'll also need your help in obtaining the materials I'll need."

"We have to trust you. Is that it?" Her sarcasm was obvious.

"Yes. Just as I have to trust you. It can't work any other way."

She considered this for a moment. "Okay. Let's assume that we agree to your requests. How soon can you do this?" She was matter-of-fact, as if she were negotiating to have her house painted.

"It depends on how quickly you can get me what I need. Then probably a month or two to finalize the plan. And, of course," McKay added, "the final date depends on his schedule."

"Okay, Frank. I'll get back to you. Tomorrow." Jane smiled again and kissed McKay on the cheek. "Now walk me back to my car, my big muscle man. You know some of these parks aren't too safe for a girl."

McKay didn't move. "There's one other thing." He paused and matched her stare. "I want five million dollars."

Once again, he was surprised at her reaction. She neither smiled nor threatened. Her face was neutral.

"Let's talk tomorrow."

———

They met again, the following morning, in a park in Alexandria, Virginia. Once again they chose an open field.

Jane studied him for a minute. "So you plan to be on board? How do you plan on escaping?" The tone was casual as if they were discussing the weather.

McKay's response was curt. "Let me worry about that."

There was an empty playground on one side and, on the other, two teenagers tossed a Frisbee back and forth. One of the kids yelled, and McKay and Jane turned to watch as the cold wind caught the Frisbee and it flew off course.

"We will meet your demands. Half up front and the other half after you complete your assignment."

McKay nodded. He had thought through several possible answers she might give him and had rehearsed various responses. He needed to show her that he was in control. Well, not in control exactly, but that he was....what? A formidable competitor? Regardless, her response told him they were serious. Jane, he reminded himself, was a hired gun.

"In exchange," she continued, "we have one additional requirement."

McKay waited.

"We want you to take on an associate. A partner if you will."

He had not expected this but was able to mask his surprise. One of her weapons, he had realized, was to try and keep him off balance. Sudden personality changes, shifts in direction, new demands were all part of her approach to keep him under her control. He knew that now and was prepared.

"What type of partner?"

"Someone to help you get the supplies you need. Someone to act as facilitator. Someone to protect our investment."

"Who?" McKay stood defiantly, arms folded across his chest.

Jane smiled. "Well, why don't we go meet him right now?"

Jane made a quick phone call. When she hung up, she hooked her arm through his and they started to walk towards the deserted playground. She made small talk along the way. McKay's mind was racing and he tuned it out.

Abruptly, Jane stepped in front of him.

"Why, Frank. You're ignoring me."

McKay was about to respond when she looked past him, her eyes twinkling.

"Cal! What are you doing here?"

McKay turned and was hit by a sudden wave of panic as he stared into the face of Agent Cal Mosby.

———

When he thought about it later, McKay realized that he had missed the obvious clues. He remembered the flood of panic, certain that he was about to be arrested. All the clandestine meetings with Jane were a charade. She had set him up, and now he was going to jail. In the silence that followed, however, Mosby just stood there, looking awkward—no different, McKay realized, from himself. Jane's smile had been as bright as ever as she looked back and forth between them. When she spoke, her tone was conspiratorial, as if they were sharing a secret.

"I believe you two know each other."

He and Mosby stood there like fools, while Jane seemed to enjoy the moment.

It was clear that she was in charge.

CHAPTER SIXTEEN

The motorcade pulled up below the North Portico of the White House. The doors of the lead and tail vehicles opened, and Mexican security and U.S. Secret Service agents jumped out. A dozen Mexican agents surrounded the limo and, after a quick radio conversation, the door was opened. Kendall walked forward and extended his hand to Mexican President Felipe Magaña.

"Señor Presidente. Mucho gusto. Bienvenidos a la Casa Blanca." *Mr. President. It is nice to meet you. Welcome to the White House.*

Magaña smiled broadly. "Igualmente, Señor Presidente. Es un placer estar aquí." *Likewise, Mr. President. It is a pleasure to be here.* Magaña switched to English. "I'm impressed. Your Spanish is very good."

Kendall laughed. "Thank you. But, I'm afraid those are the only words I know."

Magaña laughed and put his hand on Kendall's shoulder. "Somehow, I think we will manage, Mr. President."

"Please. Come in," Kendall said, escorting President Magaña up the steps into the entrance hall.

—

A short while later they were seated in the Map Room.

Magaña held up a box. "I have something for you, a gift from my country to yours; something to express our friendship."

Kendall smiled. He opened the box and pulled out a dagger. The silver blade was about five inches long with an ornate, swirled hilt where it met the handle. The handle itself was about three inches long made of some sort of black stone carved into the face of an Aztec god, Kendall guessed. He ran his hand along the blade, noticing that although it was pointed, it wasn't sharp. It took a moment before he realized he was holding a letter opener.

"This is beautiful, Felipe. Thank you very much." Kendall turned the gift over, admiring the craftsmanship. "The handle represents an Aztec god, correct?"

Magaña nodded. "It is Quetzalcoatl, hand-carved from obsidian onyx. He was a patron of priests and the god of creation. Some say this meant that he was the creator of mankind. Others say he was a male symbol of fertility. He is also associated with vegetation and the harvest. Like much of Mayan and Aztec mythology, his role, his manifestations, and his powers evolved and changed over the centuries. You can see that the figure represents a winged serpent. It is said that he ruled the boundary between the earth and the sky, possibly as one of the sun gods."

Magaña sat back. "It is interesting, David. I am a Roman Catholic. Similar to the Christian belief in Jesus's divine birth, the Aztecs believe Quetzalcoatl and his twin brother were born to a virgin."

"Really? I didn't know that."

"Yes. No matter what you believe, I think the symbolism is appropriate. He is a god of life." Magaña smiled. "Such a fragile thing, life is," he continued, his smile gone. "The drug problem that is affecting your country as well as mine has done so much to destroy lives. Working together, Mr. President, I hope you and I can change that."

———

After lunch, Kendall poured a cup of coffee and handed it to his guest.

"Felipe, I hope we can speak frankly. I would like to discuss our joint operation. While I agree with our predecessors' intents, I am worried that it is only a matter of time before the cartels begin to retaliate. I am afraid that this could be devastating to the citizens of your country and possibly mine as well."

"I agree." Magaña responded. "I know that there has been cartel activity in Arizona and Nevada, some drug related killings and kidnappings. It's only a matter of time before it spreads to other cities…maybe even to Washington." Magaña crossed his legs, his hands pressed together below his chin as if in prayer. "I think we have made a start, but unless we look at this systemically, we will have done nothing more than, what is your saying, waking the sleeping bear?"

Kendall nodded as Magaña continued.

"There are some in my country who applaud what we are doing. But many more are not happy. They see the same thing that you and I do and fear the violence will get worse. There are also some who are upset that I am allowing foreign soldiers to operate on Mexican soil. They point to your country and ask why more is not being done about the demand for drugs. And about the weapons and guns your citizens smuggle into my country and sell to the cartels."

Kendall nodded again. He had been briefed and had been expecting this. "I understand your position, Felipe, and I agree it's something that we need to discuss further. I also think we need to consider what we can do to address the support your police and your armed forces provide to the cartels. My country believes that it will be difficult to make meaningful progress unless that issue is confronted."

So much of this is a dance, Kendall thought. Although he was no stranger to negotiation, the diplomatic exchanges between nations were very different from deal making in the business world. Today, their initial dance was part of the mating ritual, the intent to see if, hopefully, they were compatible dance partners. The goal was to inform each other of their respective viewpoints and the key issues affecting each of their nations. The real discussions would come later between their diplomatic teams. First though, Kendall and Magaña had to find a way to dance together without stepping on each other's toes. That was difficult when both men wanted to lead.

"Yes, David. We can discuss that too. But there is a related issue that is equally as important. There are many in Mexico who are not happy with the wall that you have built between our countries."

"We are concerned about the immigration issue as well,"

Kendall responded. "I believe there are challenges on both sides of the border. What can be done to develop more economic opportunity within Mexico?"

"I have some thoughts." Magaña frowned. "But to make a difference—a real difference—well, it's not possible without your help, David."

"No," Kendall agreed. "But it will require significant changes in how *both* of our countries approach this problem."

Both men sat for a moment, sipping their coffee. Magaña put his cup down and Kendall held up the silver urn. Magaña nodded.

As Kendall refilled the cup, Felipe Magaña smiled. "I think you and I can work together, mi amigo."

CHAPTER SEVENTEEN

March

The black Ford Taurus made its way down the dirt road. The driver, dressed for a day of fishing, looked like an ad for L.L. Bean. A coffee thermos sat on the passenger seat next to a wicker fish basket. As the car bounced over the ruts in the old logging trail, the driver glanced at his mirrors.

Despite recent forecasts, the sky was overcast and held the threat of rain. Typical mid-March weather, thought the fisherman. He glanced out the side window again and sensed that the forest was about to come alive. The trees would bud soon, and the many varieties of fern and groundcover would soon blanket the forest floor. The car rounded a bend, entered a small clearing, and coasted to a stop about fifty feet from a stream. He turned the car off and listened to sounds of the stream and the occasional ping as the engine cooled. It wasn't quite 7:00 a.m. He was early.

The fisherman inspected his mirrors one more time and, confirming that he hadn't been followed, grabbed his fish basket and thermos and stepped out of the car. He turned, as if admiring the scene. Satisfied that he was alone, he opened the trunk and grabbed a fishing rod and tackle box. He glanced once more down the dirt road then shut the trunk.

He carried his gear over to the stream. The spot he chose was a large flat boulder, overhanging a deep pool of gently flowing water. Perfect, he thought as he laid his gear on the rock. He had a view of both the stream and, with a small turn of his head, the dirt road. He poured himself a cup of coffee, took a sip, and then began preparing his pole. He took his time rigging a new fly. When he finished, he stood and pulled some line out of the reel with his left hand while he swept the pole back and forth in long arcs with his right. Each arc began behind him and finished out over the water, and with each cycle, he let out a little more line. He let the fly fall gently into the stream. He fed more line as the current pulled it downstream.

Although he had never been fly fishing before—in fact it had been eighteen years since he last held a fishing pole, and that time it was an inexpensive spin-cast model his father had given him on his tenth birthday—he appeared adept at his task. The thirty minutes of instruction he had received at Bass Pro Shops had paid off. But he had no interest in catching fish.

He glanced at his watch again, adjusted the slack in his line, and then squatted to pick up his mug of coffee. He hesitated, the coffee mug inches from his mouth. As the steam swirled below his chin, he glanced down the road. After a moment, he bent down, placing his mug back on the rock. He didn't have to wait long. A green, late-model Crown Victoria rounded the bend in the road and pulled up next to his car. Two men climbed out and, like him, admired the scene before retrieving their gear.

———

He studied the men as they walked toward the stream. One was short with olive skin, his Mediterranean heritage evident in his features. His companion was a tall black man, powerfully built. Like him, both men were dressed for fishing. Each carried a pole and a tackle box. The black man also carried a wicker fish box, similar to the one by the fisherman's feet.

"Good morning," the black man called with a smile. "We'll head upstream a bit so we're not in your way."

The fisherman smiled tentatively. "Be my guest."

The black man placed his wicker basket on the rock next to the fisherman's and scratched the back of his head. "Any luck?"

"None yet"

"How long have you been out here?"

"About an hour."

The Mediterranean remained silent, his eyes darting around. The black man made a show of hitching up his pants with his right hand while he balanced the rest of his gear in his left. There was a red band wrapped around the handle of the man's pole, before the reel.

"Is that a White River pole?"

"Sure is! First time I'm using it, though. It's a present from my wife." The black man's mouth smiled, but his eyes didn't.

"I'm impressed."

"Don't be. I think she just wants me out of the house."

Both men laughed, finally relaxing. The exchange had confirmed their identities.

"My name's Vernon, by the way, and this here's Mike," the
black man said, extending his hand.

"I'm Bob," the fisherman replied as they shook. Both knew
these weren't their real names. The Mediterranean, Mike, smiled
weakly, but didn't offer his hand. Vernon bent down and picked
up one of the wicker baskets.

"Well, we'll get out of your way."

"Good luck," Bob called as they walked up the path.

Vernon turned and caught his eye. "Good luck to you too."

He was going to need it, Bob thought.

———

Twenty minutes later, Bob pulled his cell phone from his pocket
and made a show of reading the message. He shook his head,
closed the phone, and began to reel in his line. Fifteen minutes later, he was in his car, heading back down the dirt road.
He smiled as he thought about how cleanly the switch had been
made. Although he hadn't caught any fish, the morning had
been successful. At least so far.

CHAPTER EIGHTEEN

Bob followed the dirt road for about ten minutes but before he reached the intersection, he pulled to the side, his car hidden in the shadows. He removed his vest and flannel shirt and stuffed them in a duffel bag. Below, he wore a plain, dark blue T-shirt. He pulled off the Duck Boots and slipped on a pair of running shoes. Appearance altered, for now at least, he turned onto the paved county road.

A half hour later, he was on a state road, heading north through the mountains of West Virginia. A short while later, he spotted the gas station and pulled in. There was a small convenience store, and, around the side, a payphone. There were no other customers.

He paid cash. The old man behind the counter hardly glanced at him; he seemed more interested in the TV on the counter. After turning on the pump, Bob climbed back in the car and opened the wicker basket. Inside he found a pack of fishhooks, a single piece of paper, and, on the bottom, a key for a storage locker. The paper was old and weathered, as if it had been there for many years. Bob unfolded it.

The Lake Bug – The fisherman's best friend. Fish can't seem to resist the Lake Bug. I invented it when I lived in Coeur d'Alene and it's the best lure I've ever used. I'm sure that you'll be so pleased with the Lake Bug, that in thirty days, if you're not completely satisfied, I'll refund your money. Happy fishing!

On the bottom was the name of the manufacturer: BCS Zurich, Seattle, Washington. There was a ten-digit number listed below. He flipped the paper over and saw what appeared to be a phone number, written in pencil. Bob slipped the key and paper into his pocket, and climbed out of the car. He finished pumping, then, using the payphone, dialed the 800 number. Seconds later he was connected with a teller in New York. He read the ten-digit number and could hear the teller typing. After several seconds, the teller confirmed that two and a half million dollars had been deposited into a new account in his name in the Banque Commerce Suisse in Zurich, Switzerland twelve hours ago. He gave the teller instructions to wire the funds to another bank in the Cayman Islands. After confirming the instructions, he hung up, then dialed another 800 number, this one from memory. He was connected to the bank in the Caymans and confirmed instructions that, when the money was received, it was to be wired to a third bank in the Cook Islands.

As he climbed back into the car, he considered the information he had received. The message told him to proceed according to plan.

———

The game warden crept silently down a path that paralleled the stream and snuck up behind them.

"Gentlemen, may I see your fishing licenses?"

Startled, both Vernon and Mike turned.

Vernon recovered and flashed a smile. "Well, we're not exactly fishing now, are we?" he replied, pointing to their gear on the ground beside them.

"So you don't have licenses?" The game warden's voice was stern.

"No, we don't. But like I said, we're not fishing."

"Gentlemen, the law is pretty clear here. With all this gear, you obviously intend to fish. I'm going to have to issue citations."

Vernon and Mike looked at each other, then pulled out their credentials.

"I'm Treasury Agent Vernon Jackson and this is Agent Michael Malouf."

The warden frowned. "Well, Treasury agents or not, you still need a valid fishing license in the State of West Virginia."

"Officer, we are currently on duty," Vernon calmly replied. "We are here as part of an ongoing investigation."

"Investigation? What the heck could you possibly be investigating out here?"

Vernon's smile faded and he stepped towards the game warden. "This is an official investigation. Obviously, I can't share details with you. Now, I'm asking you to leave before our investigation is compromised. If you don't leave, I will arrest you for interfering with the official duties of a federal agent. Do I make myself clear?"

"Hey, I'm just doing my job, fellas. How was I supposed to know you guys were cops?"

Vernon relaxed and smiled again. "Look, we probably should have informed local authorities, but we didn't think we would need any assistance, nor did we think we would be getting in anyone's way."

———

After dropping off the rental car, Bob retrieved his own car from the short term lot at Reagan National Airport. Thirty minutes later, he pulled up to the guard booth at the entrance to Andrews Air Force Base. He had his military identification card in his hand as the sentry waved him forward to the checkpoint. He didn't recognize the guard on duty.

"Can I see your ID, sir?" Bob handed the card over. The guard studied the card and then peered into Bob's face. Satisfied, he handed the ID back.

"Welcome back, Lieutenant McKay."

———

In cryptic terms, the caller explained the problem.

"Can he identify you?"

"Not by name. We used fake IDs."

"But he saw your faces." It was a statement, not a question.

The caller didn't respond. Not that it mattered. The fact was, the meeting had been compromised. There was only one solution.

"I think you know what needs to be done."

CHAPTER NINETEEN

Matthew Richter yawned as he walked into the command center at the end of his shift. It had been a long, boring day filled with hours of standing watch outside the Oval Office. He preferred the excitement of travel. It didn't matter if it was a trip to New York or a short ride across Washington. Anything beat standing watch. He was anxious to get to the dojo tonight, or maybe go for a long run.

"Hi, Tim."

Tim Jacobs, sitting in front of three displays—what before the digital age would have been called the switchboard—slipped off his earphones. "Hey, Matthew. Done for the day?"

Richter nodded as he sat down in front of a computer terminal.

He logged on and checked his inbox. There were the usual threat updates and suspect profiles. He studied the pictures. Although he read his email on his Blackberry, he liked to review the pictures of people who might pose a threat to POTUS on a larger screen. He saved the message. He would review them again tomorrow before the start of his shift.

The next email was a reminder to submit his expense report. He sighed. He would have to come in a little earlier tomorrow than he had planned. Following that was a list of recent promotions, changes in assignment, new hires, and other personnel announcements. He scanned the list but didn't recognize any of the names.

Richter logged off and then glanced up at the mail slots. Email had virtually eliminated paper mail, so he was surprised when he spotted something in his mailbox. He opened the envelope and pulled out a registration form for a race, a ten-kilometer run on Memorial Day weekend. There was a yellow Post-It stuck to the bottom.

Hi! I thought you might be interested in this. The course is relatively flat and there are some nice sections along the river. I plan to run it again this year. Hope you can make it. Stephanie.

Richter smiled for the first time that day. *Oh, I'll make it*, he thought. *I'll definitely make it.*

———

The following morning, Richter headed for the monthly staff meeting. He grabbed a cup of coffee, walked into the crowded conference room and found a spot along the wall.

Keith O'Rourke began the meeting, as usual, by reading through various announcements. Richter half listened as O'Rourke explained changes to Thrift Savings Plan, the federal government's version of the 401K plan so popular with private employers.

O'Rourke flipped a page on his note pad. "Okay, next. There will be a couple of changes to shift assignments."

There was a collective groan in the room. O'Rourke read through half a dozen changes and Richter was happy not to hear his own name. There was a smattering of applause for some agents and the usual bantering with the rest who had been reassigned.

"Okay." O'Rourke continued when the noise died down. "Finally, effective today, Cal Mosby is being transferred back from the vice president's detail and has been assigned to POTUS once again."

Shit, Richter swore to himself. He scanned the room and saw Mosby against the far wall. Mosby nodded to several people then stared at Richter for a brief moment, a scowl flashing across his face.

CHAPTER TWENTY

He couldn't have asked for a better night. This far out in the country, with no moon and overcast skies, the night was pitch black. He lay on his belly in a shallow ditch about fifty yards from the small cabin. The night-vision goggles amplified the ambient light several thousand times, providing him with an eerie green image. It didn't take long to determine that there was no one outside of the house. The intelligence he had received indicated that the occupant lived alone.

The lights inside went out. He checked his watch, the numbers exceptionally bright until the goggles adjusted to the change in light. He would wait a little longer.

Thirty minutes passed before he decided it was safe. He crept toward the cabin, his steps falling silently on the ground. Crouching by the stone chimney, he listened. Satisfied that there was no movement within the house, he took off his goggles and stuffed them in his backpack. He waited for his eyes to adjust to the darkness, and then began to climb up the side of the chimney, like a cat, using the gaps between the protruding stones as footholds. Big as he was, he was surprisingly agile. The wind began to pick up and whistled through the trees; the cabin creaked and groaned. So much the better, he thought.

He reached the roof and put one foot on the edge, where the roof joist and the wall below would bear his weight without much protest. His nature was to be careful. He slowly transferred his weight from the foot on the chimney to the foot on the roof. When no noise betrayed him, he planted his other foot on the roof. The intruder took off his pack and set it on top of the chimney. He pulled out a gas mask, slipped it over his face and adjusted the straps. Next, he pulled out a small metal canister, no bigger than his thumb, attached to fifty feet of nylon string. He twisted the top of the canister, lowered it into the chimney, slowly letting out the line. After twenty seconds, he heard a soft, metallic clank as the canister hit the flue. He froze and counted to sixty. When he was certain that there was no movement inside the house, he continued.

The string went slack as the canister landed on the floor of the fireplace. He draped the excess string over the side of the chimneystack and then secured a small tarp to the top. Satisfied that all was in order, he climbed back down. He jogged back to the ditch, took off the gas mask, put on the goggles and lay down to wait. He let another thirty minutes pass before he took off the goggles and put the mask back on. Then he climbed up the side once more to retrieve the tarp. Moments later, he was at the front door. The lock didn't present much of a challenge and, within seconds, he was inside. He got his bearings and headed straight for the bedroom.

The game warden was in bed, his eyes wide open, face frozen in terror. The intruder checked for a pulse and, finding none, gently closed the warden's eyes. He opened the bedroom window several inches to air out the room. It was warm enough this time of year that sleeping with a window open wouldn't appear unusual. He opened windows in the kitchen and the living room as well. Any remaining traces of the nerve gas would be gone by morning. It would appear that the warden had suffered a heart attack. The particular nerve gas he'd used—a combination of three different gases—was virtually undetectable in the body. On the outside chance that an autopsy was ordered, the standard toxicology tests performed at the morgue would show nothing unusual.

He retrieved the canister from the fireplace, closed the top, and placed it and the nylon string into a special pouch, which he sealed and stuffed into his backpack. He walked through the house one more time, careful to make sure that there was no evidence that he had been here. He locked the front door on his way out.

In all likelihood, no one would discover the body for several days.

———

She glanced at the display on her cell phone. It was about time.

"Yes?"

"Our problem has been resolved. All loose ends have been accounted for. We're back on track."

"Good. Let's keep it that way."

Click.

———

Lieutenant Francis McKay put a ten-dollar bill on the bar.

"My treat, Andy," he insisted.

Chief Master Sergeant Brandt picked up his beer and raised his glass in salute.

"Thanks, Lieutenant. What's the occasion?"

"Besides the Orioles game tonight?"

Brandt chuckled and took a sip of beer. Both were avid fans of the Orioles and the Redskins in their adopted hometown. They carried their beers to a table in the back of the upscale bar. The place wasn't normally frequented by personnel from Andrews. Most of the airmen and Marines preferred the smoky honky-tonks that surrounded the base. And despite the fact that the Air Force frowned on fraternization between officers and enlisted personnel, Brandt and McKay occasionally spent time together, catching a ball game or discussing sports.

"Hey, I almost forgot." Although there was no one near their table—most of the crowd congregated around the bar— Brandt lowered his voice. "You remember the problem with the fuel management system that you asked about? I think I figured out a way to trigger it."

"That's great. I just need a chance to shine in front of Colonel Zweig."

Brandt shook his head. It seemed that all that McKay talked about the last month was a promotion. Brandt knew that the Officer Evaluation Report went a long way to convincing the Promotions Board that an officer was qualified for the next level.

Oh well, Brandt thought, he liked the lieutenant and it couldn't hurt an enlisted guy like him to have friends in high places.

He leaned forward conspiratorially. "Okay, here's how you do it…."

CHAPTER TWENTY-ONE

April

"How are the plans coming along?" Vice President Rumson yelled as he steered the boat up the Severn River, the broad expanse of the Chesapeake Bay behind them. The wind and the roar of the motor guaranteed their privacy. Fifty yards to their starboard, in an identical Wellcraft Cabin Cruiser, four Secret Service agents kept pace with the vice president. Fifty yards behind them were four more agents in a third boat.

It was late in the morning on the first Saturday of April, early for boating season. For most people. In his yacht club, Rumson was always the first in the water and the last one out.

He was a power boater through and through. He never understood the attraction of a sailboat. They seemed to float around, aimless, always waiting for the wind to take them somewhere. There was no sense of power. That was certainly not the case on his boat. He loved the sound he heard when he fired up the big block inboard engine; a low growl bubbling up from the back, all that power waiting to be unleashed. He always felt a thrill when he pushed the throttle forward and the boat seemed to leap out of the water. No, none of that wimpy sailboat shit for him.

Against the advice of the Secret Service, he not only continued to boat in the sometimes crowded Chesapeake Bay, he further refused to let his bodyguards accompany him. After a brief stalemate, he ultimately allowed his agents to shadow him in a separate boat. The Secret Service purchased two boats identical to Rumson's and had them retrofitted to accommodate their unique needs. The fact that they selected the same model boat was a calculated decision designed to confuse any would-be assassin.

As Jane gave him an update, Rumson steered around an island.

"Okay. When?"

"I'm still working on that. Three or four weeks, I think."

Rumson mulled this over. "Are you sure you have the right people working on this? We can't afford any mistakes."

"There are always risks in a mission like this, but I've done everything I can to minimize them. I have the right people. They're intelligent and they're motivated. We can do this."

Rumson studied her face. "There can be no trail."

"There won't be. I have that covered."

He saw nothing but confidence in her eyes.

———

"Sir, next week is your trip to Seattle for the trade summit with China," Howell began as Arlene Reardon handed the president an agenda. "This is a follow-up to the last G-7 meeting. You need to make a few opening comments before the delegates sit down to hammer out the details. Stress the importance of trade fairness, mention our concern about China's manipulation of the currency markets, our concern about human rights and sweat shops and how they relate to the products we import; all very subtly of course. The big thing to mention is our support for the Global Free Trade Alliance."

"This is at the University of Seattle?"

"Yes, sir. After that, you're scheduled to meet with Bill and Melinda Gates."

Kendall nodded. The Gates's charitable foundation had recently announced that education was a top priority, and this was a great opportunity to see how the private sector was tackling the issue.

Howell continued, "Thursday night you'll have dinner with Governor Lange, and, on Friday morning before you depart, you'll tour Old Peninsula Clothing Company."

"Is Lange looking for anything specific?"

"From what her people told me, just an opportunity to meet you. I've asked for a list of topics she's likely to bring up. I should have that from her staff shortly."

"Okay. And the clothes company? What's this, a store?"

"It's a four-year-old manufacturing company that is one hundred percent employee owned. They have over two hundred employees, all of whom were formerly unemployed. Everyone is a shareholder. This is a great small business success story in an industry where we have a significant cost disadvantage. If the

Global Free Trade Alliance is ratified, they're well poised to begin exporting American-made products overseas. That would be a very interesting turn of events for an industry that has virtually disappeared in the U.S."

"All right, I like that."

"We leave on Wednesday, the twenty-first, in the afternoon, and we're back here by 5:00 p.m. on Friday."

"Friday the twenty-third?"

"Yes, sir."

"Good," Kendall nodded then turned to Arlene. "I've been meaning to take Maria and the girls to Camp David for a weekend. What about after I return from Seattle?"

Arlene handed the president another piece of paper. "It will have to be late, sir. Angela has a ballet recital at 7:00 p.m."

The president glanced at the program. "Is this new?"

"Yes, sir. Mrs. Kendall informed me this morning."

"Okay. Please order some flowers for me." He remembered the last recital. Every other father had given his daughter a bouquet.

"It's already taken care of, sir," Arlene answered. "I can arrange for the helicopter at 9:30. Would that work?"

"That would be great."

After Arlene and Howell left, Kendall walked to the windows. Despite the bright sunshine, he felt anxious. For some reason he couldn't quite identify, he was not looking forward to this trip.

CHAPTER TWENTY-TWO

Thursday, April 15

Catherine McKay handed her ticket to the agent at the check-in desk and watched as he flipped through her passport. She was a nervous traveler, especially since this was her first time in almost thirty years.

She had initially resisted when her son had proposed the trip almost two months before. But Francis had been persistent. Outside of some distant cousins in Ireland, he argued, they only had each other. With his work schedule, they never seemed to have time to spend together. She was getting older, after all, and opportunities like this weren't always easy to find.

"Why don't you get yourself a nice young lady?" she had asked him. "Why do you want to travel with an old woman?"

"Because I want to see Ireland, Ma. And I know you do too. You've talked about it ever since I was a kid."

He had an urgent look on his face. She could tell he was worried, particularly so over the last few months. As much as she had wanted to refuse, he was her son.

"I'm not getting on no airplane," she insisted. "It's a wonder more of those things don't fall out of the sky. I don't care that you fly around in them all day. I'll go by boat. That's how my parents came here, and that's how I intend to go back."

The gate agent smiled and handed back her documents. "You're all set, Mrs. McKay. We'll be boarding in one hour. Have a pleasant cruise."

She put her passport and ticket in her purse. This she put inside a large travel bag before walking to the waiting lounge. She was traveling alone. Francis's work schedule had changed at the last moment, but he had promised to meet her in Waterford when her ship arrived.

"What happens if your schedule changes again? Are you going to leave me stuck over in Ireland by myself?"

Her son had patted her on the shoulder. "Don't worry, Ma. I'll be there. But just in case, two of our cousins from your side of the family will meet us in Waterford. They're excited to show us around."

She clutched her travel bag to her chest. Last night she had looked inside, just to make sure she was ready. Francis had thought of everything. There was an itinerary with descriptions of all of the activities available to her during the six-day cruise with circles around things he thought she might like. She also found the names and numbers for her cousins, as well as those of relatives who lived in Dublin. In an inside pocket, in an envelope, was a stack of Euros as well as a debit card. Two thousand in total, she had counted. So much money.

There was also a cell phone. "Just in case," her son had said.

The last item was a smaller envelope. On it he had scrawled, *To be opened in Ireland*. She had resisted the urge to peek inside. Francis had told her there was a surprise and that it had to wait until they were together. *This must be it*, she reasoned.

Although she was apprehensive about traveling, she was also excited. She hadn't told Francis, but she was looking forward to spending ten days with him in Ireland and learning more about her family. With her health, this might be the last time she could make such a trip. She had sensed that this was important to him, too. He was under too much stress from work and needed a break. Although she hadn't told him, she was pleased that he had asked her instead of some girl. Her son needed her now and she was, above all things, a mother.

———

"United Airlines Flight 201 to Seattle is now boarding at gate D2."

Two well-dressed men stood and joined the boarding line. They didn't draw any unusual attention as they handed their boarding passes to the gate agent. They proceeded down the jet way and nodded to the flight attendant standing in the door of the plane. The two men found their first-class seats. After stowing their luggage, the flight attendant offered them drinks. The tall man asked for coffee. His companion shook his head. *Another pair of harried business travelers off to yet another meeting*, the flight attendant thought as she poured coffee.

They didn't look like fishermen today.

CHAPTER TWENTY-THREE

Saturday, April 17

At seven-thirty in the morning, two C-5 Galaxy transport planes taxied to the runway and, one after the other, took off from Andrews Air Force Base. The planes were loaded with six armored limousines, almost two-dozen armored Chevy Suburbans, millions of dollars' worth of electronic equipment and an impressive arsenal of weaponry. The president's advance detail sat in the forward section of each aircraft with members of the White House Military Office who were responsible for maintaining most of the vehicles. The advance detail was comprised both of agents and members of the Technical Services Division, and their job was to ensure that Seattle was safe for the president well before he arrived.

The advance detail had a tight schedule. Over the next three days, they had to meet and coordinate with local law enforcement and review and test-drive multiple routes for the motorcade and assess the risk of each. They would also perform security assessments of all the stops on the president's schedule, secure the hotel rooms to be used by the president—both from physical threats as well as electronic—ensure local medical facilities were ready and equipped for any emergency, and review potential disaster scenarios and contingency plans. The local Secret Service field office had been working with the Seattle Police for the last several weeks. They had already reviewed the threat list, and agents were in the process of tracking down people of interest for a quiet conversation.

If everyone did his job properly, by the time the president arrived, any potential threat would be minimized and the trip would go seamlessly.

At least, that was the theory.

CHAPTER TWENTY-FOUR

Wednesday, April 21

Chief Master Sergeant Andrew Brandt, clipboard in hand, climbed the ladder and peered into one of the four engines of his aircraft. The fact that the Chief was a mechanic and didn't legally hold the title to the plane was irrelevant. In true Air Force tradition, the Chief owned the aircraft he was assigned to and, not surprisingly, had become as possessive and protective of his charge as a mother hen was of her chicks.

In Brandt's case, his aircraft was a specially configured Boeing 747-200B sitting in a heavily guarded hangar at Andrews Air Force Base. Unlike the typical 747, this airplane was furnished for VIP travel and, accordingly, few luxuries were spared. Accommodations included an executive suite with a dressing room, lavatory, and shower, an office, and a combination conference room/dining room. The plane was equipped with special electronic equipment for secure data and voice communications, allowing passengers to maintain continuous contact with their ground-based offices. There were separate accommodations for the entourage that always accompanied the VIPs when they traveled.

Brandt's 747 was one of two identical planes that belonged to the 89th Airlift Wing, part of the Air Mobility Command located at Andrews Air Force Base. Although the Air Force distinguished the two planes by their tail numbers, Chief Master Sergeant Brandt referred to them as *The Princess* and *The Bitch*. However, when the president was on board either plane, it didn't matter which one, it was called Air Force One.

The Princess, or tail number 28000, was first deployed in September 1990. The plane's performance and trouble-free operation during air trials had impressed the Air Force brass. However, tail number 29000, delivered three months later, proved to be a paradox. That Boeing engineers could produce two identical aircraft on the exact same production line with the exact same specifications, and yet one always seemed to be plagued with minor malfunctions mystified Brandt.

Today, he was working on The Bitch.

Each plane had a flight crew of twenty-six and was capable of carrying seventy-six passengers. The Princess, and The Bitch too for that matter, when she wasn't under repair, had a maximum range of over eighty-three hundred nautical miles. However, in-flight refueling capabilities and a spare crew allowed Air Force One, in the case of an emergency, to remain airborne indefinitely. Both planes were powered by four General Electric jet engines, each capable of developing almost fifty-seven thousand pounds of thrust. Each plane had a top speed of six hundred thirty miles per hour, a hair below the speed of sound, according to Boeing, but neither had been pushed to the max. Not yet anyway.

"Good morning, Chief."

Brandt pulled his head out of the engine in time to see Sergeant Albert Morales wheeling another food supply cart to the aft loading bay.

"Mornin', Al," Brandt responded with a lopsided grin. "What's for dinner today?"

Morales grinned back. "Black Angus steak with a peppercorn sauce, braised carrots with baby onions, fresh sourdough rolls, and a garden salad with a vinaigrette dressing. If you don't like that, we have poached salmon and risotto, or fettuccini with portobello mushrooms in a garlic sauce. Or pretty much anything else your little heart desires. Oh," Morales added, "and a bottle of merlot. Actually, a case of merlot, some chardonnay, some cabernet, and a few other wines I can't pronounce."

Brandt shook his head. "Must be nice."

"Don't give me that, Chief. You get to eat too."

"Oh, sure. I'll eat the steak. But I can't have any wine."

"My heart bleeds for you." Morales laughed. "Hey, so where's the boss off to today?"

"Seattle," Brandt replied as he stuck his head back in the engine. "I got to make sure The Bitch will fly first, though."

———

As usual, the crew arrived at the hangar five hours before the flight, allowing ample time for the preflight briefing. Although the manifest listed fifty passengers, from their viewpoint, there was only one that mattered. Given that, no detail was overlooked. The pilots and flight engineer studied the weather forecast and conditions at their destination—on this trip, Seattle-Tacoma International Airport. They reviewed their planned flight path and, as an added measure of safety, plotted the airports and air fields along the way that could be used in case of emergency.

Next, they studied the maintenance records, noting that although there had been some minor issues with both the electrical and fuel management systems, the necessary repairs had been made. Finally, they performed the walk-around: inspecting the control surfaces, the tires, the engines and other critical components, ensuring the plane was airworthy.

Members of the press were usually the first passengers to arrive, and today was no exception. After passing through both Air Force and Secret Service security checkpoints, they boarded the plane and found their seats. Despite the fact that the press section was in the rear of the aircraft, it was as well-equipped and comfortable as the first class section of any commercial airplane.

As the press settled in, Air Force stewards provided coffee, drinks, and snacks. Half an hour later, Representative Pete Ortega, Senator Jane Wentworth, and Senator Peter Dykstra from the state of Washington arrived, each accompanied by one or two staff members. They took their seats in a section of the cabin reserved for special guests of the president. This was directly in front of the Secret Service section, which, Senator Dykstra noted with a chuckle, would keep the press at bay.

The president's staff arrived next: speechwriter Nancy

Hartwig, National Security Advisor Michael Breen, Commerce Secretary Felicia Jackson, and White House Counsel Linda Huff. Moments later, Wendy Chow, the Press Secretary, joined them. Each was accompanied by the usual entourage of aides. They took their seats in the front half of the cabin, which was reserved for the White House. With its plush seating, individual and group work areas, enclosed conference room, and private dining area for Cabinet and senior staff members, this section more closely resembled a four-star hotel than an airplane. Throughout were numerous flat-screen TVs, secure telephones, and connections for computers.

The section in the very front of the plane was reserved for the president and contained a private office as well as a private bedroom and bathroom. Next to the president's office was a fully equipped medical facility, which could serve as an operating room, if required. The main galley, situated between the medical facility and the senior staff, was where the chefs, Air Force crewmembers, individually prepared meals for each guest.

With a sophisticated communications system, which allowed the president to maintain audio and video contact with the White House and, if necessary, to place a secure call to virtually anywhere in the world, he was able to transact business as if he were sitting in the Oval Office. This, more than anything else, made Air Force One a flying White House.

———

"Sir?" Charles Howell stood at the door. "Marine One is ready."

The president grabbed his travel bag and walked toward the

door. As he stepped outside, he saw Tyler Rumson waiting.

"Have a good trip, sir."

"Thanks, Tyler. See you Friday."

"Don't worry about a thing here. I'll hold down the fort."

As Kendall and Howell walked out on the South Lawn and headed for the waiting helicopter to Andrews, it struck him. After several weeks of nothing but deferential, respectful behavior, he was sure he had seen the hint of a smirk on Rumson's face.

———

Twenty minutes before the scheduled departure, inside the hangar conference room, the head of the Secret Service advance detail, Sean Tully announced, "POTUS is ten minutes out. Colonel, nothing negative from my end. Are we still a go?"

"We are a go, Mr. Tully," Colonel Zweig answered. Zweig was the pilot and highest ranking officer on Air Force One.

After a brief conversation, Zweig stood, then he, Major Tammy Lewis, his co-pilot, and Captain Wes Thomas, his flight engineer, left the conference room. Lewis and Thomas proceeded to the crew staircase. Zweig stood at the base of the main staircase, waiting.

Marine One touched down nine minutes later and taxied to the hangar entrance. Once the blades stopped spinning, Kendall and Howell exited, followed by Agents Lansing, Sartori, and Richter. The president and Howell were ushered inside the hangar. Air Force personnel stood at attention; Kendall returned the salutes.

"How are you, Colonel?"

"Excellent, sir. We should have a good ride out. No major weather issues today. We do expect some bad weather on the West Coast tomorrow and Friday. Nothing the crew can't handle, though."

CHAPTER TWENTY-FIVE

Derek Middleton bit his tongue as he watched Jack Walsh study the trail map. Friends since the fifth grade, Derek had realized years ago that Jack would never change. Methodical, cautious, and a bit nerdy, Jack was everything Derek wasn't.

"You need to live more," he used to tell Jack when they were in high school. "Be spontaneous! Let whatever happens happen and just enjoy it!"

But Jack had never wavered in his approach to life. Despite that, and despite the fact that their lives had gone different directions—Jack was now in medical school down in Boise, while Derek still lived at home with his mother—Jack was his best friend. And this, he thought as he looked out over the vista before them, was one of their shared passions.

Jack put the map away then pulled out a handheld GPS, pressed a button and locked in their current position. Apparently satisfied, he stowed the GPS but then pulled out a compass. Derek suppressed a grin. *Talk about redundancy*, he thought. Using carabineers, Jack attached his water bottles to the straps on his pack then tied a bandana around his head.

Jack scanned the gray sky yet another time. "What's the forecast?"

"It's supposed to get up to the high forties, but it will probably drop below freezing at night."

Jack frowned at the sky. "No rain or snow?"

"Not that I heard." It wasn't a lie, but it wasn't the truth either. He hadn't checked the forecast despite promising that he would. It wasn't intentional. As usual, he had been running late and decided, after a quick look out the window, that conditions were good for backpacking. Unfortunately, the window was in his mother's house, one hundred and thirty miles away.

"Ready to go?" Derek asked.

"Ready as I'll ever be." Jack grinned.

Derek resisted the urge to say something sarcastic.

They began their ascent at the Blackhawk trailhead, which, according to Jack's GPS, was just over six thousand feet above sea level. Their goal for the day was to get to Sable Point, about seven miles away by trail. Their planned route would take them through a series of small descents and ascents over the first four miles, and then they would descend by a series of switchbacks down to about four thousand feet where they would cross Sable Creek. The final leg, only a mile long, was the toughest as they would have to climb almost two thousand feet to Sable Point. They planned to camp somewhere below the peak.

After spending the night at Sable Point, they would hike another eight or nine miles to Granite Peak the following day. If they still felt good and, if conditions permitted, on day three they would trek twelve-plus miles down to Red River Hot Springs, and then, on the fourth day, they would return to Blackhawk.

Hikers usually ventured out in the Nez Perce from midsummer through early October, since the winter months could be harsh and snowmelt in the spring made crossing the streams treacherous. But Derek had pleaded with Jack.

"You only have a week off from classes and we haven't been for a while. Come on, man, don't wimp out on me."

Both men loved Nez Perce National Forest and the Salmon River Mountains and so, while most college students headed to warmer climates down south, Jack had finally agreed to spend his break in the spring thaw of the Idaho wilderness with Derek.

During the summer hiking season, it would take about three or four hours to reach Sable Point. More like five to six hours today, Derek estimated, as they had to navigate over swollen streams and deal with the remnants of the heavy winter snowfall.

He slowed his pace to let his friend catch up. Jack wasn't out of shape by any means, just careful. Derek didn't complain, at least not out loud. In his mid-twenties now, he had come to appreciate their differences. Jack had always been there for him: helping him study back in high school, providing a shoulder to cry on after his father died, even bailing him out of jail once.

Left to his own devices, Derek would throw on a backpack at the spur of the moment and head off for a four-day hike by himself. But Jack had to double and triple check all of his gear and plan out his route. He was worse than a little old lady, Derek mused, which was precisely why he had ushered Jack out of the trailhead shelter before he had a chance to read the entries other hikers had made in the logbook.

Hikers were required to sign in at the trailhead and indicate their planned route, length of stay, and probable camping areas. All too often, U.S. Forest Service Rangers were called on to rescue stranded and missing campers, and often the only way to find them was to follow their planned routes. Unless the lost campers happened to be like Jack and considered GPS devices and cell phones essential hiking gear.

The search and rescue job had become more difficult over the last five years as budget cuts had decimated the U.S. Forest Service and, in many parks around the state, ranger patrols had been scaled back or eliminated. These days, most rescues were made by other hikers or by the military, which viewed a lost, hurt, and often difficult-to-reach hiker as a training opportunity.

Earlier, when Derek had signed them in, he had noted that previous entries in the logbook warned of ice and heavy, packed snow above the six thousand foot mark. One camper had scrawled: *Crampons and snow gear recommended.* That entry was a week old, and Derek knew that if Jack had seen it he would have backed out, especially with the threat of a storm evident in the menacing clouds. Surprisingly, Jack didn't question the ominous sky.

Well, Derek thought, *what he doesn't know won't hurt him.*

———

Lieutenant Francis McKay was one of two crewmembers whose duty station included the lower deck. Although it was primarily used as cargo space, it was also the way to the middle or passenger deck. To reach the main cabin, most passengers had to climb a staircase to the rear door on Air Force One, where, once inside, they encountered yet another stairway connecting the lower deck to the middle deck.

McKay's duties included greeting passengers as they initially boarded the plane and directing them up the staircase to the main cabin. Even though the cargo hold was pressurized and climate controlled, the Air Force did not want passengers getting lost and wandering around.

McKay was more than a glorified doorman, as some of the crew had joked. He was also an on-board technician who would troubleshoot and make temporary repairs in the aircraft's flight systems while the plane was in service.

"Secure the boarding doors." Major Lewis's voice came over McKay's headphones. He closed and locked the rear hatch, then climbed the staircase to the passenger deck, securing the door to the cabin behind him. He took his seat next to Brandt in the back of the press section.

———

Immediately after takeoff, Richter unbuckled his seatbelt. As he stepped out into the aisle, Mosby shot him a look then turned away. That's weird, Richter thought, as he began a routine security patrol.

Mosby had been acting different recently. They hadn't been on the same shift—Richter needed to thank O'Rourke for that—and usually only crossed paths in the command center, or, like now, when the president traveled. Mosby hadn't extended the olive branch by any means, but he had been far less hostile than usual.

When Richter reached the White House section, he spotted Stephanie sitting outside the president's office.

She looked up. "All clear here."

Richter nodded and turned to head back when she pointed to the open seat.

"Why don't you join me for a second? POTUS is in the office with Howell and Breen."

Richter did a quick scan of the cabin and then sat. Both agents were on alert even as they chatted.

Sartori frowned. "You look like you've got something on your mind."

Richter laughed. "Am I that transparent?"

"Sometimes."

He hesitated. For the Protective Detail to be effective, they had to trust each other, and he didn't want to jeopardize that by bad-mouthing other agents. But Mosby was different, and this was Stephanie he was talking to.

"I don't know," he said, his voice low, "but Mosby seems to be acting strange."

She frowned. "I've noticed that. Rumor has it you two don't get along." When he nodded, she continued. "The guy's an asshole. I think he's threatened by younger agents like you and me. He barely gives me the time of day."

"You too?"

"Yeah. He doesn't get along with too many people."

Richter shook his head. "It's not that. If anything, he's been less of an asshole these last few weeks."

Sartori looked at him. "I heard that O'Rourke's been on his back." She patted Richter's arm. "I also heard that he might be retiring."

Richter smiled. "Boy, wouldn't that be nice?"

———

Shortly before dusk, Jack and Derek were about three hundred yards from the peak of Sable Point. Their hike had taken longer than planned as they were forced to navigate around Cobb's Creek. Normally only a trickle and often dry in late summer, the stream was swollen this time of year, forcing them half a mile off their planned route to find a safe crossing. The sun was setting when they reached their destination. They used the remaining daylight to find a suitable camping spot, set up their tent, gather firewood, make dinner and prepare for the cold night ahead.

CHAPTER TWENTY-SIX

Thursday, April 22

Unlike the pressed chinos and sports shirts he typically favored when not in uniform, McKay was wearing baggy cargo jeans, and an oversized plain blue tee shirt. While he may have looked odd to his fellow officers, he was dressed like many other males between the ages of thirteen and thirty. As he left the hotel, he donned a pair of sunglasses and pulled a baseball cap over his head.

Earlier that morning, during breakfast with the crew, Lewis had invited him to a matinee in the theater district. Zweig and Thomas had accepted Lewis's invitation but McKay had declined, stating that he wanted to visit a sports memorabilia store. If he had time, he would stop by the store later in the afternoon, but for now, he had work to do.

McKay dodged the throngs of shoppers as he walked to the center of the mall. Minutes later, he found the large balcony overlooking the food court below. He stopped by the railing, across from the escalators, and casually surveyed the scene. There was the usual assortment of fast food restaurants surrounding a communal dining area. He watched the parade of people carrying orange trays, the mothers pushing strollers, and the groups of teenage girls talking excitedly to each other as their thumbs played across the screens of their phones. McKay's eyes continued past the diners and the restaurants to the far wall, where he spotted the restroom sign at the entrance to a hallway. The right hand side of the hallway held a row of storage lockers.

He followed the balcony around past the escalators and stopped again. As he looked down this time, he noticed two police officers talking as they sipped cups of coffee. He studied the cops for a moment or two before stepping on the escalator.

He threaded his way through the crowds over to the lockers and found number sixty-seven. Without looking around—he didn't want to appear nervous—he opened the locker and retrieved the small blue bag with the Nike emblem on the sides. As he made his way back to the escalators, he noticed that the two cops hadn't moved. They seemed more interested in their coffee and their conversation than the crowds streaming around them.

Outside the mall, he let out the breath he had been holding and hailed a cab. He had over seven hours until dinner. He would return to the hotel and review the bag's contents, go over his plans again, and then find somewhere safe to store everything. Then he should have more than enough time to visit the sports store. After that, maybe a workout, and if he still had time, a ballgame on TV. He would need something to keep his mind occupied.

———

The man known as Vernon Jackson sat at the table, sipping a cup of coffee. The food court was noisy, the vaulted design of the atrium causing the sounds of hundreds of conversations to echo off the largely tiled and glass surfaces. The occasional high-pitched shrieks of pre-teen girls pierced the air. He sipped his coffee again as his eyes scanned the crowd, stopping for a moment on the two police officers before moving on to a group of teenage boys. The boys kept glancing over their shoulders at the table with four teenage girls, trying, Vernon guessed, to get up the nerve to go over and say hi. His eyes continued on to a group of moms and strollers, clustered around three or four tables. A few young mothers were snuggling sleeping babies to their chests while others were discreetly nursing theirs below small blankets.

To anyone watching, he was just another bored husband taking an opportunity to rest his feet while his wife wandered around one store or another. His eyes passed over the cops again then onto his right where a steady stream of people were either coming from or going to the restrooms—and the storage lockers that lined the wall beyond them. He glanced at his watch, took another sip, and then he saw what he had been waiting for. The young man with the sunglasses, cap, and cargo pants made his way over the lockers. Jackson studied the young man's face. Despite the obvious attempt to disguise himself as a younger, hipper college-aged kid, the young man's movements and mannerisms gave him a way. He was military. And despite the disguise and angle, Jackson saw enough of the young man's face. He was the one.

Less than a minute later, he watched as the young man disappeared into the crowd at the top of the elevator. Jackson pulled out his phone and typed *Pickup complete* onto the text screen then pushed send. He waited another minute before rising, throwing out his half empty cup and making his way over to the escalators.

Game on.

———

As usually happened, people were excited to be so close to the president. Today was no exception. Richter scanned the crowd, quickly examining each face, noting the expressions, watching the hands, wary of sudden movements. His eyes passed over a group of college students in jeans, all wearing smiles, most clapping. Then, a professor in a sports coat pointing, a child at his side. Next was a young man with a beard and leather jacket, waving. Then an Asian businessman dressed in a suit—no smile, but hands folded, respectful. And in the back, a tall, black man, muscular, arms folded across his chest, a faint smile on his face. Richter looked again at the hands, then the face. Despite what appeared to be a smile, the man's eyes were cold.

———

President Kendall took another step along the rope line when a young man wearing a heavy blue sweatshirt and a Seattle Mariners cap grabbed his outstretched hand in both of his own, all the while shouting. Richter's eyes darted from the black man to the Mariners fan.

"Mr. President! Mr. President! I'm so glad you're here! I

really need to speak with you, Mr. President!"

The Mariners fan was in an almost hysteric fervor, all the while rapidly shaking the president's hand. Kendall, having been coached well, smiled warmly. Although the man was likely just excited to meet the president, alarm bells sounded in Richter's head. The man didn't even realize that he was gripping the president's hand like a trophy he had just won. But Agents Richter and Lansing did.

Before Kendall had a chance to say anything, Lansing grabbed the president's arm while Richter reached down and flicked the man in the testicles. No one in the crowd saw Richter's hand, and even the Mariners fan wasn't sure what had happened. Involuntarily, he released the president's hand as Lansing pulled it away. After Agents Lansing and Richter moved the president away, another agent stepped up and handed the man a card.

"I'm sorry but the president's running late. If you'd like to speak to him, why don't you email or write to him at this address and he'll get back to you."

The Mariners fan, barely able to contain his excitement, took the card.

Richter and Lansing continued to move the president down the line towards the waiting limousine for a ride over to Bellevue and his meeting with Bill Gates. Agent Richter glanced back to the crowd, but the tall black man was gone.

———

Later that afternoon, Charles Howell and President Kendall sat in the back of the limo as the motorcade made its way through the rain-soaked city.

"I think things went well today," the president said. "I got a note from Felicia. She believes the Chinese may consider softening their trade position."

Howell looked up from his notebook and nodded. "I heard the same thing, sir. I think the fact that they were willing to sit down with us at all is a big win."

"Please schedule time for me to debrief Felicia on the trip home."

"Yes, sir." Howell scribbled a note.

"The meeting with the Gateses went well. You'll need to coordinate with them on the timing for a visit to Washington."

Howell made another note. "Are you ready for your dinner with the governor?"

"I think I'm set. Education is number one on her list, then foreign trade. We should have a lot to talk about. Is she looking for anything else?"

"Not that I'm aware of, sir."

The president sat back and looked out the rain-streaked window. The gray clouds were ominous and foreboding. He had heard something about a storm that was forecasted to hit the area. This must be the start of it, he guessed.

So far, the trip had gone well, he thought, then chuckled to himself as he remembered his apprehension a week earlier. *Where did that come from?* he wondered. Oh well, even with the bad weather forecasted, he was sure that the Air Force would get him home safe and sound tomorrow in time for Angela's ballet recital and their weekend getaway to Camp David.

CHAPTER TWENTY-SEVEN

"So how was the show?" McKay asked as he joined Major Lewis, Colonel Zweig, and Captain Thomas at the table. The Indian restaurant was crowded.

"I thought it was enjoyable. A very nice production." Lewis replied.

"I should have come with you instead," Colonel Zweig stated. "Total chick play. The captain and I were the only guys in the audience."

Lewis looked hurt for a moment. "No, it wasn't, and no, you weren't."

The waiter arrived and took McKay's drink order.

"So…that bad, Colonel?" McKay asked after the waiter left.

"The estrogen was so thick you could have cut it with a knife." Zweig replied. Both Thomas and McKay laughed.

"You wouldn't know culture if it bit you in the ass." Lewis countered, frustrated. She turned red and added in a much softer voice, "Colonel."

"At ease, Major," Zweig replied. "I'm just yanking your

chain." He waited a second until she relaxed. "Actually, I enjoyed the show," he said. "I'm not sure if I would have chosen it on my own, but I'm glad I went. Thanks."

Lewis smiled. "You're welcome, sir." Feeling better, she turned to McKay. "Did you find anything special at the baseball card store?"

"Oh, it was much more than a baseball card store." McKay smiled despite his unease. "They had lots of autographed items: uniforms and jerseys, Super Bowl game balls, helmets, pucks from the Stanley Cup, the bat A-Rod used in the last World Series. The place was incredible."

"A-Rod?" Lewis asked.

"Alex Rodriguez," Captain Thomas answered. "New York Yankees."

Lewis shook her head.

The waiter returned with McKay's Diet Coke. "Are you ready to order?"

"What do you recommend, Colonel?" Thomas asked as he scanned the menu. "I wouldn't have a clue what I was ordering."

"You all okay if I order for the table?"

"Sure, why not." Lewis said closing her menu and handing it to the waiter. "I guess if you can tolerate my choice in theater, the least I can do is let you choose the meal."

McKay half listened as the Colonel ordered. He had been feeling anxious and queasy since his trip to the mall. Secretly, he had been hoping that the storage locker would be empty, or that the key wouldn't work. He should have declined the dinner invitation. Ever since the trip to the mall, he felt like a freight train was speeding towards him and he couldn't jump out of the way. He took a sip of his soda and told himself to calm down. Everything was set. It was only pre-game jitters. He just had to focus on getting through the evening. Thankfully, no one noticed his growing anxiety.

———

It was 9:45 p.m. when the president returned to his suite. Agents Richter and Sartori took up their posts in the hall outside his room. Richter glanced at his watch. Fifteen more minutes to go before his shift ended. He hadn't eaten yet and considered asking Stephanie to join him for a sandwich in the hotel restaurant. He only wanted dinner and a chance to sit and talk; he wasn't interested in anything more. Or so he kept telling himself.

But would she say yes? Stephanie was driven and very serious about her job, but she had a human side too. She could be playful at times. Not quite flirting with him, but what? He wasn't sure. Maybe she felt at ease with him, the way many people do when they worked together, especially after sharing some intense and challenging moments. But every time she began to let her guard down, to show him she might be interested, she seemed to catch herself.

She's only being friendly, he chastised himself. *Forget about her and do your job.*

The trouble was, he couldn't.

———

Colonel Zweig turned on the TV when he got back to his hotel room. He burped twice as he undressed and got ready for bed. *I'll need to work this dinner off,* he thought, as he set his alarm clock early so he could go to the gym.

His thoughts were interrupted by the TV.

"A series of Pacific storms will hit the western half of the U.S. over the next few days and we can expect to see near blizzard conditions and dangerous if not impossible travel conditions in much of the northwest."

"Blizzard conditions? This is a little unusual for this time of year, isn't it, Katy?"

"Right you are, Wayne. And this is going to be a big one. The National Weather Service has issued a winter storm warning for several western states effective this evening through Sunday morning."

Colonel Zweig studied the weather map on the TV.

"This will affect parts of Washington, Oregon, Idaho, Utah, Colorado, Wyoming, and Montana. The brunt of the storm front is expected to pass through northwestern Oregon and southwestern Washington between 2:00 a.m. and 10:00 a.m. and southwestern Idaho between 7:00 a.m. and 3:00 p.m. on Friday. And Wayne, check this out. Portions of Idaho and Montana could see two to three feet of snow above four thousand feet and three to five feet of snow above seven thousand feet. In some areas, we can expect wind gusts up to eighty miles per hour."

"Three to five feet? Sounds like a good idea to stay home, Katy."

"That's right, Wayne. Travelers should expect delays and possible road closures along Interstate 15, Interstate 80, Interstate

90, and along the many state and county highways in the region. The Montana State Police have advised us that some mountain passes will be closed. Travelers are urged to use extreme caution and avoid travel if at all possible. If you do need to travel, carry chains, a shovel, blankets, and a winter survival kit."

"Thanks, Katy. We suggest that you stay tuned throughout the weekend as we continue to update you on this storm."

The colonel reached for the room phone when his cell phone rang. Dropping the receiver back in its cradle, he answered his cell. "This is Colonel Zweig."

"Colonel, this is Major Nelson from McCord Air Force Base. Sir, the National Weather Service has issued winter storm warnings for the Pacific Northwest and surrounding states."

"I'm watching the news right now, Major."

"Yes, sir. I'm sending you the details. At this point, it looks like you should be fine getting out of Seattle tomorrow. The forecast calls for freezing rain and winds of ten to fifteen miles an hour at Sea-Tac. The heavy snow will be concentrated further east from Spokane down through southwestern Oregon, throughout much of central and southern Idaho into Montana about as far as Bozeman."

"Thanks, Major. Anything changes call me ASAP."

Colonel Zweig hung up and dialed Major Lewis's room. She answered immediately.

"Major, I want to meet one hour earlier, let's say zero four thirty. It looks like we're going to have to earn our pay tomorrow."

———

Richter pushed the button for his floor. As the doors began to close, Stephanie stepped in.

"Gee, thanks for waiting for me." She playfully punched him in the arm.

There it was again.

"Sorry, Stephanie, I didn't see you."

"Oh, yes you did. You were trying to get away. Had too much of me for one day, did you?"

Richter didn't hesitate. "Okay. You caught me. How about I make it up to you and buy you a sandwich? There's a great deli around the corner."

"Agent Richter?" She feigned surprise. "Are you asking me out on a date?"

"A date? Who said anything about a date?" He smiled then hesitated a moment before continuing. "I'm sure you haven't eaten yet, and neither have I."

"You know, you're cute when you're embarrassed." She smiled then paused, uncertain, as she studied him for a moment. Then she smiled again. "I have a better idea. How about I order some sandwiches from room service?"

Richter was surprised. "That sounds great."

The elevator door opened and Stephanie stepped out. "Okay. Why don't you come by in thirty minutes?"

CHAPTER TWENTY-EIGHT

Friday, April 23

It had been snowing for the last twelve hours, and Jack was not happy. Derek watched him in the flickering light of the small candle lantern. The lantern, a tube no bigger than a roll of quarters with a retractable, reflective dome on top, swayed gently above their heads. Shadows danced on the walls of the tent.

"Let's at least wait until its light out, Jack. It's five-thirty in the morning for Christ's sake."

Truth be told, Derek wasn't happy either, but he was not about to admit that to Jack. What made it worse was that Jack was right. They didn't have the gear for this weather. Without ice gear and snowshoes, it would be foolish to continue their planned route. They didn't even have the right clothes, Derek realized, at least not for the blizzard outside.

Jack had been packing his gear since returning from a morning nature call. Thinking he was overreacting as usual, Derek had unzipped one of the window flaps and peeked outside. Although he knew it was snowing—sleeping in a tent, he never had to guess the weather—he was surprised at how much snow had fallen already. There appeared to be at least a foot on the ground, and it was still coming down.

"Look, Jack. I agree it doesn't make sense to continue in this weather."

Jack glared over his shoulder.

"We have two choices. We can pack our gear and head back. Right now. In the dark. In this storm." He let that thought sink in. "Or we can wait until its light out and see if the weather breaks." Derek reached into his pack and pulled out a small coffeepot. "I can make some breakfast in the meantime."

"A cup of your lousy coffee and a frozen granola bar." Jack smiled for the first time that morning. "Actually, that sounds pretty good." The tension inside the tent eased.

Derek smiled back. "Why don't you set up the stove? I'll go fill the pot up with snow."

"Just make sure it's not yellow," Jack joked as Derek crawled outside.

At least he's in a better mood, Derek thought as he tried to orient himself in the darkness and the swirling snow. They were going to have trouble enough finding their way today.

———

"You haven't said much this morning, Lieutenant. Are you okay?"

It was still dark as the shuttle bus drove over to the Air Cargo section of the airport, where Air Force One was under heavy guard.

McKay grunted. "Dinner tasted much better last night than it feels right now."

"So that's why I didn't see you in the gym this morning," Captain Thomas responded. "I thought studs like you liked spicy food."

"Give him a break," Major Lewis ordered. "Lieutenant. Here....catch."

McKay caught the package of Pepto Bismol. He closed his eyes and concentrated on breathing slowly. He didn't feel well, but it had nothing to do with last night's meal.

———

Richter woke, and it took him a couple of seconds before he realized where he was. He cursed silently.

He got out of bed, careful not to make any sound. Grabbing his clothes, he tiptoed to the bathroom, silently closing the door. He started to put on his pants then hesitated. He felt conflicted. Part of him was upset. He knew he had broken a professional code. He told himself that it was a mistake. That it would never work.

Then another part of him said, *So what? You need to enjoy life more!* He had one leg in his pants when he realized that this was the first night in a long time when the nightmares and bad dreams hadn't invaded his sleep. He had slept well.

He sat on the edge of the tub for a few moments. Then he took his pants off and tiptoed back to bed.

He lay down and pulled the sheets up, trying not to make any noise.

Stephanie rolled over into his arms.

"I was hoping you'd come back."

———

Four hours before the scheduled departure of Air Force One, an E-3 Sentry Airborne Warning and Control System, or AWACS aircraft, took off from Tinker Air Force base in Oklahoma and headed northwest. The plane, based on a Boeing 707-320B airframe, had a flight crew of four in the cockpit with eighteen AWACS officers operating the highly sophisticated electronic systems in the rear. In addition to assisting in the monitoring of all commercial, civilian, military, and private aircraft in its sector as part of the North American Aerospace Defense Command, or NORAD, whenever Air Force One was in the air, the E-3 provided surveillance and threat detection and coordinated the communications with and control over other Air Force assets assigned to defend and protect the president.

Two and a half hours later, when the E-3 reached its station over central Oregon, it began to fly an oval pattern.

———

Air Force One sat on the tarmac at Seattle Tacoma International Airport, waiting for clearance from the control tower. Unlike commercial aircraft, which had to wait in a queue, Air Force One was always given priority clearance by Air Traffic Control. They didn't have to wait long.

"Air Force One, you're cleared to taxi to runway Three Four Right via Bravo."

Colonel Zweig stowed the flight plan while Major Tammy

Lewis keyed her mic.

"Roger Sea-Tac Ground. Air Force One taxi to Three Four Right via Bravo."

Zweig eased the throttles forward, the four engines instantly responding. Eight hundred thousand pounds of metal, instruments, fuel, and people began to move down the taxiway as the ground crew, standing at attention in the freezing rain, saluted.

As Zweig entered the runway, Lewis glanced again, for the third time, at the preflight checklist. Despite the fact that she, Thomas, and Zweig had completed the pre-flight over one hour earlier, she found herself checking again. Double, triple, even quadruple redundancy was the norm. She glanced at Zweig and gave a thumbs-up, signaling that they were ready to depart.

"Air Force One, you're cleared for takeoff on Runway Three Four Right. Have a pleasant flight and do come back and see us again real soon."

"Roger, Sea-Tac Tower. Cleared for takeoff on Three Four Right. Thanks for the hospitality." Lewis shared a quick grin with Zweig and then turned her attention to the numerous control gauges and warning lights on the instrument panel as Zweig gently pushed the throttles forward to full power. The aircraft began to accelerate down the runway.

Once airborne, Colonel Zweig began a slow turn to the east. The flight plan called for a route across the state of Washington, into Idaho and then Montana. They would pass over South Dakota, Iowa, and Illinois, where they would fly south of Chicago and follow a direct path to Washington, DC.

And so, the fateful flight of Air Force One had begun.

CHAPTER TWENTY-NINE

Lieutenant McKay checked his watch. It was time. He keyed his radio. "Colonel, I've got to hit the head."

"Last night's dinner still bothering you?" Zweig joked.

"A little, sir." He let out an audible breath. "I'll confirm when I'm back on station. Out."

Brandt glanced up from his magazine. "You okay, LT? You don't look so good."

"Something I ate yesterday. I'll be fine." McKay walked to the restroom. Compared to a commercial airliner, the lavatories on Air Force One, even in the press section, were spacious. McKay removed a plastic garbage bag from the cabinet below the sink and stuffed it in the toilet. He folded the top of the bag over the rim. It took him several minutes of pushing to force the soft plastic container out of his colon. Not a pleasant experience by any means, but it foiled the security screens that the Secret Service made everyone, including the flight crew, pass through. The container dropped into the plastic bag in the toilet.

McKay retrieved the plastic container, gently washed it, then stuffed it into the pocket of his flight suit. He cleaned up the bathroom and returned to his seat.

"Colonel, I'm back on station."

"Roger, Lieutenant. Do you need someone to relieve you?"

"No, sir. I feel much better now. Out."

———

As the door to the president's office opened, Sartori stood then followed the president as he limped over to the medical facility. Major Diane Camden frowned.

"Your knee again, sir?"

Kendall nodded. "Flying always seems to make it worse. Got any Tylenol?"

Camden returned with two capsules and an ice pack.

"Sir, you really should put this on it. Keep it elevated."

Kendall shook his head as he took the pills. "I'll grab some ice on the way back. I need to speak to the press first."

———

Twenty minutes later, the president was back in his office with Howell and the White House Counsel. He had an ice pack on his knee. Sartori sat at her post outside the door. Richter, wearing his usual on-duty mask, took the seat next to her.

He glanced into the cabin. The National Security Advisor was discussing something with an aide. The Secretary of Commerce and the Press Secretary were leaning over a table reviewing papers. A handful of people were watching C-SPAN. Everyone was engrossed in something.

Richter turned to Stephanie, unable to hide his grin. As he struggled to put his mask back on, he leaned toward her, speaking softly.

"Listen, I can't stay long."

Stephanie nodded, fighting to hide her own smile.

"I just wanted to say that last night was wonderful."

"You're turning red again, Agent Richter." She patted his arm, but he could see that her face was red also.

"It was wonderful for me too," she whispered.

He coughed, made a show of checking his radio, then glanced into the cabin again. Thankfully, no one was paying them any attention.

"I better go. But first, I wanted to ask you out on a real date. What are you doing after work tonight?"

———

Major Lewis began another scan of the instrument and warning indicators, a process so well ingrained from thousands of hours of flying that it had become second nature. The fuel gauges caught her attention. The starboard wing tank registered one hundred and thirty-eight thousand pounds of fuel remaining, while the port wing tank had one hundred and forty-four thousand pounds. The imbalance, some six thousand pounds, was beyond the acceptable margin. Normally, the plane's engines pulled equally from both tanks to maintain an even weight distribution across the airframe. She scanned the panel. All four engines were running within specifications, and they didn't appear to be dumping fuel. Something was wrong.

"Colonel, the fuel gauges indicate we're out of balance."

Colonel Zweig glanced at both gauges and frowned.

"Do you want me to pump fuel from the port tank to the starboard?"

"No," the colonel responded. "I don't think the gauges are right. Have McKay check the level capacitors and the transfer pumps for both tanks. Reset them if necessary."

"Yes, sir."

Zweig glanced over his shoulder at the Flight Engineer. "Captain, was there anything in the service record that indicated clogged or leaking fuel lines or other problems with the fuel management system?"

Thomas already had the binder open. "The system was reset, and they replaced the fuel relay switches." Thomas looked up. "Looks like routine maintenance."

"Okay. Do a manual calculation and let me know how much fuel we should have. Also, check the computer. The flow rate could be miscalibrated."

"Roger, sir."

Major Lewis keyed her microphone. "Lieutenant?"

In the rear of the aircraft, McKay checked his watch and took a deep breath. Showtime.

"Yes, Major?" He listened as Lewis described the problem.

"Lieutenant?"

"Ma'am?"

"Are you feeling well enough to do this?"

"Yes, ma'am."

McKay unbuckled his seatbelt, stood, and grabbed his toolkit from the storage bin over his seat.

In the cockpit, Zweig turned to Lewis. "Maybe Brandt is right."

Lewis raised an eyebrow.

"He calls this plane 'The Bitch.'"

———

Stephanie couldn't stop thinking about Matthew and, every time she did, she felt her face redden. *It was just one night*, she told herself. *What did one night even mean?* God, that's something she hadn't done since college! And remember how well that turned out? *Take it slow*, she told herself. *You're not twenty-one anymore.* She needed to get to know him better. *But, still,* she thought with a smile as she watched him walk away, *he just asked me out on a date!* She turned her head, feigning concern over something; a few seconds to regain her composure.

It was hard to concentrate. *Matthew Richter*, she thought. What did she really know about him? He was athletic. He was intense, very driven at work. But away from here, he was a nice guy; funny and cute as hell when he smiled. This was the first time a man had asked her out in….Lord, she couldn't remember. She thought about the upcoming evening. A dinner, just the two of them. Maybe they would share a bottle of wine. They would get to know each other better. Heck, neither of them had to work tomorrow, so they could stay out late! Then after dinner, who knew? *Be serious, girl,* she thought with a grin. More than likely, they'd skip the dinner part. She felt her face redden again.

But could it last? Not while they were both guarding the pres-

ident; that would never work. Did she want it to last? she wondered. And what did that mean exactly? She thought of her
sister, happily married for the last ten years, two young girls, her
nieces. So different from her own marriage, she thought. Maybe
she hadn't been ready then. And maybe, she thought, it was the
wrong guy; her ex-husband was nothing like Matthew.

God! This is happening way too fast!

———

McKay closed the door to the passenger cabin and descended
the staircase to the cargo hold. He stepped through the bulkhead and maneuvered around the luggage bins and stored goods
to the center. Noting the time, he figured he had five minutes
before Lewis would call him again. He removed the four screws
in the access panel on the floor. Setting the cover to the side, he
pointed a small pen light inside. It took a few seconds to confirm that he had found what he needed: the main power feeds
for all of the aircraft's systems.

McKay glanced at his watch. A minute and a half had
elapsed. He pulled the soft plastic container from his pocket,
opened it, and extracted the Semtex. He rolled the plastic explosive back and forth between his palms for a minute, then broke
off a small piece, putting it back in the container.

Checking his watch, he saw that two and a half minutes had
passed. He pulled a handheld diagnostic computer from his
toolkit and hurried over to another electrical panel located on the
bulkhead. He opened the panel and plugged the USB lead into
the port on the fuel management system control board. With

several keystrokes, he reset the flow rates for each tank. Once the computer confirmed the new rates, McKay unplugged the connection and closed the panel cover.

———

That's better, Lewis thought. "Colonel, the gauges look correct now. Both read just over one hundred and forty-one thousand pounds remaining."

"I concur," Thomas added. "I've manually calculated the burn rate. We're on target. It looks like the flow rates in the system were incorrect and we were getting false readings. The lieutenant must have reset them."

"Okay," Colonel Zweig replied. "Let's make a note to have the system checked thoroughly when we get back to Andrews."

Thomas nodded. "Roger."

———

"We've narrowed the list down to eleven potential running mates. I have a page on each person with their picture, biography, and curriculum vitae, as well as the initial ranking I assigned based upon the criteria we established last week." Huff handed binders to both Howell and the president.

"Okay, first is Juan Garcia Mendez. As you know, he's the Governor of New Mexico. He has an interesting background. He was born in Los Angeles, but his mother died when he was an infant. His father wasn't able to take care of him and sent him to live with relatives in Mexico. Three years later, his father was killed, apparently in a dispute over money. Governor Mendez grew up poor. His only options were to work the farm, like his family had done for generations, or join one of the growing drug cartels. He broke the cycle thanks to an uncle who lived in California. He came back to the U.S. when he was twelve."

"I met him once when I was a senator." Kendall winced and shifted the ice pack on his knee.

Huff continued. "He learned the language and, in high school, he focused on school and sports and avoided the Latino gangs that many young Mexican men fall into in Southern California. He graduated number three in a class of almost two thousand." Huff looked up for a moment. "Not bad for a kid who didn't speak a word of English just five years before."

President Kendall grimaced again.

"Is there something I missed, sir?"

The president waved his hand. "No. I think he's worth considering." He stood up. "I'm sorry, Linda. Let's regroup later."

———

McKay froze at the sound of footsteps. He placed the plastic explosive in his toolkit, closed it, and prayed it wasn't Brandt coming to check on him. He let out a breath when Mosby stepped through the bulkhead. The two men nodded at each other, neither speaking. McKay pulled the plastic explosive back out, while Mosby walked over to one of the bins and began to unstrap the netting that held the luggage in place.

McKay inserted two testing probes into the digital multi-meter. The meter was an electrician's device for measuring current and voltage, checking circuits for continuity, and other tasks particular to their trade. While the device McKay held would indeed function as a multi-meter, should any one bother to inspect it, McKay had inserted a clock chip and modified the wiring leading to the testing probes. Now, it would also function as a timer. His degree in electrical engineering had served him well. After connecting the testing probes to the fuse, he turned the meter on and watched as the digital display blinked several times before settling to zero. He set the timer for twelve minutes.

Mosby removed some luggage, creating a small space in the middle of the bin. He opened one of the bags, and McKay placed the bomb inside. Crouching in front of the bin, he checked the connections one more time. He pulled his hand out, looked at his watch again, then at Mosby, and then back down at the bomb. His life has come to this, he thought. He could feel his heart hammering in his chest and felt the sweat running down his face. He felt a sudden pang of guilt as he realized the price that would soon be paid to ensure his own survival. The butterflies in his stomach, the surge of adrenaline, made him queasy.

"Come on, McKay! There's no backing out now," Mosby growled.

McKay wiped the sweat from his forehead, took a deep breath, reached into the suitcase and pushed a button on the multi-meter. He pulled his hand out and started the timer on his wristwatch. Mosby did the same. Their watches, preset to twelve minutes in the "Timer" mode, began to countdown.

CHAPTER THIRTY

The president nodded to Richter and Sartori as he limped over to the medical facility.

Major Camden stood. "Sir, are you sure you don't want something else?"

Kendall shook his head as he handed her the ice pack. "No thanks, doc. I think I want to walk around a bit." He turned to Richter. "What was the score of the game last night?"

"I didn't catch it, sir, but I read that the Flyers lost. Four to three."

Sartori stood guard while the president and Richter discussed the game. Half listening, she scanned the aisle for any sign of a threat. Although an attack on the president was unlikely while he was on Air Force One, training and the ultimate fear that something would happen on her watch, a fear shared by every agent, kept her vigilant.

———

Mosby pulled two parachute harnesses from the storage bin by the rear bulkhead. He checked the bin again and found the par-kas. He put on one of the heavy coats, strapping the parachute harness over it. The pack was awkward, and he felt restricted in the confined space. *That's okay*, he thought, as he pulled out the oxygen mask and goggles. *I won't have too far to walk anyway.*

———

"We've got what…another three and a half or four hours?"

Richter checked his watch. "About three hours and forty minutes, sir."

The president grimaced again.

"Are you sure you don't want something from the doctor, sir?"

The president shook his head as he flexed his knee. "No. I need to move around a bit."

"Well, if you want something different to do," Richter said with a grin, "we can always go over the emergency evacuation procedures."

"Didn't we already do that on an earlier flight?"

"We covered the basics, sir. I can give you a more detailed briefing, but we would have to visit the cargo hold."

"Great. Let's do it."

Richter hesitated. "Sir? I was just…" He glanced at Steph-anie then turned back to the president. "We'll have to use the stairs, sir." He hesitated again. "With your knee….are you sure?"

"I think I can manage that, Mr. Richter. Let's go."

Richter nodded. Sartori lifted her cuff to her face. Moments later, Lansing joined them. He looked at Sartori for an explana-tion.

She shrugged and whispered. "POTUS wants a demonstration of the emergency evacuation procedures."

Lansing seemed to consider this for a moment. After a second, he shrugged and nodded, a subtle confirmation that only Sartori could see.

Richter held the door, letting Sartori lead the way down the steps. He gestured for the president to follow then fell in behind him while Lansing brought up the rear.

———

McKay knelt in front of the rear hatch. He broke the remaining piece of Semtex in two and began kneading one of the pieces into a shaped charge. He placed the charge, no more than one-half an ounce of explosive, over the lock mechanism. He connected a fuse and rigged a second modified multi-meter and set the timer to four minutes.

———

"The plane is equipped with some pretty sophisticated equipment, sir," Richter said as they reached the bottom of the stairs. He led the president to a bin in front of the bulkhead near the crew door. Lansing stepped through the bulkhead into the main cargo hold while Sartori stood just on the other side with Richter and the president.

Richter opened the bin and pulled out two items.

"We have portable oxygen systems and smoke goggles in case of fire."

He handed the president the goggles and mask.

"We have these upstairs, too," he continued as the president inspected the googles. "But there are some pieces of equipment that are only kept on this deck."

"Such as?" The president asked.

Richter pointed back into the bin. "Flotation devices, rafts, wilderness survival kits, and..." He fingered the shoulder strap of a large backpack. "Parachutes."

"Really? I thought that was urban legend."

Richter shrugged. "Frankly, sir, I can't think of any situation where we would need them. It's impossible to jump out of a plane traveling over six hundred miles an hour at thirty-five thousand feet. But chutes are standard for the Air Force, sir. All of their planes—tankers, bombers, fighters—have them. On the other hand, I suppose the survival gear would be useful if we ever crashed in a remote area."

Kendall grinned, shook his head, then held the goggles up to his eyes.

"Would you like to try them on, sir?"

———

The bundle consisted of wires of various thickness and color. McKay snipped the plastic wire tie that held the bundle together, then separated seven wires from the rest. In one smooth motion, he severed all seven wires, disconnecting power to the Cockpit Voice Recorder and the Flight Data Recorder, as well as the radio and satellite communications systems. The black boxes had backup power systems, he knew, but it would cause momentary confusion in the cockpit. The loss of the communication systems would add to the confusion, and that's precisely what he wanted.

———

Major Lewis frowned. "Colonel, I've got lights indicating a malfunction with the data recorders."

Zweig glanced at the instrument panel. "See if McKay is back yet."

After several unsuccessful attempts, Lewis shook her head.

"No response, sir. Maybe he's in the head again?"

———

McKay had just pushed the wires back into the access hole when he heard voices. He fought the wave of panic that washed over him and squinted through the netting. The bulkheads and luggage blocked his view. He checked the time. Less than two minutes to go. He quickly replaced the panel cover, not bothering with the screws, and hurried to the back of the plane.

"There's someone down here," McKay whispered.

"I heard. Let's move." Mosby handed McKay a parka and then helped him strap on his parachute.

McKay pulled on the oxygen mask, attaching the bottle to the front of his harnesses. He adjusted the smoke goggles over his eyes, then turned and squatted on the forward side of the rear bulkhead. The rear hatch and his second bomb were on the other side, ten feet away. He looked at his watch again. They were cutting it close.

They might have made it undetected if not for Mosby's parachute. When he squatted, his harness snagged on the cargo bin's cover. It slammed shut with a bang.

———

Richter flinched at the noise. He grabbed President Kendall and turned towards the stairway, while Sartori stood protectively in the doorway of the bulkhead, blocking access. Lansing stepped farther into the cargo hold.

———

McKay jumped at the bang of the cargo bin lid. *Oh, God*, he prayed as a wave of panic washed over him. He just needed another twenty seconds! He just needed to get off the plane! At least then he'd have a chance, with a plan, a running start, and two and a half million dollars. He would never see the rest—he knew Jane would never let him live long enough to collect. But that didn't matter. He had a plan and the most important part involved avoiding Jane and her henchman once he did their bidding. The little she had paid him was enough and he had made sure his mother was safe. Now he had to make sure that he was too. *One step at a time*, he told himself, *and the next step is to get off the plane in one piece.*

He glanced nervously towards the front of the cargo hold when the plane was rocked by a tremendous explosion.

CHAPTER THIRTY-ONE

The blinding flash rocked the airplane, and Richter reflexively shoved President Kendall up against the bulkhead, using his own body as a shield. He shook his head, trying to clear the clouds and muffled ringing. *What the hell?* Wind rushed through the cargo hold, raining debris down on their heads. Time seemed to warp, the seconds flowing like molasses. Despite the wind, he smelled burning plastic and rubber. Something was on fire. He shook his head again, and somewhere deep in his foggy brain a voice—his own voice—screamed. *The president!* He struggled to focus, and POTUS suddenly appeared. Richter saw the blood streaking down the president's face, on his goggles, on his mask, before being whipped away in the windstorm. It took him some time to realize that the blood was his own. He could see the terror in the president's eyes as darkness crept across the edges of his own vision. Christ! He couldn't breathe! The president lunged for him, and he watched in horror as Kendall's eyes rolled into the back of his head. Richter reached out, frantically searching for the valve on the president's oxygen supply. He struggled with the stuck valve for what seemed like an eternity before realizing that he was turning it the wrong way. As his vision darkened, the president began to respond, slowly coming to.

POTUS was alive, but for how long?

———

The aircraft pitched violently, and Colonel Zweig struggled to maintain control. The cockpit instantly filled with fog as the air pressure plummeted, and Zweig batted away the cups and paper that sailed past his face.

"Explosive decompression!" Lewis yelled as she reached for the oxygen mask.

Fighting the debris storm, she helped Zweig pull on his mask, then reached for her own. Captain Thomas punched a button, and a stream of chaff and flares were ejected from the wings and fuselage. These were designed to foil radar and heat-seeking guidance systems on potential inbound missiles.

At the same time, Zweig banked sharply to the right. The evasive maneuver had turned the aircraft one hundred and eighty degrees, and they were now heading west.

———

McKay held onto the netting as the tornado rushed through the cargo hold. He kept his head down to avoid the debris—papers, luggage, pieces of metal, and plastic—rushing at gale-force speed towards the hole in the rear door. The plane began to buck and shake, first banking sharply to one side and then the other.

He lifted his head and glanced through the fog at Mosby. The man had a pained look on his face as he slapped at his ears. McKay had been prepared and was wearing earplugs. Even with the earplugs, the roar of the blast had been deafening. He could only imagine what it must have been like without them. Good. He wanted Mosby confused and disoriented. It would make things easier later.

Now it was up to Colonel Zweig. He prayed the colonel wouldn't let him down.

———

On the main deck, Secret Service agents sprang into action, six agents running to the front of the plane, another six running to the back. Both groups headed to the stairways that led to the lower deck, fighting their way through the fog, the screaming passengers, and the flying debris.

Colonel Zweig's evasive maneuvers sent agents and passengers tumbling into the aisles.

———

"Emergency descent!" Zweig yelled as he applied the speed brakes and yanked the throttle to idle.

Even though his initial reaction had been to jink, to evade potential missiles, logic told him they were too high for a ground-based threat and, with AWACS coverage, an undetected airborne threat was impossible. Besides, there had been no warning tone in his earphones signaling that they were being tracked. No, the explosion had come from on board the aircraft, Zweig realized.

His priority now was to get the aircraft down before the president—the only passenger that mattered—succumbed to oxygen deprivation.

———

As his vision grew darker, Richter franticly felt around for the cargo bin. He forced the cover open and thrust his hand inside. The vise around his chest continued to tighten as he searched for the mask. He began to slump and screamed at himself. *Don't quit now! Do your job!* After what seemed like an eternity, he felt the cylinder, yanked the mask out and fumbled to strap it on.

———

The fog began to clear as Lewis keyed the radio again. "Mother Goose, this is Air Force One. Over." She waited a moment. "Mother Goose, this is Air Force One. Do you read? Over." Lewis frowned at the radio. "Mother Goose. This is Air Force One. We've lost cabin pressure. We are descending to twelve thousand feet. Please confirm. Over."

The major switched frequencies and tried again. Something was wrong with the radio. She switched to the civilian frequency.

"Seattle Center. This is Air Force One. Do you copy?"

All she heard was silence.

———

When he took the first breath of oxygen, Richter felt as if a huge weight had been lifted off his chest. The darkness that had crept across his vision began to recede. After a while—no way to tell how long—he felt strong enough to stand on his own. Through the fog and howling wind, he saw President Kendall, terrified, but alive and breathing. He reached into the bin again, searching for another pair of smoke goggles.

———

In the press section, agents climbed over the bodies in their way. Several fell, succumbing to the debris—flying china, cell phones, laptops—and the lack of oxygen. Three agents made it to the door. The force of the explosion had not only blown a hole in the rear hatch but had traveled in the opposite direction, buckling the rear staircase and partially crumpling the frame around the door to the passenger compartment at the top of the steps. The first agent to reach the door cursed, finding it jammed.

———

Richter felt the airplane pitch forward and shudder. They were descending, he realized. The debris storm and the fog began to subside, but the wind continued to howl through the hold. The cargo netting and their clothes flapped like flags. Must not be anything left to get sucked out.

That's it! He realized. There's a hole in the plane—a door, a window, he didn't know what—but they had suddenly lost cabin pressure. The realization hit him like a ton of bricks. There must have been some sort of explosive device, like a bomb or a missile.

His eyes shifted to the doorway and there was Stephanie, crumpled on the floor, her arms and legs tangled in the cargo nets. Her white blouse soaked in blood, red streaks trailing away along the floor. Even in the dim light, he could see that her face was grey. He gasped. *Oh, God! Stephanie!*

He and President Kendall had been protected from the brunt of the explosion by the bulkhead. Agent Sartori, standing just inside the bulkhead doorway at the time of the blast, had not been so lucky. As the explosion blew a hole in the door of the aircraft, thousands of pieces of shrapnel—lethal projectiles— flew down the narrow walkway through the bulkhead doors. A split second later, there was a tremendous flow in the opposite direction as the higher pressure air in the cabin began to rush towards the hole in the rear hatch. Sartori had been hit in the head and neck, her carotid artery severed.

Richter choked back a sob. *Stephanie! Stephanie!* He shook his head again. *Stop!* His brain screamed. There was nothing he could do to save her. He had to save the president.

———

In the rear of the cargo hold, McKay felt the rapid deceleration and leveling of the aircraft. Tentatively, he stood. The wind, still rushing through the hold, was less violent now. He signaled Mosby to wait as he cautiously stepped through the bulkhead. There was a basketball-sized hole in the rear hatch, where the locking mechanism used to be. Bracing himself, he kicked the door, but it opened just an inch or two, then slammed shut in the wind. The plane was still going too fast. *Shit!* He swore to himself. They were running out of time. He pulled the remaining Semtex from his pocket, broke it in two, shaping each piece before placing one over each of the hinges. He used the last of the fuses and multi-meters, quickly rigging the shaped charges and setting the timer to fifteen seconds. He hurried back to the other side of the bulkhead.

———

Richter's eyes avoided Stephanie's body as he glanced through the doorway. Twenty feet away, he saw Brad Lansing, his arms and feet also tangled in the cargo netting. Lansing's head was tilted back at an abnormal angle, his face bloody, his eyes bulging and his tongue, swollen and black, protruded from his mouth.

———

In the White House section of the plane, the agents fought their way through the windstorm, climbing over the bodies in the aisle. As normally happened on Air Force One, passengers had been up walking or standing when the explosion occurred. Many of those who had been sitting had not bothered with their seatbelts. More than half of the passengers had been tossed to the floor. Most were hurt and bleeding, adding to the confusion. Like their fellow agents in the press section, more agents fell, victims of oxygen deprivation and flying debris, before the remaining agents thought to put on masks.

The front stairway hatch wasn't as severely damaged, and the lead agent was able to free the stuck door after repeatedly slamming his body into it.

———

Richter turned back to the president, forcing himself to think. *Okay, what do I do?* Holding the president with one hand, he opened the cargo bin again and peered inside.

Without warning, he was slammed into the president again as a second explosion rocked the plane.

CHAPTER THIRTY-TWO

"Deploy chaff and flares!" Zweig yelled as he wrestled with the controls. His instincts were to evade, to bank sharply, but he caught himself, knowing they couldn't descend anymore. They were already at the minimum safe altitude, and only a few thousand feet separated them from the mountains below. There was nowhere to run.

Once again, there had been no warning.

Major Lewis yelled over the noise. "There's no sign of fire in the engines or anywhere else on the aircraft!"

"Call it in!"

"Mayday! Mayday! Mayday! This is Air Force One and we are declaring a Mayday!" Lewis made the call two more times before switching frequencies and trying again.

"I'm not getting anything, sir! The explosions must have knocked out the communications!"

———

McKay peered around the bulkhead and saw the large hole where the rear hatch had been. He stepped up to the door and braced himself in the opening. He glanced over his shoulder at Mosby standing right behind him, said a quick prayer, then jumped out into the airstream.

———

The agents at the top of the staircase in the front of the plane were thrown to the ground by the second blast. The passenger cabin was filled with yelling and screaming as panicked, bleeding passengers called for help or began to pray. Some of the people who had fallen unconscious earlier when the cabin decompressed at thirty-five thousand feet, began to stir.

———

"We need to find the closest airfield now!"

Captain Thomas glanced at the GPS and then scanned his notes. "The closest airport that can handle us is Missoula! Runway is ninety-five hundred feet." He glanced back at the display. "One hundred and twenty miles to the north, bearing zero-one-five."

Zweig nodded as he banked the aircraft, slowly circling around again until they were heading northeast. "Missoula. Zero-one-five."

———

Holding the president with one hand, Richter turned, his eyes avoiding Stephanie's body, and cautiously peered through the bulkhead door. The hold was full of twisted metal, wires hanging from the ceiling, the cargo netting whipping in the wind. Through the debris, he saw a man wearing a parachute harness standing by the jagged hole in the fuselage at the rear of the plane. The man glanced his way before disappearing through the hole.

For a brief second, Richter thought he recognized Cal Mosby.

———

"Captain, what is our ETA to Missoula?"

"At this speed, twenty-eight minutes, sir."

"Watch the radar closely. We'll be crossing over the Bitter-root Mountains. Plot the peaks, Captain, and find us a way in. And find me some alternatives!"

Zweig turned to Lewis. "Major, prepare for an emergency landing."

"Roger, sir. God, I hope ATC is on the ball. We'll be coming in unannounced."

"I know. Keep trying the radios."

Lewis nodded. "Yes, sir. Colonel, all four engines appear to be working. Hydraulics, electronics, stabilizers…everything appears to be normal. Except for lost power to the recorders and communications systems and the cabin pressure, nothing else seems to be affected."

"I'm worried about the structural integrity of the airframe."

Lewis cringed. They were flying a potentially damaged air-craft at a low altitude, with precious little room to maneuver and no way to communicate. *God help them*, she thought.

———

The conversation moments before flashed through Richter's mind.

"Sir, we're going down! We need to get off the plane now!"

He opened the bin again and grabbed a parachute harness. The president nodded, seeming to understand. Richter hefted the parachute up over the president's shoulders, and Kendall slid his arms through. Richter fastened the buckles, tightened the straps, then checked to ensure the harness was snug. Then he quickly strapped on his own harness. He steered the president over Stephanie's and Brad's bodies, through the maze of wreckage in the cargo hold, towards the gaping hole in the back.

They stopped when they stepped through the rear bulkhead. Stepping behind the president, Richter pulled the ball of tightly folded material—no bigger than a softball—from the main pouch on the harness. He pulled the lines over the president's shoulder and wrapped the president's arms around the pilot chute.

"Sir!" Richter had to yell over the noise. "You need to hold this tightly to your chest! After you jump, you need to count to three! Then throw this away from your body!"

Despite the fear in his eyes, the president nodded.

"Count to three then throw," Richter repeated as he mimed the action.

The president nodded again.

"Okay, ready?" Then Richter, still holding the president by the shoulders, pushed him toward the large hole. Without a second thought, Richter pushed him out the door before hurling himself out into the swirling gray.

CHAPTER THIRTY-THREE

The first thing President Kendall noticed was the violent force of the wind. This was followed by sensations of extreme cold. Then, strangely, the cold gave way to a burning sensation. A million pins and needles were being stuck in his body all at once. His legs, hands, and face began to sting as the wind stripped away his body heat. He struggled to see where he was, but there was nothing but pockets of white and gray floating around him. *I must be in the clouds*, he thought. *Oh, God, I forgot to count!* How much time had passed? He pushed the pilot chute up past his face and let it go.

A second later, he felt a violent jolt as the main chute deployed. Without knowing why, he reached up and grabbed the steering toggles dangling above his head. He struggled to hear the plane, but his ears were filled with nothing but the sound of the rushing wind.

———

"Hey, Jack! You've got to see this!" From their perch on the plateau, Derek pointed out over a valley, towards a peak a half a mile away.

Jack peered through the swirling snow, struggling to see.

"Man! They're crazier than you are!"

"What do you suppose they're doing in this weather?

"Could it be a military training exercise?"

Derek squinted. "I don't know. Even those guys aren't that crazy."

They watched as the two parachutes drifted down.

Suddenly there was a bright orange flash from beyond the peak, followed by a muffled boom.

"Jesus," Derek swore. "What the hell was that?"

They watched as the parachutists, one after another, landed on the side of the mountain. A second explosion rang out, followed by a rumble that continued for twenty seconds. As the snow picked up, Derek shielded his eyes, trying to mark the location where the parachutes had landed.

"Oh God! Was that a plane crash?" Jack asked.

"Oh man! I think so! Those guys must have jumped out right before. We need to call 911. Where's your phone?"

Jack turned awkwardly in the deep snow. "It's in the lower right-hand pocket in my pack."

Derek fumbled with the zipper then pulled the phone out. He turned it on and cursed as he waited for it to power up.

———

The president landed on the side of the mountain. Over two feet of fresh snow, coupled with the slope of the hill, saved him from serious injury. He slid down the hill for almost thirty yards before the deep snow brought him to a stop. Buried up to his waist, he lay back for a moment as the enormity of what had happened began to settle in. He couldn't see and struggled with the tangle of risers and control lines that had fallen on him. He pulled off the mask and goggles and wiped his eyes. He noticed that his hands were red, covered with scrapes and cuts. Strangely, they weren't bleeding.

His parachute had crumpled and fallen twenty feet below him. *What do I do now?* he wondered. He strained to see through heavy snow, trying to get his bearings. He was on the side of a mountain. But where? He suddenly felt very alone. What happened to Air Force One? He remembered an explosion. Then Richter was pulling him through the wreckage. What happened to him? Did he jump too?

The wind shifted, blowing a swirl of snow and the parachute up the side of the hill. He struggled for a minute with the tangled lines and the canopy, finally pushing them off. The wind carried the canopy up the hill.

Through the swirling snow, he heard something. The sound was muffled, faint.

"Pull your chute in! Mr. President, pull your chute in!"

He wondered if he was hallucinating. The sound came again and Kendall recognized Richter's voice. Straining to turn his body, the snow and the parachute cords blocking his view, he finally spotted something moving farther up the slope. He raised his hand, tried to wave, before he was violently yanked out of his perch as the wind began pulling his chute, and him, across the side of the hill.

———

In the operations center of Cheyenne Mountain Air Force Station, the lieutenant sipped his soda, his third can since his shift had begun four hours earlier. He glanced at the time and wondered what was on the menu in the cafeteria. He was scheduled to take a break in the next thirty minutes. He eyes shifted back to the bank of flat panel screens. Maybe he would have the soup.

His head shot back to the center display. There was something there. He studied the screen for another two seconds and then checked the screen to the right where his priority flights were listed.

"Holy shit!" He grabbed the phone and called the watch officer. "Sir! We just lost all contact with Air Force One!"

The captain hurried over. "What? Damn! Okay. Okay. Give me the details, the last known coordinates, the list of aircraft in that sector! You know the drill! Let's go!"

———

Simultaneously, an AWACS officer on the E-3 Sentry flying over central Oregon shouted, "God damn! Colonel, we just lost radar contact with Air Force One!"

"Sir, I lost radio contact as well!" a second officer yelled out.

"They just dropped off the screen!" The first added.

"We're not tracking any threats in the area!" another officer called.

"Holy fuck! I'm getting big-time heat blooms. What the hell is that?"

"That's an explosion. Look at the size of that bloom. That's got to be a crash."

"Vampires?" the commanding officer asked.

"No, sir! No missiles detected!"

"Call it in! Now!"

———

Derek cursed as he stared at the phone. No signal. Either they were out of range or weather conditions were affecting reception. Regardless, the phone was useless right now.

"What's our exact position?" he asked.

Jack pulled out his GPS unit. He waited for the system to calibrate. When the waypoint appeared on the screen, Jack locked the position in the system's memory and then handed the unit to Derek. Derek stared at the receiver for a moment.

"I don't know how to use this thing. How far is the trailhead? How far is the car?"

Jack punched some buttons. "A little over thirteen miles."

Derek studied the adjacent mountain. "How far do you think it is to where those guys landed? Half a mile?"

Jack looked across the valley and then at the GPS, noting the contour lines plotted on the screen. "I'm guessing a quarter mile. They landed due east of us."

Derek squinted through the snow. A quarter mile as the crow flies, he reasoned, but they had to descend first and then climb back up that hill. And they didn't have the right gear.

"We can't leave those guys there, Derek," Jack said, as if reading his mind. "They're probably hurt. By the time we hike back to our car and go find help, they'll die."

Derek knew Jack was right. The car was too far away and, in these conditions, it would take two days to reach it. Then what? Elk City was still several miles away over unplowed roads. He turned to Jack and nodded.

Jack studied the GPS, calculating the waypoint where the parachutes had landed.

"We should be able to reach them in an hour, maybe less if we hurry."

"Okay," Derek responded. "Let's do it."

——

The scramble order was relayed from NORAD, headquartered in Cheyenne Mountain, through the Western Air Defense Sector at McCord Air Force Base in Seattle, Washington, to the 142nd Oregon Air National Guard Wing, stationed in Portland, Oregon.

Within seven minutes of receiving the scramble order, a pair of heavily armed F-15 Eagles leapt off the runway, banked hard to the right, and began to climb steeply. Both planes switched on their afterburners and quickly reached supersonic speeds; the sonic booms echoed over Portland. Seventeen minutes later, they were over north central Idaho. Guided by the E-3 Sentry, they searched for potential threats.

——

Minutes later, a KC-135 Stratotanker turned onto the runway and accelerated into the blinding snow. Once airborne, it slowly banked and began climbing. The Stratotanker was essentially a flying gas station designed to provide mid-air refueling, effective-ly extending the operational range and time of fighter and attack aircraft.

"Mother Goose. This is King Four. Estimate one hour and forty-nine minutes to target."

A communications officer on the AWACS keyed his mic. "Copy, King Four. ETA one forty-nine."

———

In the Secret Service Command Center, Tim Jacobs lunged for-ward, punching the keys on his computer. He stared at his screen for a moment then tapped the keyboard again. He glanced to his right at Joe Montarro, manning the satellite link. Montarro, eyes wide, shook his head.

"Horsepower to Angel. Over."

"Horsepower to Angel! Do you read?"

Damn! Jacobs cursed to himself. He jumped up, knocking his chair over in the process. He punched several more keys and glanced over his shoulder at Keith O'Rourke across the room.

"Keith!" he yelled, before turning back to the screen. "We've lost contact with Angel!" Angel was the code name for Air Force One. Jacobs pointed to the computer screen as O'Rourke grabbed the second headset.

"We've lost both audio and data links!"

"Try the alternate frequencies!" O'Rourke barked at Mon-tarro.

"I've already tried them!"

"Goddamn it! Try again!"

As Montarro pounded the keys, speaking into his microphone again, O'Rourke turned back to Jacobs.

"Have you checked with Microwave?" Microwave was the code name for the Air Force Command Center at Andrews Air Force Base.

"I'm in the process!"

O'Rourke lunged for the phone, knocking over a cup of coffee. The mug shattered on the floor, coffee splashing all over his and the other agents' pants. The three men didn't notice.

———

Richter came down the west slope of the mountain, his descent more of a controlled slide. His two-hundred-dollar dress shoes provided no traction at all, and his suit was no match for the wind.

The bitter cold began to sap his energy. His suit jacket and pants were ripped, and his hands were raw and bleeding. He knew there was an Airman's survival kit on the front of his harness and that it contained a blanket and other gear to protect his body from the elements. He also knew that he had to find the president first before he worried about himself.

He stopped for a second to get his bearings. For a moment, he felt disoriented, unsure which direction he had come from and which direction the president had been dragged away. He felt a sudden wave of panic then took a deep breath and forced himself to calm down. Fear and panic could be as deadly as the elements.

As the slope leveled off, he began traversing the face, heading, he hoped, in the direction he had seen the president sliding.

Dropping to a small ledge, he stared into the distance. Through the swirling snow, he glimpsed a flash of color. President Kendall seemed to be twisting and swinging back and forth in his parachute harness. The chute, Richter realized, had saved him from continuing to fall when it became entangled in the branches of the tree that had somehow managed to sprout up through the rocks. It took Richter almost five minutes to slip and slide down the mountain to a point where he finally saw the president again. He watched in horror as the wind repeatedly bashed the president's limp body against the rock face.

―――

Christ almighty, the lead F-15 pilot thought as he looked down at the screen.

"Mother Goose, this is Basher Two-One. We are over target now. We're not picking up any threats. Repeat, negative on threats."

"Copy, Basher Two-One. Have you located point of impact?"

"I'm picking up heat blooms consistent with a crash, but no visual. Visibility is poor. Estimate debris field two, repeat two, square miles."

"Copy, Two-One. Can CSAR get in?"

"It's going to be tough, Mother Goose. Radar and GPS indicate a mountainous terrain, elevations from four thousand feet to eighty-five hundred feet. Limited to no access roads. Weather is a bitch."

"Copy, Two-One. Maintain CAP."

"Copy, Mother Goose. Maintain combat air patrol."

"Two-One. CSAR is scrambling now. Will notify when en route."

"Copy."

As the F-15 pilot signed off, he swore under his breath, wondering what the hell had happened on Air Force One.

———

Richter grabbed onto the tree, wrapping his arms around the trunk to stop himself from sliding over the edge. He sat up, and as the president's spinning body swung by, he grabbed a leg. Bracing his back against the tree, he stood and grabbed the president in a bear hug. With his left arm around the man's waist, he felt the president's neck for a pulse. Feeling nothing, he realized that his fingers, numb and bleeding, were useless. He slid his hand up, under the parachute harness, placing his palm over Kendall's sternum, searching for a heartbeat. After a long, frustrating minute, Richter gave up. Reaching below his own harness, he pulled out his gun and held it up to the president's face.

CHAPTER THIRTY-FOUR

Finally, after almost twenty seconds, he saw it. Along the now-cold metal barrel of the gun, Richter saw the unmistakable signs of condensation forming then dissipating, then forming again. It was slow and rhythmic.

He positioned the president's body between his own and the tree. With his free hand, he fumbled with his harness, opening the pouch on the survival kit. Rooting through the contents, he found the military knife. After he cut the third suspension line, the president's body slumped into his arms. He struggled with the unconscious man, wedging him between the tree trunk and the rock face. Then he cut the remaining lines as a wind gust loosened the chute from the tree's grip. It sailed out over the side of the hill, flapping like a flag before he pulled it in with the remaining suspension line. Fighting the wind, he wrapped the chute around the president.

He leaned back against the rock face and sat next to the unconscious president, pulling part of the chute over his own body. He rummaged through the survival kit again, finding a sleeping bag and a thermal blanket. He struggled for several minutes before he was able to wrap the thermal blanket around the president and then wedge both of their bodies into the sleeping bag. He pulled the chute around and over them, forming a makeshift tent.

Richter put his hand on the president's chest again, feeling it rise and fall, slowly but steadily. He studied the president. His face was pale. One cheek was bruised, and his upper lip was swollen and cut as if he had been punched. There was an ugly scrape on his chin. He couldn't tell if there were any broken bones or internal injuries, but that wasn't his primary concern. Hypothermia was the biggest risk right now.

He put one arm around the president and pulled him tight against his body. He sat back again and stared out through the folds of the chute at the storm. His face was the trademark stony mask as he assessed the situation. For a brief moment, the mask dissolved and a sudden sob escaped from his throat.

Everyone on Air Force One was dead! He knew some of them, at least well enough to say hello: the Chief of Staff, the Secretary of Commerce, the National Security Advisor, the guys from Air Force security, the flight crew. There were many others he didn't know: the White House Counsel, the members of Congress, most of the press pool. All dead.

Sixteen fellow agents were gone. Stephanie was gone! Hands over his face, Richter sobbed. He wept for a moment until, somewhere in his subconscious, the will to live and his sense of duty took over. And with them came anger. *Goddamn it!* He had to pull himself together! He had a job to do!

His teeth began to chatter, and he knew it would take a minute or two before he felt any warmth. The president seemed to be breathing regularly, and Richter knew that he had done all he could for the moment. His mind started to clear, and he forced himself to think about their situation.

Richter was trained in what the Secret Service called "Ten Minute Medicine." Every agent had learned various first aid techniques designed to keep a victim alive for ten more minutes until emergency medical help arrived. Unfortunately, he knew that it would take far longer than ten minutes for help to reach them. He could only count on himself and his training to keep both of them alive. His next task was to find better shelter soon or both he and the president would die from exposure. He had to find a way to keep the president not only warm but dry as well. Then he had to figure out what to do. Richter's face once again turned into a hardened mask.

———

At Portland International Airport, two Pave Hawk helicopters prepared for takeoff. The HH-60G Pave Hawk was the standard rotary-wing rescue and retrieval aircraft of the 920th Rescue Wing. Known as Combat Search and Rescue, or CSAR, the air wing's mission was to locate and recover downed or injured U.S. military personnel during combat operations. The wing also supported civilian search and rescue operations in the U.S., as well as disaster relief efforts around the world.

The Pave Hawk crew consisted of five airmen, including the pilot and co-pilot, a crew chief and two pararescue jumpers, better known as PJs. Today, both Pave Hawks carried eight additional troops.

The lead aircraft took off and hovered. Twenty seconds later, the second aircraft took off.

"Jolly Sixteen. Form up."

"Roger, Jolly Twelve. Sixteen on wing."

Once in formation, both aircraft turned to the east and proceeded at maximum power to central Idaho.

Three minutes later, a Hercules H/C-130 P/N aerial tanker and support aircraft took off from Portland and headed east, soon passing the Pave Hawks. In addition to midair refueling, the H/C-130 was capable of performing tactical airdrops of pararescue specialist teams and a wide assortment of supplies to support rescue operations, including food, water bladders, first-aid bundles, zodiac watercraft, even four-wheel drive all-terrain vehicles. The fixed-wing aircraft was also capable of providing extended visual and electronic searches over land or water.

"Jolly Flight. This is King Flight. Call sign, King Eight. Our ETA to target is one hour thirty-three minutes."

"Roger, King Eight. We're right behind you. ETA is two hours seven minutes. Find us a way in, son."

"Copy, Jolly Twelve."

———

He could do this, Richter willed himself, but he needed to fully assess the situation first. The president was injured and they needed to find shelter soon. The wind had picked up considerably, and it was snowing harder now. Visibility was terrible.

The Secret Service and the Air Force would mobilize rescue units, but he doubted that they would be able to get teams into these mountains in this storm. His watch, the face cracked, told him that it was 11:21 a.m. Pacific Time. They had been flying for about an hour. That would put them somewhere in Idaho, possibly Montana, he calculated, right in the center of the storm.

He inventoried the contents of his survival kit and found windproof matches and a lighter; food packs and cooking gear; a folding shovel and a wire saw; chemical light sticks, candles and a small flashlight; fishing line and hooks; chemical hand warmers; a water purification kit and water storage pouch; a first aid kit; a signaling mirror; and nylon rope.

Richter grunted. *That's strange. There should also be a personal locator beacon.* He checked the president's survival kit and both of their harnesses but didn't find any electronic signaling devices.

He then remembered that his cell phone had built in GPS capabilities, but when he checked his pockets, it was missing. He realized it must have fallen out somewhere along the way. His radio was missing too, likely ripped from his body by the gale force winds, he realized. *Damn!*

Okay, he thought. They had sleeping bags and blankets to keep warm. They could use the parachute canopies as tents. They had food, they could make a fire…if they could find wood. They could survive, if he thought this through.

But what had happened? he wondered. That sure as hell looked like Cal Mosby. And there were…what? One…two explosions before they jumped? He remembered descending. And he was certain he had heard another explosion after he jumped and wondered whether they'd been shot down. Wait. If it was a missile, how had Mosby reacted so quickly? Why did he bail out instead of rushing to help the president?

"Son of a bitch!" Richter yelled as it dawned on him. *They had been sabotaged!* Mosby had forced the pilots to descend and then somehow created an explosion to blow the door off. *That's it! Mosby had parachuted off the plane!* But he knew he couldn't parachute from thirty-five thousand feet. He wouldn't survive. Well, he was wearing an oxygen mask, but the plane was going way too fast. He had to slow it down. He wouldn't be able to open the door because of the pressure differences inside and outside the plane. He had to slow the plane down, and even then, he had to somehow open the door. That had to be it— someway, somehow, Mosby had forced the pilots to descend and to reduce air speed.

Damn! Mosby must have smuggled explosives on board. He was knowledgeable about explosives, Richter knew, but what about parachutes? Mosby couldn't have acted alone, he realized. He had to have accomplices, and it had to be someone from the Air Force. They were the only ones who visited the lower deck while the plane was airborne. They would be able to explain how planes worked, where to set explosives, how the pilots would react in an emergency. They were trained in parachutes. And Mosby was the only one able to get the explosives past all of the security checkpoints. *Oh, shit!* If Mosby and someone from the Air Force were involved, who else was? How many people jumped off the plane?

There was no way of knowing who he could trust.

Okay. Forget that, he told himself. He needed to focus on survival. The next thing he had to do was build a better shelter. They had to get out of the wind and snow. He'd need to either build a shelter up here or somehow get the president down to where there were trees. Trees would provide some shelter from the wind.

———

Vice President Tyler Rumson was in a meeting with the House Whip when Agent Timmons, barged into his office.

"Sir, we need to leave right now!"

"I'm in a meeting!" Rumson snapped.

Ignoring Rumson's protest, Timmons pulled him to his feet and over to the door. Outside, five more agents were waiting.

Rumson suppressed a smile as the agents formed a ring with himself and Timmons in the middle. He felt Timmons' vice-like grip on his elbow as the agents, shouting, rushed him down the hall. His mind was flying. Finally!

In his excitement, he didn't hear Timmons.

"Wolf is secure."

———

Maria Kendall was in her office, in the East Wing of the White House, discussing national education objectives and policy with her Chief of Staff and the Secretary of Education. Abruptly, her office door opened and the head of her Secret Service detail, Paula Tiller, and two other agents interrupted the meeting.

"Ma'am, may I speak with you privately?"

Maria excused herself, and Agent Tiller steered her into the hallway.

"Ma'am, the president was aboard Air Force One today, flying back from Seattle. Approximately twenty minutes ago, we lost contact with his plane."

Maria's face went pale; she stared at the agent. "What exactly does that mean?"

"We don't know what it means yet. We have multiple ways of maintaining contact with the president and Air Force One at all times. We've tried them all, but we are unable to make any contact."

Maria slumped against the wall and Tiller grabbed her arms to keep her from falling.

"Ma'am, until we find out exactly what's going on, I think it's best if you come with me."

"Wait...what about Angela and Michelle?"

Tiller led her down the hall. "We're picking them up right now. They should be here in forty-five minutes."

———

Both Angela and Michelle Kendall attended the Brookfield Academy, a private, all-girls school in Arlington, Virginia. Angela was daydreaming while her teacher, Mr. Hatfield, droned on about inorganic compounds. Suddenly there were shouts, and two Secret Service agents burst into the classroom and darted through the maze of desks to her seat. Another agent stepped into the room, his gun drawn but pointed at the floor. Angela didn't notice the gasps and startled cries of her classmates. She only saw the look on Agent Barbara Sullivan's face; the hard eyes, the tight muscles stretched across her clenched jaw. Suddenly, Agent Sullivan was pulling her up from her seat.

"Angela, we need to leave right now," Sullivan commanded as she steered Angela towards the door. As they hurried down the hall, Sullivan lifted her cuff to her mouth.

"Foxtrot is secure. We're heading for the East entrance."

———

At that same moment, Michelle was running down the soccer field. Unlike most girls in her class who hated P.E. because it made them sweat, messed up their hair, and ruined their makeup, Michelle loved it. She dribbled the ball around two defenders, who made halfhearted attempts to stop her, and with a quick glance at the goalie, she picked her shot. The ball sailed past the goalie into the upper left-hand corner of the net. While a few of her teammates cheered, Michelle jogged back to center field.

Behind her, several girls screamed. Michelle turned and saw three Secret Service agents running across the field, their suit coats flapping, two of them holding guns.

CHAPTER THIRTY-FIVE

The initial shockwave from the final explosion tore a sixteen-inch hole in the right side of the fuselage. While that hole, and the damage caused to the plane from the two prior explosions, was enough to doom the aircraft, what sealed its fate was the secondary shockwave that followed the last blast. The fuselage reflected a portion of the bomb's initial energy back towards the site of the explosion. When that reflected energy met with the waves still pulsing from the original blast, the result was a more powerful and faster traveling wave of energy, called a Mach stem wave. This traveled at supersonic speeds in several directions at once, bouncing off the fuselage and racing through open cavities and ductwork, warping and twisting metal along the way. The Mach stem wave tore a large hole through the ceiling of the cargo hold into the passenger compartment and continued up through the top of the fuselage into the rushing air outside. Much closer to the detonation site, another Mach stem wave tore a hole through the left-hand side of the plane directly across from the cargo bin where McKay had placed the bomb.

This was followed by a wave of high-pressure gas that instantaneously over-pressurized the cavities of the plane and peeled back the fuselage skin as it sought equilibrium with the significantly lower-pressure environment outside. The expanding energy and gas waves buckled the airframe and broke it in half.

The passengers, already in a panic, had no way of comprehending what was happening. Their bodies were violently assaulted by the Mach stem wave and expanding gasses and the shrapnel that once again filled the cabin. Almost instantly, the top of the plane peeled back and tornado-force winds rushed through the passenger compartment.

This all occurred in mere fractions of a second and, two and a half seconds later, the plane began to break apart. The forward portion of the doomed aircraft, which contained the still intact wings, began a flat spin, the wings still providing lift. The rear portion began to plummet. As the plane continued to break into pieces, passengers and their belongings were sucked out into the freezing air.

The first portion of the wreckage, including a seat with Senator Pete Dykstra strapped in, landed five miles east of the mountainside where President Kendall and Agent Richter had landed.

———

Jack checked the GPS unit and then studied the side of the mountain.

"They landed there," Jack said pointing to the steep slope they faced, "about two hundred, maybe three hundred feet up. I think that explosion we heard was on the other side."

"Well, if that's the spot, we should be able to find their tracks in the snow."

Jack shook his head. "Their tracks are probably gone by now. Besides, we don't have the right gear. How are we going to get up there?"

The slope of the hill in front and to the right steepened dramatically to almost thirty-five degrees. Despite the slope, the side of the hill was covered in snow, with an occasional rock formation poking through. There was no way to tell how deep it was or what dangers lay hidden beneath. Even with proper gear, an ascent would be difficult.

"Did you bring your binoculars?" Derek asked.

"Yeah. In the lower right-hand pocket."

Jack turned again as Derek searched for the field glasses.

A minute later, Derek lowered the binoculars.

"I don't see any sign of them."

"Let me try."

Jack adjusted the focus and scanned the side of the hill. Beginning at the spot where he estimated the parachutes had landed, he slowly panned up the hill and then back down to eye level directly in front of their position. Seeing nothing, he continued downhill. Still nothing. He brought the binoculars back up to eye level. He was about to give up when he caught a flash of color. His heart began beating faster. He held the binoculars steady, waiting, until he saw it again.

———

National Transportation Safety Board Member Brenda Hughes

flipped open her binder to check her schedule as she walked down the hallway in the NTSB headquarters building in Washington, DC.

"Director Hughes!"

She turned to see a young staff member running down the hall. The staffer was out of breath.

"Ma'am!" he gasped. "There's been a plane crash."

Shoot, Hughes thought. *There goes the weekend.* She sighed.

"Give me the summary."

The aide finally caught his breath. "This one is big, ma'am!" He paused again, trying to find the right words.

"Well?"

"It's Air Force One!"

———

Richter was peering out between the folds in the parachute when he sensed movement. He reached for his gun as two figures appeared out of the swirling snow. Did Mosby have accomplices?

Walking across the side of the incline, they appeared to be hikers. Both wore large backpacks. Richter watched as they carefully picked their route; occasionally stopping to make sure the ground was safe. They were headed directly for him. When the two men were about thirty yards away, one of them called out.

"Hello."

Richter stuck one hand through the opening of his makeshift tent and gave a half-hearted wave.

"Are you hurt?"

"Yes," Richter yelled back. "My friend is."

Like many police officers, Richter had developed an intuitive sense, a gut feeling, about people and situations. When something didn't feel right, he found it was best to trust his instincts. He could see that they weren't carrying any visible weapons and they weren't trying to be clandestine. They were careful in their approach, clearly concerned about their own safety. They were young, in their early twenties, he guessed. He hoped his instincts and his sixth sense weren't failing him. He slid his gun back below the parachute harness but kept it ready.

The two men stepped onto the narrow ledge. The taller one pointed over his shoulder. "Jack's a doctor. And a Boy Scout." He grinned. "He'll know what to do."

"What are you doing out here?" Richter kept the makeshift tent closed except for the small hole for his head. He wanted to be sure before he let some supposed Boy Scout and his friend touch the president.

"We were backpacking. Been out here two days." The taller of the two shrugged. "We forgot to check the forecast and got caught in this storm."

The one named Jack gave him a dirty look.

"*We* didn't forget anything, Derek! *You* forgot!"

Jack maneuvered around Derek on the narrow ledge. Again trusting his instincts, Richter opened his parachute and let Jack in. Jack knelt in front of the president. "I'm not a doctor yet, I'm still in med school. But I'll see what I can do."

Jack took off his glove, checked for a pulse and breathing, then examined the president's head.

He glanced at Richter. "He's alive. How long has he been out?"

"About forty minutes. I think he may have banged his head."

Jack examined the president's head. "It was a good idea to get him into the bag and to get the blanket around him. But he won't survive too much longer up here. We need to get him into a shelter, out of this wind. You too," Jack said, nodding to Richter, and then frowning. "You look like you hit your head as well. How do you feel? Can you walk?"

Richter frowned. "I'm okay. I can walk."

"You guys were on the plane, right?"

Richter hesitated. "Yeah. We were on the plane."

———

Pat Monahan closed his binder. Today's Boston Task Force raid, the fifth so far, had gone smoothly. So far, other than cuts and bruises, assault team and Mexican civilian injuries had been almost non-existent. But Monahan worried it was just a matter of time before the cartels adapted to the new tactics. Then casualties would start to mount.

As he stepped out of the video conference room on the ground floor of the White House—today's meeting had been moved at the request of the National Security Staff—there was a commotion as a large group of Secret Service agents, Cabinet members, and senior White House personnel headed his way. One look at their faces told him something was wrong.

"Pat, you should join us," one agent said as he steered Monahan toward the Situation Room.

———

"We'll have to improvise a stretcher and carry him down." Jack yelled over the wind.

Derek nodded.

Jack fingered the parachute material. "This should work. We should be able to carry this guy..." he paused and turned to Richter. "Hey, what's his name?"

Richter hid his surprise. These guys had no idea who they were. "His name is Dave, and I'm Matt."

"Okay, Matt, let's get you out of that bag."

Richter climbed out and zipped the bag up around the president, pulling and cinching the mummy hood up around his head, leaving only his face exposed. They wrapped the president in the parachute.

"I can't believe you jumped out of that plane!" Derek said. "What happened?"

"Mechanical issues. Let's get Dave to shelter first then I'll tell you all about it."

They each grabbed a handful of parachute, cautiously made their way off the ledge, and began to trudge down the hill.

———

"Ladies and gentlemen." The White House Communications Director said. "I have a brief statement."

The director's face was pale. The room went silent.

"Today at approximately 11:14 a.m. Pacific Coast Time.... that is about one hour and fifteen minutes ago....all contact with Air Force One was lost as the plane was returning to Washington from Seattle. Information that we have right now indicates that the plane crashed into the mountains in a remote area of Idaho. Rescue teams are en route but have not yet reached the crash site. At this time, we have no word on the extent of the damage or whether there are any survivors. That is all that I have at the moment."

Pandemonium broke out, and reporters began shouting questions.

"Please. Please. One question at a time."

"Was the president on the plane?"

"Yes. The president was on the plane."

"Are you saying the president is dead?"

"No. Let me repeat that. No. I am not saying the president is dead. At this point, we have no information on his condition. As I mentioned earlier, rescue teams have been dispatched but have not yet reached the crash site."

"What happened? Is this the result of a terrorist attack?"

"At this point, we do not know what happened. All we know at the moment is that contact was lost and that Air Force One has apparently crashed. Air Force fighter planes were immediately scrambled and have confirmed the location of the crash site, but....again....this occurred in a remote section of Idaho. There is a severe winter storm in the area. Reaching the wreckage site will be a challenge."

The room erupted again.

CHAPTER THIRTY-SIX

Richter and President Kendall were huddled inside the snow cave. An hour earlier, when they had reached the tree line, Richter, Jack, and Derek had decided to build the cave below a tree for protection from the wind. The lower branches dipped down almost to the ground, effectively sheltering the cave. They had used the wire saws to cut dead branches from the trunk to make room, and then, once they had constructed the walls, they used the cut branches to form a latticework support for the roof. They layered on snow with the shovels from the survival kits.

Once the basic cave had been constructed, Jack had insisted that Matt stay inside with Dave to keep warm while he and Derek finished the roof. Richter crawled inside, checked on the president and found that he was breathing regularly. He spread the second parachute on the ground to keep the sleeping bags and their clothes from getting wet. With nothing left to do for the moment, he climbed into the sleeping bag with the president and draped the second sleeping bag over them like a blanket.

He opened one of the chemical light sticks, and the cave

was filled with an eerie green light. After several minutes of shivering, his chest and thighs begin to warm. He checked the president again. With his bruised and swollen face, he was hardly recognizable. Richter noticed a large bump behind the president's right ear. It was sticky with blood. He cleaned the wound as best he could and applied a bandage.

Kendall began to stir. Richter checked his eyes and asked him a few questions. His eyes weren't completely focused, and his speech was slurred. While Jack and Derek were still outside, Richter explained what had happened.

"This was...an assassination attempt?" The lisp was heavy; the president sounded drunk.

"I'm afraid so, sir," Richter replied. "But listen—these two campers? I think it's best if we don't reveal who we are yet. I want to get a better sense of who they are first and why they're out here in this storm before we say anything."

"What do we tell them?"

"I think we can say we are low-level government officials who work in one of the departments...why don't we say Immigration and Customs. I still have my gun, which might make them suspicious. So, I'll say I'm an Immigration Agent. You can be someone from headquarters, maybe a department lawyer or something like that. We'll say our plane developed problems and we parachuted out at the last second. Can you do that?"

"Yes." The president responded, his voice thick.

———

"Dave! You're awake!" Jack knelt in front of the president. "My name is Jack Walsh. I'm a medical student. Can I take a look?" Jack didn't wait for a response and proceeded to examine him. "Looks like you were in a fight. You were out for a while." Jack studied the president's eyes. "How do you feel?"

"Like I lost the fight."

Jack grinned. He took his time examining the president, then checking and re-bandaging the head wound. "It looks like you have a moderate case of hypothermia. But your buddy Matt prevented it from getting worse. He saved your life. He did a pretty nice job treating your head wound too."

The president smiled as Jack turned to Richter.

Richter reluctantly allowed Jack to examine him.

"You've got a nasty cut on your head, Matt. You could use several stitches. It looks like you lost a bit of blood, but you don't seem to be bleeding anymore."

Richter held up a handful of snow, stained red. "I've been applying cold compresses."

Jack smiled. "Good thinking." He cleaned the wound, applied surgical glue and a bandage.

Derek waited until the exam was complete. "So, you guys had plane trouble? What happened?"

Richter relayed their cover story.

"Was there anyone else on the plane?

"Yes, the pilots." Richter responded. "They told us to jump first. I don't know if they made it out or not." He changed the subject. "Do you guys live around here?"

"No, we live in Lewiston. Or at least I do. Jack goes to school down in Boise."

"Where's that?"

"Lewiston? About a hundred twenty-five miles northwest from here. Right on the border with Washington."

"What are you guys doing way out here?"

"Jack's on spring break from college. He came home for the week and we both decided we needed a break from our families." Derek smiled at his own joke.

"Where did you guys start your hike?"

"From Elk City. That's about ten miles from here as the crow flies, but probably sixteen miles by foot."

"Is your car in Elk City?"

"Yeah. Well, sort of. We parked off a four-wheel drive trail about five miles out of town."

"What's Elk City like?"

"Very small town. Three hundred, maybe four hundred people. It's an old mining town."

———

Within five hours and thirty minutes of the crash, the twelve members of the NTSB Go Team had assembled at Andrews Air Force Base. The team was comprised of scientists and crash investigators under the lead of Stan Burton, the NTSB investigator-in-charge. Burton was anxious to get underway. Like most team members, he felt the same rush of adrenaline he always felt as the team prepared to depart. Despite the horrors of a typical accident scene, the utter destruction, the loss of so many lives, the twenty-four-seven work schedule he would face for the next few months, this was what he lived for. It was morbid when he thought about it. However, he tended to look at the bigger picture and the role that his team played in not only uncovering what had gone wrong, but in helping to prevent future accidents. Burton checked the time again. If this were a civilian airplane crash, they would already be on their way.

"I hate this hurry up and wait shit." He was careful to keep his voice low.

"Patience, Stan." This was the second time that NTSB Board Member Brenda Hughes had accompanied a Go Team. Her role was to be the public face for the NTSB, handling the press briefings, updating the NTSB board, and managing the interagency glad-handing so often required in these things. This was her first military crash, and she suspected she would spend most of her time managing the relationship with the Air Force brass, which had primary responsibility for investigating the crash, and deftly balancing what she anticipated would be a strict communications protocol mandated by the military and the White House.

"Ms. Hughes. I'm General Bud Trescott. Is your team ready?" She hadn't noticed the general until he was standing in front of her.

She stood. "Yes, we are." Nodding toward Burton. "This is Stan Burton. He's our lead investigator."

"Mr. Burton." General Trescott said in clipped acknowledgment. "Okay. Let's board. I'll brief you in-flight."

CHAPTER THIRTY-SEVEN

In the mouth of the snow cave, Derek heated water over the camp stove.

"You guys have some nice gear," he said.

"Your tax dollars at work," Richter responded. "Just the basic survival kits carried on most government planes."

Derek had been eyeing the survival packs—he had already seen the saws, sleeping bags and thermal blankets, and some of the cooking gear—and Richter suspected that he wanted a closer look.

"Looks like pasta for us and chicken-noodle soup for Dave. Sorry, Dave…Jack's orders."

Jack smiled. "You're looking better, but I want to get some more hot fluids in you."

The president's smile was weak. "Thanks, Dr. Jack. Soup is fine."

After they ate, Derek cleaned the dishes outside.

"Do you think they'll send a search and rescue team for you?" Jack asked.

"I assume so," Richter responded. "But, with this weather, who knows how long that will take.

"Any idea how long this storm will last?" Derek asked.

"It's supposed to be bad through Sunday morning." Richter changed the subject. "You said Elk City is an old mining town? Are there any abandoned mines in this area?"

Jack opened a pocket on his backpack and pulled out a topographical trail map. He took a moment to study it.

"There's a mine about four or five miles from here, basically west from us toward Elk City. But I think I saw something closer on my GPS. Maybe a mile away."

"Do you think we could hike there in this weather? Are you still able to get a GPS signal?" Richter wanted to put as much distance as he could between the president and the crash site. There was no way to tell how big the conspiracy was, and as long as POTUS wasn't at risk of dying, it made sense to hide until he could better assess the risks and figure out what to do.

"I can check. My battery is low, but I should be able to recharge it tomorrow." Jack pointed to his backpack and the framed black and grey patterned grid on one pouch.

It took Richter a moment to recognize it.

"That's a solar panel?"

"Yes. If we can get enough sunlight, I should be able to recharge it." Jack reached into his pocket. "But I don't know about my phone. I think I got snow in it. We'll have to see tomorrow. You think we're better off in a mine?"

"Possibly. It might be warmer. We might be able to start a fire."

"I don't know. We explored some mines a few years ago. The farthest in we went was about twenty feet. Derek wanted to go farther, but I've read stories about explosive gases, people dying of asphyxiation, that sort of thing."

Richter shivered as the image of Brad Lansing, dead on the floor of the cargo hold, popped into his head. Agent Lansing couldn't help them now, but Jack and Derek could.

"These mines must have wood, building materials, that sort of thing. Right?"

"Probably. The ones we saw had formwork for sluices and bracing for the tunnels."

"What do you think about the..." Richter caught himself. "Do you think Dave can make it?"

"He's not as bad as I first thought. I think if he's looking this good tomorrow, we might be able to try. That is, if I can recharge my GPS."

———

Once the C-40B was airborne, the general organized the meeting. He introduced the Air Force investigation team, consisting of investigators, engineers and security personnel. Next, the general introduced representatives from Boeing and General Electric. Brenda Hughes let the NTSB team introduce themselves. With formalities out of the way, the general provided an overview of the mission.

"The number one priority is getting search and rescue teams in. CSAR teams have reached the area but have been unable to put people on the ground. We have a major winter storm underway dumping one hell of a lot of snow in the area. Visibility is shit with eighty to ninety mile per hour wind gusts. The temperature right now is twenty-four degrees.

"Based on infrared imaging, the wreckage is scattered over a sizable area. The majority of the wreckage, what we call the primary debris field, is in an area that's almost three quarters of a mile long by seven or eight hundred yards wide. Our estimate right now is that this only accounts for approximately eighty to ninety percent of the total debris. We expect to find a considerable amount of debris outside of this primary field, not only along the axis of flight, but also to either side due to the wind. We're mapping this now.

"This is a remote area. It's mountainous, so you can expect significant changes in elevation across the debris field; topographical data indicates anywhere from thirty-five hundred feet to over eighty-five hundred feet. The storm will make our task even more difficult, not only in getting to the site but, as the debris cools, it will be covered with snow.

"The closest town is about fifteen miles away. Elk Creek, population three hundred. With this storm, though, we can't safely land anywhere near there. For now, we will be staging in Portland, Oregon, at the Air Guard Base. We will try to transport the team to Elk City by helicopter, possibly later tonight if the weather permits. Since we don't know if we can land a helicopter near the crash site, we may have to rely on four-wheel drive vehicles, Humvees, or snowcats to get in. There are some logging roads and ATV trails, but if we're forced to go in by ground, we'll be trailblazing most of the way. Hopefully, we can land a helo closer but we won't know that until we get some men on the ground.

"Mr. Burton, for reconstruction, we're still trying to determine whether there is sufficient space in Elk City. In all likelihood, we will have to commandeer a hangar in Portland." The general turned back to the rest of the group. "Needless to say, there will be a lot of eyes watching us. I want to see everyone's 'A' Game on this one. I will not accept anyone cutting any corners. We do this one by the book. Is that clear?"

He waited until he saw heads nod in agreement.

"Okay. That's the big picture. Major Conklin will take you through the specifications, the operating history, and operating parameters of Air Force One." The general paused again and looked around the cramped meeting room on the C-40B. "This," he paused until he was sure he had everyone's attention, "is classified data."

———

Richter sighed. It was going to be a long night. Jack had lit one of the candle lanterns, and it hung from the crisscrossed branches that formed the roof support. The president seemed to be sleeping peacefully, despite Derek's snoring. After dinner, Jack had given his coat, hat, and gloves to the president, insisting he wear them. He had inspected the president's feet, then slipped foot warmers into his socks. The president was fine for now in his sleeping bag. As best as they could tell, his body temperature was back to normal and his pulse and respiration were strong.

The president had done well, Richter thought. He stuck to

the cover story and had answered Jack and Derek's questions without providing anything specific. *Well, he is a politician*, Richter reminded himself. He took it as a sign that the president was recovering.

Richter was reasonably warm in his bag with the mummy hood cinched around his head. Before he had climbed in, he had wrapped one of the thermal blankets around himself and had placed one of the hand warmers down by his feet. Comfortable for now, but unable to sleep, he watched the flickering light dance off the walls and ceiling of the cave. He studied the ceiling and walls but didn't see any signs of ice or dripping water. That was good. It meant that the air inside the cave was probably no more than thirty-five to forty degrees, the ideal temperature for a snow cave, he remembered from Army survival training years ago. They would have to be careful to avoid melting.

Jack sat by the mouth of the cave with his mummy bag cinched up around his face. He, too, had one of the thermal blankets. Still awake, he periodically used the shovel to clean out the newly fallen snow from the opening, providing much needed fresh air.

"Tell me about Elk City." It sounded like they were sitting in a soundproof room as the snow structure absorbed their words. Even so, Richter kept his voice low, trying not to disturb the sleeping men.

Jack turned. "The town sprang up in the Gold Rush, sometime in the mid-1800s, but the mining operations were shut down by the 1930s. I think the miners moved on to newer and larger discoveries elsewhere and the population dwindled."

"What does the town do now?"

"This area is mostly timber farming. This is all part of the Nez Perce National Forest, so there's not a lot of development. There are some fly-in trout fishing and hunting camps. During the winter, there's some snowmobiling. I think there's a business in town that rents them and provides guided tours. Mostly, it's a great place to hike. You can go out for a week and not see another soul, even during the summer. It's beautiful here. When the sky is clear at night, the stars are amazing."

Richter smiled. "That's pretty cool. Are there any airports close by?"

"Elk City has an airport, but I don't think they have a lot of flights. The Forest Service also has a number of air fields, but those are for small planes and they're open only from late spring to early fall. It's a very remote area."

Richter digested the information. "Is there a sheriff's office in Elk City?"

"I don't know. We never saw one."

"What about forest ranger stations?"

"The only station I ever saw was at one of the air fields. I read somewhere that many stations were closed permanently, something to do with budget cuts. Those that are left normally shut down for the winter."

"How far is the closest station?"

"I'll check my map and my GPS in the morning, but my guess is at least ten, maybe fifteen miles away."

Richter pondered this. One thing was certain. He needed Jack and Derek. These guys knew the area and they appeared to be exactly who they said they were...two hikers caught by the freak storm. He liked Jack. The kid was careful, thoughtful, even caring. Derek on the other hand was arrogant and cocky. Then again, Richter remembered, he had been too at that age. Regardless, his instinct told him that they were both good kids, and he was very glad that they had run into each other.

Elk City sounded like their only option. They could survive here, in the snow cave, for a little while, but then what? Two questions remained: besides Jack and Derek, who could they trust and where should they go?

———

The president woke with a start, and it took him a moment to realize where he was. He heard snoring, but that wasn't what had woken him. He sat quietly and tried to remember his dream. It had been unsettling. He gave up after a while and, with a clearer head, pondered their predicament. Never in a million years would he have predicted that something like this would happen. That someone would try to kill him and that he would be stranded in the wilderness, trying to survive in an ice cave in the middle of a brutal snowstorm.

Richter had told him that Air Force One—his plane—had crashed. Everyone aboard was almost certainly dead. Tears began to run down his cheeks. Charles Howell was gone. His Secret Service agents died trying to protect him. Linda Huff. Felicia Jackson. Nancy Hartwig. Mike Breen. All of his closest advisors—his friends—were dead. The Air Force crew—folks he had come to know and trust—was gone too.

His thoughts drifted to Maria and the girls. They had to be devastated. He wished that he could do something to ease their pain, hug them and tell them that everything was all right. That he was okay. The only thing he could do, he realized, was to survive somehow and make it back home. Thinking of his family, he felt hope. They were something he could hang onto in a storm. They gave him strength and the will to keep on fighting.

His mind drifted back again to the people who had been on Air Force One. As he thought of everyone who had unknowingly sacrificed their lives for him, he felt outrage; outrage and determination. He had to make it back. He had to find out who did this and make them pay.

He realized that this could wind up being one of those defining moments in history where the entire nation felt intimately connected somehow to the event. How many times had he heard people discuss where they were and what they were doing when they had first learned that President Kennedy had been shot or when President Walters had killed himself? There would be confusion, disbelief, anger, tears, and grief. The TVs would be running continual news coverage, providing the latest information, the latest theories, interviewing hundreds of so-called experts who would be only too happy to offer their opinions.

He wondered what was happening in Washington right now, back in the White House. He had lived through it once when President Walters died. But it had to be far worse now. It was probably two or three in the morning, and the West Wing would be a zoo. There would be a team in the Situation Room trying their best to figure out what had happened and what to do. There would be discussions on succession and chain of command. Rumson was probably taking advantage of the opportunity. He was probably smiling right now, not believing his good luck; probably thinking that he couldn't have planned it any better...

Oh, shit.

It took a long time for the president to fall back to sleep.

CHAPTER THIRTY-EIGHT

Saturday, April 24

"This is being treated as a criminal investigation." It was four in the morning, and FBI Director Emil Broder was in a foul mood. "I will not get caught up in petty jurisdictional bullshit. The FBI is in charge. The participation of all other federal and state criminal, investigative, rescue, and other agencies is now under the oversight and coordination of the Bureau." His dark eyes and the edge to his voice left little room to maneuver. He stared at each of the department heads and military officers seated around the table. No one dared challenge him.

"This is how it will work. The Air Force will lead the accident investigation and reconstruction, with the National Transportation Safety Board and the FAA assisting. Search and rescue efforts will be led by the Air Force, with assistance from the Idaho and Montana National Guards. I understand that both governors have mobilized their guard units and they'll be at our disposal. Idaho State Police units, as well as volunteer local search and rescue teams, will be available to assist if needed.

FEMA will coordinate and provide disaster site assistance including food, water, clothing, and temporary shelter and sleeping quarters, if required, to the teams. The FBI will lead the criminal investigation with assistance from the ATF and the Secret Service and local law enforcement officials."

Broder paused. Several people shifted uncomfortably in their seats; otherwise the room was silent.

"Pat Monahan, Deputy Director of the FBI, will be the lead in Idaho. Senior Agent Kaitlyn Pearson, from my office, will be the lead in Washington. Agent Pearson will support Deputy Director Monahan by coordinating the participation of all of the federal, state, and local agencies involved. She'll ensure that the search and rescue operation proceeds as quickly and effectively as possible. Right now, that's the priority. She will also ensure that Deputy Director Monahan has the support he needs on the criminal investigation by coordinating resources. Homeland Security has created an information clearinghouse, and Bob Mendoza from Homeland Security will be assisting Agent Pearson.

"Agent Pearson and Mr. Mendoza will explain how the overall effort will be managed, the communication and notification protocols, daily briefings, etc. Then, Deputy Director Monahan will provide you with an overview of how the on-site rescue efforts and investigation will proceed."

Broder nodded to the agent seated next to him. "Agent Pearson?"

———

Richter was surprised by how much snow had fallen overnight.

There was at least a foot of new snow below the tree. The branches had kept most of the snow from falling on their cave and were sagging below the weight. Dawn was breaking and it was still snowing. The wind was still gusting, Richter learned the hard way, as a pile of snow from the higher branches fell onto his head. He shook the snow off and carefully peered out between the branches. The snow had to be three or four feet deep. How were they going to walk through that?

The air was bitter cold, and he began to shiver. As he crawled back inside, the president was unzipping his sleeping bag.

"Nature calls."

"How do you feel?" Richter asked.

"Not bad, considering."

"I need to go too." Jack sat up. "You can stay inside, Matt. I'll go with him."

"That's okay," Richter responded. "I wouldn't mind stretching my legs again."

Moments later, wrapped in a thermal blanket, arms folded tight across his chest, he watched Jack and the president piss in the snow. Despite all that Jack had done for them, Richter still wasn't comfortable when the president was out of sight. Kendall swayed slightly and began to shake.

Richter grabbed his shoulders. "You look a little wobbly… Dave. Let's get you back inside."

Once they were settled inside, Jack pulled out the camp stove.

"I'll get a pot of water boiling and make some breakfast. You feel like something to drink, Dave? Maybe something to eat?"

"Something hot would be great." The president's teeth chattered as he crawled back inside his sleeping bag. The commotion woke Derek. He followed Jack outside.

After they left, the president leaned over to Richter and whispered, "So, what's our plan, Agent Richter?"

Richter caught the formality. That was good; he seemed to be regaining his presidential bearing.

"We need to find a better shelter. There might be an abandoned mine nearby or a forest ranger station."

"Can we make it in this weather? It looks pretty deep out there. I grew up in the Rockies, and you don't want to go wandering around in a blizzard."

"I was thinking about that. If we had snowshoes, we should be able to. I remember the instructor showing us how to make them during survival training. And Jack has a GPS, which should keep us from getting lost." Thinking out loud, he continued, "Our biggest challenge is going to be clothing. We don't have any coats or gloves or hats. It also will depend on how you feel. I would like Jack to take a look at you again."

The president nodded then glanced at the mouth of the cave. "Listen. Before the boys return, I want to share something with you." He relayed his suspicions about Rumson. "Now, I might be wrong, but…."

Richter felt his pulse quicken, then the president suddenly went quiet as Jack and Derek crawled back inside.

———

Phil Perry turned on the TV and switched to CNN and the stern face of the news anchor.

"We continue with our coverage of the crash of Air Force One. There is still no word on the status of President Kendall. Authorities tell us that search and rescue efforts have been difficult, due to the blizzard that has paralyzed Northern Idaho. We have learned that Air Force rescue crews expect a break in the weather today and hope to reach the crash site later this afternoon. The mood of those involved in emergency response is somber, and authorities have not commented on whether they believe there are any survivors, or on possible causes for the crash. One source, who remains anonymous because he is not authorized to speak about the accident, tells us it is unlikely that anyone could have survived. As a shocked nation waits for news on the fate of President Kendall, condolences and offers of support have poured in from around the world.

"While the focus has been on the president and those who were on board Air Force One, the storm has impacted thousands of residents in Idaho, Montana, and surrounding states. In Idaho, the governor has declared a State of Emergency and has mobilized the National Guard. Meanwhile, State Police have closed all major highways in north-central Idaho and are only allowing emergency and rescue vehicles through. Even with the closures, which were ordered by the Governor yesterday afternoon, many motorists have been stranded by the storm, particularly along sections of Route 90, Route 95, Route 93 and Route 12, where reports indicate snowdrifts up to eight feet deep. State Police estimate as many as five hundred vehicles remain stuck and crews have been working around the clock to reach an estimated eight hundred motorists and passengers who are still stranded.

"The National Guard and State Police are using military trucks and other heavy vehicles that can plow through the snow drifts. We now go live to Kevin Battaglia of affiliate K-DCH in Coeur d'Alene. What can you tell us, Kevin?"

Perry listened as the reporter in Coeur d'Alene, standing outside in the falling snow, rehashed the same facts as the CNN anchor. He switched the TV off. He had tried calling Rumson last night and again this morning. The news had said that he had been moved to an unnamed, secure location, and he assumed that Rumson was preoccupied with the crisis. That was understandable. He decided to give Rumson another day or two before he tried again.

———

Richter peered out between the branches of the tree. The snow had slowed to flurries, for the moment at least, but the grey skies threatened more. He could make out the steep slope of the mountain several hundred yards away. The top was hidden in the clouds. Somewhere behind the veil, he knew, he and the president had landed less than twenty-four hours ago.

He carefully let go of the branch. Something was nagging him. The president believed that Rumson was somehow behind the assassination attempt. But how were Mosby and Rumson connected? Rumson rarely acknowledged anyone below him unless it was to issue an order. Yet, hadn't he seen the vice president and Mosby—several months back—sharing a quiet word outside the Oval Office? At the time, it had struck him as strange.

What did he know about Mosby? He had been a New Jersey State Trooper before he had joined the FBI. And then he... Richter paused as he suddenly remembered the picture. His pulse quickened. It had been six months ago. He had been in the command center, and Keith O'Rourke had been holding a magazine, something from twenty years earlier. O'Rourke had waved the magazine and laughed.

"Get a load of this!" he said.

Richter and two other agents had circled around the table. O'Rourke tapped the picture and Richter stared down at a much younger Cal Mosby. Wearing his Trooper uniform, he was standing at attention behind then State Senator Tyler Rumson. According to the caption, Rumson had been at a campaign stop in the middle of his bid to become a U.S. Senator. And Mosby had been there too, providing security for the rising star.

Where was Mosby now? Richter wondered.

———

Monahan stared out the window of the FBI-owned Gulfstream G550 and noticed the faint light of early morning. He sat back and shook his head. To say that this would be no easy task was an understatement. Running a criminal investigation with hundreds of competing agencies and departments, so many he had lost count, was going to be a Herculean challenge. Not that he was afraid of stepping on a few toes or bruising a few egos in the process. In his thirty-one years with the Bureau, he had done his share of that. With the limited information they had right now, they had to assume that the crash of Air Force One was the result of criminal or terrorist activity. And, as Broder had made crystal clear, that put the FBI in charge.

He checked his watch; two hours until they were scheduled to land in Portland. He glanced around the cabin noting the seven agents with him, each handpicked to assist him in this assignment. One hundred and sixty miles behind them was another plane, much larger than his Gulfstream, carrying another sixty-five agents. More would be following shortly.

He felt conflicted. On one hand, he was excited. This was, by far, the largest, most important case he and all of the agents with him would likely ever see in their careers. And he was in charge. And yet, that was precisely why he couldn't shake the sinking feeling. With only three years to go until retirement, he had been hoping for a series of easy assignments during the twilight of his career. Now, who knew when he would see his wife or his family again? Or if he would even make it to retirement. He was a realist. The huge expectations, the tremendous responsibility, the stakes for the Bureau, and for the nation, were made very clear in Broder's terse briefing.

"You're in charge of this thing, Monahan. If you screw it up, I'll bury you myself!"

———

As Jack ate his oatmeal, he studied Dave. He definitely looked like he lost a fight, Jack thought. One eye was swollen, not quite shut, an ugly purple bruise below. His chin and cheeks were a patchwork of nasty scratches. His lips were cracked and swollen. And with the bandage wrapped around his head, he looked like an extra for a low budget horror film. Still, even in the flickering light from the candle lantern, he was certain he had seen Dave before. It hadn't occurred to him until they were both standing outside earlier.

It was more than his appearance, Jack realized. Dave seemed down to earth, and he had a sense of humor, but at the same time, he had a presence. He looked like a business executive. When he spoke, he conveyed confidence. Despite that, Dave wasn't arrogant or condescending. He seemed to be humble and wasn't afraid to ask for help.

On the other hand, Matt had the bearing of a soldier. Jack studied him for a moment. Even as he ate, Matt appeared on guard, pensive.

Dave coughed, and Matt turned, a concerned look on his face. Matt was very protective of Dave, Jack mused.

"So, what do you guys do for the Customs Department?" he asked.

Kendall nodded toward Richter. "Matt's an agent. I'm just a bureaucrat."

"You look very familiar."

The president smiled. "You have no idea how many times I hear that. I guess I have one of those faces."

CHAPTER THIRTY-NINE

The snow concealed how devastating the crash was. The most obvious sign was the enormous crater where the forward section of the plane had struck the ground at over four hundred knots. This was where they began their search. Twenty-three hours after the crash, the winds had subsided to forty-five miles per hour and the snow, while still falling, was less than the blizzard conditions the area had experienced over the past thirty-six hours.

The Pave Hawk hovered as a team of ten PJs rappelled down to a spot three hundred yards to the side of the crater. Once they hit the ground, the Pave Hawk lowered several large bundles of equipment and supplies. The weather was expected to worsen, and it was questionable if the helicopter would be able to return at the end of the day. The PJs would likely spend the night on the mountain.

As soon as the first Pave Hawk began to climb away, the second Pave Hawk discharged its crew and their supplies. Once the helicopters withdrew, the commander on the ground, Lieutenant Germaine Jennings ordered the teams to transport the provisions to a more sheltered spot and to set up camp and a mobile command post. Although it was still morning, Jennings estimated they had six hours before nightfall, and he wanted to use as much of that time as possible.

———

Jack crawled back inside the cave and made his way to an open spot along the wall.

"According to my GPS, there's a mine about one and a quarter miles from here."

"Any chance it's still operable?" Richter asked.

"No, I don't think so. Most of the mines around here were shut down a long time ago. This one's called the Old Parker-Baxter Mine. But," he hesitated a moment, "I was thinking about this. There's a chance that it might not be the type of mine you're thinking of. You know, like a tunnel in a mountain with train tracks? This might be nothing more than a big hole in the ground; I think what they call a pit mine. There were a lot of those around here as well."

Derek added, "Jack's right. It could also be a panning operation if it's located near a stream. They used to blast the side of the hill and wash the mud through a sluice. Really, there's no way to tell without seeing it."

Jack shook his head. "This one doesn't look like it's near a stream. Still, we might hike there and find out it's not what we're looking for."

Richter digested that. "Okay, what about ranger stations?"

"The GPS says there's one twelve miles southeast of us. Our

car is thirteen miles west of us. The ranger station doesn't make sense."

Derek's face brightened. "Hey, Jack. What about that old hunting shack we saw a while back?"

"Hunting shack?"

Jack nodded slowly. "I forgot about that." He turned to Richter. "Derek and I saw an old cabin a few years ago. It was locked up, but we might be able to break in."

"I think it was below Tamarack Saddle, just south of Sable Point. That's west of us, on the way back to Elk City. What do you think, Jack? About three miles from here?"

"That sounds right, but I don't think it shows up on any map. It was kind of strange to see it out here since this is all national forest. I don't recall seeing any access roads near it. It might be an old prospector's shack. Even though most of the mines were shut down in the 1920s or 1930s, people continued to search for gold over the years." Jack rubbed his chin. "It might even be a poacher's shack. Regardless, whoever owns it probably has to use an ATV or a snowmobile to get to it."

"Or hike in like we did."

Richter shifted his position. Even with the sleeping bag, the cold penetrated through the layers below, and his butt was sore. He glanced at the president who didn't seem to mind. *Could he make it three miles to the shack?* Richter wondered. *Maybe with the right gear*, he thought as he looked back at the boys.

"Have you guys ever made snowshoes?"

Jack nodded, understanding. "I read about it in a survival book."

Derek feigned surprise.

Ignoring the jab, Jack continued. "Mostly Boy Scout stuff. I've never made them myself, but I don't think it would be too hard."

———

"What do you think, Matt? Will this work?" Derek was in the door of the cave, holding two branches, both slightly longer than his six-foot frame.

"Let's see."

He started by stripping the smaller branches and needles off the main branch. When he was done, he had two pieces about six to seven feet long and a little over an inch thick at the base. Richter bent one of the branches until the two ends joined to form a large teardrop. He smiled. "I think these will work fine. We'll need six more just like this."

"No problem." The boys crawled back outside.

Richter took the large, teardrop-shaped branch and, using nylon rope from the survival kit, tied the two ends together. Laying it on the ground, he placed four cross pieces, spaced two inches apart, over the frame. He bound these to the frame with the rope. Next, he wove several smaller branch segments front to back along the frame. He held it up again. It was about two and a half feet long and a little over one foot wide.

The president watched in amazement. "That's ingenious. Think it will work?"

"I believe so. I'll make another and we'll test it first before we make a pair for each of us."

They shared a smile, then Richter leaned the snowshoe against the wall. He glanced at the mouth of the cave. *Jack and Derek should be a while*, he thought. When he turned back to the president, his smile was gone.

"We have a bigger problem, sir." He hesitated and glanced at the door again. "I think you might be right about Rumson. I think he and Cal Mosby are connected." He relayed his suspicions and the connection going back to Rumson's days as a state senator.

The president let out a breath then frowned. "He was also an FBI agent?"

Richter nodded. "For five or six years. Worked in Chicago and then Washington if I remember correctly."

The president's eyes narrowed. "Chicago? Wasn't Emil Broder in charge of the Chicago office? Before he was named Deputy Director?"

Richter felt a prickle on the back of his neck. And when Broder moved to Washington, he thought, Mosby had come with him. Then, for some reason, fourteen or fifteen years ago, Mosby had moved over to the Secret Service while Broder eventually went on to become Director of the FBI.

"If Rumson cultivated a state trooper all those years ago," Richter added, "who else might he have corrupted in the years since?"

He and the president shared a glance.

Shit!

———

"The Twenty-fifth Amendment to the Constitution addresses the transfer of power upon the president's death, as in the case of President Walters, or upon the resignation of the president, as in the case of President Nixon, or upon the removal of the president, after impeachment for example, or when the president is deemed to be unable to discharge the powers and duties of his office. However, the amendment does not clarify this last point, on what exactly constitutes an inability to discharge the powers and duties of office." Supreme Court Justice John Stanhope pointed toward the screen where examples of past successions were listed.

"For God's sake, the man is dead. Isn't it obvious? The vice president is now the president. All he needs to do is to take the oath of office."

Justice Stanhope turned to the exasperated face of Senator Broussard.

"No. It's not that clear cut, Senator. Under the amendment, for the president to be declared unfit to fulfill his duties, the president himself must declare so in a written declaration to the president pro tempore of the Senate and the Speaker of the House of Representatives. Alternatively, the amendment allows the vice president to declare the president unfit. In this case, the vice president and a majority of the principal officers of the executive departments, that is the President's Cabinet, must submit a written declaration to the same two legislative leaders."

"Okay, assuming that Rumson and the Cabinet were to submit this written declaration. What happens next?" the attorney general asked.

"The vice president would be authorized to serve as acting president."

"Acting president? What exactly does that mean?"

"The amendment only envisioned that the vice president would need to serve in this capacity on a temporary basis. The president may resume the powers and duties of his office at a later date by submitting a written declaration stating that the disability no longer exists."

Justice Stanhope paused for a second. "Gentlemen, ladies," he said, looking around the room. "It is my suggestion that we use the provisions of the Twenty-fifth Amendment to temporarily transfer the duties and powers of the presidency to the vice president immediately."

"But if President Kendall is dead?" Senator Broussard continued.

"We don't know that definitively," the attorney general stated. "From what I have been told, rescue crews are just reaching the crash site. No bodies have been recovered yet." He paused for a moment. "I think that until...pardon me...if... keep in mind that people have survived plane crashes before... so, if and when we find the president's body and he has been declared dead...until that time, David Kendall is still the president. Consequently, what we are talking about today is Vice President Rumson's ability to act in the capacity of the president. Is that correct, Justice Stanhope?"

"I think that is the correct interpretation."

The AG turned to the two people next to him. "Congressman Bolsh? Senator Pankin? Are you two okay with this approach?"

The Speaker of the House and the President Pro Tempore of the Senate responded that they were.

The AG looked up at the monitor, where Tyler Rumson was connected by video conference. Rumson nodded, his face somber.

"I'm on board, Ben."

———

By the time they finished testing the four pairs of snowshoes, it was after three. With less than two hours of daylight left, they decided it was too late in the day to attempt the hike to the cabin.

Richter and Jack spent the rest of the daylight hours fashioning ski poles from pine branches. They filled their water bottles and, as the sun began to set, they sat inside the cave and discussed their plans.

"Matt, we're going to have to make you guys some coats or something to keep you warm during the hike," Derek said.

"I've been thinking about that. We could rig up some makeshift ponchos using the thermal blankets, the sleeping bags, and the rope."

"Yeah, that might work. You'll need hats and gloves too. I have an extra long-sleeved shirt that you can use as a hat. You can wrap it around your head and use the sleeves to tie it on like a bandana."

Jack added, "I have an extra shirt too. And some extra wool socks that you can use as mittens."

———

"Ladies and gentlemen. Fellow Americans. It is with profound sadness and pain that I address you tonight. As you know by now, President Kendall's plane crashed yesterday in a remote, mountainous region of Idaho. As you also know, this area has suffered severe winter storms, and rescue efforts have been hampered. Search and rescue teams have been mobilized, and I'm told that they have only recently been able to reach the crash site. We have no word yet on the president's condition."

Rumson wiped away a tear. "President David Kendall was… is my mentor and my friend. We will spare no expense to find him and to find…and help….the other passengers and crew members who were traveling with him.

"I ask that you pray for him. For his safe return. I ask that you pray for Maria Kendall and for their daughters. I ask that you pray for the many passengers on the plane and for the Secret Service and Air Force personnel who were with the president. Pray for their safe recovery. Pray for their families. Give them the strength they need to survive this ordeal."

Rumson paused for a second, staring at the camera before he continued. "America will endure. We have been through crisis before, and we have always emerged a much stronger nation. This is our history and this is what makes us stand out as the leader of the free world. Right now, I will be in charge of the executive branch of government, of the White House, until we have more information on President Kendall's condition."

Rumson paused again and looked down at his notes before lifting his head and speaking again. "At this point, we do not know why the president's plane crashed. I want to be clear about that. We do not know what caused the crash of Air Force One. It's too soon for speculation." He stopped, seemed to hesitate, and then stared hard at the camera. "But let me assure you this. If this tragedy was due to an act of terrorism I will not rest until the cowards behind this are brought to justice. Make no mistake. The full force and might of the United States will be brought to bear, and we will find you. We will find you and you will pay!"

"God bless David Kendall. God bless America. Good night."

CHAPTER FORTY

Sunday, April 25

They were a strange-looking group. While Richter and the president appeared normal, except, maybe, for their snowshoes, Jack and Derek looked bizarre in their makeshift ponchos, rag hats and sock mittens. They had insisted that Matt and Dave use their gear and had traded their Gore-Tex coats, gloves, and wool hats for the improvised clothing. Richter had protested until he realized that his Sig Sauer would be useless below the sleeping bag and parachute wrapped and tied around his body. His instinct told him that even in the remote mountains, in the deep snow, he needed to be on his guard. He had to be prepared for the unknown, and in this case, the unknown was Cal Mosby.

Mosby would have landed somewhere in these mountains, he reasoned. He may well have had someone waiting for him with a snowmobile. Or, more likely, the freak storm had interfered with his plans, and he had been forced to find shelter and wait it out. He would be looking for the opportunity to make his way to the closest town, probably Elk City, and make his escape. Mosby's accomplices had to be waiting somewhere nearby.

The conversation with the president yesterday left Richter even more worried. Who knew how big the conspiracy was? Could there be people involved in the search and rescue whose real agenda was to make sure the president was dead? Or to ensure that any evidence that this was anything other than an accident was destroyed? The conversation had validated his belief that their best option was to put as much distance between themselves and the crash site as possible.

Ultimately, Richter had accepted Derek's offer. As they continued on their way, he felt the reassuring weight of his gun in the coat's outside pocket. He wanted to be ready, and if that meant wearing Derek's nice, warm coat, well, so be it.

———

Even with the snowshoes and ski poles, walking in the snow was a challenge. Although the improvised snowshoes worked well—preventing them from sinking into the deep snow—it was physically demanding as they had to navigate the ever-changing landscape, all the while facing a constant headwind. It took them five hours to cover two miles. Worried about Dave, Jack had insisted they take frequent breaks.

An hour later, they came to a swiftly flowing stream. They stopped for a moment, staring at the rushing water, the opposite bank some fifteen or twenty feet away. After a quick discussion, Jack and Derek set out in opposite directions, searching for a safer crossing while Richter and the president rested against a tree.

A short while later, Derek returned, then moments later, Jack.

"I can't find anything that way." Derek said, pointing down-stream.

"There's nothing upstream either." Jack added. "At least as far as I went." He rummaged in his pack, pulled out protein bars, and passed them around.

"Wait," Derek said. "Didn't we cross this same stream… what, four days ago? Isn't this Cobb's Creek?

"I think you're right." Jack responded. He pulled out the GPS and waited a moment as it searched for satellite signals. "We crossed farther north, about one point four miles upstream from here." He punched several buttons. "Right now, we're about one mile from the cabin. If we go back to where we crossed before, it would be about three point two miles total." He shook his head. "I don't think we'll make it before dark."

"Okay," Derek responded, "why don't we go as far as we can today while there's still light? We might find somewhere to cross along the way. If not, we'll go all the way back to where we crossed before. If it starts to get dark before we reach the cabin, we'll build another snow cave and hunker down for the night."

"I think that might be our only choice. What do you guys think? Dave, do you think you can make it?"

"Let's give it a shot."

———

"Idaho State Police. This is Sergeant Williams."

"Sergeant? My name is Rhonda Walsh. My son is missing… he hasn't come home yet."

"Where are you calling from, ma'am?"

"I live in Lewiston."

"Ma'am, are you aware that many of the highways and secondary roads have been closed, especially in your area? There are hundreds of people stranded, and we are working as quickly as we can to get to them all. There are shelters being set up all around the state."

"I don't think he's stuck on the side of the road."

"Why do you say that, ma'am?"

"Because, they were going hiking. He was with his friend Derek. They were supposed to be home Friday."

"Where were they hiking, ma'am?"

"In the Nez Perce National Forest. They left here Wednesday, and I think they were starting their hike in Elk City."

"Nez Perce?" The sergeant felt a chill.

"I know. I know. I've been watching the news. I…I…think they might have been there…where the plane crashed."

The Sergeant heard crying on the phone.

"Ma'am, if they were, we have hundreds of people out searching in that area right now."

"Have you found anyone alive yet?"

"I don't have anything specific on that. Why don't you give me your name and information on your son? I'll make sure that it gets to the right people."

———

They came upon a large tree that had fallen over the stream. Although the deep snow covered the banks, the large irregular shapes on either side indicated that this was a narrow channel cut between large boulders. On both sides of the stream, the banks sloped steeply down to the water. Derek stopped and considered the tree for a moment.

"I think this might work."

He took off his pack and removed his snowshoes. Sitting at the top of the bank, he sank into the deep snow and carefully slid about five feet down to the tree trunk, displacing a large volume of snow along the way. As he stood up on the trunk, more snow fell into the rushing water four or five feet below him. He studied the tree. The trunk was wider than his shoulders, but the tree sloped up to the opposite bank where the upper portion had landed. To cross, he would have to walk uphill almost twenty feet before reaching the other side.

"I don't know, Derek. That water's moving really fast. If you slip and fall in..." Jack didn't finish the thought.

Derek studied the stream. Jack was right. If he fell in, his wet clothes would quickly rob his body of heat, and hypothermia was a certainty. That is, if he made it out before he drowned or was bashed unconscious on the rocks. He patted the sleeping bag and parachute wrapped around his body. A wet sleeping bag would act like an anchor. Going across with the packs would be tricky. Still, he reasoned as he considered the tree, it didn't look that difficult.

"Toss me one of the ski poles."

Using the stick for balance, Derek was able to walk across without too much difficulty.

"I think we can do it."

"I think it's too risky." Jack stated. "I don't think everyone can make it as easily as you."

———

Richter listened to the exchange for a moment as he studied the log. Then, reaching into his pack, he pulled out the nylon rope. He tied one end of the rope securely to the base of a tree.

"Hey, Derek. I'm going to toss this to you."

Richter took off his snowshoes and slid down to the base of the tree-bridge, using the rope to control his descent. Bracing himself, he tossed the rope across to Derek, who tied it to another tree, about shoulder height, pulling it taut.

———

The president tentatively stepped out onto the tree. With the boys calling encouragement, he shuffled forward. The log was wide and, with the rope to hold onto, it was much easier than he expected. Soon, he was halfway across. He took another step and then it happened. A section of the trunk was coated in ice, courtesy of the splashing water below and the sub-freezing temperatures. His right foot slipped and he fell to the side. Suddenly he was plunging toward the stream—certain he was going in—when he was abruptly jerked to a halt. He bounced up and down like a yo-yo before Richter grabbed his harness.

"I've got you…Dave." Struggling, Richter pulled the president up until he got his feet back on the log. Kendall was breathing heavily.

"That looked like fun," Derek called. "Can I try it next?"

Kendall let out a breath. He was too old for bungee jumping, he thought, but thank God for the harness. After watching Derek and Jack slip and slide their way across several times as they carried the gear over, Richter had fashioned a safety line using the parachute harness. He had looped the suspension lines over the rope support and secured the ends to either side of the harness.

Kendall took a deep breath, stepped over the icy section and began to inch forward. Richter, in a second harness and with a steady hand on his boss's shoulder, followed.

———

It took them another two hours to reach the strand of pines. They stopped and rested for a moment after the strenuous climb. After some water and more protein bars, they set out again and twenty minutes later emerged from the trees. A shack, constructed from rough-hewn planks, stood in the middle of a clearing, fifty yards away. A single window faced them, but it appeared to be shuttered. A pile of cut wood stood to the right of the cabin, in an area that had been cleared.

"Hey, we finally made it!"

Suddenly, Richter grabbed the president and turned back to the trees.

"Back in the woods!" he hissed. "Right now!"

Confused, Jack and Derek trailed to a spot behind a large spruce.

"What's wrong?" Jack whispered.

Richter ignored him as he stared through the tree branches at the woodpile, then up at the roof. There was a black metal chimneystack rising above the cabin. Even in the wind, the smoke was visible.

Richter tapped Derek's shoulder then pointed at the president and then the forest. Without a word, Derek took Dave's arm and led him and Jack deeper into the trees. Richter watched until they disappeared. He studied the cabin for a moment then turned and followed. He caught up several minutes later, and they found shelter below a large spruce.

Richter nodded at Jack and Derek.

"Stay here with Dave," he ordered.

"What's going on?" Jack asked.

Richter ignored Jack again as he peered through the snow-covered branches. Then he took his gloves off, handing them to Derek.

"If anything happens, I want you to take Dave back the way we came. Get as far away from here as you can. Understood?"

Confused, Derek nodded nonetheless.

———

Richter made his way back to the edge of the forest. He stopped to observe the cabin again. Other than the smoke drifting up from the chimney, the cabin was still. Holding his gun with both hands, he moved forward. His instinct was to run in a half-crouch, zigzagging from tree to tree for cover. Instead, he plodded along, awkward in the snowshoes, exposed, on top of the deep snow. Every three or four steps, he paused to scan and listen.

He was twenty feet from the shack when, to his right, a figure suddenly appeared from around the corner, gun in hand. All he saw was a torso; the figure apparently was following a path through the snow. Richter, struggling to maintain his balance in the snowshoes, twisted his upper body like an acrobat as he tried to follow the figure through his gun sights.

The figure froze in midstride then, with lightning speed, spun around toward him.

The boom of several gunshots echoed through the woods.

CHAPTER FORTY-ONE

Jack flinched. "Holy shit!"

Derek stood, grabbed Dave's arm, and pulled him up. "Come on! Let's go!"

Jack hesitated. "Shouldn't we help him?"

"No!" The president hissed over his shoulder. "There's nothing we can do. Come on!"

The three trudged deeper into the trees and, ten minutes later, they reached the other side. Derek stopped and peered back through the foliage.

"I don't think anyone's following us." He turned. "What do we do now?"

"We keep going."

"Wait!" Jack pleaded. "What if he's hurt?"

President Kendall grabbed Jack by the shoulders. "No. We're going to do exactly what Agent Richter told us to do."

Jack stared at Dave for a moment before the realization hit him.

"Oh my God!"

———

Richter pushed the snow off his face and sat up; he swung his gun back and forth, certain his attacker was coming. After several seconds of silence, he peered over the top of the snow and saw a head disappear to his right. The head reappeared a second later, closer to the woodpile. Richter swung his gun and fired. Seizing the moment, he sat back and removed his snowshoes. He rose and peeked above the snow again and, seeing nothing, dropped back down. Using the snowshoe, he began to dig a trench toward the cabin.

"Give it up, Richter! You're fucked!"

Ignoring Mosby's taunt, Richter continued digging. After several minutes, he crawled back to the spot where he first dove into the snow and peeked over the edge again. He ducked back down as the snow exploded behind him and another shot rang out. Mosby was behind the woodpile.

"You saved yourself, didn't you?"

He crawled back down the trench and began digging again.

"You left him on the plane to die, didn't you?"

A minute later, he reached the cabin and then began to tunnel along the side, moving out of Mosby's line of sight.

"You're oh for two, Richter! That's a hell of a record!"

Richter continued digging until he reached the corner of the cabin. Peering over the trench, he couldn't see the woodpile any longer.

"You froze! You choked!"

He stood and continued digging and plowing his way through the snow around the side of the cabin.

"I'm going to kill you, Richter!"

When he reached the next corner, he peered around the side. There was a small covering, hardly a porch, over the front door. A trench ran from the door then curved to the right where it forked, one path disappearing around the next corner. That must lead to the woodpile, Richter guessed. The left-hand fork continued straight into the trees to what appeared to be an outhouse.

"You couldn't save the president, and you can't save yourself!"

Richter dug his way to the trench by the front door. He dropped to his knees again, and pulling his stinging hands up into the sleeves of the coat, he began crawling to the outhouse. Mosby continued to taunt him. When he reached the outhouse, he stopped and peeked over the snow. Mosby was kneeling behind the woodpile thirty feet away, his back to Richter.

"You're a coward, Richter!"

Richter stood and pointed his gun at Mosby.

"I'm coming to get you!" Mosby taunted

Mosby poked his head above the woodpile, then stood. His gun was pointed at the spot where Richter had been when they exchanged gunfire. He turned and began to follow the trench back toward the front of the cabin.

"Stop right there, Mosby!"

Mosby spun, and several more shots rang out.

———

Derek peered out through the branches of the tree.

"Someone's coming," he whispered as he ducked down.

There was no way they could hide; their tracks gave them away. He looked back at Dave. They couldn't run either. The president was lying in the snow, his face contorted in pain, while Jack massaged his knee.

Derek looked up again and watched as the shadow moved through the woods. After a moment, he recognized the coat.

"It's Matt!"

They watched Richter approach, his face a mask of stone.

"Are you okay?"

Ignoring the question, Richter nodded toward the president. "What happened?"

Jack gently touched Kendall's leg. "He twisted his knee."

Richter nodded. "Let's get you to the shack. We should be okay there for a little while."

In the fading light, Richter and Derek helped the president to his feet.

They began to make their way to the strand of trees once again. Jack and Derek were too stunned to talk, but the president asked the question on everyone's mind.

"What happened?"

"There was only one, sir." Richter paused. "Mosby."

———

The cabin appeared to date back to the mining days; nothing more than a single room with an old woodstove in the center. Three rough, handmade chairs were arranged around a similarly constructed table against the wall. Wooden pegs on one wall held a coil of weathered rope, a two-man saw—its blade rusted brown—and an old miner's lantern.

There were two folded cots stacked against another wall, below a propane camping lantern hanging from a wooden peg. Two fishing poles were standing in the corner, next to a tackle box. A nearby shelf held several boxes of twelve gauge shotgun shells and a box of .22 caliber ammunition.

Below the single shuttered window was a counter, constructed from the same rough-hewn wood as the furniture. A large sink, the enamel chipped and scratched, sat in the middle. The drain line ran into a five-gallon plastic bucket on the floor. A camping stove was set up next to the sink. On a shelf below, there were half a dozen small propane canisters, various cast iron pans and pots, and a one-gallon jug of water. Old newspapers, hung as insulation, covered the walls. Most dated to the early 1900's, and the articles and ads provided a glimpse into mining life at the turn of the century.

A third cot was set up against another wall, and an Air Force sleeping bag lay neatly on top. The table was covered with the food packs and assorted gear from a survival-kit. It was obvious that Mosby had been staying here.

Richter took off his snowshoes, stood, and signaled Derek.

"I need your help outside."

Derek hurried to remove his snowshoes and then stood, uncertain. Jack stood as well but, after glancing at Richter, sat back down.

"He's dead, Jack. There's nothing you can do for him."

Jack sighed. When Richter opened the door, a cold wind blew in and both Jack and the president shivered. After the door closed, Jack hugged himself for a moment to warm up.

The president pulled off his last shoe and tried to stand, but Jack stopped him.

"Here, let me." Jack stacked the shoes against the wall. "Does your knee still hurt?"

Kendall shook his head. "It's nothing, Jack."

"Let me take a look."

Kendall waved him away then pointed to the chair. "Have a seat and warm up."

Shaking his head, Jack sat. He glanced at the president for a moment and shook his head again.

"I can't believe I'm sitting in an old mining cabin with the President of the United States."

"Jack, believe me when I say that I never expected to be sitting here either. But we are here and we need to figure out how we are going to make it out of this alive."

"So, this wasn't just an accident. Someone tried to kill you....?" Jack hesitated. "What are we supposed to call you now? Dave seems too weird."

"Dave is fine." The president patted him on the shoulder. "And yes. Someone tried to kill me."

"God. I don't know what to say. How could this happen? Do you know who's behind this?"

"I have my suspicions, but I think for now it's best if I kept those to myself."

"But that guy outside? That guy Matt shot? He was a part of it?"

"Yes. We believe he was."

"Won't they be looking for you? You know, the Secret Service, the police, the Army?"

"I'm sure they are. But right now, I think we're safer here."

———

Richter stared down at the body. Mosby's lifeless eyes stared back. There were two neat holes in the center of his forehead. He wanted to scream. *I didn't freeze that time, did I, asshole!* The tension of the last few days was like acid in his stomach. *What the hell possessed you to do it? You betrayed your country! You killed them all! You killed Stephanie!* He felt the rage inside growing. *I'm going to find out who else is behind this. I'll find them and, if it's the last thing I ever do, I'm going to kill them myself.* He took several deep breaths and watched the flakes fall for a moment before looking back down. *You're one cold bastard.* He suddenly laughed as he remembered something Brad Lansing had said: *That man has ice in his veins.* Well, if he didn't before, he would soon!

"Jesus!"

He turned at Derek's voice. Ignoring him, he knelt and pried the gun from Mosby's hand and stuffed it in his pocket. As he began to undress the body, he called over his shoulder.

"Bring that wood to the cabin and then come back and help me."

———

Richter dumped the clothes on the table and began to examine them.

"So what did you do with him?" the president asked.

"I stripped the body and buried him in the snow."

The president nodded.

Richter held up Mosby's flight suit and parka. "Sir. I think you and he are the same height."

There was a stain on the hood, and the president realized that it was Mosby's blood. He was about to say something but hesitated when he saw Richter. He saw a warrior looking back at him, a soldier on a mission. Richter had done what he had been trained to do, which was to keep him alive. He was doing a damned fine job of it especially under the circumstances, Kendall thought. Richter had no choice in shooting Mosby, but it was a brutal reality that he found tough to fathom. Kill or be killed. It was one thing to read about it or discuss it in an academic sense, but it was entirely different to be thrust into the middle of it. It was survival of the fittest. He was glad that he didn't have to face these kinds of decisions himself. Still, to survive, he had to start thinking like Richter, to always be one step ahead, anticipating the next threat.

As if reading his thoughts, Richter left the clothes on the table and sat down. "Sir, I don't think we can stay here for very long."

He waited for Richter to continue.

"Mosby had to have someone waiting for him, an accomplice to help him escape."

He frowned. "You think they may be near here?"

Richter nodded. "This is a good shelter, for now, but we're sitting ducks here."

The president considered this.

"When the boys come back, we need to discuss our next steps," Richter continued

"Where are they?"

"They're filling the water bottles."

He frowned. "Jack knows who I am. I'm sure Derek does too by now."

Richter held his gaze for a moment. "It was bound to happen eventually, but right now, I'm not sure if that's a good thing."

———

"You don't really work for the Immigration Department, do you?" Derek asked. "You're a Secret Service agent, right?"

Richter nodded. "Yeah, I'm a Secret Service agent."

"Why didn't you tell us earlier?"

Richter glared at him; Derek flinched as if stung.

"Hey, I'm just asking. I didn't mean anything by it."

Richter took a breath. "Look, my job is to protect the president at all costs. I didn't know who you were at first. There are more people involved in this than that guy outside." He paused. "I had to be sure."

Derek considered this for a moment. "I guess that makes sense. So what do we do now?"

That was the question, Richter thought. According to Jack, the car was still a good distance away, seven or eight miles at least. The trek today, only half that distance, had taken more than eight hours. To reach the car would take them two days at least and then what? The car was still five miles from Elk City, buried below four or five feet of snow. The forest service roads would be impassable. They had no choice but to head toward Elk City. *But what then?* he wondered.

CHAPTER FORTY-TWO

Monday, April 26

President Kendall woke to the sound of creaks and groans and the whistle of the wind. His knee throbbed in rhythm with his heartbeat. He had ignored the pain yesterday, but the strain of the hike had taken its toll. As he listened to the sounds of the cabin, the pain intensified, and he realized that he wouldn't be able to fall back asleep.

The fire had died out during the night, and the cabin was cold. He pulled his sleeping bag up around his chin and rolled over on the cot. The movement sent a sharp pain up his leg and he gasped.

"Are you all right, sir?" Richter whispered.

"Yeah."

Richter turned on a flashlight and opened the survival pack. "There should be some painkillers."

Jack and Derek woke up. While Derek restarted the fire, Jack lit the propane lantern. It took several minutes for the cabin to warm up.

"I'm sorry." The president's grin was sheepish. "I didn't mean to wake everybody up."

"That's okay," Jack answered. "Let me take a look."

Jack slid the president's pant legs up and studied both knees. The right knee was noticeably swollen.

"You did this yesterday?"

The president shook his head. "No. It's an old injury. It's been hurting for the last week, but I must have overstressed it yesterday."

Jack proceeded to examine the knee.

"How did you hurt it originally?"

"Skiing…" He winced as Jack probed below the kneecap. "Maybe fifteen years ago."

"Well, I don't think you broke any bones, and the ligaments seem fine. My guess is it's either a strain, which means you partially tore a muscle or tendon, or you injured the cartilage or meniscus by twisting your knee. The delayed swelling would tend to indicate that you have inflammation in the joint and might be more indicative of a meniscus or cartilage injury." Jack pulled the president's pant leg back down. "Either way, I think you need to rest it for a while. We'll need to get it elevated and get some ice on it."

———

"Have you found the president yet?"

Since Monahan arrived in Portland two days before, every phone call with Broder began the same.

He sighed. "No sir. Not yet."

"That has to be a priority," Broder continued, his voice gruff. "I know you're leading the criminal investigation, but we have to find the president. We can't leave the country hanging like this."

"I understand, Emil. As I told you yesterday, we weren't able to land a CSAR team until two days ago. These guys are dealing with some very challenging conditions."

"That's what they're trained to do. Do you have enough resources?"

"I think so, but you have to give them some time. There's a lot of ground to cover."

"How many bodies have you recovered so far?"

Monahan shook his head. Was Broder even listening? "Nineteen as of this morning. You have to remember that it didn't stop snowing until early yesterday morning. The bodies we found so far were frozen and below several feet of snow. We need to be cautious so we don't disturb evidence. It's a delicate balance."

"Are you sure no one survived the crash?"

"I don't see how it's possible. The teams are using some pretty sophisticated technologies to search for survivors. Did you receive the pictures I sent you last night?"

"Yeah."

"You saw what the crash did to the bodies." Monahan took a breath. "Emil, the images and the data are one thing, but I toured the crash site. Not only did I fly over with the CSAR team, but I was on the ground. It's absolutely devastating. I don't know how anyone could have survived this crash. And on the one-in-a-million chance that they did, there's no way they would have survived the weather. I think we need to consider shifting our focus from search and rescue to recovery only. "

"Dead or not, you need to find him, Monahan. Now. Not tomorrow, not next week. Now."

"Okay. Okay. I hear you."

"Have you identified any of the bodies?

"Only tentatively." Monahan paused. "But I'm absolutely certain that the president isn't among them."

———

They adopted a routine. Jack and Derek filled their time gathering wood, keeping the fire lit, and refilling the water bottles. Derek prepared the meals, careful to ration their remaining supplies. Jack periodically checked the president's knee while Richter studied the topographical maps. Every two or three hours, Richter strapped on the snowshoes and walked a large circular trek around the cabin. The president had little to do except sit in front of the fire with his knee elevated. He kept the conversation going.

Jack and Derek peppered the president with questions about his family, life in the White House, how Washington really worked, and about the many issues in recent news. The president indulged the boys, but after a while, turned the focus of the conversation back onto them.

Richter opened the shutter and looked out the window. Although he had just returned from a patrol, he felt edgy, defenseless in the cabin. He glanced over at the president, sitting in front of the fire, his injured leg resting on another chair. Derek put two more logs in the stove, adjusted the damper, then sat next to Kendall.

"So anyway, after high school, I had a couple of different jobs, but now I'm working in a warehouse."

Richter, too anxious to sit, turned back to the window and only half listened to the conversation. Jack had found a book on the mining era and was reading.

"Did you ever consider college?"

Derek hesitated. "I wanted to, but I was never able to make it work."

President Kendall nodded. "The cost?"

Derek hesitated. "That was part of it." He seemed to struggle with the next words. "I did some stuff back in high school. I got into trouble."

Richter turned, a frown on his face.

"Stupid stuff."

Derek shifted in his seat. He looked at the floor for a moment, then at Richter before turning back to the president.

"I didn't hurt anyone. It was stupid, teenage stuff." He took a deep breath. "Anyway, I had to go to court, then my dad got sick, and my mom wasn't able to take care of him herself."

The president nodded with empathy. "I'm sorry to hear that, Derek. What happened?"

"My dad died from cancer two years later. That was almost three years ago. I was paying restitution—I still am—but when my dad got sick, we found that his insurance didn't cover all of the costs for his treatments. I got the job in the warehouse because it was closer to home, and it's been just me and my mom ever since."

Richter was about to say something, when he caught the president's glare.

Kendall put his hand on Derek's shoulder. "I'm sorry about your father. Do you think you'll ever go to college?"

"I would like to. There's a community college in town. But…" Derek looked at the floor.

"What did you do, Derek?" Kendall asked softly.

Another deep sigh. "A friend and I stole a bus from the senior center. We took it for a joy ride across the state line. On our way home, we had an accident, slid off the road and hit a tree. We were okay, but the bus was a mess. We were able to drive it back to Idaho, but we were afraid of getting into trouble." Derck sighed yet again before he continued. "So after we got back to Lewiston, we left it behind an abandoned building, hoping the police wouldn't be able to connect us to it. But they did."

Richter looked at Jack, who held his palms out and shook his head.

"I'm not proud of what I did. Anyway, because I was a juvenile, and it was my first offense, I didn't have to go to prison. I was put on probation, had to pay restitution, and had to perform community service."

President Kendall squeezed Derek's shoulder.

"That took all my college savings, then when my dad got sick…" Derek's voice trailed off.

Richter stared at Derek and began to wonder if his judgment was failing.

———

Maria slipped on her jacket and looked at herself in the mirror. She straightened her blouse then fussed with her hair. Nervous energy she knew; something to keep busy. She looked in the mirror again, this time studying her face. Despite the makeup, she was pale; nothing could mask the pain in her eyes. She was wearing a gray knee-length skirt, conservatively cut. She refused to wear black.

She walked to the girls' rooms to see if they were ready. The prayer vigil was scheduled for 8:00 p.m. and they had to leave soon.

Twenty-five minutes later, there was a knock on the door. She slipped on her overcoat and turned to the girls. "I know you don't want to do this. But please do it for me. Do it for Daddy." Angela and Michelle both nodded, tears running down their cheeks. Maria opened the door.

"Are you ready, ma'am?" Maria took a deep breath, shuddered, then nodded at Agent Tiller.

———

President Kendall's thoughts drifted again, as they so often did, to Maria, Angela, and Michelle. He was overcome with grief and, without warning, began weeping. They had to be suffering terribly right now, and the only thing he wanted to do was to hold them, to comfort them.

Be strong, Maria. Be strong, girls. I will come home. I promise you.

He didn't notice when Richter ushered Jack and Derek outside, leaving him in privacy to grieve alone.

———

"We pray tonight for all of your servants who were on Air Force One. We pray for their families, that they may be strong and find solace in your blessing. It is often difficult to understand such tragic events……"

Maria tuned out the voice. Sitting on a large stage in front of the Lincoln Memorial, she looked out over the Mall, noticing the crowd for the first time. A sea of faces bathed in a soft glow. *That's odd*, she thought, then realized that the glow was coming from the tens of thousands of candles held by the crowd.

She held Angela's hand and draped an arm around Michelle. She felt Michelle's head on her shoulder and hugged her tightly as she squeezed Angela's hand. She felt herself warm in the glow from the candles, somehow feeling a small sense of comfort in the soft light. The candles seemed to grow brighter, and Maria felt a stirring in her chest. Suddenly, she sensed that Dave was somehow reaching out to her. She didn't know how she knew, or how it was even possible, but she knew nonetheless. Her mind spun as she tried to understand the feeling. She so desperately wanted to believe, to hope. But there were facts and logic and so many photos of the devastation in the mountains of Idaho that said such hope was foolish. Yet the feeling remained. She couldn't explain it to herself, but a sense of calm seemed to flow through her body.

Oh, David. Come home.

CHAPTER FORTY-THREE

Tuesday, April 27

The dogs started barking when Tim Shelton reached the summit. He let the dogs lead him to a strand of fir trees. They had been out for the last three hours and he was tired. The sky was still overcast, the temperature not quite twenty degrees, and trekking through the snow had proven difficult for both Shelton and the dogs. The dogs were circling a single fir tree, disturbed by something. The trunk was almost three feet in diameter, the upper branches towering some two hundred feet above. It was probably over two hundred years old, he guessed. He circled the tree, searching for what had excited the dogs. In the fading light, he spotted something in the branches, way above his head.

"Rescue Seven to base."

"This is Base. Read you loud and clear, Seven."

"Base, I found something."

———

Seven miles to the west, Richter watched through the window

as Jack and Derek brushed snow off a fallen tree. Despite the stack of wood outside, the boys were feeling restless and had grabbed the old two man saw off the wall and headed outside. They struggled for several minutes before they found a rhythm. He watched for a moment more before turning back to the president.

"Elk City might be a problem."

The president raised his eyebrows in question.

"According to Jack, it's the closest town to the crash site. It must be overrun with search and rescue personnel: state police, NTSB," he paused, frowning. "And FBI." They shared a glance before Richter continued. "There's also bound to be Air Force and Secret Service agents all over the place. As long as you haven't been found...your body I mean...the people behind this will be getting nervous. There has to be someone waiting nearby for Mosby and any accomplices."

The president nodded. "What are you thinking?"

"We can't go to anyone in the Service, not even the director," he concluded with a frown.

The president looked skeptical. "You think he may be involved?"

"Kroger? No. I don't think so." He paused and considered this some more. "Heck, I don't know, sir. But even if he isn't, he'll dispatch a team of agents to pick us up. Maybe I'm being paranoid, but anyone on that team could be part of this." His eyes narrowed. "The same goes for the FBI. Whoever we contact could easily send a message to whoever is here, whoever is waiting for Mosby, to finish the job before they arrive. We can't take that risk, sir."

The president nodded.

"If we can find a group of state cops or possibly a National Guard platoon in town, we might be safe. They can protect us until we figure out what to do next." He paused. "Or, somehow we sneak out of town and head to the closest large city—maybe Boise—and go to the state police there. That would be my choice, sir; to get as far away from this area as possible before we turn ourselves in."

The president sat quietly as he considered this. "What if we went to a reporter?" he said after a moment. "Leaked a story?"

Richter stood and walked over to the window. Jack was stacking wood onto Derek's outstretched arms. He glanced back at the president. "Perhaps. But we would still need protection."

They were silent for a moment, both lost in thought.

"Do you know Pat Monahan?" the president finally asked.

Richter frowned. "I've met him."

"He's a good man."

"He's with the FBI." Richter said; the point obvious. He hesitated. He had met Monahan on a handful of occasions. He had a reputation for being a straight shooter. Based on rumors, Monahan wasn't enamored of the FBI Director. Then again, he sighed, most people in the FBI weren't. Was that a good sign, he wondered, or a bad sign?

"I've met with him several times," the president said then hesitated. "I've been thinking about replacing Broder."

Richter nodded. So Monahan was on the president's short list of candidates.

"Have you done a background check yet?" he asked. The FBI, he knew, assisted the White House Counsel's office in researching a potential appointee's criminal past. The fox in the hen house, he thought.

The president nodded. "Linda Huff used the Justice Department." He waved his hand. "They have some special unit that does investigations." He paused, his gaze firm. "The man's clean. We can trust him."

Richter frowned and glanced out the window again. Jack and Derek, loaded down with wood, were making their way back to the cabin. If they could make it out of Elk City without being discovered, he thought, they could head down to Boise. That is, assuming they could somehow find a car. They could go to the state police in Boise or possibly try to contact Monahan. But could they trust him to help them without tipping off the people behind this? Accidently or otherwise?

"Assuming I agree to this, sir—and I'm not saying I do—how do we contact him? You don't have a direct number, do you?"

Kendall shook his head. "No. I don't."

They discussed this for a while, considering possible conduits.

"What about Arlene?"

The president frowned. "I don't know her number. It's on my Blackberry, but that was on the plane. She's unlisted. I think she told me that you guys suggested that for security purposes."

He sighed. "We probably did. We'll have to find someone else, preferably someone who isn't connected to the government;

someone whose trust is unquestionable."

"There might be someone…" President Kendall said after a moment.

———

Tim Shelton watched as the Pave Hawk appeared over the ridge. Minutes later, it began to circle the tree. He turned his head to avoid the mini snowstorm caused by the downdraft from the rotors.

It took the Air Force Search and Rescue team two hours in the fading light to recover what was caught in the tree. They lowered the forest penetrator down by hoist cable. The device, so named for its ability to penetrate thick trees to reach a survivor, had three folding seats and straps to secure the victims. The PJ was sitting in one of the seats as it was lowered. Thankfully, the wind for the moment was light, and the helicopter was able to maintain a hover above the tree.

Shelton watched the recovery from forty yards away as he listened to the conversation between the rescue crewmembers on his radio.

"Sarge, looks like we have a body. Cold and stiff. Appears to be male." The radio crackled. "Appears to have parachuted into the tree."

"Copy, Ed. The Feds want photos before you recover. Think you can accommodate?"

"Roger, Sarge." The PJ took pictures from different angles. It took him several minutes to maneuver through the branches and parachute lines to get shots from all sides. "Pics done. Securing body now."

The men on the ground watched as the PJ struggled to strap the frozen body into the seat. He then cut the chute lines. After he strapped himself in, Shelton heard the radio again.

"Ready, Sarge. Bring us up."

As the penetrator began to rise from the tree, the FBI agent grabbed Shelton's arm. "Tell him he needs to recover that chute and whatever else he finds in the tree as well."

———

Richter spotted Jack by the wood pile when he returned from another patrol. He walked over and grabbed an armful of wood.

"How much longer before he's ready?"

"One or two more days, I think. His knee's still swollen, although it's not as bad as yesterday. But it's still quite tender, especially when I probe certain areas. He's in more pain than he says."

Richter frowned. "We can't stay here much longer. It's only a matter of time before we're discovered."

Jack shook his head. "I don't think he'll make it too far, Matt. You saw how he's hobbling. I think that hike really strained it."

Richter sighed. "Okay. We'll give it another day, two at the most. If he's not able to walk by then, we'll need to figure some other way to get him out of here. We may have to improvise and make a stretcher or something."

Jack nodded as they carried the wood back to the cabin.

———

Pat Monahan hurried into the morgue, General Trescott on his heels.

"What do you have?" He asked.

Before Major Conklin could respond, FBI Special Agent Meg Connolly spoke up.

"We think this is Lieutenant Francis McKay. He was a steward on Air Force One." Connolly ignored Major Conklin's glare. "It would appear that he parachuted from the plane before the crash. We believe that he may have been knocked unconscious when he hit the tree and died from exposure."

Monahan cringed as he considered the implications.

CHAPTER FORTY-FOUR

Wednesday, April 28

The sun was beginning to break through the clouds when Lieutenant Jennings arrived at the scene. It was eight in the morning and the early appearance of the sun, Jennings thought, was a promising sign.

"What do you have, Sergeant?"

The airman pointed into the hole in the snow. "Looks like one of the recorders, sir."

"Okay, excellent work. Have you called it in to the NTSB team yet?"

"No, sir. I waited for you."

"Sit tight, Sergeant."

"Yes, sir."

Stan Burton arrived twenty minutes later with two members of the NTSB team. "Which one is it?"

"It looks like the cockpit voice recorder, sir."

The sergeant stepped out of the way as Burton and his team gathered around the hole. A bright orange metal box poked out from below a twisted and scorched piece of airplane skin. There were scorch marks on the recorder as well. He hoped it had survived the fire.

"Okay," he said, addressing his team. "Let's record the location, get some pictures and then get it out of here." He turned. "Lieutenant, we're going to need a helo."

"Already ordered one, sir. They're about two minutes out."

———

"We'll be back." Derek said as he put on his coat.

Richter nodded as the two boys headed outside. He picked up his gun, checked the safety, then ejected the magazine. He removed the slide, the guide rod and the barrel, laying each piece on the table, then picked up the dishtowel. Without the proper cleaning supplies, he would have to improvise as best he could. He kept Mosby's gun loaded and within reach by his side.

President Kendall was sitting in front of the stove.

"You seem okay with Derek."

Richter considered the statement; not so much a question as an observation.

"Yes, sir. He could have lied or glossed over his past. It took some guts to share that with us." He paused, thinking. "He's been nothing but reliable and trustworthy since we've met him."

"I see you're even letting them do some of your security patrols."

Richter grinned. "Yeah. They need something to do, and they're pretty good in the woods. Derek hunts, and you can see that he knows how to be quiet. Anyways, I've showed them what to look for."

"What about Jack?"

"He's cautious by nature. Now that he knows we're hiding, he's extra cautious. And he learns fast." He gave the president a weak smile. "Those two have some interesting stories about growing up in Idaho."

"Beyond Derek's escapade with the bus?" the president asked.

Richter smiled, then his face became serious. "We need to talk to them, sir."

"I know," Kendall responded. "Let me handle that, okay?"

Richter nodded, turning back to his task. He peered through the barrel for a second and then wiped off the built-up carbon with the dishtowel.

"What about you?" Kendall asked. "Where did you grow up?"

He placed the barrel on the table and picked up the gunstock. "A small town outside of Columbus, Ohio, sir."

"Do you still have family there?"

Richter turned, gunstock in hand.

"Hey, don't stop what you're doing."

He nodded and studied the stock for a moment, inspecting it for damage.

"Yeah. My parents and my sister."

"Do you get to see them often?"

"I visited during the holidays."

The president smiled. "You're not married, are you?"

"No, sir."

"Anyone special in your life?"

Richter flinched and his face darkened. "No."

He sat still for a moment then began to reassemble the weapon. He placed the slide back on the gun, snapping the retainer pin in place, the sounds sharp in the silence.

"I'm sorry, Matthew, I didn't mean to pry."

"That's okay, sir. It's just that....." He told himself to let it go, that if he said anymore the damn might burst, but the sudden need to share was overpowering. "I was kind of seeing someone...when all of this happened." He slid the magazine back into the gun. *Stupid!* He had too much to deal with right now without the added burden of confronting his loss. The tears and grief would have to come later.

"I'm confident that between you, Derek, and Jack, we will make it out of here. You'll be back in DC in no time, and you can pick up where you left off."

"I don't think so, sir." His voice was barely a whisper.

The president nodded and seemed about to say something else, but thankfully didn't. Richter took a deep breath, his sigh filling the room.

———

"Chemical analysis on Lieutenant McKay's body indicates traces of Semtex. The highest concentrations were found on his fingers. On both hands."

"Okay. Any theories?" Monahan looked around the room at the assembled team. No one wanted to voice what appeared to be an obvious, but troubling hypothesis, especially with Major

Conklin glaring at the end of the table.

Meg Connolly leaned forward. "Well, the fact that McKay parachuted from the plane indicates that he had advance knowledge of the explosion and the crash. The Semtex could indicate that there was an explosive device on the plane. We need to do some research to see if there is any other possible explanation for the traces we found on McKay, but I think one theory that we need to follow is that McKay may be somehow involved in the intentional sabotage of Air Force One."

Major Conklin turned red.

Monahan nodded. "I would agree. Okay. This is our working theory right now. Excellent work, folks. Let's pursue this, but…" Monahan paused and looked at the assembled team of agents and Air Force officers. "Don't automatically rule out other possibilities. We need to be completely thorough here. Okay?"

He looked around the table as heads nodded.

————

"They still haven't found the body."

Rumson's face clouded. "I know. The FBI has been briefing me several times a day. I'm getting worried. Mosby hasn't turned up yet either." His eyes narrowed. "You were supposed to deal with him."

"He hasn't turned up because of the snow. My men are still on site. When he shows up, we'll take care of it."

Rumson said nothing as he stared at her.

"One man has already been taken care of. And I'm confident we'll get the other."

"What about Kendall? Why hasn't the search crew found him?"

"Give them some time."

He studied her for a moment. "By the way, how did McKay know to wire transfer the funds? That's not something most people are familiar with, let alone some military grunt. I know the kid was smart, but come on."

"I would guess that Mosby showed him how. He did the same thing, you know, although he moved the money through Luxemburg, where we lost the trail."

Rumson frowned.

"The Secret Service are experts in money transfers, wire fraud, and things like that. They used to be part of the Treasury Department."

"And what about your two errand boys?"

"I'll take care of them myself when this is all over."

————

The Flight Data Recorder was discovered later that day by an Idaho National Guardsman. The soldier called his squad leader over.

"I think this is it, Sarge. Looks like the pictures you showed us this morning."

The sergeant patted him on the shoulder. "Good work, soldier."

————

Jack pulled the president's pant leg back down and placed the plastic bag of snow on his knee.

"What do you think, Dave? You seem to be walking better."

Kendall smiled. "Well, you haven't let me move much these last few days and you have me popping pills like they're candy. So other than a sore butt and being a little restless, I'm feeling pretty good."

Jack laughed. "It seems to have worked. The swelling is down and it's not as tender. And restless is good."

"When do you think we can try?" Richter asked. "Tomorrow?"

Jack frowned. "I think so. Let's see how it looks in the morning. We'll have to wrap it up first and maybe make some sort of crutches for the snow."

"I don't think I'll need crutches. The ski poles should be fine."

"Jack's right," Derek interjected. "We still have a long way to go. The car's at least seven miles from here." He grinned. "Besides, it will give me something to do."

"Okay. Okay." The president chuckled. "Make the crutches."

Derek stood. The president waved him back down.

"Before you go, I need to ask you guys a favor."

Both men nodded. "Sure. Anything."

"Well first of all, I want to thank you for everything you've done for me. I would not be here if it weren't for you. You guys saved our lives." The president put his hand on Derek's shoulder. "We will escape from here. I know this isn't my area of expertise, but with you two and Agent Richter working together,

I have no doubt that we'll get out of here." He paused until both men nodded. "I also know you guys have lives to go back to. Jack, you need to get back to school. And Derek, I know you need to get back to work. Your families are probably worried about you and must be thinking the worst right now." He paused a moment. "It will most likely be dangerous, but I need you guys to help me until we're safe."

After a moment, Derek nodded. "You're afraid that if we go home, we'll tell someone that you're alive."

The president held his gaze for a moment. "Yes."

Derek smiled. "Dave...sir. This is going to sound stupid, but this is an adventure for me." He blushed. "Stupid and immature, I guess." He hesitated a moment. "I drive a forklift in a warehouse. I load trucks. The guys I work with are pretty cool. But compared to this? Trying to help the president? Look, even before I knew who you were, I wanted to help you. I know there's a dead guy outside and that this is dangerous, but if you're asking me to tag along, then I'm definitely in."

Jack shook his head and grinned. "That's why I love Derek. Without him, my life would be boring."

They all chuckled.

"Dave. Mr. President. Sir. I understand what you're asking, and I'm willing to do whatever I can to help you. You have my commitment."

"You don't know how much this means to me, guys. Thank you."

CHAPTER FORTY-FIVE

Thursday, April 29

Emil Broder slammed the door and barked at his driver.

"Back to the office! Now!"

He rubbed his chest, popped a couple of Tums in his mouth, and waited for the burning to subside. He'd been FBI Director for almost eight years and, the truth was, he had turned the organization around. Compartmentalized and plagued by infighting when he took over, the Bureau had been slow to change with the times. He had fixed that. He had streamlined the Bureau, cutting out the dead wood, and centralizing the decision-making. And in the process, he had become feared throughout the organization. People referred to him as J. Edgar—behind his back, of course. He viewed it was a compliment. He ran the FBI with an iron fist and, in that respect at least, he was like the first FBI Director, who had built and commanded the Bureau for almost four decades. But now, all of the progress he had made seemed to be for naught.

As the driver turned onto Pennsylvania Avenue, he pondered

his next move. Rumson had summoned him once again and had demanded to know why his vaunted FBI had not yet recovered Kendall's body. He had failed to acknowledge any of the progress they had made over the last five days. To Rumson, the priority was on bringing an end to the uncertainty surrounding President Kendall, not on the criminal investigation.

"I don't pay you for excuses, Broder," Rumson had said. "I pay you for results." There had been no mistaking the scorn in his voice.

He sighed. It was time to call Monahan. Shit ran down hill.

———

Despite the wind and snow, the smells were overpowering: a mixture of jet fuel, burnt plastic and rubber, and worse, burnt flesh and death. Brenda Hughes had only spent four hours at the actual site, but the smell seemed to follow her. Even now, two days later, she could still smell it in her clothes, in her hair, and in her room on the base. Despite repeated washings. She remembered her first accident investigation three years ago. She had made an offhand comment about the lingering odors to other members of the team and they had smiled in a strange way and told her it was normal. The smells even haunted her dreams.

This was a brutal job, and she wondered how people like Burton did it. It didn't help that she spent the better part of the day inside an aircraft hangar, with the growing collection of debris, or in the adjacent hangar, which had been converted into a temporary morgue. She remembered from her first investigation that uncovering what had gone wrong—what had caused a highly sophisticated, multi-million dollar aircraft traveling at over four hundred knots to break apart in mid-flight—was a laborious and time consuming task. The larger pieces had been extracted first, raised up by cable and winch to hovering helicopters and then flown to Portland Air Guard Base. Tens of thousands of pieces of twisted metal, upholstery, cables and wires, luggage, pieces of laptop computers, shards of glass and dishes, pieces of clothing and unidentified debris had been recovered so far. These, too, were flown to Portland.

As bad as that was—the growing evidence of a major devastation—the bodies were the worst. Many were burnt beyond recognition by the explosion as the fuel-laden wings impacted the ground at over four hundred knots. A large number of bodies that weren't burnt were naked, their clothes stripped off by the tornado-force winds that had ripped through the passenger compartment as the plane broke up. Many were missing a hand, or a leg, or sometimes a head. These they found separately, if they were found at all. A severed foot still in its shoe. A hand and a portion of an arm, the wristwatch intact. She would never get used to the magnitude of the death, the wholesale destruction of human lives on an unimaginable scale. It was one thing to read about it in the papers or hear about it on the news, but to see the devastation to what once were living, breathing human beings; well, that was almost too much to bear. Thank God there were no children.

———

Cursing, Monahan crushed his cup and threw it against the wall.

It bounced and fell to the side of the can. He took several deep breaths as he watched the half dozen coffee splatters snaking their way down to the floor.

The call had not gone well. He took several more deep breaths and, as he thought about it, realized that he should have seen it coming. For the last several days he had sensed Broder's growing frustration. And today the volcano had erupted.

"For Christ's sake, Monahan! I've got the Attorney General on my ass! I've got Congress on my ass! The vice president's dragging me to the White House at least once a day! It's been almost a week! How tough is it to find one fucking body?"

He had brushed it off—or tried to anyway—and told Broder about their progress: the number of bodies recovered, the identifications made so far, the lead on Lt. McKay. And while Broder had listened, what really set him off was the NTSB's speculation—a speculation he now fully supported—that they would never recover all of the bodies.

"Emil, there's evidence that at least one passenger may have been sucked into one of the jet engines. It's also likely that some passengers may have essentially been cremated. Keep in mind the wings were loaded with fuel, so depending on where they were when the plane struck the ground....."

Broder never let him finish the thought.

Monahan sighed again, stood, took another deep breath, then left in search of paper towels to clean up the mess he'd made.

———

In the large hangar on the guard base, the painstaking task of reassembling the airplane had begun. As Stan Burton had explained it, they were essentially assembling a large three-dimensional puzzle. Once they had enough pieces, they could analyze each fracture, each point where the airplane had separated, to determine why it had come apart. Their preliminary suspicions, Burton had told her, were that there had been a high-energy event, which had initiated a cataclysmic chain of events, leading to the inevitable crash of Air Force One. A high-energy event. Brenda Hughes shivered at the thought. That meant an explosion, a bomb.

They should be able to validate their theory in the next day or two. The black boxes were currently being analyzed. If it survived the crash, the cockpit voice recorder would provide clues to the crew's stress levels and their reaction, assuming they had had any warning at all. The Flight Data Recorder would tell them how the aircraft was functioning up to the point of the crash. In all, almost one hundred and fifty separate parameters were measured over periods of time, including airspeed, altitude, direction and bearing, the performance of the power plant or jet engines, the positions of the flaps and stabilizers, and control and actuator positions.

Her thoughts were interrupted when Pat Monahan and General Trescott arrived, followed thirty seconds later by Stan Burton and Major Conklin.

———

Richter stopped every minute or two and scanned the area with binoculars. So far, there had been no signs of anyone else in the forest. He was careful to follow the same route each time, not wanting to leave any more tracks in the snow than he had to. As he plodded along in his snowshoes, the only tracks he saw, other than their own, belonged to deer and other animals. He was relieved to see that Derek and Jack had followed his instructions and had stuck to the patrol route. Although he had showed them what to do and what to look for, and although they were experienced hikers and familiar with the area, he wasn't comfortable unless he made at least one round per day.

His patrol route was a large loop around the cabin, the president no more than a quarter mile away. He knew he was taking risks, leaving the president with Jack and Derek and leaving tracks in the snow that led back to the cabin. And while he trusted Jack and Derek, it was difficult to leave the president exposed, with no one protecting him. He had considered leaving Derek Mosby's Sig Sauer but was not comfortable with the thought of someone else with a gun—someone he'd met only days ago—so close to the president when he was so far away.

Sitting in the cabin, the president was an easy target, with no defensive position and no easy way to escape. That left him no choice but to accept the risk of periodic patrols. It was unlikely that search and rescue personnel would be anywhere near the cabin. He had studied the hiking maps and had plotted the likely crash site. Based upon that, the search and rescue operation would be focused on an area nine or ten miles to the east. It was also unlikely that he would encounter any recreational sportsman. The snow was far too deep for hunters or hikers and, while snowmobilers or cross-country skiers might be tempted by the pristine snow, access roads were likely impassable. Snow cleanup would be focused on the major roads: the interstates first, then the heavily traveled state and county roads. It would be some time before the fire roads and forest service roads, currently buried below four or five feet of snow, would be plowed, if they were at all. Besides, according to Derek and Jack, this area was sparsely populated. No, he had to assume that anyone he might encounter in these mountains was a threat, and he could not sit idle while the president recuperated, hoping they wouldn't be discovered.

He began walking again, scanning his surroundings, following the path into the trees. He was in the middle of a grove of spruce when the growl of an engine broke the silence. He dropped to the ground then snaked himself below the snow-covered branches of a large spruce. The sound echoed through the mountains, seemingly coming from one direction one moment then another the next. He cursed as he calculated how far he was from the cabin.

The sound grew louder then became steady, coming from his right. Richter held the binoculars to his eyes, searching for movement, for a flash of color. The growl of the engine grew louder still, seemed to peak, then suddenly dropped. Over the sound of the wind, he could hear the sporadic low rumble of the motor idling. He crawled forward for a better view and, gently pushing a branch to the side, noticed a clearing twenty yards away. He scanned the area but saw nothing. The engine revved again, and a few seconds later a vehicle emerged from the trees into the clearing. With a large red, enclosed cab, and tracks instead of wheels, the truck reminded Richter of the trail-grooming machines on ski slopes. Shit! A snowcat!

The snowcat stopped in the middle of the clearing, fifty yards away. A second later, a man jumped out, sinking into the waist-deep snow. He was partially hidden behind the open door, but Richter could see a dark blue wool cap and a matching one-piece tactical jumpsuit. The man was speaking to someone inside. After a moment, he closed the door, then began to survey the clearing. The other door opened and a tall black man jumped out. Similarly dressed, the black man held his hand to his eyes, shielding his face from the swirling snow. He, too, began surveying the clearing. Richter felt his pulse quicken as first one, then the other, looked in his direction. Thankfully, they continued on. A moment later, both men turned and Richter cursed silently. In bright yellow letters, the back of their jumpsuits proclaimed they were federal agents.

The noise of another engine startled him and he crouched lower. Moments later, a second snowcat pulled into the clearing. One man, dressed in a grey jumpsuit instead of blue, hopped out. The two federal agents looked over expectantly. The man in the grey jumpsuit shook his head. As he turned to climb back into the snowcat, Richter read the words on his back. State Police.

Shit, he swore silently. *Could they be part of the search and rescue effort?* he wondered. Yet, something didn't feel right. What would they be looking for here? He flinched again, this time at the sound of a cell phone. He watched as the black man fumbled with his glove before reaching into his pocket.

"Yes?" The man's deep, baritone voice was surprisingly loud.

He studied the man's face and felt a prickle on the back of his neck. There was something familiar about him, but he couldn't put his finger on it. He had met many federal agents in his career, but his gut told him that wasn't it. Why did he feel that he'd seen that face before?

"No. He's a no-show."

Richter felt a chill run up his spine, suddenly remembering the tall black man in the crowd at the University of Seattle.

"We're at the primary site, but there's no sign of him." There was a pause. "No. We checked the alternative rendezvous points, but nothing."

Alarm bells started going off in Richter's head.

The black agent shook his head. "No. Maybe he never made it off the plane?"

———

"Lab analysis shows traces of RDX and PETN." Monahan flipped through his notes. "These were found on numerous pieces of luggage, on the bottom of Senator Dykstra's seat, and on portions of the fuselage, particularly on the peeled back skin on the starboard side." Monahan nodded to Burton. "Looks like you were right, Stan. The isolated holes below the VIP cabin would appear to be the main blast site."

"Hang on," Hughes interrupted. "What are PETN and... the other one? Explosives?"

Monahan nodded. "PETN stands for pentaerythritol

tetranitrate. It's used in military and industrial-grade explosives. It's also used in certain heart medications. We know that Senator Wentworth suffered from angina and was taking a drug containing PETN. The key here is the RDX. This is a nitroamine and is also used in the manufacture of high explosives. When RDX is mixed with PETN and several other agents, they form a plastic explosive called Semtex."

Hughes' face went pale. "Is there any other possible explanation for these compounds?"

"The lab boys tell me that the odds are slim. Based upon the ratio of PETN to RDX, the levels or amounts that we've found so far, where they were found, the analysis of the scorch marks on the luggage and on the aircraft skin, the isolated holes on both the starboard and port sides of the aircraft as well as the hole in the passenger cabin, all in very close proximity, it is highly probable that this plane was brought down by an improvised explosive device."

"Could it have been a missile?" Hughes asked.

"No." Major Conklin answered immediately. "We had an E-3 up. There was no missile launch."

"So, we come back to Lt. McKay," Monahan continued. "With the traces of Semtex on his hands, understanding his role in this is crucial." He turned to Burton. "We need to find the triggering device. ASAP."

"We're on it," Burton responded, the frustration evident in his voice. "You know my team has been working around the clock."

"I know, Stan. I know. But the sooner the better. Okay?"

Burton nodded.

"Anything else?" The general barked.

"Yes. We didn't find evidence of any chemical taggants, which indicates that the Semtex was fairly old, produced before 1991." Monahan noticed the questioning looks. "Due to the increased use of Semtex by terrorist organizations in the seventies and eighties, all Semtex produced after 1990 contains chemical taggants to aid in detection. Once we suspected that this was the explosive used, it begged the question of why screening by both the Air Force and the Secret Service didn't detect it. This may help explain why. Our next step is to determine exactly where this Semtex came from. Semtex was widely sold on the black market, and numerous terrorist organizations and rogue states were suspected of acquiring varying quantities over the years. The IRA. Libya. Various Islamic terrorist organizations in the Middle East. The list goes on. It may take us some time to trace the source. But we will find it. I'm confident of that."

———

Jack glanced out the window.

"Matt's coming."

"Good." Derek replied. "Just in time for dinner."

The door burst open and Richter hurried in, his face dark.

"We need to leave! ASAP!"

CHAPTER FORTY-SIX

Friday, April 30

They could hear the throaty hum of the generators from a distance and continued in the direction of the noise. Midnight had come and gone, but the half-moon against the cloud-free night sky provided ample light. They continued hiking and soon noticed a shimmer through the trees. The glow intensified as they moved forward, careful to stay in the shadows. As they got closer, they saw a large dump truck through the trees.

"That definitely wasn't here before." Despite the noise, Derek spoke softly.

Jack checked the GPS. "You're right. We went right past this point when we hiked in last week."

They studied the scene for a moment before Derek nodded. "This is a construction site. No doubt about it. They have portable lighting systems so they can work at night. Those are the generators we hear." He pointed to the dump truck. "And that right there looks like a yuke truck."

"A yuke truck?" Richter look puzzled.

"It's a heavy-duty dump truck, made for rough terrain. I worked for a construction firm for a while, mostly building roads. The guys always called them yukes. I'm not sure why, but that's what they called them."

Richter nodded as it dawned on him. "They must be building a road into the crash site."

They continued to study the scene, but despite the generators and the lights, the area appeared deserted.

"Let's head this way and see if we can get a better view." Richter led them forty yards to the right behind another large tree. The truck was sitting on the side of a newly cut road that ran at a forty-five degree angle across the path they had been on. It looked like a logging operation, with several large piles of log sections lining the clearing and a front-end loader parked on the other side.

"I think we might be able to steal that truck." Derek grinned.

Richter turned. "You know how to drive it?"

"I've never driven a yuke before, but I've driven regular dump trucks, bulldozers, even front-end loaders. How hard can it be?"

Jack shook his head. "We don't have the keys, Derek."

"That shouldn't be a problem. The crews normally leave them inside."

Richter studied Derek for a second before turning to Jack and the president. "You two stay here. Stay in the shadows behind the trees. We'll check it out."

———

Richter hesitated at the steps to the cab. Even with the sound of the generator, he could hear the chainsaws, trucks, and bulldozers close by. Every second they spent here, in the clearing, below the work lights, was a risk.

Derek, wearing an orange safety vest and a hard hat, sat in the driver's seat. The president, sitting next to him, wore a heavy brown work coat and a hard hat. Richter studied them for a moment. Up in the cab, away from the work lights, they might not draw a second glance.

Richter handed Derek the radio.

"The channel should be clear, but maintain radio silence unless it's urgent."

Derek nodded.

Richter climbed into the bed of the truck and joined Jack below the tarp.

—

The yuke bounced its way across the ruts and uneven ground. Richter swore as he banged his head again. His watch said they had been driving only thirty minutes, but it felt like two hours. They passed below another portable light system and, for a brief moment, he saw Jack's face. He was miserable too, Richter realized.

They rode in silence for another five minutes before the radio hissed and he heard the president's voice.

"Okay. We're coming up on Main Street. Lots of police cars and army trucks and flashing lights."

Shit! Richter reached into his pocket, resting his hand on his gun. The truck slowed as Derek downshifted. Richter's radio clicked twice and he began to hear background noises. When he heard the screech of the brakes over the radio, he turned the volume down and held it to his ear.

———

As Derek eased the truck forward, President Kendall saw the dozen or so cops and soldiers standing at the intersection. Nervous, he glanced at Derek and saw the grin as the red and blue flashing lights illuminated his face. Across the intersection, a large green canvas tent had been erected. Numerous Humvees and military transport trucks were parked at various angles outside. On the left, a front-end loader with forks instead of a bucket sat by stacks of steel girders, truss supports and steel panels.

The cops and soldiers glanced their way but seemed unconcerned. Behind them, a man wearing a hard hat and a safety vest stepped out of the tent and walked past the cops to the middle of the road. He waved to Derek, directing them to the side of the road. Derek braked and lowered his window.

"Good morning," he called down.

"Good morning." The man pointed towards the front-end loader. "Back it in and we'll get you loaded."

"We're not here for that," Derek said, nodding towards the steel girders. "The boss needs a load of gravel."

"Oh. Okay. Hey listen, on your way back, stop by and I'll fix you guys up with some coffee."

Derek smiled. "Thanks!"

The man turned and walked back to the tent. Derek put the truck in gear. He gave the cops a nod as he maneuvered the large truck onto Main Street.

The president watched the side view mirror as the man they had spoken to emerged from the tent again. The cops and soldiers turned. Kendall felt a wave of relief when he saw the man hand the cops two thermoses.

He slapped Derek on the shoulder and smiled. "That was pretty quick thinking." In the dim light, he caught Derek's smile.

———

The man known as Vernon Jackson flashed his identification as he drove past the road block. A former federal officer, he had cultivated the penetrating gaze that cops around the world, especially those in positions of authority, used to get what they wanted. With the look and a badge, he knew, he could go anywhere. It didn't matter that the badge was fake.

Even at this early hour, he noticed, there was a constant stream of traffic on Main Street as mostly trucks and off-road vehicles headed out to or returned from the unpaved fire roads, marked ATV trails, and Forest Service roads that snaked through the mountains. These roads, Jackson had learned, brought them no closer than fifteen or sixteen miles to the crash site. From there, they had to rely on snowcats and the new road segments currently being hacked out of the forest and mountains. Over the last two days, he had seen modular bridge sections being carried in on flatbed trucks, which indicated that the Army Corps of Engineers were constructing temporary bridges over the many streams and gullies between Elk City and the crash site.

The federal government had taken over the town of Elk City

and its airport and was using every available public and private structure to support the search and recovery efforts. Although they had a rented room in the one motel in town, Jackson had wisely realized that Elk City, the closest piece of civilization to the crash site—if it could be called that—would soon be overrun. They had moved out just as the rescue teams began to descend on the town and were now renting a trailer in an RV park twenty miles away. Whoever had planned to bring Air Force One down over a remote section of Idaho hadn't foreseen that this tiny town would be crawling with hundreds of people, with more traffic in a single day than they probably saw in a year. Apparently his contact, a woman he knew only as Jane, hadn't.

Jane, he thought. She was a piece of work. He had met her a few years after he had been fired. Even though the charges were dropped, the Secret Service had kicked him out anyway, and he knew he would never be able to work in law enforcement again. His former fellow officers, men and women he had worked with for years, had turned their backs on him, even though he knew for a fact that two of them had done the same thing. It had taken a while, but he had gotten his revenge.

He had met Jane when he began doing freelance jobs for a private security firm. Jane, it seemed, handled some of the unadvertised services the firm offered—services that no one would admit to. And so he had taken on the odd job like breaking into the office of a tech startup to steal the prototype for a new cell phone they were working on, or planting a bag of cocaine in the hand luggage of New York's First Lady. That had been fun to watch when she was detained by airport police. And then came the more unsavory jobs: breaking the leg of a ballet dancer, making a particular cop disappear, and, later, silencing the witnesses to a rape. It was the type of work that someone with a moral compass like his didn't lose too much sleep over. And each time, Jane had paid him well.

Jane was tough, he had to admit and, in a way, he respected her. But at the end of the day, he had no loyalty, not to her certainly. His only loyalty was to himself. He had learned long ago that the people he thought had his back didn't.

As he drove past the airport road, he glanced out his window at the noise and watched the helicopter lift off, hover momentarily, then turn and fly east. He craned his neck, watching through the windshield as it passed almost directly over his car. Several seconds later, it was swallowed by the darkness. He glanced back at the road and slowed as a dump truck pulled in front of him. Crews were working around the clock, both at the airport and at the edge of town, where the forest roads disappeared into the woods. The glow from the large portable lighting systems stretched for more than a mile into the forest before fading into the darkness. The air was filled with the constant hum of generators, trucks and equipment, but now, after several days, he was able to tune it out.

Maybe something had gone wrong, he thought. Jane had only shared certain details with him, but he was able to piece together the bigger plan. And, through Jane, he had been kept current on the search and recovery efforts. So far, there had been no sign of the man they were supposed to meet. Maybe the plane had crashed far closer to Elk City than planned? With

Elk City overrun by police and rescue teams, their contact may have been forced to hide, waiting for a safe time to make his way to one of the pre-established rendezvous points. They had checked each site daily, at the prescribed time, but so far, there hadn't been any signs of him. *Oh well*, Jackson sighed. Their role wasn't to plan but to clean up, so to speak, and they had recently learned that their job had gotten easier. Two days ago, Jane had told them, nature had taken care of one of the men they were supposed to meet. He suspected that either nature or the plane crash had taken care of the other, but Jane insisted that he keep checking until there was definitive proof that their contact wasn't walking out of the mountains alive. As she had stressed repeatedly, they could not afford any loose ends.

So far, their cover story seemed to be working, and they were able to lose themselves in the chaos that had descended on Elk City. But even with their federal IDs and even with the look, it was only a matter of time before someone started asking questions.

Jackson watched the large yellow, six-wheeled dump truck drive up Main Street. What a clusterfuck this was turning out to be. It was almost 4:00 a.m. and he had one more hour on watch before Malouf relieved him. Then he would make the drive back to their trailer for a few hours of sleep.

———

Derek grinned as he turned onto the side road three miles out of town.

"Where are we going?" the president asked.

"I have an idea," Derek responded. He shifted back up to high gear. "We can't drive around in this thing forever. It's too slow and we stand out. We need to find a car, and I know where we can get one."

The president smiled. The kid was quick on his feet. Several minutes earlier, they had passed through a second roadblock at the edge of town and Derek nodded and waved as he drove through. *Act like we belong*, he had said. No one had challenged them.

Ten minutes later, they pulled into a junk yard. Next door was a used auto lot with a dozen cars, all buried in snow. Derek drove the truck around the side of the yard, along a chain link fence with green slats, many broken with age. The truck bounced along the ground until they came to the end of the fence. Derek turned right and drove the yuke thirty to forty yards along the back of the fence before he stopped.

He keyed his radio. "You guys can come out now."

By the time they climbed down from the cab and walked to the back of the truck, Richter and Jack were climbing out.

Richter turned in a full circle. "Where are we?"

"At a junk yard, six or seven miles from Elk City. We need to find a car."

Richter walked over to the fence and peered between the gaps, seeing nothing but mounds of snow.

"The last time we were here," Derek continued, "Jack's car broke down and we needed to buy an alternator. We didn't have a lot of money, so the mechanic in town sent us here. I bargained with the owner and he let me rummage around in the

junkyard until I found the right one. It only cost us ten bucks."
He pointed behind them. "He has a small cabin about a half a
mile that way, back in the woods. The guy's drunk most of the
time. I don't think he'll notice anything's missing for a day or
two."

Richter was skeptical. "Is there anything besides old wrecks
here?"

"Yeah. Out front. Give me a few minutes and I should be
able to get us one."

Richter hesitated for a second until he caught the president's
look. He turned back to Derek and nodded.

Derek grinned, then turned and followed the yuke's tracks,
slipping and sliding as he went. He disappeared around the corner. Five minutes later, he appeared again, this time waving them
over.

"We're all set. Let's go."

They followed him around to the front where they saw the
old Jeep Cherokee idling in the lot. The Jeep was a patchwork
of parts with different color doors and panels. Derek explained
that the owner of the junk yard repaired old cars with parts sal-
vaged from wrecks then put them up for sale.

The president shook his head. "That kid has many hidden
talents."

Richter frowned. "Yeah. And grand theft auto is one of
them."

CHAPTER FORTY-SEVEN

The snow was piled over ten feet high on the sides of the road. Derek drove slowly, negotiating the almost constant twists and turns as the road wound through the hills, following the river. It was an hour before they saw the sign for Route 95. Jack and the president were dozing in the back while Richter watched the mirror, looking for signs they were being followed. As they approached the highway, the sky began to brighten with the new day.

"Get on the highway and head south."

"Okay." Derek signaled for the on-ramp. "Why south?"

Richter ignored the question. "We'll need to stop somewhere and find an ATM."

Derek pointed to the dashboard. "We're going to need gas soon, too. And I need some coffee."

Richter felt bone-weary. He wanted to close his eyes and surrender to the waves of exhaustion that swept over him but knew that, if he did, he would be out for a while. And that wouldn't be good. When they stopped, he thought, he'd relieve

Derek and drive awhile.

"You seem to have a knack for stealing cars," he said.

"I didn't think we had a choice." Derek tone was defiant. "What would you have done?"

"Probably the same thing." Richter smiled weakly. "But, Derek? You just made the President of the United States an accessory to a felony."

———

"What's the matter?" Richter asked.

Derek explained the problem.

"So you only have one hundred?"

"Yeah. Sorry. That's all I have in my account," Derek answered somewhat embarrassed. "I only keep enough for lunch and pocket money: I transfer the balance to my Mom's account to cover living expenses, and the rest goes to restitution."

"What about you, Jack?"

"It wouldn't give me any cash." Jack was frustrated. "The ATM says I'm overdrawn, but I know I'm not."

Richter scanned the street. "This looks like the only bank in town. The hundred should be enough to get some gas and food." He sighed. "We'll have to try again later."

———

Their luck wasn't any better in the next two towns. Frustrated, they climbed back into the car.

"Ahh, shoot," Jack said once they were back on the road. "What's today's date? The twenty-ninth? The thirtieth?" He shook his head. "It must be my tuition bill. That gets deducted automatically. I must have forgotten to transfer cash before we left." He sighed and shook his head again. President Kendall patted him on the shoulder then exchanged a glance with Richter in the rearview mirror. Richter let out a breath then nodded.

An hour later they pulled off the highway again and found the bank. Reluctantly, Richter pulled out his own card. When the machine dispensed his money, he grabbed it and stuffed it in his pocket without counting. It was risky, he knew, but they didn't have a choice.

"Where to?" Derek asked as Richter climbed in the Jeep.

"We need to get rid of this car."

———

Rumson frowned. "Are you sure about that?"

"Yes, sir," Justice Stanhope responded. "Technically, you're still only acting president. Absent finding his body, the only way around this, that I can see, is to have President Kendall legally declared dead. That would need to be done by the court."

Rumson shook his head slowly. "You are the court," he said after a moment. He kept his tone even, but there was no masking the condescension.

"With all due respect, sir, I am a justice of the Supreme Court. My job is to rule on motions brought before the court. I can't bring motions to the court. You would need to file a motion before a lower court and have a federal judge rule on it. No doubt there would be challenges. Ultimately, it might end up in my court, for a ruling."

Rumson absentmindedly picked up the letter opener that was lying next to the blotter on the desk. His desk now, but there still seemed to be some technicalities getting in the way. He studied the letter opener for a moment. It was heavy. With its black stone handle—carved in the shape of an Aztec figure, he had heard—and the ornate silver blade, it looked like a dagger. It belonged to that prick Kendall, who, even dead, was still causing him grief. He laid it back on the desk.

Not only had Rumson moved into the Oval Office, he had also insisted on being addressed as "Mr. President." Given the circumstances, no one argued the point with him. As each day passed, the twenty-four-hour news coverage, with its continual visual reminders coupled with the pessimistic commentary of the newscasters and analysts, only served to diminish any hopes the public may have once had. The more detailed briefings that most senior governmental officials received were bleaker still, and most had already resigned themselves to the fact that President Kendall was gone.

Rumson looked up at the Attorney General. "Can the Justice Department file this brief?"

"We'll have to do some research. But…"

Rumson's eyes narrowed, but Kiplinger held up his hand.

"Sir, please hear me out. We're dealing with the Constitution here. If we approach this wrong, there will be challenges. We've never faced this situation before, and it's not clear. The last thing you want is a procedural misstep. I think it's best to wait for the recovery teams to find his body."

Rumson was silent for a moment. "What if they don't find

him? The FBI is telling me that there's a possibility that they never will."

"Then that will be the basis for the motion we file before the court. We would need the investigators to declare that, in their expert opinion, the president's body was destroyed in the crash."

And who knew how long that could take, Rumson thought. He frowned.

"Tyler…Mr. President, we'll cross that bridge when we get there." Kiplinger paused. "From what I've been told, the recovery teams have done an incredible job in a very short period of time. They're still finding bodies. I suggest that you give them another week."

Rumson sat back. Kiplinger was right. He had to let the investigation play out. He would still keep the pressure on—the American public needed closure, and he would use that. But it was better not to rush things. It had taken a long time to reach this office, a lot of planning, many small steps. The snowstorm was just one more obstacle and a small one at that. The acting part of his title was just a formality. He was the president.

He glanced up at the two men and nodded.

———

President Kendall didn't recognize the face in the mirror. His beard and mustache were peppered with spots of grey. His cheeks were sunken, one still bruised, and his dark eyes reflected the tension. He looked like he had aged ten years. With a Budweiser baseball cap on his head, and a green and blue flannel shirt, he couldn't have looked any less presidential than if he had hired a Hollywood make up artist. God, he looked like a redneck, he thought. But he was alive.

He rubbed his face. Even though he had groomed it, his beard still looked awful. Richter, however, wouldn't let him shave it off. He sighed as he looked around the motel room, noticing it for the first time. The carpet and curtains were stained, the bed springs squeaked, the tiles in the bathroom were cracked, and the place smelled musty. But after the snow cave and the miner's shack, it was heaven.

They had arrived at the motel on the outskirts of Boise, Idaho, late in the afternoon. The president had headed directly to the shower. It had felt good and he wanted to stand below the hot water forever. But Richter had come knocking with a new set of clothes and a couple of pizzas.

Their trip down from Elk City had taken almost eight hours. Along the way, they had learned the latest news on the crash and the recovery from the car radio, from newspapers, and from a copy of Time Magazine. President Kendall shivered when he read about the crash and the latest theories and speculation of what had happened to his body. He was stunned by the horror and devastation captured in the pictures. He read the list of names of all those, passengers and crew alike, who had been aboard Air Force One. He turned the page and saw the pictures of his family attending the candlelight vigil. His wife, his Maria, looked grief-stricken and his daughters crushed. They were holding onto their mother as if trying desperately to make sure that she too would not be taken away. His heart ached, but at the same time, he was angry. He vowed to do everything within his power to find the people responsible.

He glanced up at Richter standing by the door. His appearance had changed as well, he realized. Gone was the clean-shaven, well-dressed young man who favored designer suits. He looked more like Derek and Jack than a federal agent. With sweatpants, a matching zippered sweatshirt and running shoes, he might be on his way to play soccer or softball with his buddies. Except for his eyes, Kendall thought. If anything, they made him appear even more formidable, more intense.

———

The president seemed far away, and it took a moment for Richter to get his attention. He handed him a newspaper, pointing to the front page article.

"Pat Monahan's heading up the investigation," he said. "That might work to our favor, but it may be very difficult to get a hold of him."

The president glanced at the paper and nodded.

Richter sat on the edge of the bed. They had, against all odds, made it to Boise. Now, he had to figure out their next move.

"I can try calling the main FBI number. We can get that at the local library. The problem, though, is that there's no way they're going to give me his cell phone number; they'll connect me to his voice mail or maybe to his secretary." He shook his head. "But I'm not about to leave a message."

The president frowned. "What about a local FBI office. They should be able to reach him."

Richter shook his head. "Too dangerous. Even with my credentials, it will probably take some effort to convince them who
I am. And there's no way to prevent them from notifying people
up the chain of command." He paused as his eyes narrowed.
"All the way to Washington."

"We might have to take that risk," the president said.

Richter could hear the doubt in his tone.

"Mosby and Rumson have a history together," Richter countered. "And Mosby seems to be connected to Broder too. Besides, those two federal agents I saw in the woods? For all we
know, they're real and they're from the local office." Richter
shook his head again. "For the same reason, we can't go to the
state police either."

The president was still frowning, but after a second he nodded. "Okay. So, it appears Rumson's tentacles are everywhere,"
he said. "What do we do next?"

Richter let out a breath. "You mentioned a reporter that you
know. In Colorado?"

Kendall nodded.

"We go to Colorado."

———

"We've completed the review of the data recorders." Stan Burton handed out the transcript. "This shows the timeline and
sequence of events as we understand them so far. At 10:58 a.m.
local time, exactly fifty-nine minutes into the flight, the flight
data recorder indicates an apparent malfunction in the fuel gauges. The gauges indicate an unequal feed from the port and star-

board fuel tanks. These tanks are located in the wings and, if this were true, it would indicate an imbalance across the airframe. This appears to be an anomaly. Data on the engines and the fuel system indicate normal operation, everything within specs.

"The cockpit voice recorder indicates that the crew noticed the problem almost immediately. The transcript of the conversation is in front of you. Colonel Zweig and Major Lewis discuss the situation and then order Lieutenant McKay to check the level capacitors and the transfer pumps. They discuss the maintenance brief. Colonel Zweig then orders the Flight Engineer, Captain Wes Thomas, to check the computers and to manually calculate the fuel state. At 11:02, Lewis reports that the gauges appear to be correct, and that they indicate approximately one hundred and forty-one thousand pounds of fuel in each tank.

"Four minutes later, at 11:06 a.m., the flight data recorder indicates an interruption to the main electrical supply to the data recorders and to the communications systems. The data recorders have backup power systems and continued recording. We don't know yet why the main power supply failed.

"At 11:09, there appears to be an explosion. The FDR indicates that the rear hatch is breeched. The crew suspects they're under attack and begins evasive maneuvers, deploying chaff and flairs to confuse any potential inbound missiles. At the same time, they immediately lose cabin pressure; in the transcript, you can see Colonel Zweig refer to an 'explosive decompression.' They don oxygen masks and immediately begin an emergency descent to the minimum safe altitude. Although they're not exactly clear what occurred, the crew reacts quickly and professionally. They've turned and are now on a westerly course of two-five-three degrees.

"One minute later, at 11:10, Lewis unsuccessfully attempts to contact the Air Force E-3 Sentry that is controlling the flight. She then attempts to contact Air Traffic Control, again, unsuccessfully. The aircraft continues to descend and, at 11:11, they level off at eleven thousand, nine hundred feet.

"There is another explosion. The crew deploys chaff and flairs again but does not take evasive action. It would appear that Colonel Zweig reacted appropriately, given the low altitude and the elevation of the mountains they were over. They radio a Mayday and discuss their options. They decide to try for Missoula, Montana, which is one hundred and twenty miles away. The aircraft turns north to heading zero-one-five.

"At 11:14 a.m., there is another explosion and the CVR ends. The FDR continues to record for another twenty-seven seconds and indicates major malfunctions in multiple systems, hydraulics, electrical, power plants, control surfaces. This is where the recordings end."

Monahan waited until Burton was done and then looked around the room. "The critical question is: what exactly was Lt. McKay doing when he was sent to investigate the fuel gauge problem?"

CHAPTER FORTY-EIGHT

Saturday, May 1

The call came in the morning, minutes before seven. After working through the night, Pat Monahan had just closed the door to his office and was heading to his trailer for a few hours of much needed sleep. Wearily, he answered the call.

"Mr. Monahan. This is Brett Donahue from San Antonio."

Monahan remembered Donahue when he was transferred to Texas to become the Special Agent in Charge of the San Antonio office five years ago.

"Sir? I've got something down here that's going to interest you. We discovered a body in a house about fifteen miles west of Laredo. Male, age and identity unknown, decapitated. Our initial inspection of the corpse suggests he's of Mexican heritage. At first glance, this looks like the modus operandi for the cartels, a retaliatory killing. However, we found something with the body that suggests otherwise."

Monahan rubbed his head, unsure where this was going.

"In a briefcase next to the body, we discovered two pounds

of Semtex, plus timers, fuses, and various fake IDs." There was a pause. "Sir?"

Monahan felt the hair standing up on the back of his neck. "Yes."

"We also found classified spec sheets and diagrams of Air Force One and the president's itinerary for his trip to Seattle."

———

Behind the dirty strip mall south of Salt Lake City, they found what they needed: another Dodge Grand Caravan, from an earlier model year, but with a similar color pattern. They had watched the strip mall for some time and noted very little traffic. The mall was located on a side street and had lost its customers to the more heavily traveled and newer thoroughfares. There were vacant lots on either side of the strip mall and the few small clusters of retail activity on the other side of the street appeared to be hanging on for dear life. Except for the wino out front, even the liquor store a block away looked abandoned.

In the strip mall, six of the storefronts were vacant. Of the businesses that had somehow managed to survive, there was a tax preparation service—a sign indicating it was closed—a computer repair shop, a printer, and a vacuum cleaner repair shop. There were three cars in the front parking lot and, in the back, a handful more, presumably belonging to the owners and employees. On the far end, they spotted the minivan. It was covered with a thick layer of dust, and rust was eating through the sides. A rag was stuffed into the hole where the gas cap had once been. One tire was flat, and the crack in the back window was held together with duct tape.

It took Derek two minutes to remove the license plates. The odds were in their favor that no one would notice that the seemingly abandoned minivan behind the seldom-used strip mall no longer had plates. Or so they hoped.

———

Henry Amalu frowned. "Do the intelligence services have anything to support this? The CIA, the NSA?"

"No sir," the agent answered. "Not to my knowledge."

Emil Broder sat back, only half listening. He knew the answer. Other than the body found in San Antonio, there had been no other indication that the Mexican cartels were involved in the downing of Air Force One. At least for the moment. But that wasn't unusual. Libya's planning and preparations for the bombing of Pan Am 103 over Lockerbie, Scotland, in 1988 had somehow slipped through the intelligence nets. The USS Cole attack, the bombing of the World Trade Center in 1993, and countless other terrorist attacks, including 9/11, had slipped through the nets as well. It wasn't until well after the events that the intelligence services were able to connect the pieces of the puzzle. Yes, the federal intelligence and law enforcement services were reorganized after 9/11, and the Department of Homeland Security was created; the goal being to ensure that coordination and information sharing across almost two hundred separate federal agencies were not impeded by bureaucracy and the desire to protect one's own turf, something all too common amongst the agencies involved. Still, there were billions of pieces of data to sort through and somehow connect: cell phone and wire intercepts, satellite images, emails and blogs, news reports, data gathered by agents and operatives...the list went on. New data mining software helped, but it was a daunting task.

Were the Mexican Cartels behind this? he wondered as he rubbed his chest. They had a history of targeting the police and the Army in retaliation for raids and arrests. They also targeted informants, local government officials, and political candidates, going after the political structure behind the Mexican government's war on drugs. Was this retaliation for Project Boston? Could they be sending the U.S. a clear message to stay out of Mexico's drug battles? Or was it a matter of survival, fighting back to protect their livelihood? So far, their response to the Boston raids had been subdued.

He popped another Tums in his mouth as he turned his attention back to the meeting. As he listened, he began to notice several stolen glances in his direction. It was time to end this.

When he sat forward, a hush came over the room. "This is clearly a lead that we need to pursue."

———

With their first task done, they drove to Walmart where they purchased more clothes, several newspapers and magazines, some food, more painkillers, and a knee brace. Derek tossed the Idaho plates into the dumpster behind the store. Back in the car, they continued south. Two hours later, they pulled into a roadside motel.

CHAPTER FORTY-NINE

Sunday, May 2

"Sir, we got something."

Monahan turned to see Agent Connolly. His mouth full of bagel, he nodded and pointed toward the conference room. This was his third bagel and it was only 5:00 a.m.; the night wasn't over yet. Eating like this, he knew, would kill him. He swallowed, refilled his coffee, and followed Connolly into the room.

"What do you have?"

Connolly sat at the computer and clicked the mouse. "We found another body," she said over her shoulder. "He was discovered quite a distance from the crash site."

Finally some good luck, Monahan thought. Frustrated that they hadn't recovered more bodies, he had asked General Trescott to expand the search.

He leaned over Connolly's shoulder and examined the picture, noting the circle of light around the body fading into darkness. This was a nighttime shot taken with a lighting system.

"When was this taken?"

"Forty minutes ago."

The CSAR team, Monahan knew, was working around the clock. Connolly pointed to the screen.

"That's how they found him, naked and buried below the snow."

Well that wasn't so unusual, he thought. Many passengers had been stripped naked by the gale-force winds that had torn through the plane. And almost all had been buried in the snow.

As if reading his thoughts, she continued. "A number of things make this significant. First, he was found about nine miles west of the primary debris field." She walked over to the large map on the wall and stuck a red pushpin in it. "Right about here." She traced her finger east across the map to a blue push-pin. "The next closest body, Lieutenant McKay, was found seven miles to the east, right here." She tapped the map. "Senator Dykstra was found another mile further east."

Monahan nodded as Connolly returned to the computer.

"He was buried in the snow outside of an old mining cabin. It appears that he was purposefully buried. What's more disturbing is that it appears that he was shot," she added.

Monahan studied the picture, grabbed the mouse, and clicked through several shots. Other than the dark holes in the forehead, there didn't appear to be any other significant injuries to the body.

"Could it be an injury from the crash?" He felt obligated to ask.

"I don't think so. I told the coroner that this is a priority, so we should know soon. As for the cabin, it appears that someone has been camping out there."

Monahan clicked the mouse again until the cabin appeared. He studied it for a moment and then clicked back to the pictures of the body.

"Have you ID'd him yet?"

"That's the disturbing part. We compared him to the eight missing passengers. Three of those, as you know, are female. Of the remaining men, he bears a striking resemblance to Secret Service Agent Cal Mosby."

"Shit. Really?"

She nodded soberly. "Yes, sir. We should know for sure soon."

Monahan shook his head. The investigation had just taken another ugly turn.

———

They arrived in Durango, Colorado, in midafternoon. After driving along the river for several miles, they turned into town and, minutes later, pulled up in front of the public library. As Jack climbed out, Richter caught his eye.

"We'll be back in half an hour."

Jack nodded then jogged towards the door. Once he was safely inside, Derek put the car in gear. As they pulled out of the lot, he turned to Richter and grinned.

"Time to go car shopping again?"

———

Rumson considered the news. Mosby had been found; apparently shot and killed and his body dumped. He was certain that wasn't part of the plan. It sure wasn't part of Mosby's plan. In fact, disappearing in South America was. But he had known Mosby for over twenty years and, despite the fact that he was trained to be skeptical, Mosby had been easy to manipulate. Like a pawn on a chessboard, it had been easy to move the hapless agent in the direction that best suited his purposes.

It had started small, years ago, a series of tests to see how far across the line Mosby was willing to go. Each time, he had pushed Mosby a little further: fixing a ticket, leaving certain facts out of an official report, presenting false testimony at a trial, planting evidence to frame a local politician. When he joined the FBI, the stakes had risen. Mosby had helped to steer the investigation into an Ohio gubernatorial candidate's alleged misuse of campaign funds—to, among other things, pay for hookers— into the poor records maintained by an inexperienced staffer who, unfortunately, had died weeks earlier in a car crash. The candidate won, served two terms as governor, and was now the Ambassador to Japan. And that was another chip that Rumson could cash in whenever he needed.

When Jane began doing private security work, he had decided that Mosby might be more useful to him in the Secret Service. Even back then, his ultimate goal was the White House, and he started planting the seeds early, unsure at the time when or how he would use Mosby in the future. He only knew that he could. When he moved into the White House, he had maneuvered Mosby again, having him moved from the president's security detail onto his own. Mosby, who had always been moody and irritable, had grown bitter over the years, upset that he hadn't risen further in the Service. Rumson had been able to use that against him. A loner now—his wife had died ten years ago from breast cancer—it hadn't taken much effort to harness Mosby's anger and resentment.

When he shared with Mosby a confidential reorganization plan drafted by the Director of the Secret Service, at first Mosby had been stunned. The plan—a fabrication, complete with organizational hierarchy charts—included a list of older agents who would be let go. Mosby's name was on the list. Rumson had promised to see what he could do and Mosby had stewed for a week. When they met again, he had shaken his head and watched as Mosby's eyes burned with anger. Then, he offered Mosby a way out, and the disgruntled agent had jumped at the opportunity.

He frowned. Mosby would have died anyway, but it was supposed to appear that he died in the crash—or at least it was supposed to be assumed. Just like that Air Force guy. But something had gone wrong and, now, they would have to do some damage control. He glanced at his phone. He needed to speak to Jane.

He had to admit, her plan was brilliant. Frame the Mexican drug cartel. If they did it right, not only would he avoid any suspicion falling on him, it would give him an excuse to bring the full might of the United States military to bear against the cartel. Instead of merely lopping off a few heads—which, like the Hydra of Greek mythology, only sprouted more as other criminal elements moved in to fill the power vacuum—he could not only avenge Kendall's death, he could significantly reduce the flow of drugs from Mexico. That alone would guarantee another term and further ensure that history would judge him as one of the great ones.

Now, the challenge would be to somehow connect Mosby and the Air Force guy to the Mexicans. He would have to speak to Jane. But she would have to scramble to connect the pieces for the FBI before the investigation got too far off track.

In the meantime, he thought, it would make sense to rattle Broder's cage a little. There was no way he could derail the investigation into Mosby, or into his connection to the Air Force, or his likely motivation. Now that Mosby's body had been discovered, the FBI would be like a dog with a bone. But he could slow them down a little and give Jane some time.

He picked up the phone.

"Get me Emil Broder."

———

Three hours later, they were in a motel room watching the news. They sat in silence as pictures of the crash site flashed across the screen. The announcer told them little they didn't already know.

Richter stood, lifted the curtain, and peeked outside. He was on edge. The irony wasn't lost on him. A little over a week ago, he was part a team of over one hundred Secret Service agents plus scores of local police protecting the president. Sections of Seattle had been virtually shut down as they carefully orchestrated the president's visit and interactions with the public. Mostly, they managed the risk by limiting his exposure to people. Now,

Richter was by himself, guarding the president while he ate a barbecued pork sandwich in a cheap motel room. Hiding in plain sight.

He watched a pickup truck pull into a space across the lot. A young man climbed out, a six-pack in one hand and a pizza in the other. After the man disappeared into his room, Richter stared out at the dark lot for another minute.

They had made it to Colorado—they were a thousand miles from the crash site—but he was still nervous. The face kept coming back to him: the black man in the crowd in Seattle, the federal agent in the mountains of Idaho. He knew he had seen the man before, somewhere, sometime, years ago. Was he on the Threat List? Was he really an agent? And in the mountains, he had partners. He hadn't recognized either of their faces, but they were two more on his growing list of people to worry about.

He glanced at the president. He could see from the president's eyes that he understood. While the world held its breath and waited and wondered what had happened to the president, they had successfully eluded the thousands of people who were searching for them. They had also eluded those who were somehow involved in the downing of Air Force One: a group that seemed to be growing and one whose tentacles seemed to reach far and wide. There was no way to tell how much of the latter had infiltrated the former.

But they couldn't run forever. The more he thought about it, the president was right: Monahan was their best opportunity.

———

"If you need more people, you've got to let me know!"

Monahan took a breath before he answered. He was both exhausted and frustrated, and it took all of his effort to hold his tongue. "Emil, the last thing I want is more people tramping around the mountain. This is a crime scene, for Christ's sake, and we're already running the risk of compromising evidence as it is."

"God damn it, Monahan! You need to manage both!"

There was a silence on the line, but Monahan resisted the urge to fill it. It was a second or two before Broder spoke again.

"Canada has one of the best cold-weather search and rescue teams in the world..."

"Are you serious, Emil? I have too many people here right now and you want to send more? Jesus, if you want to help, send Pearson out here! Let her manage the coordination from the ground while I focus on the investigation! That would be a hell of a lot more effective!" He took a breath, forcing himself to calm down. "Look, we're doing everything we can. We're using body-sniffing dogs, infrared and heat detection, acoustic and seismic imaging, fiber-optic cameras, and biometric detection probes." He felt his anger rising again and took another breath. "We're using robots that can burrow through the snow. I even commandeered an NRO satellite and a Predator Drone." He sighed. "We've been through this already, Emil! We're working as hard and smart as we can, but you've got to accept the fact that we may not find him."

Broder exploded. "Are you fucking insane! We cannot tell the nation that the president's body just disintegrated!"

The frustration and fatigue had been mounting, and Monahan erupted. "What the hell do you want from me? I haven't slept in I don't know how long, and I am going to start losing people if I drive them any harder! But if you think someone else is more capable than I am...if you think that they can somehow magically produce a missing body out here...well, then for Christ's sake, take me off the case and send them out here instead! It's your call!" He knew the moment the words were out of his mouth that he had crossed the line.

There was a long pause before Broder responded. "That's exactly what I intend to do. You are now off the case, Monahan! I'm sending Kaitlyn Pearson to replace you. When she gets there, you're to brief her, introduce her to the team, and then get your ass back here ASAP. Do you understand me?"

"Loud and clear!" Monahan slammed the phone down. *Screw him! Jesus! What an asshole!* He tossed his pad of paper on the table and sat back, exhaling loudly. Sure, people in Washington were demanding results, but it was Broder's job to manage that so that the investigators could focus on their work. He had never known Broder to cave in to political pressure before.

Monahan walked over to the map, covered with notes and clusters of pins. On one hand, he understood Broder's frustration. The nation needed closure. It would be horrible if they declared that the president's body was consumed by the crash, only to have some hiker discover his remains later. That was one of his worries. But the search had been exhaustive, and his gut told him that there were no more bodies to be found.

He shook his head and sighed. This was not how he wanted

to end his career.

———

Jane arrived at eight o'clock and was escorted into Rumson's study.

She gave him a quick peck on the cheek. "Your security has increased considerably since I was here last."

"Are you surprised?"

She ignored the condescending tone and sat on the couch.

"You sounded troubled on the phone earlier."

He glared at her for a second before sitting. He gave her an update on the investigation.

"Do the investigators know who shot him?" she asked.

"Your men weren't behind this?"

"I'll need to check, but I don't think so. They would have disposed of the body, unless….." She hesitated a moment as she considered the possibilities.

"Unless what?"

"Unless they were interrupted and had to go into hiding themselves." She frowned. "This does present a problem." She stood up and began to pace.

Rumson watched her. "This thing can't come back to me, Jane." His eyes were dark. "You know that."

She stopped. "No operation ever goes as expected. But I can assure you that there is no trail back to you."

"Except through you, Jane. Except through you."

She stared at him, unfazed, but said nothing. After a second, she began pacing again. He watched her.

"We need to connect Mosby to the Mexicans," she said without breaking stride.

He watched as she paced back and forth once more before she came around the couch and sat.

"There are two ways to do that," she began. "One is through the bank account. The second is through his cell phone." She explained what she was thinking.

This time he smiled. "How soon can you do that?"

"Tonight."

He looked skeptical.

"I still have a team in Texas."

He nodded. Jane was good. As he studied her, he had no doubt the matter would be taken care of. But there was still one issue that was weighing on him.

"They still haven't found Kendall's body. Or that of his Secret Service agent. That troubles me."

"Are you suggesting that the president somehow managed to survive the crash and the weather? I think the odds of that are astronomical."

"Do you have any better explanation?"

"My guess is that Mosby was shot by my men and for some reason they had to abandon his body quickly. As for the president and his agent, as you told me yourself, depending on where they were when the bomb exploded or when the plane crashed, their bodies may have been destroyed. There may be no traces."

Rumson's face clouded. "You always tell me that you don't like coincidences? Well, this is one big fucking coincidence, don't you think?"

She frowned as she considered this. "I see your point."

"Then I think we need to assume that this is a possibility. So long as there is any chance of him being alive, we need to do everything we can to prevent him from being found."

———

Although the sun had already set, the frantic pace in Elk City continued. *This is getting too risky*, Jackson thought as his phone vibrated.

"Yes?"

"Where are you?" He recognized the angry voice.

"Elk City." He resisted the urge to add: *Where the hell do you think I am?*

"Why didn't you call me?"

He was confused. "What the hell are you talking about?"

"Your second target has been discovered with two holes in the head."

Damn! "That wasn't us. Where was he found?"

Jane filled him in. "Something doesn't make sense," she added, then silence.

He waited for her to continue.

"What's the standard-issue weapon for the Secret Service?"

"Most carry a Sig Sauer P229, which uses a .357-caliber SIG cartridge. Why?"

"According to the FBI, Mosby had two .357 SIG slugs in his head. They can't find his service weapon and believe he was shot with his own gun." More silence.

While he waited, Jackson watched a convoy of trucks disappear into the forest. His instinct told him to let Jane wrestle with the various pieces of the puzzle herself.

"Okay. Tell me what's going on there."

Jackson let out a breath. "Same as yesterday," he said, then explained that the town was a massive construction site, and the engineers continued to work on the roads and bridges.

"Okay. Go back to the trailer, pack your stuff and wait there. I think it's no longer safe for you in Elk City."

CHAPTER FIFTY

Monday, May 3

Jackson lay in bed, unable to sleep. He was thankful that Jane had pulled them out of Elk City. He had begun to wonder when their luck would run out and someone would demand to know exactly what it was that two federal agents were doing chatting with the local cops and the construction crews. He also had the nagging suspicion that something was going on and Jane hadn't told him everything. From the fold out couch in the living room, Malouf's snores filled the trailer. At least someone was getting some sleep. He sighed.

Their task—to break a couple of links in the chain—had taken care of itself. He wondered what their next assignment would be.

The phone rang. *It's about time*, he thought, reaching for his phone. Despite his dislike for Jane, he was anxious to complete this assignment.

"I need you to go to Council, Idaho," she said. "On Friday, someone withdrew four hundred dollars from Matthew Richter's account at an ATM. Although the odds are against it, we need to consider that they survived, and if they did, you need to see if they're still in town. I want a copy of the video from that ATM." She paused, then: "I think they're on the run."

Jackson pulled out a map, searching for Council. There it was. "Richter? How could he have survived?"

"That's irrelevant. You need to check it out."

He sighed. "It's one in the morning. The bank's not open now."

"Get there when it opens. You have the credentials you need to get that video." It was a statement, not a question.

"Okay, okay," he finally said as he rubbed at the pain that had begun to throb in his temples.

"Call me as soon as you have it."

"I will. But hang on. You said 'they.' You said 'they're on the run.' Who else are you talking about?"

"The president, of course."

———

Bill Daniels clicked on the save button. Feeling good that his column was complete, he wrote a quick email to his editor, attached the file and sent it on its way. He checked the clock and was happy to see that he still had more than enough time to hit a few balls on the range before his bi-weekly golf game. Life was good.

After working for almost thirty years in the newspaper business, he had risen from an intern all the way up to editor of the Denver Record. But after nine years at the helm, he had grown tired of the newspaper business. The constant deadlines and the late nights, while exciting as a cub reporter, had taken their toll. To make matters worse, the business had been on a steady decline for the last twenty years. They had continued to lose readership and circulation as first magazines then the internet encroached on what was once sacred space. The declining advertising revenues that followed only added to the pain. On top of that, he found it taxing to manage a diverse team of independent-minded writers, always having to hound them to get their copy in on time.

So when he was offered the job as editor-in-chief of the Boston Herald, he had begun to mentally pack his bags, even before he told his wife. Even though he had lived in Colorado all his life, the idea of moving to a new city had seemed exciting.

He had almost accepted the offer, and would have, if not for Peggy. Always the voice of reason, his wife had asked him one crucial question that had stopped him from making the call. What would change? Sure, Boston was a nice city, and they had enjoyed vacationing there years ago. Living there would open up a new world of cultural opportunities. However, for six days a week, his normal work schedule, what would really change?

When he analyzed it, what he enjoyed about the newspaper business was writing. He had been good once, but at some point in his career he had made the shift from columnist to editor. He was part of the management team. That was a move that he always regretted.

And so, five years ago, he said no to the job offer in Boston. He also, to the publisher's dismay, resigned from his job at the

Denver Record and became a columnist again. It was funny how life sometimes went full circle.

After leaving the Record, he and Peggy realized they were no longer tied to Denver. He could write from anywhere. Although they loved the city, it had changed over the years as the growing population brought with it urban sprawl and traffic. While family wouldn't keep them in Colorado—their children were both grown with families of their own: one living in Hawaii, the other in Atlanta—the many friendships they had built over the years would be difficult to give up. In compromise, they decided to semi-retire to the town of Cortez.

Cortez, a small town of eight thousand, was nestled in the Four Corners region of Southwestern Colorado. While visiting Mesa Verde National Park on vacation, they had fallen in love with the town and had discussed buying a second home there. Some of their closest friends had already done it, a few of them making Cortez their permanent home. With nearby ski resorts and hunting, hiking, biking, camping, and fishing, Cortez cultivated an active outdoor lifestyle. The city of Durango was forty-five minutes away. With double the population of Cortez, it offered more in the way of culture with restaurants and nightlife that catered to tourists. Then there was Santa Fe to the south and Arizona and Utah almost next door. Cortez couldn't have been any more different from Boston. That suited Bill just fine. Colorado was his home.

His life now entailed writing a weekly column, a tongue-in-cheek poke at the national political scene. After four years, he was syndicated and carried in over one hundred and fifty newspapers around the country. It was strange how things sometimes worked out. He was much happier now and was making more money than when he was in charge of the Record.

Yes, life was good, he thought as his phone rang.

"May I speak to Bill Daniels please?"

Daniels didn't recognize the voice. "This is Bill."

"Mr. Daniels. My name is Mike Johnson. I work in the White House. I understand that you're a friend of President Kendall."

Daniels was surprised. "Yes. I am. Or I was when he lived here. I haven't spoken to him for about a year, maybe longer. What is this all about, Mr. Johnson? What can I do for you?"

"Mr. Daniels, you no doubt have been following the news. I'm in Colorado handling some matters for the government related to this tragedy. I need to speak to you. Are you available today?"

Although the reporter in him was curious, Daniels was cautious. "What is this all about? What does this have to do with me?" Instinctively, he grabbed a pad of paper.

"This is confidential, and I think it's best if we discussed this in person. Are you available today?"

Daniels hesitated. "What is it that you do, exactly, Mr. Johnson?"

"I work for the Justice Department. I have been asked to follow up on some legal matters related to the president. I can't go into the details on the phone. Are you available at one?"

Daniels frowned. There's a story here. He hadn't done any investigative reporting in years, but his instincts told him there was far more to Mr. Johnson's request. He was intrigued. Besides, David Kendall was a friend. Still, it was odd. Why would a Justice Department…what…a lawyer, he guessed…want to speak to him?

"Mr. Daniels. This is urgent."

"Okay. Okay. Let's meet at La Cantina San Miguel. That's in Cortez, on East Main Street."

By the time he hung up, Daniels was more than curious. Although he was a good judge of character, the restaurant was a reasonable precaution and would allow him to size up the man in person.

He glanced at the notes he had scribbled on the pad then frowned as he remembered something. *Looks like I won't be golfing today*, he thought.

———

Richter summarized his conversation for the president. "He was suspicious, of course."

Kendall smiled. "He's a reporter. That's his nature. You'll need to be honest with him. Otherwise, he'll know something isn't right and that might backfire on us. We need to trust the man." They had debated this before, but Richter was still leery. He glanced at his watch; he had to leave soon and, in the little time left, he needed to learn as much about Daniels as he could.

———

"I'm in Council. I have a copy of the video." They were parked in front of a small restaurant half a block from the bank.

"Is it him?"

"I don't know. The height and build look right, but I'm not sure about the face." The bank video was black and white, grainy. The color photo she had emailed him was probably from the identification badge system, he guessed.

"I emailed you a digital copy of the video. Maybe your people can enhance it."

"Good thinking. Okay. I'm going on the assumption that it's him. They may have stolen a dump truck in Elk City. The truck was discovered in a junk yard close by. A Jeep and a set of plates were stolen from the junk yard. I'm sending you a description and plate information."

Jackson hung up and went to wake Malouf. Searching for the car, without leveraging the local sheriff or the state police, would be tough. They would have to canvass the streets in town and then the surrounding countryside, all without attracting attention. There were so many places that a car could be hidden. He sighed. Well, he thought, it beat government work.

———

Bill Daniels studied the man at the door. He appeared to be in his mid-thirties and was dressed in jeans and a grey, zippered sweatshirt. He didn't look like he was enjoying his visit to Cortez. *Must have had a fight with his wife or girlfriend*, Daniels thought.

As a reporter, he was an unapologetic people watcher and, living in Cortez, there was normally a steady flow of visitors to feed his hobby. There were several other diners at nearby tables, and the man glanced at each before his eyes settled on Daniels.

It can't be him, Daniels thought. Yet the man walked directly over to his table.

"Mr. Daniels? I'm Mike Johnson."

Daniels gestured to the chair across from him.

"I'm surprised, Mr. Johnson. I was expecting you to be wearing a suit. Instead you look like you're out running errands."

"I apologize. Normally I do wear a suit." *At least that's not a lie*, Richter thought. "Listen, is there some place we can talk?"

Daniels studied the man. He was fit, and his eyes had a certain look, like he could be dangerous if cornered. There was also something else: a sense of urgency, but at the same time a wariness, perhaps. Regardless, his instincts told him that this man meant him no harm.

They found a table in the empty back room. After the waitress brought drinks, Daniels sat back, waiting.

"So what can I do for you, Mr. Johnson? What is so urgent that someone from the Justice Department comes all the way out to Cortez to meet me…dressed like he was going to The Home Depot?"

"Do you remember a meeting you had with our mutual friend eight years ago? It was after he sold his company and began to focus on Social Security reform."

Daniels stared back for a second before he nodded. There had been several such meetings.

"Your paper had run a front page article on him, and you wrote an editorial supporting his push for reform."

Daniels nodded again, remembering the editorial. He had written that while he couldn't evaluate whether Kendall's plan would work, at least he had brought a comprehensive proposal to the table and had started the public dialogue on finding a solution versus merely adding to all of the chatter about what was wrong.

"Our friend asked to meet with you. You had dinner."

"Yes. That was the first time I met him personally."

"Right. You challenged him that night. You told him that if he wanted to accomplish something, he needed to do it from inside the system."

Daniels nodded again. "Yes. I told him to…"

"You told him to put his money where his mouth is. You told him about the soon-to-be-open Senate seat, which wasn't yet public knowledge. You encouraged him to run."

Daniels sat back, thinking. "Yeah. I remember. But what does all of that have to do with this…with why you wanted to meet with me?"

Richter held up his hand. "Do you remember what he said to you that night?"

Daniels nodded again. "Yes. He…"

"He told you, off the record, that he wasn't sure if he wanted to put his family through the scrutiny that comes with public office. He also shared something very personal with you that night: that his wife had breast cancer. That this was why he sold his business."

Daniels felt a shiver crawl up his spine and his head began to spin.

"You told him that your wife had a cancer scare too, years earlier, and you would understand if he decided not to run."

The prickles reached his neck; Daniel sensed something big coming.

"I shared all of that with you, Mr. Daniels, so that you know I'm for real. Our friend Dave did not reveal that conversation to anyone else other than to his wife and to me."

Mr. Johnson held out a leather wallet, letting it flip open. "My name is Matthew Richter. I'm a Secret Service agent. I was on that plane eleven days ago."

———

After four hours of driving through the streets of Council, Idaho, and then through the various state and county roads, they found the Jeep in an RV park northeast of town. There was little of value inside the car: no scraps of paper, no garbage, nothing. Even the glove compartment was empty. They had even taken the car's registration and insurance certificate.

He pulled out his cell phone. "We found it," he said when she answered, then gave her the details.

"They must have stolen another car in the area. Stay where you are. I'll check and call you back shortly."

After twenty minutes of waiting, they drove back to town for coffee. They had just climbed back into their car when the phone rang.

"There's no report of any stolen cars in Council or nearby towns. Either it hasn't been reported yet or they're hiding out. You need to check the trailer park. See if there has been any suspicious behavior, if anyone noticed anything."

CHAPTER FIFTY-ONE

"My God, Dave! I can't believe it's you!" Bill Daniels hesitated, then hugged the president.

"I know. I know. I look like hell." Kendall smiled. "But it's good to see you, Bill."

"I don't know what to say! Wow!" Daniels shook his head. "What the heck happened? What's going on? I've got a million questions."

They were in the bedroom of a cheap motel in Cortez. The president steered his friend to the armchair next to the bed.

"I'm sure you do, but here's the short version. This was an assassination attempt. Agent Richter figured it out beforehand and rescued me. We were stranded in the wilderness, in that blizzard that I'm sure you heard about. I would not be alive now if it weren't for Agent Richter."

"Wow! How did..." Daniels stopped, shook his head. "Dave, what do you need me to do?"

"I know." Kendall patted his shoulder. "This whole thing has been surreal. I need your help, Bill."

———

"Did you find anything in the trailer park?"

"No. No one saw anything. And there's no sign they hid here. It looks like it was just a place to dump the car."

Jackson waited for instructions.

"I think they might be in Colorado. There was a car reported stolen about seven miles north of Council. That same car was found this morning at a truck stop outside of Durango, but it looks like they switched plates. My guess is that they're still somewhere in the Durango area. You need to get down there now and check it out."

"What about the bank video? Is it him?"

"My people are still working on that. How long before you can get to Durango?"

He checked his watch. It was 5:15 p.m.

"I'm not sure. I don't know how far it is. We probably won't be able to get there until tomorrow morning."

He heard a curse on the other end of the line.

"Okay. Get on the road now. Call me when you're there."

Before he could say anything, she hung up. He sighed. It would be another long night.

———

Peggy Daniels threw her arms around the president. "Oh, Dave! I can't believe you're alive! When Bill told me…well, thank God you're okay."

Kendall returned the embrace. "It's good to see you, Peggy."

She let go, stepped back and wiped the tears from her face. "I'm sorry. I'm forgetting my manners. Please introduce me to your friends." She laughed. "Hey, can I still call you Dave?"

Kendall laughed, told her she could, then made the introductions.

"It's nice to meet all of you. Can I get everybody something to drink?" There was a beeping noise from the kitchen. "Excuse me. That will be the lasagna. Bill, would you see what everyone wants?"

Peggy headed towards the kitchen.

"Okay, gentlemen, what can I get you? Soda? Beer? Wine? Something stronger?"

As Bill served drinks, the smell of the lasagna wafted in from the kitchen. Moments later, Peggy called them to the dining room for dinner.

Dinner was a surreal event for the four men who, for the last week and a half, had been living in the wilderness on dehydrated food and then fast food as they fled across the country in stolen cars. Peggy proved a charming conversationalist and kept a dialogue going throughout the meal, learning about Jack and Derek, then sharing stories about her children, about Bill and the life they now had in Cortez.

Peggy turned to Richter. "Matt," she playfully scolded him. "You haven't touched your wine."

He smiled. "Sorry, ma'am. If I drink any more, I'll fall asleep. The lasagna was incredible, though. I haven't eaten a home-cooked meal like that since...well, I can't remember the last time."

"Do you work for the government too, Matt?"

Richter gave a weak smile. "Guilty as charged."

"Tell me about yourself. Where did you grow up?"

After chatting for several minutes, Richter excused himself and left with Bill to tour the property and to assess the security. Jack and Derek took the opportunity to help themselves to more lasagna. Peggy smiled as she watched the boys eat. The sound of a door opening interrupted her thoughts, and she turned and watched as Richter and her husband stepped outside. She turned back to Kendall and frowned.

"Matt's with the Secret Service, isn't he?"

Kendall nodded. "He saved my life more than once over the last few days."

"He's a strong man, but it's obvious he's under incredible pressure. You too, Dave." She took a sip of wine. "So, what happened?"

"Peggy, there's a lot I can't tell you for obvious reasons. Okay?" He patted her hand. "And frankly, my coming here puts you and Bill in danger. I'm truly sorry about that."

She brushed away the concern. "You know we would do anything for you and Maria." She gasped. "My God! Maria! Oh, the poor thing. I saw her on TV the other night. They had a prayer vigil for you and for everyone on the plane. The camera kept coming back to Maria and the girls. Oh, Dave! I feel so bad for them!"

Kendall wiped a tear from his cheek. "I do too."

CHAPTER FIFTY-TWO

Tuesday, May 4

It was 7:45 a.m. when they turned onto Route 160. Called Main Street in Cortez, Route 160 continued straight east through town about a mile and a half, and then on for another forty-five miles to Durango.

Jackson woke up when they stopped at the traffic light. He stretched and yawned then checked the time. Only five hours of sleep. He was stiff and sore from the car.

"Where are we?"

"Cortez, Colorado. Durango is another hour further."

"Let's stop here. I need to take a piss."

They spotted a gas station on the next block and Malouf pulled in. Next door was a donut shop. Jackson climbed out, stretched again, then walked toward the donut store. He called over his shoulder, "You get gas. I'll get us some breakfast."

Five minutes later, he walked out of the shop and stopped on the sidewalk for a moment, basking in the sunshine. The skies were a deep blue and, although chilly, the sun felt good. The TV in the donut shop said the temperature would climb to sixty-five degrees today. After the last ten days in the cold and snow, this was a welcome change. He noted that the town was an eclectic mix of architectural styles, from the dark-brown, rough-wooden structure that sold western wear to the Mexican adobe facade of the local cantina to the Greek style of the turn-of-the-century bank building. There was a single-screen cinema with a marquee that jutted out over the sidewalk, a microbrewery, two antique shops, and several restaurants.

He began walking back to the gas station as the light at the intersection changed. Glancing at the traffic driving by, he noted three pickup trucks and one minivan passing by and, coming toward him from the other direction, a battered and rusty SUV, another pickup truck, and at the end of the line, a dark green Ford Explorer.

Jackson stopped short, staring at the driver. He had the beard, like the man in the video, and the distinctive jaw line was clear. What grabbed his attention were the eyes. They were continually shifting; studying the surroundings. Jackson had seen those eyes before. Usually on soldiers. Sometimes on the police. Always on Secret Service agents. As the car passed, the man turned and their eyes met for just a second. His eyes were dark and hard. Suddenly the Explorer sped up and turned off Main Street.

He tried not to spill the coffee as he ran back to the car.

———

Sitting at the stop light, Richter felt the hairs on the back of his neck stand up. He glanced out the passenger window, scanning the people on the sidewalk. Then his eyes shifted to the mirrors and the cars turning at the intersection. What had spooked him? His eyes continued across the intersection to the pedestrians on the other side road. The light changed and he edged forward at the same time his eyes locked on the tall black man holding the cup of coffee. As he passed, the man turned and hurried down the sidewalk and Richter felt a wave of panic. At the next intersection, he made a split-second decision and turned right onto a side road and sped up as he drove north. As he raced up the street, he remembered where he had seen the man before.

"Where are we going? What's wrong?"

Ignoring Bill's questions, he scanned the mirrors and eased off the accelerator as he approached the speed limit. He wanted to put some distance between himself and the man, but he didn't want to attract the attention of the local cops. Moments later a black Chevy Suburban turned sharply off Main Street behind them. Richter cursed and began looking for options. On their left was a residential neighborhood and on the right a park or a school with a large expanse of green lawn. The approaching traffic light was red. He waited until the last second to brake and, with no cross traffic, he ignored the light and made a sharp right-hand turn. In his mirror he watched as, seconds later, the Suburban ignored the light as well. *Shit. Not a good sign.*

"Bill." Richter kept his voice calm. "I recognized someone back there. He's following us."

Daniels glanced in the side view mirror. "The black truck behind us?"

Richter nodded. "Do you recognize them?"

Daniels shook his head. Richter's eyes darted back and forth from the mirrors to the road ahead. There was a parking lot ahead on the right.

He pointed. "Is there another exit to that lot?"

"Yeah. " Daniels pointed past the building. "On the side street running perpendicular to us."

Richter pulled in and, seeing the other entrance at his two o'clock, turned and sped across the spaces, ignoring a horn and angry stares from two women in a minivan. In his side view mirror, he saw the Suburban pull into the lot behind them, then the blaring of horns as the Suburban raced across the lot.

"Hang on!" he yelled.

He stomped on the accelerator and the Explorer leapt forward, its engine growling. When he reached the exit, he slammed the brakes, turned left onto the side street then punched the gas again. They were racing back toward the road they'd just been on. The light was green, and Richter made a sharp left-hand turn, tires squealing on the pavement as he accelerated. A moment later, the sound of horns and tires squealing told him the Suburban had reached the intersection.

He sped up the block, then hit the brakes hard, taking the first right turn, then another right on the first side street and then a left. He began racing north, passing another residential area on the right and a hospital on the left. Half a mile later, they roared through another intersection and the town faded behind them.

In his rearview mirror, he saw the Suburban a quarter of a mile back.

The engine growled as the speedometer hit seventy. Richter glanced from his mirrors to the road ahead, considering the narrowing options. He could continue to lead his pursuers away from the president, acting as a decoy, but he wasn't sure if the men behind him were working alone. He felt a growing unease as he drove farther away from the man he had sworn to protect. There was only one option.

As the Suburban narrowed the distance, Richter spotted a road on the right that seemed to disappear into the hills.

"Where does that go?"

"There was on old airfield out here years ago," Daniels answered. "It's been shut down for some time now. I think that's the access road."

Richter broke hard, turning onto the narrow lane. The back end of the Explorer began to slip on the sand and dirt that had blown across the seldom-used road. He eased off the gas until he found traction then accelerated again. In their wake, a large dust cloud billowed up behind them.

Two miles down the road, Richter let off the gas and scanned his mirrors searching for the Suburban. For a moment, he was afraid he lost them, then the Suburban emerged from the dust. He began to alternatively tap the gas pedal and shift from drive to neutral causing the car to buck.

"Get down! Now!" Richter yelled as he continued to buck the Explorer, hoping that it would appear that they were having engine trouble. The Suburban came up behind them, filling the

rearview mirror. Richter watched and waited. *Come on! Come on!*
He coaxed. Suddenly, the Suburban swung out to the other lane,
as if to pass. Richter slammed on the brakes and turned the
wheel sharply to the left, catching the Suburban's rear bumper.
The larger vehicle spun across the roadway in front of them,
tilting precariously up on two wheels before straightening and
spinning the other way.

By the time the Suburban came to a stop, forty yards away,
Richter was out running, his gun pointed at the driver. The Suburban suddenly spun around and, tires sliding on the sandy black-
top, accelerated towards him. Richter dropped into a shooting
stance and fired twice, then dove out of the way as the Suburban
flew past before veering off the road into the scrub brush where
it stopped. Richter jumped up and charged the truck, his gun
now pointed at the passenger.

"Put your hands where I can see them!" He shouted twice
more before the black man put his hands on the dashboard.
Richter, still yelling, continued around the side of the truck and
yanked open the door.

"Get out! Get out! Move it! Get on the ground now! On
the ground now! Hands behind your head!"

The black man stumbled out, hands in the air, then lay face
down in the dirt.

"Hands behind your head! Lock your fingers! Get your face
in the dirt!"

When the man was slow to respond, Richter stomped on
the back of his head. The man screamed in pain as his head
struck the ground. Reflexively, he pulled his head up, and Rich-

ter struck him again. Then he stepped between the man's spread legs and kicked him once more. He stepped back, panting, as the man curled into a fetal position. He took a deep breath and glanced back down the road, confirming they were still alone. Holding the man's head down with his foot, Richter holstered his weapon, then checked the man's pulse and breathing. Satisfied that he was only dazed, Richter yanked the man's arms behind his back and, using the man's own handcuffs, secured his wrists.

After searching his prisoner, he placed the gun on the hood of the Suburban. He flipped open the two billfolds, shook his head, and then dropped them on the hood as well. He turned to the driver. The man's face was a mess of blood; one lifeless eye stared vacantly at nothing. He pulled the body out, letting it fall like a rag doll to the ground. Like his partner, the dead man had a gun, a pair of cuffs and two billfolds. Richter placed everything on the hood then searched the Suburban, finding two more guns, extra clips of ammunition, various fake IDs and a newspaper. Everything went on the hood of the truck.

Richter turned as Daniels walked up. Daniels stared at the body then glanced at Richter. He doubled over suddenly and threw up.

CHAPTER FIFTY-THREE

Several hours later, they drove down the dirt road to what Daniels referred to as his ranch. The Daniels lived on a thirty-seven-acre spread, south of town, close to Mesa Verde National Park. They passed the main house and drove up to a large sheet metal building that housed Daniels' motor home and boat. Daniels opened the large sliding door, and Richter pulled the Explorer inside.

Climbing out, he heard noises behind him and turned as Derek, Jack, and the president joined them.

"What happened to you guys? We were getting worried—Jesus Christ! Are you okay?"

Richter, aware of the blood on his shirt and pants, ignored Jack's question as he stepped around them and closed the shed's door.

The president grabbed his arm. "Are you hurt?"

Richter shook his head. "No, sir. We had a run in with some guys who were following us. But we're okay."

Kendall nodded soberly. "So, they know we're alive."

Richter nodded, then gave them an abbreviated version of

the tense morning, leaving out the part where they hid the driver's body and the blood splattered Suburban in a dilapidated building at the old airfield.

"Do you think there are others?"

"I don't know yet. But we're going to find out." Richter walked to the back of the Explorer and opened the hatch. He dragged the hooded figure out. "Bill, I'm going to need a chair and some duct tape."

———

As Monahan climbed out of the car, he heard laughter and shouts—the high-pitched, excited voices of girls coupled with the bluster and banter of boys. He glanced down his tree-lined street and saw the group of children rounding the corner. Two or three were on skateboards, most had iPod wires dangling from their ears, and all were laden with backpacks. They seemed happy, carefree as they made their way up the block. He glanced at his watch. It was 3:00 p.m. He shook his head and smiled.

He nodded to his driver then made his way up the front walk. He had met with Broder and, despite that or maybe because of it, he felt better than he expected. It was the sense of relief, he decided; the feeling that he wasn't carrying around the weight of the world—or at least the weight of the FBI and it's overbearing director—on his shoulders. He had postponed the meeting a day, partly because he had spent most of the prior day in bed after arriving home at two-thirty in the morning, but more so because he needed time to sort through the emotions and jumble of thoughts in his head.

He was frustrated that he had been pulled off the case, especially after the progress they had made. They had uncovered evidence that pointed to a conspiracy involving the Secret Service, the Air Force, and the Mexican drug cartels. How many others were involved? He felt an obligation to uncover exactly what had happened and to obtain justice. But he wouldn't get that chance now.

Surprisingly, Broder hadn't fired him. Instead, Broder told him he was on administrative leave, whatever the hell that meant. Even more surprising, he had been allowed to keep his credentials, his gun, and his driver. *If this was the limbo the nuns had warned about back in grammar school*, he thought with a smile, *maybe it wasn't such a bad thing.*

He had just stepped into his house when his phone rang. He debated for a moment whether he should answer, whether he should even check the display to see who was calling, but thirty years of habit won out. He glanced at the number: Brett Donahue, the SAIC from San Antonio.

"What can I do for you, Brett?"

There was an uncomfortable silence. "Sir, I know you're no longer on the case, and I'm sorry to hear that."

There was another pause and Monahan sighed. It was the first of a string of pity calls, something he should have expected, but also something he had no desire to hear right now. Before he could say anything, Donahue continued.

"I thought you would want to know about something else we just came across." Donahue sounded excited.

Monahan felt his pulse quicken. "What have you got?"

"Early this morning, we found a pickup truck about ten miles from where we found that body. It was on a ranch about two miles from the border, hidden in some brush. Mexican tags." There was a pause. "We found a head inside: male, decomposing...."

Having witnessed some gruesome scenes in his years as an agent, Monahan had a good idea of what the inside of the truck must have looked like.

"We're doing the DNA testing now, but it looks like it belongs to the body. But even more importantly," Donahue continued, "we found a cell phone. We've been reviewing the contact list and call log all day and, so far, two numbers are very concerning."

Monahan glanced up. His wife was in the hallway. He held his finger up and shook his head. It was a signal that after thirty-two years of marriage she knew all too well. A bit put out, she turned away.

"Go on," he prodded.

"One of the numbers is for a cell phone that belongs to Secret Service Agent Cal Mosby."

Monahan felt a sudden excitement, the rush he always felt as the pieces of the puzzle began to come together.

"And the second is for a bank in Luxembourg. In the contact details, there was an account number. We contacted the bank. It took some effort, a lot of twisted arms, and some help from Interpol, but we found out that the account belongs to Cal Mosby."

———

Bill and Derek spent the afternoon acquiring the items on Richter's list. They weren't ready until almost 9:00 p.m.

The black man sat in a wooden chair, his arms handcuffed behind him, his legs duct-taped to the chair. A bandanna covered his eyes. Richter sat across from him. He placed the man's cell phone on the table between them and connected it to a digital recorder, then sat back and studied his prisoner. He had confirmed his suspicions earlier in a private, somewhat physical conversation. The man's real name was Joe Reed.

Richter leaned over. Reed flinched as he felt Richter's hot breath on his face. Richter let him stew for a moment.

"Okay, Reed. One more time."

After Reed finished, Richter stood, then without warning thrust his straightened fingers into the man's solar plexus. Reed doubled over, as if kicked by a mule, his face contorted in pain. After several seconds, Richter pulled his hand away. He watched Reed wheeze and struggle to breathe. It took another fifteen seconds before his breath finally came in a series of shallow pants.

Reed shook his head, tears running down his cheeks. "Okay! No more! Please!"

Richter studied him again. Earlier, after seeing Reed's bloody face and apparent broken nose, the president had pulled Richter aside.

"I want him alive. I know you had no choice with Mosby and with that other one. But I want him to face justice. I want to know who's behind this." The president's tone was stern. "I will not condone torture, Agent Richter."

Richter wanted Reed alive as well. He had been trained to

subdue a person without inflicting permanent physical damage. And if he needed to inflict a little pain? Well, he thought as he studied Reed, the president wasn't here now.

When Reed finally recovered, Richter sat down. "Are you ready to make the phone call?"

The blindfolded man nodded. Richter stuck an earphone in his own ear and dialed the number. The call was answered on the first ring.

"Where the hell are you? You were supposed to call me this morning!" Richter heard the fury and watched as Reed stiffened.

"I tried to call you, but I couldn't get through. Then my battery died and I had to go and buy another."

"Why didn't you call me from a land line?"

"You told me never to use a land line."

There was silence. "Do you have anything?"

"Nothing yet. We visited most of the motels and hotels in town and quietly checked around to see if anyone fitting that agent's description had checked in. We spoke to the local police, too, but there's nothing on the car. We checked the hospital as well."

"Why the hospital?"

"It struck me that they may be injured." Richter watched as Reed paused for a moment. "Were you able to confirm that it's him? In the bank video?"

"Yes. It's him. And if he's alive, then the president is alive as well. What are you doing now?"

"We're going to check into a motel to get some sleep. We've been up for over forty hours. Then, tomorrow, we're going to check surrounding towns."

Richter nodded. Reed was following the script.

"Keep your phone on tonight. I'll check surrounding towns to see if anything has been reported stolen." The phone went dead.

———

It was just after midnight when Monahan jumped out of bed, grabbing his phone. He checked the caller ID. Area code 970. No name. He stepped into the hallway, closing the door behind him.

"Monahan speaking."

"Mr. Monahan. My name is Bill Daniels. I need to speak to you about the crash."

"Mr. Daniels, do I know you?"

"No. I'm a newspaper columnist."

Damn. Another media vulture. *For Christ's sake*, he wanted to scream, *it's midnight!* Instead, he took a breath. "Look, I'm not prepared to make any comments or answer any questions. You can try calling the FBI Media Affairs Office."

Monahan was about to hang up when he heard something. He put the phone back to his ear.

"…I have some information related to the accident."

"Say that again please."

"I said I'm not calling as a journalist. I'm calling as a friend of…let's call him Dave. I have some information on the accident which I think you'll want to hear."

Five minutes later, Monahan hung up, stunned. His mind

raced as he wrestled with the implications. The caller, Bill Daniels or whoever he really was, had mentioned several things that only a few people were supposed to know. Daniels knew about Project Boston and Monahan's meetings with the president. More disturbing, he had confidential information about the crash investigation, including the fact that Agent Mosby had been shot and killed and the location of his body—exactly where they had had found it outside the miner's shack. Was there a leak in the FBI? Monahan wondered. What was most chilling was the man's response when asked how he learned this information.

"There's only one way, Mr. Monahan. Our friend Dave told me."

The caller had insinuated that the president was alive and that he had seen him recently. *This could be a crank call*, Monahan realized. They had received so many false tips over the last week. Most of the callers were insane, with theories of aliens, the Russians, or Mafia involvement, and even one who swore that a descendant of Lee Harvey Oswald was responsible. Of the hundreds of calls they had received so far, over ninety percent had been discounted immediately. The rest were assigned to a team of investigators, but as of yet, no credible leads had surfaced.

No one could have survived that crash. He had not only flown over the debris field by helicopter, he had walked through sections of the crash site with the NTSB investigators. He had seen the size of the crater and the torn and twisted metal of the airplane. He had seen the bodies, or what was left of them. Even though both McKay and Mosby had survived—for a short while at least—logic told him that the president was dead.

But then how did Daniels know about Project Boston? How did he know about his conversations with the president? How did he know about Agent Mosby? And how did he get Monahan's cell phone number?

In the kitchen, Monahan made a pot of coffee as he contemplated what to do. Daniels told him to expect another call within thirty minutes and not to speak to anyone until then. While he waited, he did some research on his Blackberry and found that the area code was in Colorado. He made a note to have the number traced. He also learned that Bill Daniels was a syndicated newspaper columnist, living in Colorado. As Monahan poured a cup of coffee his Blackberry buzzed. Same area code, different number.

"Monahan speaking."

There was a long pause, then: "Pat. It's Dave. I realize that this is tough to swallow, but it's me."

Monahan recognized the voice. "But…how?"

"I can't go into that now. Suffice it to say that one of my friends, Matthew, saved me. I'm sure you know who I'm referring to. He's on the line with us by the way."

"Sir, where are you now? Why don't you go to the local police? They'll protect you until I send my people."

"This is Matthew. You need to understand our reluctance to share that with you. There appear to be a number of people involved in this…situation. More than you can imagine. We ran into two more today. One of them used to work in Dave's house. At this point, I don't trust anyone."

"Okay. I think I understand." Monahan paused. "What are

you proposing?"

"We need to find out who's behind this. Then we need to figure out how to get Dave home."

"Okay." Monahan was unsure what to do next. "Do you have any ideas?"

"I recorded a phone call that…our visitor made."

"Matthew, if I understand you correctly, that recording may not be admissible…."

"I don't give a shit right now about rules for search and seizure or rules for evidence! I don't care about Miranda rights! I need to know how big this thing is and who I can trust!"

"Okay. Okay. I understand. How do you want to do that?"

"I'm going to give you a phone number. I want a wiretap on it ASAP, within the next hour."

Monahan jotted down the number.

"I want to know who this person calls and who calls them and what they say. As soon as you have anything, call us back."

"Okay. I can do that."

"One last thing. Whoever handles this must report to you and you alone. I don't want anyone else involved yet. Not even your boss." A pause. "Especially not your boss. Are we clear?"

CHAPTER FIFTY-FOUR

Wednesday, May 5

Like a soldier, Richter woke instantly, his body tense as he scanned his surroundings. He reached for the phone, noting the time. 3:30 a.m. He had been dozing on and off in a recliner for the last several hours, waiting for the call.

"Matthew. This is Pat. I have some information. There was only one outgoing call from that number. Not good news. They're expanding their search. They've added more.... resources."

Richter sighed. "Okay. I was expecting that. Anything else?"

"Yes. What time was the call that you recorded?"

Richter picked up Reed's phone and scanned the call log. "8:33 p.m."

"Are you in Mountain Time?"

Richter hesitated. "For the moment."

"I thought so. We accessed the record of calls made before we put the tap in place. There were two calls last night, both to the same number. The first was at 11:07 p.m., Eastern Time.

That's thirty-four minutes after your visitor's call. The second was at 11:59 p.m."

"Who did she call?"

"That's the disturbing part. I'd rather not say over the phone."

"I assume this goes all the way up, possibly to the number two man."

There was a pause. "Yes. How did…..? Never mind."

"Continue to monitor the number, but don't do anything else. I'll contact you later." Richter hung up and hurried to the president's room. Kendall woke with a start.

"Sir. We need to leave. Right now."

———

At 10:00 a.m., as they were nearing Albuquerque, New Mexico, the president placed the call. He heard the phone click but didn't give the other person a chance to speak.

"Hi. It's me. No names. Okay?"

"Okay." There was a brief pause. "You got a new phone?"

"Yes. We picked up several."

"That was smart."

"I'll pass that on. Listen. I'm sure you understand now how big this might be."

"I do. But, sir, I'm at a disadvantage. I'm only using one person, and she reports directly to me. The phone we're monitoring is a cell phone. If I could put some men on the ground, with the technology we have, there's a good chance we would be able to chase this person down."

"First things first. From the calls that you listened to, do you have enough evidence to tie this back to the source?"

"Not yet. We need to complete a voice analysis. I would also like to monitor the number she called. And it would help if we could pick up the caller and interview her. Then we might be able to build a case. Right now, I don't think we have enough to directly tie your...assistant to this."

"Hang on." The president relayed the information to Richter. "Okay, continue to monitor the caller's phone. Can you monitor the recipient's phone without anyone else finding out?"

"Yes. I think so."

"Do it now."

"Yes, sir."

"I need you to do something else as well."

"Absolutely, sir."

"I need you to commandeer a plane."

It was a moment before Monahan answered.

"Okay. I should be able to do that."

"Do it. I want you to assemble a team of agents. Four or five other people that you trust completely, that are loyal to you alone. And I don't want anyone else to know about this. Can you do that?"

"Yes. I can."

There was no hesitation, the president noted. "Good. We told you about our visitor yesterday. The one who made the phone call for us?"

"Yes..."

"I'm going to tell you where to find him." The president

gave Monahan an address. "I want you to pick him up. I want him in your custody. You're going to want to talk to him. Personally."

"Yes, sir."

"Good. I want you to leave right away, within the next hour if possible. I'll call you later."

CHAPTER FIFTY-FIVE

The FBI-owned Gulfstream G550 landed at Durango-La Plata Airport shortly after 4:00 p.m. and taxied to the private terminal. Monahan had to pull a few strings to arrange the flight on such short notice. That hadn't been difficult, given his position as deputy director. His administrative leave, apparently, was only between Broder and himself.

Monahan and a team of four agents were met at the terminal door by the gate agent. "Mr. Monahan, welcome to Durango. Your two cars are right outside in spaces seven and eight. Here're the contract and keys. Do you need any directions?"

"No, thank you." Monahan handed a set of keys to another agent as they walked out into the bright sunshine. Twenty minutes later, the cars pulled into the fenced lot of the self-storage facility, drove past four aisles before turning between two rows of storage units. They stopped halfway down, in front of number fifty-one. The team of agents climbed out then turned expectantly to Monahan.

"Wait here." He walked to the end of the row of lockers and

found the garbage can around the side. He tipped the can over and found the key taped to the underside. He jogged back to the locker. "Let's close off this row."

Two of the agents moved the cars, one to each end of the driveway, parking them sideways to block access to the aisle. Another agent handed Monahan a pair of latex gloves. He opened the locker's garage door. Inside was a dark green Ford Explorer with a mangled front end. An agent with a video camera began to record the scene while two other agents opened the doors. They heard noises in the back and opened the tailgate to find a bound and gagged man lying in back. He struggled against his restraints.

"Get him out now. Check his condition and get him some water but keep him cuffed."

As one agent tended to the man, another handed Monahan an envelope.

"This was on the front seat."

Monahan's name was written on the front. He pulled out the hand-written note.

This is Joe Reed. He is a former Secret Service Uniformed Officer who was fired for stealing from the White House and the First Family. He and his partner were chasing us. They knew we were alive. I suspect that their contact was providing detailed updates on the investigation. They were able to track us from Idaho to Colorado, probably by tracing stolen automobiles and ATM withdrawals.

You'll find Reed's partner in Cortez, CO, in a hangar at the abandoned airfield north of town. He's KIA.

In the glove box, there are various IDs and weapons that these two were using.

An agent handed Monahan two Zip-lock bags.

"We found these inside, sir."

Monahan held the bags up and examined them in the light. One contained various shields and credentials for federal agents including, it appeared, the FBI. He swore. The second bag contained three handguns. He turned to the young agent.

"Put all of this in evidence bags."

Monahan turned to the prisoner. "Are you Joe Reed?"

The man nodded.

"Mr. Reed. You are under arrest for treason and for the attempted assassination of the president of the United States." Reed sagged and an agent pulled him up. Monahan turned to another agent. "Read him his Miranda rights."

Monahan spent the next thirty minutes questioning Reed. When he was done, he stepped outside and pondered his next move. What Reed told him was chilling. His contacts knew that the president and Agent Richter had survived the crash and had instructed Reed and his accomplice to track them down. When Monahan asked him why, Reed shook his head, refusing to answer.

Monahan's phone vibrated and he stepped away before answering.

"Hello."

"Hello. Where are you?"

"At the storage locker."

"How is our friend?"

"Fine. I've had a short conversation with him. Obviously I would like some more time, but—"

"There's no time. How many seats are there on your plane?"

"Eight. But I have four men with me, plus our friend. That leaves two open seats," Monahan added hopefully.

There was muffled conversation on the line.

"Okay. I want you to take our friend and fly to Amarillo, TX. I'll call you in two hours."

———

"What's the status?"

The transmission was garbled; her voice cut in and out.

"What was that?" he asked. He had to wait a few seconds for the reply.

"I said I can't reach either of my men."

He was confused. "Are you referring to the first team?"

"Yes. The first team."

"Well? Do you know what happened?"

"No. The second team is in Durango now. So far they haven't picked up any leads."

Shit! He cursed silently. The more he analyzed it, the evidence pointed in one direction. Despite all odds, it appeared that Kendall was alive. And he was running.

"Put every resource you have on this," he ordered. "You need to find him pretty damn quick. And you need to end this!"

After he hung up, he sat back and considered the implications. It now seemed more and more likely that Kendall was alive and running. And now two of Jane's men had disappeared. Could they have been picked up by the police or the FBI? If they had been, would Jane be able to get to them? They needed to resolve that loose end quickly and then find Kendall. He reached for the phone. He knew someone at the CIA, someone he had placed there years ago. Someone who, like Jane, had performed various delicate jobs for him in the past. Someone, he knew, who could help clean up this mess.

He hesitated. It would be risky to bring in another player. He put the phone down. He would give Jane some time.

———

Although tense, Richter didn't let it show. He checked his watch.

"Okay. Bill and I need to go. Are you okay here?"

Kendall nodded. "We'll be fine."

The motor home was well-equipped and comfortable, but for the last several hours there'd been nothing to do but wait. After a while, it began to feel crowded.

"Derek, I need you outside for a moment." Richter grabbed a duffle bag on his way out.

Daniels and Derek followed. They walked past several other travel trailers and motor homes to the picnic tables near the central fire pit. Thankfully, all of the other campers had chosen to sit in front of their own fire pits and they were alone.

"I don't like leaving him, but I don't have a choice." Richter pulled out a fanny pack then turned to Derek. "You said that you hunt, correct?"

Derek's eyebrows went up. "Yes."

Speaking softly, Richter held up a fanny pack. "This is a nine-millimeter pistol. The magazine is full and there is a round chambered. I'm also giving you a spare magazine." His face went dark for a second. "Derek, I don't want you to take this out unless you absolutely, and I mean absolutely, need to. This is illegal, but I can't leave him unprotected. If something doesn't seem right, I would rather that you take him and run before you use this. Okay?"

Derek nodded soberly.

Richter slid the pack across the table. "Do you have the keys for the car?"

Derek patted his pocket. "Right here."

Richter patted him on the shoulder. "Good. I know I can trust you, Derek."

Derek smiled briefly then caught himself, the stony look he had seen on Richter's own face now reflected on his. "Thanks, Matt"

"I'll call within two hours. If I don't for some reason, Bill will. If you don't hear from either of us by midnight, take Dave and run."

"I won't let you down."

CHAPTER FIFTY-SIX

Vicky Jensen clicked the icon on her computer and the recording played again. As she listened through her earphones, she studied the spectrogram on the screen. The monitor showed a graphical depiction of the frequency and amplitude of the speaker's voice over time, in this case a recording of a twenty-seven-second phone call. The spectrogram essentially represented a voiceprint of the speaker, which, much like a fingerprint, was unique.

Agent Jensen was an FBI "techie" and was considered an expert in voice printing. But, unlike some of her peers who had advanced degrees in linguistics and sound-wave theory, her credentials were a training course eight or nine years ago taught by two FBI experts and a scientist from Bell Laboratories. She learned the basic theory behind voice printing and identification and the law enforcement application of voiceprint analysis, its use in criminal investigations, and its admissibility in court cases. The course had given Jensen enough information to be intrigued or, as one instructor put it, enough information to be dangerous.

She had analyzed many recordings over the ensuing years,

and although she always reviewed the recordings and her analysis with one of her more learned colleagues, she had yet to be proven wrong. This time though, Deputy Director Monahan had been very explicit that she perform the analysis herself without seeking a second opinion. She had been an agent for fourteen years, more than enough time to understand that sometimes, even within the FBI, certain investigations were compartmentalized for a multitude of reasons. In this case, the fact that she was analyzing phone calls made to and from a cell phone that belonged to the vice president was sufficiently dangerous that she clearly understood the logic behind Monahan's instructions. The fact that the wiretap and resulting recordings were obtained without a warrant, but under the guise of the Patriot Act was disconcerting by itself.

The theory of voice identification was based on the premise that every individual's voice was uniquely characteristic, sufficiently so to enable it to be distinguished from others through voiceprint analysis. Every person's voice was a unique pattern—a combination of pitch, tone, cadence, and harmonic level—driven by differences in not only their vocal cavities but in their teeth, tongue, lips, and palate. This could be viewed graphically in a spectrogram.

The advent of the digital age had brought with it very sophisticated computer software that significantly enhanced the field of voice printing and, at the same time, put it in the hands of more law enforcement professionals. Over the last several years, the software had become Jensen's second opinion.

After listening a third time, she then loaded another sound

clip, this one a speech made by Vice President Rumson a week ago. It was one minute twenty-four seconds long. *That's more than enough*, she thought. She clicked her mouse again and, as she listened, the spectrogram displayed on her screen.

When the recording finished, she then clicked the compare button. The program utilized a special algorithm to compare the two samples. Two seconds later, she had her answer.

———

The RV Park was seven miles northwest of Amarillo International Airport, close to the highway. Their site not only provided a view of the entrance, but was far enough away from the other campers to afford some privacy. Earlier, after checking in, they drove to the airport and rented two cars, one in Bill's name and one in Peggy's.

Now, as Richter drove one of the cars back to the airport, he quizzed Daniels once again. By the time they approached the airport, Richter was satisfied. He dropped Daniels off at a restaurant a mile away, then continued on to the TAC Air terminal. TAC Air was an FBO, or fixed base operator providing services to private aircraft, located next to the main terminal. As he pulled into the airport lot, he couldn't help but notice that the flag was at half-mast. He picked a parking spot with a clear view of the TAC Air terminal door. Twenty minutes later, he saw a plane begin its landing approach. He watched through binoculars and was able to read the tail number before the jet disappeared behind the terminal building. They were right on time.

Five minutes later, Monahan exited the building and walked

to one of the rental cars in the lot. Moments later, he pulled out onto the access road. Richter waited twenty seconds to see if anyone followed Monahan before he put the car in gear. Traffic was light, and he was able to spot Monahan's car several hundred yards ahead. He punched the speed dial button and when Monahan answered, he instructed him to drive to a shopping center several miles away. As Monahan pulled in, Richter drove past and pulled into the carwash next door. He watched as Monahan parked. After five minutes, and no sign of a tail, Richter dialed again.

"I want you to leave the shopping center and drive back to the airport. Keep the phone line open."

Richter let several cars pass before he pulled out and followed. Several minutes later, Monahan stopped at a traffic light. Richter was three cars back.

"Pull into the restaurant on your right. Keep the line open." With a second phone, Richter punched the speed dial button. Daniels answered immediately. "We're here."

Monahan parked, and Richter pulled in three spaces away. Daniels exited the restaurant, spotted Richter's car, and walked over. Richter climbed out, scanned the parking lot again, and then approached Monahan's car, his Secret Service credentials open in his hand.

Richter climbed in the back. Monahan looked in the rear-view mirror and nodded.

Richter nodded back. "Are you armed?"

"No. I followed your instructions."

"Are your men still on the plane?"

"Yes. Guarding Reed."

He studied Monahan in the mirror. He was nervous, which was understandable, but he kept his hands on the steering wheel. That was smart.

"What's the plan, Agent Richter?"

"We're going to take a drive and have a chat. Based on how that goes, I'll tell you what our next steps are."

———

An hour later, they pulled into the RV Park. With Richter directing, Monahan drove up to the lone RV at the end of the row. He parked and watched as a scruffy young man wearing a fanny pack stepped out of the motor home. The man disappeared around the car then reappeared in Monahan's side view mirror. Another car parked two spaces away and a slightly overweight, older man stepped out. He too wore a fanny pack.

He caught Richter's eyes in the mirror.

"It would be a mistake to underestimate them, Mr. Monahan."

Monahan nodded.

"Let's go."

Monahan climbed out and allowed Richter to search him, not that he had much choice. Then, he was led up the steps, escorted inside, and told to sit at the table. He took a deep breath. He had been preparing himself for this moment since the phone call with Bill Daniels last night. He was both excited and nervous.

Richter stood behind him. "We're ready."

Monahan's eyes went wide as the president stepped out of

the rear bedroom.

———

Frustrated, Rumson stood. Minutes later, flanked by the Secret Service, he climbed into the limo. He was still living in the Naval Observatory, having decided that it wouldn't look good if he forced Kendall's family to move out of the White House. Not yet anyway. As the motorcade pulled through the White House gate, he stared out the window at the lights of Washington. He hadn't heard back from Jane yet. He would have to call her when he got home.

The challenge was that there was a nation to run. He had security briefings, Cabinet meetings, phone calls with foreign leaders, meetings with congressman and staffers and governors, and a myriad of other responsibilities that he had to focus on throughout the day. The crash investigation, while still the number one priority, only occupied a portion of his time. And on top of all of that, Jane and her people had to find Kendall. What the bomb on the plane had failed to do, they now had to do themselves. Kendall had to be shoved back into whatever hole he had crawled out of, along with whoever was helping him. Rumson had to put all of this behind him, and he had to do it soon.

One of the signs of a leader, he knew, was how well he dealt with setbacks, with crisis, with problems that suddenly arose and threatened to unravel carefully crafted plans. He again considered calling his CIA contact, but, once more, decided against it. While things looked dire at the moment, he had faith in Jane. She was resourceful. She would find a way to resolve this. She had never let him down.

———

"Hi, Pat."

Monahan tried to stand, but Richter pushed him back down.

"Mr. President...Sir? I'm at a loss for words."

The president sat across from him. "You understand the gravity of the situation I'm in, don't you?"

"I do, sir."

The president's eyes narrowed as he studied the federal agent for a moment. "Are you here to help me, Mr. Monahan?"

Monahan grimaced. "Yes. Of course, sir."

The president smiled briefly. "Good. There's one thing we need to clear up first." He paused, his eyes narrowing again. "Agent Richter is calling the shots. He's in charge. You and your men will not do anything without his knowledge or approval. Understood?"

Monahan glanced at Richter then nodded again. "Yes, sir. I understand."

The president smiled. "Okay, then. Agent Richter has some questions for you."

Richter sat next to Monahan. "Take us through the crash investigation, the evidence you've gathered over the last twenty-four hours, everything."

Monahan told them about McKay and Mosby, about the body in Laredo and the briefcase, about the cell phone they discovered in the pickup with Mosby's number and the bank account in Luxembourg.

Richter and the president exchanged a glance.

"Do you believe the Mexico angle?" Richter asked.

Monahan frowned. "I did, but after listening to the phone calls, I'm wondering if all of that was just a plant." He described the calls they had recorded and told them that they were now monitoring the vice president's cell phone, but, as of early this evening, there hadn't been any additional calls made by or to that number. Then he described his interview with Reed.

"We haven't picked up the body in Cortez yet," he said at the end.

Richter nodded then changed gears. "How quickly can you do a DNA analysis of blood and hair samples?" He explained what he wanted. "I want it witnessed by at least one other agent. This way, no one can allege that the samples came from before the crash or were obtained from the bodies recovered from the crash."

Monahan nodded. "We should be able to confirm identity in a day, if I push it."

"Push it, Mr. Monahan."

———

The security guard checked Monahan's ID.

"He's an agent as well," Monahan said, nodding toward Richter.

The guard nodded and opened the gate. Monahan drove out onto the tarmac, directly up to the plane. As they pulled up alongside the wing, the stairs descended and two agents climbed down. Richter climbed out of the car and scanned the area. It was shortly before 10:00 p.m. Thankfully, there were no other planes or people about.

He stopped at the foot of the stairs and nodded to the agents. "He's inside?"

The agents nodded back and, with Monahan trailing, Richter bounded up the steps. In the back of the cabin sat a hooded man, his hands and legs cuffed. Two FBI agents stepped out of the way. Ignoring them, Richter walked up to the prisoner. The man appeared to be sleeping. Richter yanked off the hood. Joe Reed blinked several times as his eyes adjusted to the light. When he saw Richter's face, six inches from his own, his body stiffened and his eyes went wide.

"You're going to make another call for me, Reed."

———

Jane didn't recognize the number. She hesitated for a second, debating whether to let the call go to voice mail, but on the fourth ring, she answered.

"Hello?"

"It's me."

She exploded in anger. "Where the hell are you?"

"We ran into some problems. My partner's dead."

"What? How did that happen?"

"He had a heart attack. I just left the hospital."

"Why didn't you call me right away?"

"I couldn't. My phone's broken."

"You're a total fuck-up, Reed!"

"Look. He collapsed and stopped breathing. My phone was on the ground next to me. I called 911 while I was performing

CPR. I think one of the paramedics stepped on it. I bought a new phone as soon as I could."

She mulled over the implications and her next steps. Reed continued talking.

"He was dead on arrival. It's been hectic ever since. I had to talk to the doctors and the police."

"How did you identify yourself?"

"I didn't use any law enforcement credentials if that's what you mean."

"What about your partner?"

"I took his creds and gun before the ambulance arrived."

Jane digested this. "Okay. Are you still in Durango?"

"No. Santa Fe. We were following a lead."

"Give me your address."

Jane jotted it down.

"Stay where you are. I'll call you back."

She hung up then leaned back, thinking. Something didn't feel right. That was two days in a row that he'd been out of touch. That was one coincidence too many. She made another call. The phone was answered immediately.

"I need you to send a man down to Santa Fe. There's a loose end I need taken care of."

CHAPTER FIFTY-SEVEN

Thursday, May 6

It was three in the morning when Monahan hung up the phone.

"The plane arrived back in Washington two hours ago. Reed is now in a safe house. My men are guarding him."

Richter nodded.

"We have a problem. He's demanding a lawyer. We arrested him at the storage locker, read him his Miranda rights. He hasn't been processed or formally charged. This is going to get sticky. I need to speak to a U.S. Attorney."

Richter ignored the veiled request. "What about the wire taps? What's the status?"

"The tap on Rumson's phone's in place. So far, there's been only one call, and that was to the woman, to 'Jane.' We've compared the voice with known voice records for the vice president. It's him."

The door to the motor home opened and Peggy stepped out. Richter lowered the window.

"I made coffee for you guys."

Richter took the two mugs. "Thanks, Peggy."

After she went back inside, Monahan continued. "One problem is that they have not specifically mentioned the president or the bombing." Monahan flipped on the map light and handed Richter a yellow legal pad. "This is a transcript."

Richter read for a moment. "…'Put every resource you have on this. You need to find him pretty damn quick. And you need to end this!'…That sounds pretty damned incriminating to me."

"It does, but I would like to hear him mention the president's name."

Richter flipped off the map light and rubbed his eyes. "Yeah, but we might not get that chance."

"I know. Separately, you know that Jane has dispatched another team to look for you. Again, she never mentioned the president by name or even title, so we have no direct evidence tying her back to the bombing. She's getting nervous though. Shortly after Reed called her, she instructed her second team to locate him. I suspect that she now sees him as a liability. Either way, I think we need to consider locating her and picking her up for questioning. I'll need to get more resources to do that."

Richter was silent for a minute. His first priority was to protect the president and get him back to Washington safely. And with Monahan, his men and the plane, they could do that. But they couldn't just walk back into the White House, could they? And didn't he have an obligation to uncover how widespread this conspiracy was? To make sure those behind it paid the price?

"We need to set up a sting operation. We need to get Rumson to admit that he's behind this. If we pick Jane up, can we get her to wear a wire?"

Monahan shook his head. "She's likely to refuse, but on the chance she agrees, she's going to want a deal. We would have to get the U.S. Attorney involved. We can't cut plea deals on our own. I think that's the same thing Reed is now thinking."

Richter rubbed his eyes again. "Shit."

"Agent Richter," Monahan paused, "Matthew...what you've done is nothing short of amazing. You got him off the plane. You kept him alive in the wilderness, in the middle of a blizzard. My initial reaction was that you were crazy for not turning yourself in to the search and rescue teams. But, with what you knew at the time and what we know now, I can see why you didn't. Your instincts were right. You survived a run-in with Agent Mosby and another one with Reed. I know that you're not only focused on protecting him, you want to hold these bastards accountable as well." Monahan took a breath and shifted in his seat. "Look. I know you don't trust anyone. You don't even trust me. Not completely. I get that. But let me help you. Once we get the president back to Washington...I assume that's what you're planning on doing when the plane returns...what's your next step?"

Richter stared back but said nothing.

Monahan continued: "If you haven't figured that out yet at least let me give you a couple of options."

In the darkness, Richter studied Monahan's eyes. After a long moment, he finally nodded.

———

With seven people, the motor home was crowded, but no one complained. Monahan was sitting at the kitchen table, facing the president and Richter. Derek and Jack were perched in the driver's and front passenger's captain's chairs, which had been turned backwards and now faced into the living area. Bill and Peggy sat on the couch.

"The plane is due to arrive in two and a half hours." Monahan checked his watch. "A little after seven thirty. We need to decide who's coming and who's staying."

"Everybody's coming with us."

Everyone turned toward Richter.

"I know we haven't discussed this yet, but if you stay here, you'll need to be placed into protective custody. There are still people after us, and we've put you all in danger."

"Bill, Peggy," the president interrupted, "I'm sorry, but Agent Richter's right. We can't leave you behind unless Mr. Monahan can provide for your security."

Bill laughed. "Mr. Monahan would have to arrest me to keep me from coming."

The president smiled and turned to Peggy.

"I'm coming as well." She pointed her thumb at Bill. "I'm not going to let him have all the fun."

"And I know Jack and Derek are with us all the way. Right, guys?"

Derek, half asleep, gave a thumbs-up. Jack smiled.

———

Jane wrestled with calling her uncle. The news wasn't good.

There was no sign of Reed in Santa Fe. Her instinct told her it was a false lead. The question was, why? Why would Reed mislead her? Why had he been out of contact over the last two days? His excuses, while plausible, had started to smell bad.

The other troubling fact was that they had lost any trail of President Kendall and Agent Richter. There had been no new information, no leads since the stolen car had been discovered in Durango several days ago. It was a guess on her part that the stolen cars were connected to the president and Richter. Between the dump truck, the cars, the switched plates, and the ATM, she could plot their path on a map. While it was conceivable that it was a series of coincidences, she didn't like coincidences.

So, she came back to the question of Reed. The only explanation that made sense was that he had been picked up by the police and coerced into providing her with misleading information. The question, then, was by who? Certainly not the local police in Durango or Santa Fe or wherever he really was. More likely it was the Secret Service or the FBI. If this was the case, she reasoned, then they were probably trying to track her down. And if Reed had called her, besides trying to mislead her, could he have been trying to set her up? Could they have been monitoring the call? She found that possibility very disturbing.

The other question she had to answer was how? How had the Secret Service or the FBI—or whoever had Reed—how had they found him in the first place? From the reports and updates her uncle had given her, and from her own sources, she knew the investigators were under tremendous pressure to find the president's body. The current theory was that the president and Richter and a handful of other passengers had either been sucked through an engine as the plane came apart or incinerated in the inferno when the plane crashed. From everything she had heard and read, those two theories were plausible.

Consequently, there was no reason for the investigators to suspect that the president and Richter were alive. Unless, she realized, they too had questioned the stolen truck in Elk City and the trail of stolen cars that led to Durango. That didn't make sense, though. Why would they concern themselves with a handful of stolen cars? They would be preoccupied with the crash, not with a rash of auto thefts. Especially when they didn't believe there were any survivors.

And then it dawned on her.

———

The plane landed in Manassas, Virginia, shortly before one in the afternoon and taxied to the private terminal where eight black Chevy Suburbans were waiting. Once the plane stopped, the Suburbans drove up. After the stairs were lowered, two agents jumped out of each vehicle and quickly formed two lines extending from the stairs to the second Suburban. Monahan descended, and after conferring with agents on the ground, signaled to an agent on the plane. The agent escorted the prisoner, hands cuffed, head bowed, and face hidden by a sweatshirt hood, down the steps to the waiting vehicle. Then a second agent escorted another prisoner to the same Suburban. The doors were slammed shut and, as if choreographed, the line of Suburbans pulled forward twenty feet.

Four more prisoners were escorted down the steps, one after another, and loaded into the SUVs.

———

Jane walked out of Walmart with two new cell phones. Her old phone was in a trash dumpster several miles away. In the trunk of her car, she had two suitcases and a duffle bag with everything she needed. Everything else she had left in the apartment. She had prepaid the six month lease three months ago. It would be a while before anyone noticed she was missing.

She was still unsure what to do, which, she realized in a moment of self-reflection, was very uncharacteristic. She would run and hide, that much was certain. Working as she had for a private security firm, she had availed herself of some of the shadier services they had occasionally offered some of their clients. A new identity and a place to hide wouldn't be a problem.

Should she warn her uncle, she wondered. It wasn't so much a question of morals as it was a question of practicality. She genuinely felt loyal to him, justifiably so since he had always been loyal to her. He had made sure she was taken care of after her father died. The question of right versus wrong wasn't a question she spent much time pondering. He'd told her once that one of her strengths was that she didn't let such questions cloud her thinking.

What would her uncle do with the information? If the FBI had been monitoring her phone, it was possible they suspected his involvement. She had spoken to him several times over the last few days, each time using her cell phone. If they were being monitored, there was nothing he could do. While she could run, he couldn't. Telling him might not accomplish anything, except maybe to hasten his downfall as the tension of knowing that the noose was tightening might cause him to act irrationally. Well, maybe not irrationally but uncharacteristically. If they had already connected Reed to her and her to him, then he was fucked. But what if they hadn't made the next connection? She should warn him. Although unlikely, there may be information and records that he would want to destroy. Besides, she needed to tell him herself that she was going to disappear for a while.

———

The line of Suburbans turned into a private drive in the Virginia countryside. The gates closed automatically after the last one. The road disappeared into the forest, and Richter spotted the occasional security camera in the trees. After a minute, the forest gave way to a long manicured lawn, a large house and several outbuildings. The convoy pulled up the circular drive and stopped.

Richter and Monahan jumped out. After conferring with a group of agents, Richter opened the door. President Kendall smiled as he stepped into the sunshine. He stood still for a second then whispered to Richter.

"My God! It feels good to be this close to home."

Under the watchful eyes of two dozen FBI agents, Richter and the president followed Monahan into the house.

CHAPTER FIFTY-EIGHT

Jane scrolled through the list on her computer and found the number. She hadn't had time to transfer her contacts to her new phone yet. She dialed the number and stared out the windshield at passing traffic while she waited. After eight rings she hung up.

She pulled back out into traffic, heading south.

———

Everyone had gathered in the ornate library by the time Richter arrived. The president, clean-shaven and smiling, wore khaki pants, a golf shirt, and loafers. Despite his knee—he was still limping—he was in good spirits. Jack and Derek were dressed in sports shirts and jeans, while Bill and Peggy, like the president, looked like they were ready to tee off. Richter rubbed his own face. A shower, a shave, and new clothes would be nice. For a second, he wondered what the FBI had picked out for him to wear. He shook his head. That would have to wait.

Richter watched the FBI agent hand the president a drink. The agent turned and nodded. Richter nodded back. Special

Agent Wayne Elms had attended a Secret Service training course that Richter had taught years ago.

Elms walked over. "It's damned good to have you guys back, Agent Richter. Can I get you something to drink?"

"Just a water, please." Richter knew Elms wasn't here because of his bartending skills.

Monahan arrived and they all sat down in comfortable leather chairs.

"I see you all have had an opportunity to visit your rooms."

Everyone smiled.

"We're working on bringing this to a close. Right now, I think we'll only be here for a day or two. I'm not making promises, but that's what I believe. In the meantime, you'll be comfortable. You're free to roam around both inside and outside at your leisure." He pointed around the room. "I'm told that this is an extensive library with a wide range of books. We also have subscriptions to numerous newspapers and magazines."

Richter half listened as Monahan described the estate, with its exercise facilities, pool, tennis courts, and hiking trails.

Monahan checked his notes. "Dinner is scheduled for seven. The kitchen staff can accommodate any special needs. Anyway, they'll fill you in on all of that later."

———

Rumson hung up and sat back, staring at the ceiling. Where the hell was Jane? His phone rang again. He picked it up but didn't recognize the number. He let it continue ringing until it stopped. Something struck him, and he scrolled through the call log. The same number had called before. Only a few people had this number. He dialed it. After six rings, he hung up.

He sat back and stared at the ceiling again. Over the last few days, he'd found himself preoccupied with the plaster medallion of the Presidential Seal in the center of the curved ceiling. He had heard that it had been handcrafted back in 1934 when FDR had personally overseen the redesign of the West Wing and the construction of what was now considered the modern Oval Office. Each president since then had left some form of personal imprint here. While many of these changes were temporary, like the paintings and the furniture, which were replaced with each occupant, some were more lasting. Truman was the first to install carpeting that bore the Presidential Seal. Although the carpeting eventually gave way to rugs, the concept of the Seal as a centerpiece in the floor remained. Rumson looked around the room, his eyes stopping on the ornate fireplace and the potted ivy sitting on the mantel. Kennedy had started that tradition.

He would leave his own imprint here as well. He had worked hard for this: to be sitting in this office, behind this desk. He ran his hand across the smooth surface. Fashioned from the timbers of the HMS Resolute, it had been used by so many of his predecessors. They had sat behind this very desk as they had made some of the toughest decisions in history.

It was his desk now. And he had his own decision to make. As much as he didn't want to get anyone else involved, Jane needed help. He glanced at his watch and reached for his phone.

———

After everyone left, the president, Richter, and Monahan sat in front of the fireplace. "We've lost contact with Jane. The last call she made was to her team in Durango. She sent one of her men down to Santa Fe to look for Reed. We know she called from Fairfax, Virginia. We have it narrowed down to about a ten-block area, but—"

Richter interrupted. "She must have deactivated the GPS in her cell phone. She probably pulled the chip or has a jammer. We've seen this before."

Monahan nodded. "We have as well. We were never able to get a GPS signal from her phone. That's why we couldn't track her before, except to the closest cell tower. I have several teams with microwave receivers driving around Fairfax right now. If she makes a call, they can triangulate on her exact location." Monahan frowned. "I don't think that's going to happen, though."

"She's spooked," Richter responded. "She's not using her cell phone anymore. She either has it turned off or she trashed it."

"Right. The same goes for the person she sent after Reed last night. We've designated that contact as T-1 for now. We were unable to find a GPS signal on T-1, and he hasn't used his phone either, not since this morning. He called Jane at 8:00 Eastern Time. We were able to trace the call to Santa Fe. He said there was no sign of Reed. Here's the transcript."

When Richter finished reading, he passed the transcript to Kendall.

"That was the last call made to or from her phone. It's also the last call to or from T-1's phone. That's odd given what's at stake for them. So your theory that they got rid of the phones is probably right." Monahan checked his notes again. "Oh. I also have teams in Colorado and New Mexico right now. If T-1 uses that phone again, we'll be able to pick him up."

Richter rubbed his eyes. "What about Rumson?"

Monahan handed Richter another piece of paper. "He received one call today at approximately 9:45 a.m. from Phil Perry. That's the transcript. Prior to that, the last call was with Jane last night."

Richter read it, then handed the paper to Kendall. "From this, it doesn't sound like Perry's involved."

"I would agree, but we should question him anyway."

Richter turned to the president. "Sir? I think we have to move on Rumson now. If Jane's spooked, you can bet he's spooked as well. While he can't run, he might start destroying evidence."

The president was quiet for a moment. "This woman, Jane… she's the key to all of this, isn't she?"

"We think she is, sir. Our guess is that she's Rumson's go-between; a single point of contact, if you will. She was probably the one to arrange the bombing with McKay and Mosby and also the one to send Reed and his friend after us."

"If we can't locate her," Kendall responded, "that will hamper our ability to determine who else is involved….other than those people we already know." Kendall counted on his fingers. "Rumson, Jane, McKay, Mosby, Broder, Reed, his partner, and this, what do you call him? Tee One? These people in Colorado or New Mexico, looking for us. That's all we have so far?"

"That's correct, sir. We know two Secret Service agents were involved. Pardon me. One current agent and one former uniformed officer. We also know that one Air Force officer was involved. What we don't know is if there are others involved. Frankly, that's scary."

"So, the only way to uncover who else is involved is through Jane and Rumson…"

"Yes, sir. There are a few other leads we're following." Monahan turned to Richter. "We recovered the body in Cortez. We'll run his fingerprints and, if we can identify him, it may fill in some of the blanks. We told the local authorities that this was a drug-related killing and is related to a case we are currently working on and that we have jurisdiction. They're mad as hell, but…tough."

Richter smiled weakly. "Anything else?"

"I have our profilers working on T-1's voice. We'll see what comes up. And, finally, we found a connection between Rumson and Lieutenant McKay. It seems they both attended the same high school in Newark, New Jersey, although there was some thirty years between them. What's even more interesting is that when McKay applied for admission to the Air Force Academy, Rumson wrote the Letter of Nomination."

The president and Richter exchanged a glance.

"I think we need to proceed with the plan we discussed, sir."

CHAPTER FIFTY-NINE

Friday, May 7

Half a dozen blocks from the White House, Attorney General Kiplinger was sitting behind his desk at the Justice Department when he heard a commotion in the outer office. He stood as three men barged into his office.

"Sir? FBI. I'm Special Agent Wayne Elms. You need to come with us immediately, sir. We have a national security incident."

Kiplinger stepped back. "What the hell is…?"

"Sir, we don't have time."

The agents grabbed Kiplinger by the elbows and led him towards the door. He was hustled to the elevator and, one minute later, they exited into the parking garage where he climbed into the waiting Suburban. The doors were slammed and the Suburban drove off, raced up the exit ramp and out onto the street.

Fifteen minutes later, they drove through the gates of Washington Executive Airport and drove directly up to the waiting helicopter. Kiplinger, still protesting, was manhandled onto the chopper. As an agent secured his four-point harness, he looked up into the confused faces of the Secretary of Treasury and the Secretary of Education.

They arrived at the Virginia country estate shortly after 9:00 a.m. and were hustled into the library under the watchful eyes of a dozen agents. Elms followed them in. "Gentlemen, I'll need your cell phones, your Blackberries, and any other communication devices. Right now."

The three Cabinet members loudly protested, but Elms was adamant.

By 10:00 a.m., they were joined by the Secretaries of Defense, Energy, Labor, Agriculture and Veterans Affairs. Used to barking orders and not being barked at, the assembled officials were angry, especially as their numbers grew. By 11:20 p.m., the majority of the President's Cabinet and the President Pro Tempore of the Senate and the Speaker of the House were sitting in the library. A screen showing six separate video connections with the remaining Cabinet members, all of whom were currently traveling, stood against one wall. The agents-turned-guards ignored the threats and demands for information.

The door opened and the room quieted as everyone watched Monahan walk to the center of the room.

"Ladies, gentlemen. Most of you know me. I'm FBI Deputy Director Patrick Monahan. I'm sorry for abruptly pulling you away from your schedules. And I apologize for taking your cell phones. You'll understand why in a moment. What I can tell you right now is that we have a national security incident, and your presence here is absolutely critical."

There were several shouted questions.

"Where the hell are we?"

"You can't detain us like this!"

"Is Director Broder aware of this?"

Monahan held up his hands until the room quieted. "Please bear with me, folks. Director Broder is on his way. So is Henry Amalu."

———

Richter felt all eyes on him as he entered the room. He scanned the faces, spotting several that he knew, including the Director of the Secret Service, Gerry Kroger, whose eyes had gone wide.

"Ladies and gentlemen. My name is Matthew Richter. I'm a Secret Service agent assigned to the president's protective detail." He paused and looked around the room. There wasn't a sound. Richter took a breath and continued.

"What I'm going to share with you is highly sensitive information. You will not discuss this with anyone outside this room. Are we clear on that?"

There was a flicker of comprehension and a mixture of hope in some faces, while others seemed confused. Heads slowly nodded.

"Two weeks ago, I was on duty, guarding President Kendall as he flew on Air Force One back from Seattle."

There was a collective gasp in the room. Richter held up his hand.

"As I believe you all know or suspect, there was a bomb onboard the plane. President Kendall and I managed to escape before the bomb was detonated." The room erupted, but Richter held up his hands until there was silence. "Because this is an ongoing criminal investigation, I cannot provide any details. But I will say this. Based upon the nature of information that we had at the time, we were forced into hiding. We were finally able to make it back here with help from Deputy Director Monahan and the FBI."

The room again filled with shouts and demands.

"Where is the president now?"

"Is he okay?"

Richter held up both hands again. "Please hold your questions for a moment." He turned and nodded to Monahan.

Monahan stepped forward. "Agent Richter and President Kendall have provided blood and tissue samples that the FBI lab has analyzed and compared to known samples for these two men. That is, we compared them to samples taken before the crash." Monahan paused a second. "I have a certified statement by the FBI lab that the DNA matches." There was a stunned silence as Monahan handed copies of the statement to Harry Bolsh, the Speaker of the House, and to Joyce Pankin, the President Pro Tempore of the Senate. "I point this out only because I don't want any doubt whatsoever about their identities." Monahan waited for this to sink in, then turned again and nodded to the agents at the door.

As if on cue, the room stood and turned. The doors opened and a collective gasp escaped as President David Kendall, flanked by six FBI agents, stepped into the room. The room erupted in applause as Kendall, dressed in a suit, limped to the center. He stopped and scanned the faces around him before breaking into a smile.

"You don't know how good it is to see you all again. Obviously, these last two weeks have been a huge challenge for our country and a huge challenge for me personally." His voice cracked, and he wiped away a tear. "I would not be here before you today if it were not for some truly remarkable people, who, at some point I will make sure you all get a chance to meet." He took a deep breath and, in a much stronger voice, continued. "We have some urgent business that we need to address immediately. I understand that twelve days ago, under the provisions of the Twenty-fifth Amendment, you, as members of my Cabinet and as leaders for our legislative bodies, temporarily transferred presidential powers to Vice President Rumson." The president turned to Representative Bolsh and Senator Pankin. "I understand that powers were transferred because I was presumed dead, or at the very least, severely injured and therefore unable to discharge the powers and duties vested in me as president. I understand and respect that decision." The president held his arms out, much like a preacher before his flock. "But I stand before you now to assure you that I am both mentally and physically able to discharge the powers and duties of the office of President of the United States."

The president pulled an envelope from his suit coat. "Mr. Speaker, Madam President. Under the provisions of the Twenty-fifth amendment, I am now submitting to you a written declaration stating that no inability exists and therefore I am now able to reassume the powers and duties of the office of the president." Kendall walked over and handed each a copy and then another copy to the attorney general.

Joyce Pankin looked up from the letter and turned to Harry Bolsh, who gave her a nod. She stood up; there were tears in her eyes. "Welcome back, Mr. President." The Cabinet members jumped to their feet and the room was filled with cheers and thunderous applause.

As the president exchanged hugs and reunited with his Cabinet, Richter noticed Broder, his eyes dark, making a beeline toward Monahan. Four FBI agents stepped forward, blocking him.

"Get the fuck out of my way," Broder hissed.

Instinctively, Richter stepped beside the president as Kendall's voice boomed, and the room went silent.

"Mr. Broder." The president signaled with his index finger. "Come here."

Broder, red-faced, complied.

"Mr. Kroger. You too, please."

Kendall glared at Broder for a moment. "I want to make this crystal clear. Agent Richter is in charge and both the FBI and the Secret Service are now effectively under his command." He paused. "Mr. Broder, is this going to be a problem for you?"

Broder turned even redder. "Sir, with all due respect, Agent Richter does not understand the bigger picture nor does he have the breadth of experience to deal with this."

"I'm not giving you a choice," the president snapped back. "If you can't live with my decision, you'll be relieved of your duties immediately."

Broder, his eyes smoldering, shot Richter a look, then nodded.

The president turned. "Mr. Kroger, the same goes for you."

After a moment's hesitation, a tight-lipped Kroger nodded as well. "Yes, sir."

The president stepped back. "Agent Richter?"

Richter stepped forward. "For now, I'm satisfied with the security arrangements that Mr. Monahan has put in place. Mr. Kroger, at this point, I do not want anyone in the Secret Service to be informed of the president's status. No one, Mr. Kroger. Is that clear?"

Kroger glanced at the president and then glared at Richter. "Very clear, Agent Richter."

Richter studied him a moment before speaking. "Director, I need you to find out where the vice president is right now and what his schedule is for the rest of the day. Discreetly, please."

CHAPTER SIXTY

When the fire alarm sounded and the lights flashed, most people in the West Wing looked up for a second or two in annoyance before turning back to their work. *A fire at the White House? Be serious!*

It took the Secret Service twenty-five minutes to clear the offices. The staffers were hustled out to the South Lawn, complaining all the way. They joined a growing group of people: chefs and cooks in their white aprons, Marine guards in full dress uniform, gardeners and maintenance personnel in coveralls, ushers and staff from the residence, and hundreds of annoyed people in business suits, arms folded across their chests. Only the press was happy.

Agent C.J. Timmons gathered Rumson's detail outside the Oval Office.

"I want all of you stationed outside on the South Portico. Wolf will remain in the Oval Office. I want all entrances manned. No one is allowed back in until the 'all clear' is given." He glanced at his watch. "Once the Uniformed Division gets a complete headcount to make sure everyone is accounted for, they'll let us know." He handed a note to one of the agents. "Give that to the uniformed boys. The only ones inside are three in the command center, myself by the Oval Office guarding Wolf, and Agent Winston in the East Wing." Timmons scowled. "Fucking fire drills."

His men walked outside. When he was alone, he felt a moment of doubt, but shook his head. He trusted Kroger, and if the man wanted the building cleared, then so be it.

He raised his hand to his mouth. "Wolf is in the Double O. Crown is clear."

———

With Kroger in the lead, more than twenty FBI agents escorted the two men through the tunnel that connected the Treasury Building to the White House. Attorney General Ben Kiplinger and Monahan brought up the rear. Originally constructed as a bomb shelter for Franklin Delano Roosevelt during World War II, the tunnel saw many uses over the ensuing years, including, it was rumored, as a covert means for sneaking Marilyn Monroe into the White House for late night trysts with President Kennedy.

Despite the fact that they were indoors, the two men wore dark sunglasses, hats and bulky coats. When they reached the vault door that opened into the East Wing of the White House, Director Kroger signaled for the group to stop. After a quick radio call, the heavy vault door was opened by a single Secret Service agent. His eyes went wide.

"Not a word, Agent Winston." The young agent nodded, stepping out of the way as Kroger led the group into the vacant hallway.

Ten minutes later, after a somewhat circuitous trip through the White House, the group was escorted into the president's private dining room, adjacent to the Oval Office. Agent Timmons was waiting. He looked from one to the other in confusion and then surprise as the room filled.

Kroger nodded towards the door. "Is Wolf still in there by himself?"

"Yes, sir."

An FBI agent helped the president take off his coat; then the president took off his hat and sunglasses. He straightened his tie, smoothed the sleeves of his suit coat, then nodded to Monahan. "Okay, let's do it."

———

Kroger led Kiplinger and Monahan into the Oval Office.

Rumson, sitting behind the desk, staring at the phone in his hand, was startled.

"Kroger! What the hell do you think you're doing, barging in here?" Seeing the men behind Kroger, he stood and leaned over the desk, his eyes menacing. "What the hell is going on?"

Monahan stepped forward. "Mr. Rumson. Sit down please."

Ignoring Rumson's glower, Monahan placed the digital recorder on the desk and pressed the play button.

What's the status?

"What the hell kind of stunt is this?" Rumson thundered.

Monahan rewound the recording and hit the play button again.

What's the status?

What was that?

I said I can't reach either of my men.

Are you referring to the first team?

Yes. The first team.

Well? Do you know what happened?

No. The second team is in Durango now. So far they haven't picked up any leads.

Put every resource you have on this. A pause. *You need to find him pretty damn quick. And you need to end this!*

Monahan pressed the stop button.

Rumson looked at all three men in turn before his eyes settled back on Monahan. "What the hell is that?" he said dismissively, pointing to the recorder.

"Mr. Rumson," Monahan said. "I am placing you under arrest for murder, for conspiracy to commit murder, and for treason."

Rumson stared at him, unblinking. "I didn't hear anything on that recording about murder or treason."

Rumson's eyes went wide for a second as David Kendall and Matthew Richter stepped into the room.

Kendall stepped up to his desk. He stared at Rumson, feeling nothing but disgust and loathing for the man before him. Rumson, his face clouded, his surprise gone and his eyes defiant once again, stared back at him. There were no signs of remorse, Kendall noted. *How many people did you kill?* He wanted to scream. *You corrupt, power-hungry bastard!* Instead, he shook his head then turned to Monahan.

"Get this asshole out of my office."

Monahan, holding a pair of handcuffs, stepped around the desk. Instinctively, Richter stepped forward next to Kendall. Rumson sat frozen. His eyes dark, he looked up at Kendall and shook his head.

"You son of a bitch," he said quietly. Then he lunged out of the chair, grabbed the letter opener and launched himself across the desk.

CHAPTER SIXTY-ONE

On the second floor of the White House, Maria Kendall was crying. She knew. Ever since the prayer vigil, she knew. Somehow, someway, she sensed David had connected with her. She didn't know what it meant at the time and tried not to hold onto false hope. It had been so hard, and the feeling had been so strong. She never told anyone about the feeling that had come over her that night, not even the girls. But she had prayed. She didn't even know what she prayed for, but she prayed nonetheless. She hugged Angela and Michelle. Both were crying; overcome by the rollercoaster of emotions.

Agent Tiller put her hand to her ear, listened for a second and nodded. "Ma'am?"

The door opened and David Kendall stood on the threshold, tears streaming down his face. Maria and the girls let out a sob as he limped into their arms.

———

"In stunning news, President David Kendall has been discovered alive. The White House and federal authorities have not provided any additional information, except to say that President Kendall is alive and has returned to Washington today. We have also learned that, after an emergency meeting of high-ranking officials, including the President's Cabinet and Congressman Harry Bolsh and Senator Joyce Pankin, under the provisions of the Twenty-fifth amendment, presidential powers have been transferred from Vice President Rumson back to President Kendall. We are told that President Kendall will be addressing the nation tonight. This is an absolutely stunning turn of events for a nation still in shock over what was thought to be the tragic loss of a great man. There is no word yet on exactly where President Kendall has been for these last two weeks or how he survived the crash of Air Force One.

"In related news, we have also learned that Vice President Tyler Rumson has been rushed to the hospital. Details are sketchy and, at this time, his condition is unknown. We turn now to our White House Correspondent, Betty Hoffman for the latest details."

CHAPTER SIXTY-TWO

Richter watched on the monitor as President Kendall, his jaw set, his eyes intense, strode into the East Room. His limp was barely perceptible, Richter noticed, but he knew it had more to do with the man's will than with the brace he was wearing or the pain medication he had taken earlier. There was no mistaking that he was in charge.

Standing in the adjoining Green Room, Richter watched as Kendall waved to the crowd while nervous FBI agents trailed closely behind. The president did not stop to shake hands, did not stop to share a few words or a hug with those he knew. That would come later, Richter knew. The president headed directly for the podium. After a full ten minutes and many repeated attempts, he was finally able to quiet the room.

"Ladies and gentlemen. Fellow citizens," the president began. "You don't know how good it is to finally be back home."

The crowd jumped to its feet again, and the room overflowed with noise. It was another two minutes before the crowd took their seats again. The president glanced down. He only had a few hastily scribbled notes, Richter knew. There hadn't been time for speechwriters and teleprompters.

"Two weeks ago, an attempt was made to alter the very fabric of our democracy. An attempt was made to change something very dear to our hearts, to change the core of who we are as Americans: the right for each of us to determine our own fate. An attempt was made to take away our ability as citizens to determine, through democratic process, who will lead us."

President Kendall paused and looked out over the assembled congressmen and women, at his Cabinet, at the assembled government officials, and at the White House staff and the reporters who had been crammed into the East Room. When he spoke again, his voice boomed through the room.

"I stand before you tonight, confident that our democracy has been restored!"

With a roar, the crowd jumped to its feet once more. As the president held his hands up again, Richter turned and nodded to the FBI agent in front of the door. The agent stepped aside and Richter entered the small side room. The two FBI agents inside looked up but said nothing. Jack and Derek were watching the president's address on the monitor. It took a moment before they noticed him.

"You know why you're in here and not out there…" he began.

"The investigation?" Jack offered.

Richter nodded. The boy was bright. He started to say something but suddenly found himself tongue tied. The words he had prepared a moment ago so his emotions wouldn't get the better of him were gone.

There was a thunder of applause from the other room. They all glanced at the monitor, at President Kendall, behind the podium. Back in the White House. Back where he belonged. Richter took a deep breath then smiled.

"Jack, Derek. I don't know where to begin," he said. "It's been one hell of a journey and the odds were against us most of the way. But we did it." He shook his head. "You guys were amazing." He gestured towards the monitor. "The president would not be alive today if it weren't for you." He shook his head again. "Heck, I wouldn't be alive today…" He took another breath before continuing. "Being an agent, you need to rely on your partners to cover your back. Well, I couldn't think of anyone else I would want protecting me but you two."

Jack's face flushed red and he wiped away a tear.

"It's been an amazing adventure," Derek said, his voice cracking.

"It has been, but unfortunately," Richter said as his smile faded. "It's not over yet. They're going to want to talk to you," he continued with a nod to the two FBI agents. "There'll be depositions and Congressional Hearings…" he waved his hand.

"Yeah," Jack said. "They told us."

"Well," Derek said with a grin. "This is our first time to Washington. I'm sure between all of that we'll get to see the sights."

"Unfortunately, over the next few days, you'll be spending most of your time behind closed doors. But I'll make sure the FBI gives you the grand tour." He smiled. "I'll make sure they show you things tourists never get to see."

Jack and Derek smiled at that.

Richter gestured toward the TV again. "Listen, he wants to meet you later tonight, after the media circus is over. Are you guys okay waiting around?"

"Are we okay?" Derek spread his arms wide. "Where else do you think we'd rather be?"

Richter smiled. There were things he wanted to say, that he had to say, but he knew he couldn't. Not tonight. He stepped forward, his hand out.

"Thank you..."

Jack ignored the outstretched hand and suddenly his arms were around Richter's shoulders. A second later, Derek joined them. Richter suddenly felt the tears running down his cheeks. After a moment he pulled away and forced himself to push all the emotions back down. *Not here. Not now.*

"Listen, I need to go," he said as he wiped his eyes. "The next few days will be hectic, but I'll make sure I check in on you guys from time to time to see how things are going."

Jack and Derek nodded and Richter turned away before anyone said anything else. He stepped back into the East Room.

After a moment he caught Monahan's attention and nodded. Ignoring the eyes on him, he stepped out into the hall. Spotting him, the reporters and photographers who had been relegated to the TV monitors set up hastily in the hall, pushed forward only to be blocked by a team of FBI agents who formed a protective ring around him. Pat Monahan pushed his way through the crowd. They shared a glance.

In a voice that betrayed his weariness, Richter mumbled,

"I'm going home."

Monahan nodded then spoke to one of the agents. He and Richter shared another glance then Monahan squeezed Richter's arm and nodded again.

Five minutes later, Richter found himself in the back of an FBI Suburban. His face a mask, he said nothing to the agents sitting beside him. Twenty minutes later, the car slowed, and he glanced out the window and saw that they had stopped in front of his building. He stared out the window and, for a moment, the building felt unfamiliar and cold and he wondered how he had ended up here. He shook his head, then realized someone was talking to him. He turned and noticed for the first time that Special Agent Wayne Elms was next to him. Elms asked him again and Richter frowned then shook his head.

Elms nodded. "Wait here a moment please."

As Elms climbed out, Richter sat back and closed his eyes.

Sometime later—five minutes, maybe more—Elms returned.

"The door's open. The apartment's secure." Elms paused. "I'd like to post some of my men inside your apartment," he added.

Richter shook his head. Then he climbed out.

A minute later he shut the door to his apartment, not bothering with the bolt. Elms and his men, he knew, would be right outside. He glanced at his sparsely furnished apartment: at the sofa and chair he had purchased with little thought, at the remote sitting next to a TV that he had so rarely used, at the jar full of cooking utensils by the stove, some still wrapped in the plastic they came in, and at the cheap Ansel Adams print he had hung on the wall in a vain attempt to make a place that he spent so little time in feel like home. He couldn't shake the feeling that he was an intruder. He leaned back against the wall and closed his eyes.

Slowly, he slid down the wall until he was sitting on the floor. His face buried in his hands, his body shook as he began to weep.

CHAPTER SIXTY-THREE

Thursday, May 20

It was a hot Carolina morning when Matthew Richter turned into the driveway of the small house in Greensboro. He parked the car and sat for a moment studying the brick ranch, the well-manicured lawn, and neatly tended shrubs. Richter took a deep breath and climbed out of the car. The door opened as he walked up the steps. The woman smiled, but her eyes betrayed the pain.

"Ma'am, I'm Matthew Richter. I called earlier."

"I know. I recognize you…from TV. Please. Come in."

Richter followed her into the living room.

"Please have a seat. Can I get you something to drink? I made some fresh ice tea."

"Thank you, ma'am. That would be nice."

Richter looked around the room. Pictures of Stephanie were displayed on end tables, on the mantel and the walls. Stephanie posing with friends. Stephanie, in cap and gown, at her college graduation. Stephanie holding a trophy after, Richter guessed, a track meet. Stephanie, eyes vigilant, standing behind President Kendall as he shook hands with President Magaña of Mexico. On the table next to him, there was a memorial card from Stephanie's funeral. He flipped it over and read:

To know even one life has breathed easier because you have lived. This is to have succeeded.
—Ralph Waldo Emerson

He let out a breath, placed the card back on the table, then stood as he heard voices coming from the kitchen. Mrs. Sartori walked in carrying a tray. A tall, distinguished looking man with gray hair followed her in.

He stuck out his hand. "I'm Ted Sartori."

"I'm Matthew Richter, sir."

"Please, have a seat."

While Mrs. Sartori poured drinks, Richter picked up a picture frame. "I didn't realize Stephanie was a track star. She never told me that."

"She ran in high school. Mostly long distance." Pointing to the picture, Mr. Sartori continued. "That was after she completed her first marathon. She was still in college then. She didn't win." Mr. Sartori smiled at the memory, then shook his head. "But I had a trophy made up beforehand, and we gave it to her when we finally met up with her at the finish line." Mr. Sartori paused, the words stuck in his throat. "She was our only child."

Mrs. Sartori touched his arm and then turned to Richter. "Mr. Richter. I didn't ask, but I hope you like sweet tea. It's how we serve it in the South."

"Please, call me Matthew." He took the glass. "Thank you, ma'am." He took a sip. "This is very good."

He put the glass on a coaster.

"I appreciate your seeing me on such short notice. I know this is a very difficult time for you. I worked with Stephanie and...I had come to know her quite well. I realize you're probably wondering what happened."

Mrs. Sartori nodded. "No one has told us much. The president called to offer his condolences and to thank us. He told us Stephanie saved his life." Mrs. Sartori reached for a tissue. "Did she?"

Richter's felt his eyes well up. "Yes, ma'am, she did. Stephanie was a hero."

CHAPTER SIXTY-FOUR

June

Matthew Richter looked around the empty apartment one last time. His footsteps sounded loud as the noise echoed off the bare walls. He paused by the window for a moment and sighed. Two months of endless sessions with investigators, of testifying before Congress, of painstakingly recounting their ordeal had left him drained.

Rumson was dead. In the scuffle with Richter, he had fallen on the letter opener, and the blade he had intended for Kendall had pierced his own flesh instead. There was little anyone could have done, and by the time the doctor arrived, he was gone. The woman named Jane, investigators had determined, was someone Rumson had befriended as a child. Like Mosby and McKay, she was one of many that Rumson had apparently cultivated over the years. She had vanished. As investigators learned more about her background, they realized that finding her would be a challenge. Joe Reed refused to speak, his lawyer claiming that he had been tortured and that anything he said had been under duress. His demands for a plea bargain fell on deaf ears. The investigation into the Air Force, the Secret Service, and the FBI continued; Emil Broder loudly protested his innocence. Yet the questions remained.

Richter turned from the window, and stopping by the door, glanced back once more. Even with his FBI detail, the reporters still hounded him, trying to win a few minutes of his time, telling him he was a hero. They shouted their questions over the tops of his agents. One question, above all, had struck a chord.

"How do you feel?"

How did he feel? He stared at the apartment. *Like this*, he thought. *Empty. Hollow.* Stephanie was gone. She and Brad Lansing and so many others had done their jobs. Yet, the Service had failed them. The Service had failed him.

With a sigh, he shut the door.

Fifteen minutes later, a ball cap pulled low over his face and driving his own car for the first time in months, he merged onto Rt. 495. It was seven hours to Columbus. He would spend a week with his family, maybe two. Where he would go after that—what he would do next—he wasn't sure. But one thing was clear, there was nothing left for him here.

He glanced in his rearview mirror and watched as Washington, DC, faded in the distance.

For a preview of *An Eye For An Eye*, the sequel to *In Sheep's Clothing*, continue on . . .

An Eye For An Eye

As he made his way through the cantina, Pablo Guerrero could hear the cries of the crowd, calling for blood. He tugged at the cap, pulling it low over his face. Dressed as he was in a laborer's clothes, and not the designer fashions he'd grown accustomed to, he wasn't recognized.

Stepping out the back door, he threaded his way through the crowd to the side of the ring. He caught the eye of the boy standing in the middle. The boy, no more than thirteen, nodded briefly then held the black rooster up for the judge to inspect. After checking for injuries, the judge held out his hand and the boy handed him the one-inch curved blade. The judge inspected this, first looking then sniffing for the tell-tale signs of poison. Although he didn't detect any, he wiped the blade with a lemon—a long-standing practice to guard against cheating. Satisfied, the judge tied the blade onto the rooster's leg then stepped back.

The boy moved to the center of the ring, thrusting the bird in front of him, letting him see his opponent. Across from him, an old man holding a white rooster did the same. Guerrero watched as his rooster twisted and writhed in the boy's hands, clucking and hissing, anxious to fight. A slight grin crossed his face then disappeared. The judge signaled; the boy and the old man retreated to opposite sides of the pit.

The judge eyed the crowd and called out once more. "Apuestas!" *Bets.*

Guerrero signaled and handed the judge one hundred pesos, nodding in the boy's direction.

"El negro." *The black one.*

The judge nodded, held the hundred pesos in the air and called out to the crowd again. When all bets were placed, he signaled to the boy and the old man. They stepped forward again, thrusting their roosters at each other several times as the noise grew. The spectators, those wagering and those just watching, began to shout and chant, excited at the imminent battle. The judge called out again and the roosters were placed on the ground. Like prize fighters, they danced around each other for a second or two before the black rooster charged. Wings flapping, the birds pecked at each other, clawing and fighting as they'd been trained.

The black rooster jumped, fluttered a foot above the ground for a moment, and then dove at his opponent. The white rooster turned, swung his right claw out. As the chants and calls rose to a din, the black rooster crumpled to the ground.

For a second, Guerrero didn't move. Then he glanced at the old man holding the white rooster aloft, smiling, triumphant. He looked at his own bird lying in the dirt, the dark stains of blood appearing almost as black as the feathers. Guerrero stared at the old man again; his eyes dark. As he turned to leave, he caught the boy's eyes once more and nodded.

The old man would be found three days later, the dismembered white rooster sitting on top of the man's brutally beaten body.

Acknowledgements

I began this journey in the early 1990's, but it wasn't until 2010 when the many twists and turns in my life left me with an opportunity to complete this book—a book that had been patiently waiting for such a time when I might be able to finally grant it my full attention. Along the way there have been so many people who have offered their time, their expertise, their encouragement and their support that I can't possibly mention them all here. You know who you are and you have my eternal thanks.

For Jeff Lewis and Peter Cake, for telling me to follow my dreams. For Jennifer Stolarz, who offered not only her editing skills but her on-going encouragement as well. For Kevin, Lori, Allison and Jeff—Beyers all—for support and encouragement above and beyond the call of duty and for enthusiastically reading my early drafts. For Amani Jensen, who helped me see the trees in the forest. For Pat Galizio and Andy Yin, who willingly jumped on board in the beginning and whose advice, edits, suggestions have been too many to count. For Kevin Hoffman, who, with tape measure and shotgun, proved that, yes, it could happen that way.

For Lt. Raymond "Blaster Tad" Godsil USN (Ret.) for educating me on military flight. For Captain David Leahy, 767 pilot extraordinaire, and for Chuck Mullins, pilot, retired FAA Inspector and former hockey buddy, both of whom helped me get the lingo and technicalities right. For Pat Heder, a Beyer in all but name, for answering various technical questions about one random thing or another.

For Suzanne Berube Rorhus and Carlos Fontana, fellow authors, and for Steve Hyde for advice on the business side of writing.

For understanding how an Air Force Combat Search and Rescue operation functions, I relied on such well written accounts as *Heart of the Storm* by Col. Edward Flemming.

For an understanding of the elaborate process and the many challenges in protecting a president, I relied on *Confessions of an Ex-Secret Service Agent; The Outrageous True Story of a Renegade Agent* by George Rush, *The Secret Service Story* by Michael Dorman, as well as numerous documentaries on the Discovery Channel and the History Channel.

For an inside look at the Presidency and the White House, I turned to *Inside the White House* by Ronald Kessler, *My Life* by Bill Clinton, *The Reagan Diaries* by Ronald Reagan, *Decision Points* by George Bush, *An American Life* by Ronald Reagan, and *Unlimited Access — An FBI Agent inside the Clinton White House* by Gary Aldrich.

The technical guidance I have received has been top notch.

But it was up to me to translate what I learned into the story that unfolds. Any errors are mine and mine alone.

For Faith Black Ross, my editor and for Lindsey Andrews, who designed the cover, my thanks for your invaluable help in taking my ramblings and ideas and helping to turn them into a real book.

Finally, for Kaitlyn, Kyle and Matthew, great children all, who each contributed immeasurably with their edits, thoughts and suggestions, and for my wife, Mona, who personally read and edited more drafts than I can count—none of this would have been possible without your belief in me.

L.D. BEYER is the author of two novels, both part of the Matthew Richter Thriller Series. His first book, *In Sheep's Clothing*, was published in 2015 and reached the #4 spot on the bestseller list for Political Thrillers on Amazon Kindle.

Beyer spent over twenty-five years in the corporate world, climbing the proverbial corporate ladder. In 2011, after years of extensive travel, too many missed family events, a half dozen relocations—including a three-year stint in Mexico—he realized it was time for a change. He chose to chase his dream of being a writer and to spend more time with his family.

He is an avid reader and, although he primarily reads thrillers, his reading list is somewhat eclectic. You're more likely to find him with his nose in a good book instead of sitting in front of the TV.

Beyer lives in Michigan with his wife and three children. In addition to writing and reading, he enjoys cooking, hiking, biking, working out, and the occasional glass of wine.

If you enjoyed this book, please consider writing a review on Amazon, Goodreads, or the platform of your choice.

To learn more about the author and for the latest information on new releases and events, go to http://ldbeyer.com.

48639214R00268

Made in the USA
Lexington, KY
07 January 2016